Something Wicked This Way Rides

From

Dark Owl Publishing, LLC

Arizona

ISBN 978-1-951716-18-9

Cover image by InvisibleNature.
Cover design by Dark Owl Publishing, LLC.

Visit us on our website at:
www.darkowlpublishing.com

ALSO FROM
DARK OWL PUBLISHING

Anthologies
A Celebration of Storytelling
The anthological festival of tales

Collections
The Dark Walk Forward
A harrowing collection of frightful stories from John S. McFarland

The Last Star Warden:
Tales of Adventure and Mystery from Frontier Space, Volume I
A return to the classic sci-fi pulp with modern twists by Jason J. McCuiston

The Last Star Warden Volume II: The Un Quan Saga
More chronicles of the Last Star Warden by Jason J. McCuiston
(Coming November 1, 2021)

No Lesser Angels, No Greater Devils
Beautiful and haunting stories collected from Laura J. Campbell

Novels
The Keeper of Tales
An epic fantasy adventure by Jonathon Mast

Just About Anyone
High fantasy comedy from the twisted mind of Carl R. Jennings
(coming September 1, 2021)

The Black Garden
An atmospheric gothic historical fiction novel from John S. McFarland
(coming October 1, 2021)

YA Novels
(Coming December 1, 2021)

Dragons of the Ashfall
Book One of the War of Leaves and Scales
An epic steampunk fantasy story by Jonathon Mast

Grayson North: Frost-Keeper of the Windy City
A totally cool urban fantasy adventure from Kevin M. Folliard

The Portal: This Set of Journeys is for You
An incredible adventure fueled by the magic of a book
by K. Lamm

Buy the books in paperback and for Kindle
www.darkowlpublishing/the-bookstore

TABLE OF CONTENTS

INTRODUCTION

The era of the Old West was a unique time in North American history. It included time before the Civil War through the 1800s until about 1912, when Arizona, the last of the mainland territories, became the forty-eighth state of the United States. The setting typically stretches from west of the Mississippi River all the way to the rugged Pacific Northwest, including the Yukon Territory of Canada. This was a time when thousands of pioneers, prospectors, and entrepreneurs chose to move out West to be more independent, find more opportunities, and better their lives and those of their families.

So, of course, Western stories usually explore themes that are unique to that era and its locations, such as the fight to keep peaceful societies, solving crimes specific to the physical and moral landscape, and protagonists who address these problems but function on the outskirts of the social norms.

The history of Weird Westerns begins in the 1930s, with the earliest horror and science fiction Western stories being printed in *Weird Tales* magazine. At its most basic, the Weird Western genre is the mixture of genre fiction—fantasy, horror, sci-fi, mystery, or any combination thereof—paired with the setting of the Old West. These stories went beyond the traditional Western but kept the themes that are unique to the genre. If you want to learn more about Weird Westerns, visit the page for *Something Wicked This Way Rides* on our website at www.darkowlpublishing.com/something-wicked-rides.

I came across the idea for this anthology when I stumbled upon a few lines written in the vein of Shakespeare's original poem from Macbeth. It was geared toward a Western theme, and it ended with the line "... Something wicked this way rides." This stuck with me. I realized how powerful that statement has become since Ray Bradbury used it as the title and theme of his dark fantasy novel. I found there is still a place for the Weird Western genre, and that its popularity hasn't waned with the genre fiction reader. So, I invited some of my favorite authors to start sending me stories.

My goal with this anthology was to embody the title while thinking outside the box when it came to common Western tropes, morals, and clichés. But it's always important to still be mindful of those elements, for they are what define the Western genre. The authors took up this mantle and didn't just run with it, but *rode* with it. Each created gritty, creepy, smart, tough, strong, unusual, frightening, and sometimes humorous story elements that both resonate wholly with the Western genre, but give us wonderful new looks by combining components from other genres, even from regular literary fiction.

To preserve the authenticity of the era, I allowed the authors to use words, phrases and situations that were a part of those hard lifestyles but are not considered acceptable today. It does not mean I or the authors approve of them. Rather, I believe history must be preserved and we must learn from it, and not repeat those transgressions. And these are certainly situations and sentiments we hope to never see anyone emulate.

Finally, as the editor, I don't usually have a dedication for an anthology. However, this one is special as I dedicate it to my father, a U.S. Air Force Lieutenant Colonel, Retired, from being a jet pilot and trainer. Dad is the one who started me on the road of genre fiction. He made me watch *Star Wars* and *Raiders of the Lost Ark* as a kid, so now I'm a massive Harrison Ford fan. *Star Trek: The Next Generation* was enjoyed as a family from the day it premiered on TV. He really loves *Back to the Future*; he is known to say that famous line about eighty-eight miles per hour when in the driver's seat of a vehicle. And he's the one who handed me the novel *Jurassic Park* when I was in high school and told me to read it. We totally geeked out when Dad came in one morning, newspaper in hand, to tell me that *Jurassic Park* was being made into a film, and Steven Spielberg was directing it.

His love for Westerns has managed to genetically ooze into my blood, especially when I discovered Weird Westerns. We thought *Cowboys & Aliens* was a fun movie, and Dad named one of the resident lizards in my parents' back yard Rango. As for traditional Westerns, I've grown a strong appreciation for them, too. I clearly remember when *Dances With Wolves* made me cry and get angry about the abuse the Natives experienced, and my dad put his arm around me for comfort as we left the theatre.

So thanks for the inspiration, Pop. And it's Dunbar, not Dumb Bear.

And thank you for picking up this book and sitting a spell to read it. We'd love to hear your thoughts on this anthology, so we ask that you leave us a review online. We hope you find these stories hearty examples of a genre that's endured for nearly more than a century.

Y'all come back now, ya hear?

Andrea Thomas
Editor
June 2021

TEARS OF WINTER
BY
JASON J. MCCUISTON

The fort was empty.

First Sergeant Malachi Wilson trotted his sorrel, Old Flash, alongside his commanding officer, Lt. William T. James. After twenty-seven years of Army life, Mal had been assigned to the young West Point graduate. Together, Mal and the white officer led a squadron sent to reinforce E Troop of the Ninth U.S. Cavalry, commonly called the "Buffalo Soldiers."

Their arrival at Fort Oglala, near the "pacified" Pine Ridge Reservation, occurred less than a year after the massacre at Wounded Knee Creek.

Mal looked at the empty wooden ramparts, the unmanned towers jutting against a sky the color of burnt iron. He'd thought this posting would be his last before retirement, and he'd return to his wife and family in St. Louis. But if the Indian Wars weren't over, sixteen troopers, mostly raw recruits, had no chance against whatever force could wipe out a fortified garrison of some ninety men. Disease was an even scarier notion. "Explains why nobody met us at the railhead in Rapid City."

"Doesn't make sense." Lieutenant James adjusted his kepi against the rising wind. "Why attack the fort instead of the surrounding settlements?"

"No idea, sir. Maybe we should go in and look around?" Inaction was death for nervous soldiers. And they were getting nervous.

"Have two men scale the wall, make certain there's not a trap in there."

"Yes, sir." Mal turned. "Bell, you and Freeman. Get up there and check things out."

Sergeant Bell scowled as he followed Freeman to the wall. Everyone knew Zeke Jackson was the best all-around athlete in the group. Everyone also knew Zeke was Mal's friend, while Bell was decidedly not.

The two troopers crossed the timber ramparts as Mal held his breath. When the windblown silence did not erupt in war whoops, zipping arrows, or gunshots, he exhaled along with the rest of the squadron. A few moments later, the gates to Fort Oglala opened.

"It feel like a graveyard at midnight." Private Lacroix crossed himself as they walked the horses into the silent courtyard.

"Spread out and search every corner." Lt. James turned his horse at the flagpole. "First Sergeant Wilson, find torches or lanterns and get us some light. It'll be dark soon."

"Yes, sir."

As the search commenced, clouds gathered overhead and the temperature dropped. A peal of muffled thunder rolled through the Black Hills to the northwest. A storm was coming.

After issuing lanterns from the supply shed, Mal made a quick round through the fort. In the empty barracks he found Sergeant Bell griping to two troopers.

"... Just our luck to get assigned to that wannabe Kit Carson. Not that I mind the whites and the redskins killing each other, but why we gotta be in the middle of it? I hear James tell his girl before we left St. Louis that he'd make a name for hisself, 'even if it is in command of cah-lahed troops.'" He finished the diatribe with a passable imitation of the New Englander's accent.

Mal cleared his throat. "That's enough, Sergeant. You'll show him the respect due his rank. Is that understood?"

Bell scowled, touched the brim of his kepi. "Yes, First Sergeant... The barracks is empty."

"Then I expect there's someplace else could use your attention." Mal looked around the darkened bunkhouse as the three troopers departed. It seemed colder inside than out. His breath formed a white mist.

A chill ran up his spine.

"Down here!" A frantic voice shouted. "Down here! In the cellar! We found one!"

Mal hurried from the barracks and joined James on his way to the dugout storehouse. "As you were!" The officer's order froze men in their tracks as they made for the cellar. "Sergeant Bell! Take charge and continue the search."

Bell snapped off a salute and did as told.

Mal followed James into the cellar. Pale lantern light illuminated the ashen faces and wide eyes of two troopers, one of them Zeke. The lamplight glistened on a naked body stretched across the sawdust floor.

"It must be an officer," James said, kneeling beside the corpse and motioning for a lantern. "He's white."

"No, sir." Zeke's voice trembled. "He's one of us. He's just..."

The lantern revealed the truth. Dusky skin shone through a thick layer of frost. Short curly hair and wide-staring dark eyes had turned to pale ice.

The man was frozen solid.

"Impossible." James took off his kepi. "The first snows shouldn't fall for another month. It couldn't have gotten cold enough to do this."

"Why is he naked?" Zeke chewed his lips. "His face... he looks... happy..."

James stood. "See to the remains, First Sergeant. Then to the disposition of the squadron. We'll lay this man to rest within the walls tonight before taking up our posts... We may be the only garrison at the moment, but Fort Oglala must be manned. I'll see if I can find anything about this in the reports. Tomorrow, I'll dispatch a rider to Fort Rice." The officer glanced at Zeke and the other trooper. "In the meantime, the less said about the condition of the body the better. Understood?"

"Yes, sir." Mal frowned until the other two men repeated the affirmation. When James had gone, Mal said, "You two get shovels and dig a grave near the flagpole. Cover him up before you take him out. Don't let nobody see him."

The fort was searched from top to bottom, but nothing else was found. No men, no animals. The squadron's horses were stabled, and the troopers moved into the vacant barracks. As the moon began to rise, the men assembled for the funeral of the unknown trooper. Lieutenant James made a somber speech about duty and honor while the fifteen men stood at attention.

The bugler played Taps. Cold rain began to fall before he was done.

The ceremony over, Mal made for the mess hall to ensure the men would have breakfast in the morning. On the building's wooden porch, Mal opened his pocket watch to check the time. The lovely face of his wife, Marina, smiled from inside the watch's lid, just as she had on their wedding day over twenty years ago. Mal always took courage from that photographed smile. He knew he'd make it back to her. Everything would be all right.

Something grabbed him as he entered the darkened mess.

"Mal! You can't be serious about staying here." In the dim moonlight, unfamiliar silver glimmered at Zeke's throat, beneath his neckerchief. But Mal was distracted by the man's next words. "Whatever this is, it ain't natural. Even if it was, there ain't no way fifteen men can hold this fort if the Sioux decide to go on the warpath. We need to get out of here."

Mal lowered his voice. "You have your orders, Corporal. If I need to repeat them, you'll spend the night in the stockade. We clear?"

Zeke stepped back. "Yes, First Sergeant."

***

The next morning Zeke was gone.

"Find him and bring him back." Lieutenant James sat behind the desk in the missing captain's office. He gave Mal the order without looking up from his paperwork. "Take Bell and two men."

Mal flexed his gloved hands against the office's chill. "Is that wise, sir? Why risk four men for the sake of one? And what about the dispatch? I'd recommend sending at least six riders. That'll leave you all but alone out here."

James glanced up. "Of this I am aware, First Sergeant. I will send three men with our fastest horses to Fort Rice. I trust you to recover Corporal Jackson within the next twenty-four hours. With last night's rain, he can't have traveled far."

Added to the fact that Zeke was the best horseman in the squadron, Mal had no interest in chasing his friend down with Bell in tow. "At least keep Sergeant Bell here. He is the next ranking NCO, sir."

James sighed. "Of this, too, I am aware. However... I don't trust Bell... At least not without you as a buffer. And I certainly don't trust him enough to send him out alone."

Mal understood. The white officer feared Bell might stage a coup under the current circumstances. Given Mal's absence and the low morale and isolation, there were better than even odds he would succeed. "We'll depart at once... Did you find anything in the reports, sir?"

"Nothing yet. Everything routine until a patrol came back from Wounded Knee about two weeks ago. A desertion occurred the next day. More followed, but this is not uncommon in these isolated situations. When one man runs and looks to get away with it, others take the same notion. Which is why I need you to succeed, First Sergeant. Bring Jackson back for justice."

"Yes, sir."

Ten minutes later, Mal led Bell and Privates Freeman and Lacroix into the Badlands of South Dakota to hunt his best friend. The troopers carried revolvers, carbines, and extra ammunition. The temperature dropping, the gray sky poured icy rain on the rolling pine- and spruce-covered landscape.

"Looks like your boy Zeke wasn't cut out for soldiering." Sergeant Bell smiled as he rode alongside Mal. "Maybe if you wasn't so dazzled by all them dime-novel tricks he showed off back at camp, you'da noticed."

"Bell, I don't need you or nobody else to tell me a damned thing about soldiering." He touched spurs to Old Flash's ribs and trotted ahead to look for sign of Zeke's passing. This wasn't difficult. The ex-cowpoke had opted for speed rather than stealth. His tracks led to the southwest, away from the res.

As the day wore on, the rain turned to sleet. The horses' hooves crunched frozen mud. Shrill winds howled out of the foothills, cutting through overcoats like knives. The sun sliding behind a bank of low black clouds in the west, Mal spotted a glimmer of fire on the next ridge.

"That's got to be him." Bell turned to Freeman and Lacroix. "Let's go get him, boys."

"Hold it." Mal raised his field glasses and scanned the vale between the two ridges. "That's rocky ground. Looks like some deep gullies." He glanced at the spitting sky. "Crossing that in the dark is asking for trouble. We'll drop back on the other side of this ridge and make camp. Set out come dawn."

Bell snorted. "We catch him tonight, we sleep under a roof tomorrow."

"We catch him in the morning, same thing. We try to cross that scrub in the dark, we might be sleeping under dirt forever."

Bell's eyes narrowed. "You heard the First Sergeant. Let's set camp."

Establishing a foul-weather camp kept the four men busy and quiet. Even if Mal couldn't hear Bell's mouth, he could feel his hateful eyes. The sergeant's dislike for him had grown since arriving at Fort Oglala. Mal knew he had to head it off before it led to trouble.

"Sergeant, walk with me." Mal's three subordinates had just settled under the scant protection of an improvised lean-to. Huddling beside the small fire, Bell gave an exasperated sigh, climbed to his feet, and joined Mal in the cold rain.

Moving out of earshot of Freeman and Lacroix, Mal said, "There's no two ways about it, Sergeant. We're in a tight spot. Even if we catch Zeke and get him back to the fort. Alone and surrounded by hostile country, you and I will be the linchpin between twelve inexperienced troopers and the white man who just hanged one of their friends."

Bell's eyes widened in the dark. "Surely you don't—"

"Lieutenant James will have no choice. Zeke deserted. Regulations are pretty clear. Besides, the lieutenant will see it as a deterrent to keep anybody else from getting homesick. But it'll do no favors for morale."

"You don't mean to catch him, do you? That's why you called a halt tonight."

Mal sighed. "I have to catch him, Sergeant. If I don't, discipline breaks down. And discipline's all we got between us and every angry Sioux in the Dakotas. So, yeah. I mean to catch my best friend, take him back to the fort, and let Lieutenant James hang him in front of God and everybody."

Bell shivered against the wet cold. "That why you brought me out here? To tell me that?"

"I brought you out here to tell you to lose that chip on your shoulder. I don't care if you hate Lieutenant James and every other white man in the world. And I don't care that you don't like me no better. All I care about is that you do the job those stripes on your sleeves say you're here to do. Namely, take care of these men."

"Yes, First Sergeant."

A high, blood-curdling scream tore through the night.

It was long and loud—drowning out the sounds of wind, rain, and the creaking pines for what seemed like minutes. Before it faded, the horses raised a fuss and strained against their tethers. Mal hurried to calm them. Returning to the campfire, he saw dread and fear mingled on the faces of the other three men.

"What was that, First Sergeant?" Freeman asked.

Lacroix crossed himself. "It was a ghost of one of them Sioux what got killed at Wounded Knee by the Seventh. I hear stories 'bout 'em ever since we get assigned to this outfit. I hear they's ghosts what hunt ever' winter, lookin' for they's lost babies, wives n' husbands." His face was ashen when he looked at Mal. "I hear they's lookin' for the soldiers what killed 'em an' left 'em out in that blizzard."

Bell chuckled. "Well, you got nothing to fear, Lacroix. Them soldiers was white."

Freeman poked at the fire. "But they was soldiers. Just like us. Maybe a ghost can't tell no difference."

Mal shook his head. "There's no such thing as ghosts. We got enough live Indians to worry about in this country without conjuring up dead ones."

No one spoke the rest of the cold, rainy night. And no one slept. Each man held his carbine in his hands, his revolver on his lap.

Mal spent the night counting the minutes and staring at his wife's lovely face.

***

The eastern sky fading from black to silver, the men got to their feet and tried to work the aches and pains from their cold joints before tending the horses. The rain had stopped, but it was even colder.

"If it don't snow by nightfall, I'm President Harrison." Freeman stomped his feet, tucking his gloved hands into his armpits as he moved around the campfire.

"More reason to finish this." Mal kicked out the fire. "Mount up."

They crossed the ridge and descended into the rocky defile as the sun rose like a gaping wound. The blood-red light illuminated the treacherous terrain, but the night's weather had added a new threat: ice. Dismounting, they led their horses along the slick boulders and brittle scrub, reaching the valley floor by mid-morning.

"He's done long gone by now," Bell growled.

"You think so?" Mal spotted a dark shape in a deep crag just ahead. Old Flash caught the scent and grunted in consternation. Mal patted the horse, soothing him at the edge of the depression. "If he is, he hasn't got far."

The carcass of Zeke's unsaddled roan sprawled in the pit, one leg jutting at an odd angle, broken in two places.

"That explains the scream." Freeman relaxed.

"Do it?" Lacroix shook his head.

"At least we've got an easy trail to follow." Mal led them along the dead horse's tracks in the slush and frozen grass until they reached Zeke's camp on the opposite ridge.

"Lord have mercy!" Freeman covered his mouth.

Zeke Jackson lay stark naked, stretched out on his bedroll beside the cold campfire. His head rested on his saddle like a pillow, a smile on his face. He was bone white, frozen solid, just like the soldier in the cellar.

Lacroix examined the neatly folded uniform lying beside the man's boots. "Did it get that cold last night?"

Mal glimpsed a slender, dark-haired figure disappear into the woods. Drawing his revolver, he gave chase.

"First Sergeant!" Bell shouted.

Mal ran through the thicket, hearing a woman's mournful song. He couldn't make out the words. They weren't English, maybe Sioux. In a clearing, he spooked a pair of deer into flight.

"She couldn't have come this way..." His lungs burned from the icy air.

A cold hand gripped his shoulder.

He spun.

Bell glared at him. "First Sergeant! What are you doing?"

"Did you see her? The Sioux woman."

Bell looked around the clearing. "I saw nobody but your dead cowboy back there. I think Freeman's right about that snow, so we ain't got time to chase ghosts in the woods."

"Ghosts... Right." Mal scanned the forest before following Bell.

They gathered Zeke's gear and supplies. Mal wrapped his friend's frozen corpse in the bedroll before lashing it to the back of his saddle. Old Flash didn't like the notion any better than he did. Zeke's body was too rigid, too light. It was like handling a bundle of cord wood.

"We'll head due north through this vale." Mal raised his voice above the howling wind. "Try to find an easier place to cross that ridge."

"That'll take us close to the res." Bell rode alongside. "You know the Sioux could have done this. Come up on Jackson in the night, made him strip down, and watched as he froze to death. Redskins are mighty creative when it comes to torture."

Mal shook his head. "It'll take longer to backtrack the way we come."

The four troopers rode through the windswept vale the rest of the afternoon. The skies darkened, thunder booming in the Black Hills to the north. The wind continued to cut and shriek. When the pale sun dipped in the west, the first snowflakes began to fall.

"It's too early for snow." Lacroix stared at the sky. "That's what Lieutenant James said."

"He ain't no prophet. He's just another white man what thinks he knows everything." Bell called up to Mal, "You plan on setting camp or riding through this, First Sergeant?"

Snow fell harder and faster.

"We'll push on to the fort. Ride through the night if we can."

"Good thing we brought lanterns."

Lighting them proved almost impossible with the hellacious gusts tearing out of the hills. After several failed attempts, they circled the horses, spread their overcoats, and created a windbreak for Bell to stand in the center and light two lanterns. By the time they remounted, the snow had started to stick.

"This is like something out of a storybook," Freeman said.

Mal realized the futility of continuing. Even with the lanterns, visibility was almost nil. Wind drove the heavy snowfall in sheets. The snow caking on top of his gloves and thighs blended with that on the ground. They were minutes away from white-out conditions.

"We've got to find shelter," he declared. "Stay close. We'll make for that stand of pines."

Reaching the tree line, they dismounted and hurried to build some semblance of shelter. Stiff, frigid fingers fumbled with hatchets. Aching eyes blinked against ice forming on wind-burned cheeks. Bodies shivered through snow-dampened uniforms. Throats and lungs burned from the icy air.

Once the lean-to was in place, Mal moved to secure the horses. He hoped that by hobbling them flank-to-flank, their body heat and blankets would keep them alive through the night. He placed Zeke a good distance from the horses, so the corpse might not keep them agitated until dawn. "Build a fire. A big one."

"It could draw Indians," Freeman said.

"Indians are too smart to be out in this, Private." Bell glared at Mal. "You heard the First Sergeant."

Later, as snow and wind howled and the horses whinnied and grunted against the cold, the four men huddled around the fire blazing in the center of their lean-to. They had draped their bedrolls over the other side to create another wall for protection. The wind billowed this like a sail until the snow melting on its outside froze into a wall of ice. The fire produced more smoke than heat, irritating already sore throats and eyes.

"All this for one man." Bell's teeth chattered.

"The lieutenant had no choice." Freeman's breath was a white fog. "If he didn't send somebody after him, they'd be somebody gone ever' morning 'til he was the only one left in that fort."

"Serve him right." Bell chuckled. "He shoulda stayed back east, took a job at his daddy's bank or newspaper, or whatever job white-folk get up to."

Mal cleared his throat, his voice a raspy whisper, torn raw by the wind. "Sergeant Bell, surely you are not advocating desertion to these men."

Bell lowered his eyes. "No, First Sergeant. Just tired and wore out. I didn't mean nothin' by it."

"Good. I suggest we all get some rest."

Settling in for the night, Mal noticed his watch had stopped. Though Marina still smiled, he found that smile less than comforting for the first time.

8

***

Lacroix was gone.

Hurrying from the shelter, Mal blinked at the blinding white world. Though the wind had abated, snow still fell. No tracks shone among the knee-deep drifts. "Spread out. Find him."

It didn't take long.

"Over here!" Freeman shook as he stared at the base of a towering lodgepole pine.

Mal and Bell shuffled through the snow to reach the young trooper.

Lacroix stood with his back frozen to the tree trunk. His long-handles and trousers crumpled at the tops of his boots, the rictus of a smile on his ashen face. His eyes were pale marbles set beneath a layer of ice. His arms formed a circle, as if he had frozen while in the midst of trying to clutch something.

"Damnation." Bell shook his head.

"I don't understand, First Sergeant." Freeman stared at his dead friend. "If it had been Sioux, why didn't they kill us?"

Mal stared at the frozen corpse, seeing accusation in its lifeless eyes. "He must've got up to make water in the night. Wandered out and got lost in the storm. Got disoriented. I've heard it happening before."

"Have you?" Bell faced him. "What about Zeke? Wasn't no storm caused that. He was in his camp, lying on a bedroll. Didn't look disoriented to me. But he had that same shit-eating grin as Lacroix, here. Same as the trooper found in the fort."

Mal tore his gaze from the dead man. "How did you know about that?"

Bell bared his teeth. "Only thing run through a camp faster than the trots is gossip, First Sergeant."

Mal stiffened. "Get him loose. We'll take him back to the fort, too."

Bell snorted. "You really want to haul two bodies through this? It'll take us all day to find our way back with the best of luck. I say we leave 'em here under this tree and come back to get 'em when the weather's better."

"With all due respect, Sergeant," Freeman said. "I ain't leavin' Nat out here. We can put him and Zeke on his horse."

Mal nodded. "Then best get to it. We're burning daylight. Sergeant Bell, you get the horses ready. I'll help Freeman."

They had to use hatchets to chip away the ice fusing Lacroix to the tree. Once they had him stretched out on the snow, Freeman went to fetch the dead man's bedroll.

Mal noticed a glint of silver in Lacroix's right fist. He tried to pry the cold fingers apart. When the pinky broke off, a small chain set with turquoise and gold slipped onto the snow.

9

Mal retrieved the necklace, recognizing it. Zeke had worn it when he had tried to get Mal to desert with him. Mal had never seen it before that night.

A woman's song drifted on the wind.

"You all right, First Sergeant?" Freeman returned with the bedroll. "You look like you seen a ghost."

"Fine, Private. Let's get him wrapped up."

Mal led the small column with Freeman guiding Lacroix's horse, now laden with two dead men, Sergeant Bell riding drag. The weather continued to worsen with heavier snow, higher winds. Huddling into his overcoat as snugly as he could, Mal felt drowsy with each of Old Flash's plodding steps through the knee-high drifts...

"You hear that?"

Freeman's words jarred Mal awake.

It was the sad chant he had heard at Zeke's camp and near the tree where they had found Lacroix. Mal could hear the woman's voice above the shrieking wind. No—the wind was her voice.

"It's beautiful!" Releasing the packhorse's lead, Freeman spurred his mount past Mal and into the grey fog of snow. "She's beautiful!"

"Private!" Mal gave Old Flash a kick and pursued. The song was his, meant for him alone. "Freeman, halt!"

Bell rode up as Mal came upon Freeman's horse staggering in the whiteout. The private had dismounted. Wading through the drifts, Freeman's shouts drowned in the lovely, melancholy song filling the sky, the wind, and the world. The soldier struggled against the snow toward another figure.

Long dark hair lifted as if caught in a gentle breeze, not a howling gale. A white buckskin dress fluttered, its pale blue shoulders and embroidery untouched by snow. A beautiful face the color of the moon smiled. Bone-white arms beckoned Freeman into an embrace, blood red lips moving in song.

Mal and Bell drew their pistols. "Get away from him!"

Both men pulled triggers. Both cartridges misfired.

"No!" Mal spurred Old Flash at the woman, pulling the silver strand from his pocket. "No! Take me! Not him!"

The woman looked up.

Mal saw a world of hatred, pain, and vengeance in her black, empty eye sockets. Her withered lips parted in a ghastly smile as Freeman reached her outstretched hands—

Mal stood on a creek bank at the edge of a large Indian camp. It was cold, but there was no snow. White men in blue uniforms corralled the miserable natives. Thin, haggard Sioux men queued at a table where an officer made notes in a ledger and a burly sergeant major took their hunting rifles, tossed them onto a growing pile. The women, children, and elders stood to the side, coughing and sniffling, encircled by a cordon of mounted troopers.

Mal saw the white buckskin with the blue shoulders among them. She was lovely and young, with a swaddled child in her arms. The silver necklace flashed in the late winter sunshine at her throat. Several troopers circled her, cruel smiles on their faces, filthy words on their lips.

A shout drew his attention back to the table. An old man refused to surrender his rifle. The sergeant punched him. A Sioux warrior raised his weapon.

Gunfire erupted in the camp.

Mal looked to the young woman with the baby. She staggered. Blood spread out on the bundle in her arms, ran down the white buckskin. Her head snapped back with the second volley. The silver necklace glittered as it fell to the ground—

"No!" Tears ran down Mal's wind-burned cheeks.

Old Flash shied away, rearing. Mal fell from the saddle, toppling into the snow.

He heard another unearthly shriek, a horse's scream, and Bell cry out in pain.

Regaining his feet, Mal knocked icy tears from his face, looked to see Freeman standing alone on the snow-covered plain. The private was frozen just like Lacroix, Zeke, and the soldier from the cellar. Still clothed, he wore the same contented smile on his face.

A few feet away, Bell lay moaning, trapped beneath his unmoving horse.

There were no other tracks in the sun-bright snow.

"No!" Mal held the necklace up to the clear blue sky. "Why him? I'm the one who had it! Why not me?"

"First Sergeant!" Bell's hoarse shout broke through Mal's confusion. "First Sergeant Wilson! Look at me!"

Mal stumbled to the frozen horse. Kneeling, he helped Bell to escape. "You saw that? You saw what happened?"

Bell looked around the barren landscape, now suddenly still. "I saw it. Not sure I believe it, but I saw it... What's that necklace got to do with all this?"

Mal looked at the strand of silver, gold, and turquoise. "I think it's haunted. One of the fort's garrison must have found it at Wounded Knee. That... ghost must've... done this," he waved at Freeman's frigid corpse, "to the entire garrison."

"I think Zeke found it on that trooper in the cellar, her last victim before we arrived. Then Lacroix must've taken it off Zeke's body. It was in his hand this morning. I thought... if I held it, I could keep you and Freeman safe."

Freeman's horse grunted, shuddered, and collapsed. They turned at the sound of another soft thud. Lacroix's horse fell, spilling its grim passengers. "The horses are freezing!"

Mal ran and grabbed Old Flash's lead, got him moving. The sorrel was shaking, weak, and exhausted, but still alive. Mal led the horse to where Bell stood on one leg above his own dead animal. "If we stand still, we die."

"There's no place to find shelter for miles. No fuel for a fire. Now we're all dead men."

Mal accepted the rebuke. "Here. Get on Old Flash. You're not going to make it very far with a busted leg."

"You could leave me out here. Why ain't you?"

Mal tossed the necklace as far as he could. He touched the watch in his pocket and thought of his wife and family, the love that must have protected him from the dead Sioux woman's wrath. "Because Freeman was right about that ghost not being able to tell the difference between us and the white men of the Seventh. She was blinded by hate, Sergeant... And that is something to think about."

GHOST
BY
BRADLEY H. SINOR

After three years of war, I thought I had seen everything.

The last thing that you expect to see on a hot afternoon in Richmond is a ghost. And certainly not one standing in the front door of the capital building of the Confederacy.

Well, I saw one.

I tied up my horse at a hitching post on the southeast corner of the building, in an area away from the main door. I had arrived a quarter hour early for my appointment with General Morgan Girard, my commanding officer. A soldier, obviously on guard duty, approached me, his rifle carried low in his left hand.

"Excuse me, sir. This area is restricted to Army officers only."

"As well it should be," I said. "Which is exactly why I'm leaving my horse here."

"Sir," he said. "It's for Army officers only. The civilian areas are around the corner." He put a special bit of emphasis on the word "Army."

Because of the nature of my work, I've been more often out of uniform than in one. There are places where a uniform would stick out as much as Abraham Lincoln walking the streets of Richmond.

I held my identification where he could see it.

"Sir, I'm afraid I can't... read," he said.

"That's all right, son. I'm Captain Adam Thorne, Military Intelligence."

He eyed me for a moment. Then snapped to attention, his rifle sliding down to rest at his side in the proper manner.

"Sir, sorry for bothering you. I've been ordered to stop any civilians from leaving their animals here."

"That is not a problem. You just keep on doing your duty. I wish more of our people were as adamant as you.

"Do you have a match, private?" I said as I pulled a cheroot from my inside coat pocket. He passed a Lucifer match to me. I had just dragged it along the bottom of my boot when I saw the ghost.

She was standing at the top of the stairway, looking off in the distance. Jenny, a vision in blue, her long red hair hung loosely on her shoulders, her parasol in one hand to protect her from the sun.

"Jenny?" I muttered, unsure of even the sound of my own voice. Not that I expected her to hear me.

"Captain? Are you all right, sir?"

The guard was looking at me with that uncertainty that a lot of enlisted men seem to have when dealing with officers. Before I could do or say anything, pain shot through the tips of my fingers. I realized that the match had burned down and was attempting to steal a few seconds more of life by using my flesh as its home. I dropped the burning ember and stamped on it with my foot.

"Captain?"

"I'm all right. My mind was elsewhere." When I looked back, she was gone. If she had ever been there in the first place.

The memory of the headstone bearing her name was as fresh as the first time I had seen it three years before. No, it had to have been my imagination; it couldn't have been Jenny.

Yet...

***

"Right on time. Not that I would expect anything less than that from you, Thorne."

Brigadier General Morgan Girard stood up from behind his desk. He was not physically a big man, standing barely five-foot-eight-inches tall, yet he always seemed to fill whatever room he occupied.

Girard had recruited me within a week of when the war for independence had begun. As a graduate of West Point, I had expected to serve our new country in the regular Army. Instead, I found my talents being put to use in other ways. Our office was attached to the Secret Service, but they preferred not to talk too loudly about the connection.

"It's always good to see you, sir," I said. "I was sorry to hear about Mrs. Girard. I know her death must have taken a great toll on you."

"Thank you, Adam. These last few months have been very hard. But thankfully, I've had the boys, George and Derrick. They've been a source of great strength for me," he said.

"I've been told it was her heart?"

"Yes, I came into the bedroom one morning and found her. She had slipped away in the night. She just lay there, peacefully. I sat with her for an hour before I kissed her cold blue lips and found the strength to summon the rest of the house," he said.

There were few things, outside of his job, that I had seen Girard care passionately about. His wife, Allison, had been one, his two sons the others.

"Well, I'm not the only one to have lost loved ones in this war, so enough about me. Let's talk about what you're going to be doing next. I think you'll find it not nearly as big of a problem as that matter in New Orleans," he said.

That would be a relief. I preferred not to dwell on the New Orleans matter any more than necessary. There were, at times, things a soldier had to do in service for his country. You didn't have to like them, but they had to be done. New Orleans had been one of them.

"I'm putting you in charge of security for Lord Anthony Case-Jones."

"I take it this fellow isn't your average traveler on a Grand Tour over here instead of in Europe."

"Far from it. He's a special representative from Prince Albert, sent here to prepare recommendations on the question of diplomatic recognition."

Girard didn't have to explain the significance of that move. Diplomatic recognition would be a godsend for this country. It could bring us aid and allies, which we desperately needed. I had concluded a few months earlier that, shy of a major miracle, there was no way that we could win this war.

This might be that miracle.

"You'll meet his lordship tonight. He's staying with an old family friend of mine, James Collins," said Girard.

"So how does his lordship feel about having a shadow?"

"It doesn't really matter what he wants or doesn't want. He will be protected," said Girard. "I'll send a carriage for you tonight at eight. We dine at nine."

I knew when I had been dismissed.

**

"Captain Thorne! Captain Thorne!"

I was just fastening the last button on my waistcoat when someone started pounding on my hotel room door. My watch indicated half past six.

"Captain Thorne! Captain Thorne!"

"A moment," I answered. After slipping on my jacket, I picked up a small pistol from the table. Just because someone knew my name and where to find me didn't mean that they had my best interests at heart. There are certain things that you must do to stay alive. Better to do them and not need them then to lay bleeding and regretful minutes later.

"Yes?" I said, standing to one side of the door.

"Captain Thorne. General Girard sent me. My name is Cole Masterson," he said.

Cole Masterson turned out to be a lanky man in his thirties. He had an odd accent; one that I couldn't place.

"I wasn't expecting anyone until eight."

"I understand, sir. However, something has happened, and the general wants you to come to the Collins house as soon as possible. He sent me with a carriage and orders to bring you there straight away."

"Can you tell me what happened?"

"No, sir. The general said he would brief you upon your arrival," said Masterson.

That sounded like him. I dropped the pistol into my coat pocket, picked up my hat, and motioned Masterson to follow me.

***

The Collins family home was an elegant, three-story affair, built at the turn of the century on the south edge of Richmond. Several rooms on the first floor were so brightly lit they fairly glowed in the fading July sunlight.

We were met by a man in his fifties, balding with a fringe of iron gray hair, whom I presumed to be the family butler. He was accompanied by a young nigger boy who took charge of the carriage without a word.

"If you gentlemen would come with me. You're expected," said the butler.

I didn't know too much about the Collins family. The great grandfather had immigrated to the United States just after the first war for independence. They had extensive mine, manufacturing, and farm holdings.

Girard was waiting for us in the entrance hall. He wore his usual grim expression, an unlit cigar in his mouth.

"Good evening, sir," I said.

"Ah, you made good time, Thorne. Masterson, I need you to take this to the Naval office." He handed an envelope to Masterson, who promptly saluted and left without a word.

"Well, Thorne, I had hoped that this evening would be a pleasant interlude for the both of us. So much for those hopes," said Girard.

He motioned for me to follow him through a pair of double doors into what proved to be the library. It was a big room with floor to ceiling bookcases and a fireplace at one end. Two oil lamps were the only sources of light.

The general gestured toward a wing chair in one corner. Someone sat there, a man in his late forties with heavy sideburns and a dark tropical tan. His eyes were milky gray stones sunk deep into his face. Only, now that I looked at him, it wasn't his face that caught my attention. What looked like a long red sash ran across the front of his jacket, up over his shirt and onto a deep gash in his neck.

"Do I take it that this might happen to be the gentlemen who you wanted me to keep alive? Lord Anthony Case-Jones?"

"Indeed."

Well, so much for that assignment. I glanced around the room, and in a dim mirror on the far side I saw the ghost again. Just for a moment, peering out from a book-lined alcove on the other side of the room. Except this time, it was wearing the black dress and white-collared uniform of a maid.

It was Jenny!

She was gone just as quickly as she had been the first time I saw her.

"Well, I don't know what recommendations his lordship had in mind, but I would say that someone did not approve of them," I said.

"Then you agree with me that this is very likely the work of Yankee agents?" said Girard.

"Possibly," I said. "Who all is in the house?"

"Just Collins, his lordship's traveling secretary named Rodney, and us. The rest of the Collins family has been living on one of his plantations near Florida for the past six or seven months. There are several hired servants, the butler whom you met, a cook, along with a couple of general handyman types," said Girard.

"What about slaves?"

"Amazingly, none. The handymen are niggers, but they've both been manumitted. I honestly hope that we find out it is a personal thing, rather than a political one. That will make it far easier to explain," muttered Girard. "But whatever the reason, I want answers as soon as possible."

"If you would get everyone in the living room, I think we can begin there," I said. "I want to have a closer look at a few things about his lordship, here. Shall we say in fifteen minutes or so?"

"Agreed," said Girard.

After he left, I gingerly slid my hands into the dead man's pockets. There was little there of interest: a handful of coins, a pencil, and several peanut shells. My manipulations caused him to slump to one side. That was when I noticed an inch or so of chain sticking clear of his shirt collar. It held a medallion of some sort. I thought at first it was a religious one, but when I drew it free, I could see a single letter engraved on each side.

"Don't you think it's about time that you came out?" I said.

There was no response, certainly not from his lordship. But he wasn't who I had been speaking to.

"I saw you in the mirror. I'm going to presume you've been listening and watching since then," I said.

To my left, I heard the slightest sound of metal creaking and hinges at work. Out of the corner of my eye, I caught sight of one of the bookcases swinging back into place.

"Can I get you a drink?" said the ghost. She looked every inch the proper ladies' maid. Her red hair had been wound beneath a white mob cap. At first glance it would have been hard to recognize her, but this close there was no mistaking my sister, Jenny.

"Yes. Scotch," I said.

She poured me two fingers of amber liquid from a bottle on a table near the fireplace, then poured herself a twin of my offering.

"I hope you don't mind drinking with the hired help," she said.

"As if you were really the hired help," I said. "I imagine the only reason that you are employed on these premises is because you wanted to be."

"A girl has to earn a living," she said defensively.

"Are you saying that Davis Walker doesn't pay his spies well enough?"

I've always enjoyed being able to pull a rabbit out of my hat and surprise my sister. The astonished look on Jenny's face was enough to prove that I had not lost my skill.

"Not bad, little brother, not bad at all," she said.

Major General Davis Walker was Girard's opposite number on the Northern side. I had encountered one of his men in Cuba six months before. We had gone to West Point together and considered ourselves friends still, despite political differences. Besides, our particular assignments at that time did not conflict, so we spent the evening drinking and reminiscing. It was somewhere past the second bottle of rum that he mentioned to me that Jenny had gone to work for Walker.

"Looks like there are two Thornes in the spy business now," he said.

"So, do you like working for the enemy?" I said.

"Adam, I don't consider what I do as working for the enemy. I'm working for the country that we were both born in. But let's not get started on any political discussions. I had enough of them with Father. How is he, by the way?"

"Still as hardheaded and stubborn as ever. You know that he considers you to be dead. He even went so far as to erect a headstone for you in the family plot."

I'd been there the day that he'd had it set in place. I suspect he would have held a formal funeral service for her, but my mother, and the local parson, had said no to that idea.

He and Jenny had disagreed on things for most of my life: slavery, politics, the proper way to respect one's parents. Their shouting matches were legend in our family. It had been her falling in love with Nathan Jackson and wanting to marry him that had driven our father and her to the breaking point. It had stormed the night she and her fiancé drove off together, four years ago. That had been the night my father had announced that as far as he, and the family, were concerned, his daughter Jennifer was dead.

So I suppose, from my father's point of view, I was talking with a ghost.

"You heard about Nathan?" she said.

"Yes, a botched bank robbery and he was in the wrong place at the wrong time. Was that what drove you to work for Walker?"

"Among other things," she said quietly.

"You responsible for this?" I gestured at his lordship.

"Hardly. We learned he was coming, and I was sent to keep an eye on him. A dead envoy will not help the United States' relationship with Great Britain. It might even be enough to drive them into recognizing you.

"Besides, it is my understanding that he was going to file a report saying that the English should stay neutral in the whole matter. Something to the effect of letting us settle our own internal matters," she said.

***

"This is hardly the way you normally investigate a murder," said Girard. "However, you all must realize this is not a normal murder. Otherwise, we would have summoned the local police at once."

Girard was pacing back and forth in front of the leather couch that took up most of the main living room of the Collins house. Our host, James Collins, was a man in his mid-fifties, but seemed older. He stood near the large bay window that dominated the room. Seated near the door was Alexander Rodney, the late Lord Case-Jones' traveling secretary.

"Sir, why are you wasting your time here?" said Rodney. "It is obvious that a Yankee agent murdered his lordship. You should be pursuing him. The fiend is no doubt halfway to Washington by now."

I didn't like Rodney's tone and his presumption.

"We are pursuing all avenues of investigation, Mr. Rodney. Not just in this house, but elsewhere, as well," I said. "Do you have a particular reason to believe that the North even knows you're in this country?"

The secretary's face burned red with anger. "Of course they know we're in this country! I have no doubt that detailed reports of our every move are making their way to Abraham Lincoln's desk in each morning's mail!

"Are you aware, sir, of the delicacy of our trip here? There are members of the government who do not want to grant the Confederacy diplomatic recognition. They want us to formally ally with the United States against you."

"The general has seen fit to brief me on your mission. I only wish I had been brought into the matter sooner. Perhaps we could have prevented this murder," I said.

"I doubt that," said Rodney.

"Mr. Collins, where were you and Mr. Rodney earlier this evening?" I asked.

"Business kept me away from the house for most of today. I had barely returned home when Morgan discovered his lordship's body. I last saw him this morning at breakfast. In fact, that's also the last place I saw Mr. Rodney," said Collins.

"Don't go trying to accuse me, sir. It was Northern assassins!" said Rodney. "In the last fifteen years I've traveled to many countries with his lordship. But this is the vilest one I think I have ever encountered!"

"General, the stories you told us of this country were enough to frighten any sane man. But all they did was make his lordship want to come here all the more," said Rodney.

"You had met Case-Jones before, General?" I asked. It was a fact that he had not mentioned.

"Yes, Mrs. Girard and I spent a year in Europe and England before the war. I believe we met him at the Burton estate in Sussex," said Girard.

"Enough of this!" said Rodney. "You must stop gibbering like old women and find the killers. They are getting farther away with each passing minute!"

"Oh, I think not."

"Really? Would you care to explain, Thorne?" said Girard.

"Actually, gentlemen, I know who killed his lordship. I have only one more matter to confirm before settling this entire affair," I said.

***

The sitting room and bedroom that had been assigned to Case-Jones was midway down the hall on the house's third floor. It wasn't locked; there was no need. So, I let myself in. If the whole thing was the work of Yankee assassins, then no doubt they were, as Rodney seemed so convinced, long gone.

Everything in the room was as neat and orderly as if the maids had just finished cleaning it. I opened the closet and found each of Case-Jones' suits perfectly arranged. Three pairs of boots, which I suspected were shined to within an inch of their lives, sat on the floor.

I was about to inspect one when something struck me hard across the back of the head. The blow didn't knock me out, but I had to grab onto the doorframe to keep on my feet. Whoever my attacker was followed with a swift kick that connected to my hip and almost sent me down.

Somewhere in that process I realized that I still had one of Case-Jones' boots in my hand. I threw it at my opponent, missing, of course, but that bought me time enough to get steady on my feet and face him.

Without really thinking, I threw myself against him, sending both of us tumbling down. What I presumed to be a knife went clattering to the wooden floor. My own pistol was in an inside coat pocket and caught between the two of us, essentially unreachable.

"I'd suggest that you boys call this whole thing off right now!"

Jenny! She was standing with a gun of her own in one hand. The expression on her face as cold and unfeeling as any I had ever seen.

"Are you all right, Captain Thorne?" she asked. Better not to acknowledge each other.

"Aye, and very grateful to you."

I looked down at the familiar face of my opponent: Morgan Girard.

***

"You're insane, Thorne," said Girard.

I'd had the butler summon the two nigger handymen who were now standing on either side of Girard. He hadn't really wanted to come back to the living room, but the barrel of the gun I had taken from Jenny and held in the small of his back provided a powerful argument in favor of doing what he was told.

Jenny had excused herself, claiming to feel close to fainting now that it was all over. Officially, she had been passing by the room, heard the scuffling, and went in to investigate. Actually, I had left her hidden in the hallway, waiting to see who might come along.

"See here, Captain Thorne, I hope that you know what you're doing," said Collins. "I've known Morgan Girard since we were both small children. I cannot conceive of the idea that he is a killer."

"Then perhaps you had best learn," I said.

"So, what it is it you're claiming? Is he a Yankee spy and killer?" asked Rodney.

"Killer, yes. But I doubt he is a Yankee spy. I have no doubt of his loyalty to the Confederacy," I said. "He just wanted us to think that a Yankee spy was behind the murder. It would keep people from realizing that it was actually a matter of jealousy, revenge and, more than likely, double murder."

"Double murder?" said Rodney and Collins at the same time. "Who?"

"Yes, I'm fairly certain that in addition to murdering Lord Case-Jones, Girard also killed his wife, Allison," I said.

"Thorne, you have become a monster. You know Allison died of a weak heart," said Girard.

"Indeed, I attended her funeral," said Collins.

"But do we know that? We have only his word and the word of a doctor who no doubt made no close examination. This morning Girard told me about discovering Allison's body. He mentioned that her lips were cold and blue. It strikes me now that that may well have indicated death by either poison or suffocation," I said.

"But why? And why kill Case-Jones?" asked Collins.

I took out the medallion that I had removed from his lordship's neck and held it out where the others could see the disk. On one side was a stylized A and on the other an M. But the M had been obliterated.

"This is significant?" asked Rodney.

"It is, indeed," answered Collins.

"You know?" I said.

"I was there when Morgan had those made. They were his wedding present to Allison, one for her, one for him." Collins face had grown still, showing no emotion.

I didn't have to look to see that Girard still wore his, under his shirt. I had seen it on several occasions before.

"I would suspect that during their sojourn in England, Allison Girard and Case-Jones began an affair. That was no doubt when she gave him the medallion. At some point Girard found out about it but opted to do nothing. Perhaps he felt having an ocean between the two lovers was enough. That was, until he heard that his lordship was being sent here as a special envoy. That was when he made up his mind to have his revenge, on them both," I said.

I had wondered why he had gotten me involved in the whole matter. The only reason I could conceive of was he thought my loyalty to him would let him conceal anything that was too incriminating.

"This is a fine tale you've spun, Thorne," Girard said. "But it is nothing but pure fantasy. It's obvious to me that you've gone over the edge, pressure of the war. I've seen it in others who've worked for me. Trust me, son, I'll see that you get the best medical treatment."

"Morgan, shut up," said Collins. "He's right. You told me yourself that you knew Allison had had an affair. You know the hidden passages and panels in this house almost as well as I do. We spent many hours prowling them when we were children. So, I would say that the best thing to do right now is to keep quiet."

I expected Girard to do something, but not what he did. Instead of making a grab for a weapon and trying to escape, he reached into his coat pocket and brought out a small enamel snuff box. With a slow dignified, manner he administered several pinches to himself.

I don't know exactly what was in it, but the reaction came a few seconds after he set the box down. He went stiff for a moment and then his head slumped forward on his chest. I didn't bother to check; if he wasn't dead, then it was only a matter of a few minutes. Perhaps this was better than the gallows or a firing squad.

Still, the whole matter left a foul taste in my mouth. I didn't say a word to Collins or Rodney as I excused myself, went out into the hallway and lit a cheroot.

A few minutes later Jenny came up beside me. "Not the most pleasant circumstances for reunions, little brother," she said.

"No, no it wasn't," I said.

Jenny reached over and plucked the cheroot out of my hand. She lifted it to her lips and took a long puff from it, then blew the smoke out in slow series of rings.

"I know you looked up to Girard. He was a good man who went wrong, somehow," she said.

"I think we all have that potential, little one," I said.

"You know, you're a pain, but I definitely like having you around. Be careful, and don't you go wrong," she said as she passed the cheroot back to me.

"I'll try." That I was speaking to empty air didn't surprise me. My big sister is good at what she does.

"Is there a problem, sir?" The butler came from the direction of the kitchen, looking at me rather oddly.

"No, no, nothing that won't eventually right itself," I said. "I was just standing here thinking."

"Very good, sir, although I did think I heard you speaking to someone a moment ago," he said.

"Actually, I was. One of the maids, the one with red hair," I said.

"Red hair? You must be mistaken, sir, we have no maid with red hair. Besides, both of them have been working in the kitchen for some time," he said. I could see the slightest sparkle in his eye.

"Perhaps I was mistaken. Who knows, maybe I was chatting with a ghost," I said.

"Quite possible, sir," he said.

BORROWED GODS

BY
GUSTAVO BONDONI

"I didn't hear no one building this. Didn't see them, either," Old Carl said for the hundredth time. "Saw it when I woke up."

Quigley had arrived just after dawn, when Carl had raised the alarm, but he'd stayed in the background as the man told each townsperson who showed up the story of what he'd discovered. It wasn't often that people listened to Carl, and he was milking it for all it was worth.

Two parallel lines originated in the middle of the road and stretched off into the distance. They traversed the dirt main street until the road turned left toward Denver and the mountains. At that point they went into the scrub, straight as a gunshot. Quigley imagined they would cut through anything that might be in the way.

"What are they?" Anna asked. It was mighty unusual to see her out and about that early, but it would have been more unusual for her to miss anything important in town. She made it her business to know what was what.

"Ain't it obvious? Those are train tracks," a cowboy, one of the Lorraine boys, said.

Carl scratched his head. "They ain't got no sleepers. What's to hold 'em together?"

Men kicked at the metal lines embedded in the ground. One dusty traveler pulled a sledge out of a wagon and gave them a good whack. "Them's more solid than any train lines I ever seen. Shinier, too. And if you go back along them, you'll find that it doesn't have joins. I looked especially. Them's just straight metal lines all the way across the desert. And they're so solid I bet they reach down into the center of the earth."

"Into hell itself, I reckon," Carl said.

Everyone started talking at once then, everyone except Quigley. He listened. And then he heard another sound, not a loud sound... but dark.

"Listen," Quigley said. "Can you hear that?"

Everyone stopped talking. They always did when Quigley spoke. Even as children, they'd listened to him.

"It's like a humming," Anna said.

"Yeah. Fills you, like. Makes your bones shake."

The guy with the sledge leaned down over the rails and screwed his eyes shut. Then he straightened and walked to his wagon. "I'll be on my way to Denver," he said. "I don't want to be here later." He nodded to where the tracks disappeared into the distance. "Those tracks, they're humming. This is the end of the line... and a train's coming."

They watched him leave with a creak of wheels and tack. Finally, Anna said, in a voice completely unlike the hoarse whisper of her coquettish nights, "Shouldn't someone go get Cooper?"

***

The town marshal placed his fingers on the vibrating tracks and then stood, glaring into the distance. "We need to get to the Parker place," he said. "Who's comin'?"

Quigley stepped forward. "I reckon I will."

Cooper didn't look happy, but he nodded. They'd butted heads but tolerated each other because they both wanted what was best for the town. The disagreement was how to go about getting it. "Who else?"

Two of the Lorraine boys volunteered, which was no surprise, and then Anna stepped forward, which was. With a stare that dared the men to argue, she said, "Tara Parker was one of mine. If there's going to be business with the old man, I'm going to be there to make sure it's fair business."

"For all we know, the old man was the one who scared Tara out of town," Carl said. "And killed all those people." He didn't glance at Quigley.

"And for all we know, he wasn't. I'm coming with you."

Cooper shrugged and, since no one else volunteered, he led them towards the town.

Most of the buildings fronted Main Street, but others, places that needed a little room, were outside the town on the grassy hills that commanded a view of the eternal plains to the east. The church was on those hills, and so was the Parker House, the last remnants of one family's glory.

The house had been built with the proceeds of cotton farming in Georgia, which had allowed Zacharias Parker to move west with his family and household staff. The man's vision was to establish a model community where people of all creeds and colors—white settlers, freed slaves, and Indians from the surrounding hills—could live in harmony, learning from one another, in a territory far removed from the arguments about free states and slave states.

But Zacharias had died within a year, and his wife weeks later, leaving his two young children to be raised in the thirty-room house by their colored servants.

Whispers about what had happened in those years had sprung up around the Parker Trading Post: witchcraft, communing with spirits, forbidden liaisons, death cults.

But the children had grown. Zebadiah Parker became, as a young man, the head of the community. Any darkness he might have been subjected to didn't make itself known. He was a good man, solid.

Until the day, twenty years before, on which his sister and her husband disappeared. On that day, he locked himself in the mansion, never to emerge again, and expelled his niece, a fifteen-year-old named Tara, who everyone believed would be the next town beauty. Homeless and penniless, with no way to contact relatives back East, she'd had only one option, and only Anna's patronage had kept her from becoming the woman of some blacksmith's apprentice or stagecoach driver.

Some said she might have been more respectable if she had.

Cooper knocked on the dry wooden door, causing flakes of ancient paint to float to the porch floor.

Footsteps within told them that their call had been heard, but it was an eternity before the door creaked ajar to reveal the deeply creased mahogany features of a man in a dark suit holding a threadbare feather duster.

"The mastah does not receive visitors," the man said in an eternal drawl that made the speech of passing Texans seem clipped and rushed by comparison.

He tried to close the door, but Cooper's foot barred the way. "I'm the law around here, and we need to speak to him."

"Town law don't apply to the mastah. That's for town folk."

"The law applies to everyone, high and low," Cooper replied.

Quigley had to smile at that. He suspected that the marshal wasn't talking about whatever was coming on that train, but it certainly fit. A train from nowhere, carrying God-knew-what, would make few distinctions of class.

"I'll tell the mastah." The old retainer attempted to close the door, but the marshal hadn't moved his foot, and if it came to a physical altercation, the enormous lawman would not find much of a challenge in the old servant. The retainer shrugged and disappeared into the gloom of the house.

Not waiting for him to return, Cooper swung the door fully open and invited himself inside. The others followed.

Quigley brought up the rear and studied the entrance hall. A chandelier, dark and covered in cobwebs, hung from the ceiling, and a two-armed staircase at the back of the room led upstairs. Wooden paneling gleamed darkly in the reflected sunlight, and the room smelled of wax. No lights burned.

The servant returned, and if he disapproved of their presence inside the sanctum, it didn't show on his impassive features. "This way, please."

They followed in silence, through a doorway, a long dark dining room with sheets over the chairs, and into a sitting room where a single candle threw flickering shadows over every wall, but appeared to give very little light.

"A delegation, no less," a strong, masculine voice said from the shadows. "To what do I owe this pleasure?"

Quigley tried to find the source of the voice, but he could barely make out the shape of a man seated in a tall armchair in the deepest of the room's gloom.

"It's a time of reckoning," Cooper replied.

"All times are times of reckoning," the man responded. "Won't you sit and tell me about it? I suspect there must be some wine somewhere."

"We don't have time for wine," Cooper replied curtly. "The time has come for you to face your sins."

"All of them?" The voice sounded amused. "I'm not certain even a true reckoning could do that. Or perhaps you're trying to assign me sins that aren't on my soul."

"I assign nothing. It's the train that will do the assigning."

"A train, you say?" Now the voice sounded more interested. "Is the railroad finally coming to our little corner of the world?"

"This is no human train. And it's coming for you."

"Ah. I see."

"Your black magic has run its course," Cooper said. "It's time for you to face the consequences so we can go on with our lives."

The figure in the corner stood with a rustling sound and Quigley gaped as the candlelight revealed the owner of the house. He'd never seen Old Man Parker before... and this was anything but what he'd expected. The man was in his early fifties, slightly going to fat but still sporting powerful shoulders. His beard, though greying, was cut short, and dark eyes peered out at them. "I admit I'm curious to see what you describe," he said. "I will go with you."

"You're already dressed," Anna noted.

He cocked his head, as if noticing her for the first time. "Anna," he said. "I never thanked you for saving Tara, did I?"

Anna turned away. "Tara would never have needed saving if you hadn't forbidden her this house."

"In that," he responded softly, "you are wrong. If she'd stayed here, she would be as dead as her mother. Dead like so many others. And yes, I'm already dressed. I felt it coming."

Quigley stared hard at the man, trying to see if his words were an admission of guilt, but found no clues in the impassive features.

They walked out of the house and stopped in the sunlight. Out there, a sense of oppression, of being constantly watched and judged, disappeared. Quigley breathed easy again.

Parker peered around the members of the group. His eyes lingered on the Lorraine boys, young, sullen, menacing. "You didn't think I'd come quietly?"

"I didn't know what we'd find in there."

"And if I didn't want to come, you would have tried to take me by force? Inside my house?"

Cooper shrugged. "I would have tried to do my job."

"You would have failed," Parker replied.

"Maybe. But then there would be no more doubts about where the evil that weighs us down is located. The town would have been free to act."

"The town is always free to act. There's no one around to keep you from lynching a lonely old man or burning his wooden house around his ears." He held each of their gazes in turn. "It's your own doubts that are holding you back."

"I don't have any doubts."

"No. You wouldn't. They say my father was like that, and look where it got him... dead, a world away from his family."

"If that were true, his family wouldn't still be here tormenting our town."

Quigley stepped between them. Parker was shorter than the marshal, but broader across the shoulders, but that would only matter if the fight remained on the physical plane. If the rumors were true... "This isn't the time to argue. There's something coming," Quigley said quietly.

"Very well," Parker replied. The marshal just nodded. Both stepped away and the group resumed its walk.

Moments later, they approached the crowd standing beside the tracks, which ended abruptly in the center of Main Street.

"It would seem to me that if a train's coming, it's not coming to my house," Parker said. "Maybe you should ask the Bank if they've been playing with dark forces they don't understand." He nodded towards the nearest building and seemed to be smiling under the beard.

"Humming is getting louder, Cooper," Carl said.

Cooper bent over the metal and stood, nodding. "Comin' closer."

"What are we going to do?" Carl said.

"We're going to meet them. Go get the pastor."

"I don't want to be here when..."

"I said, get the pastor," Cooper said.

Carl ran off toward the church.

They waited tensely until Reverend Jameson arrived, flanked by his wife. He was tall and sallow, all fire and brimstone... but the town feared Mrs. Jameson above him, and it wasn't even a contest. She ruled the congregation with an iron fist concealed behind raised eyebrows or pressed lips.

But even as they joined, the crowd thinned. Carl only returned as far as the corner, and others who'd been inspecting the tracks drifted out to watch the proceedings from windows or down the street a ways. Pretty soon, only Cooper's little group, the preacher, and his wife remained. Quigley was surprised that the Lorraine boys hadn't run for the hills. But it made a certain amount of sense: if they ran, they would lose what all respect anyone had for them, and they were too young to be able to survive that kind of humiliation. The oldest must have been twenty-one. The other, probably seventeen.

"Look," Anna whispered, pointing down the tracks.

Smoke floated in the distance. Black smoke, the darkest shade of night.

Quigley waited for the wind to dissipate the dark cloud, to turn it light and insubstantial, but that never happened. The smoke remained dark and evil even as it floated into the cloudless sky. "Should be here in a few minutes," he said.

The marshal put his hand on his six-shooter. One of the Lorraine boys walked over to his horse tied in front of the bank to retrieve a Winchester from the saddle. The wind kicked up dust and tufts of grass from the ground, a cold wind more suited to February than to May.

Then the sound arrived. Quigley had heard trains before, and this roar wasn't like those. This one was angry, a screech more than a roar, the sound of metal grating against metal, of souls being torn from unwilling bodies. His stomach turned to water, and his body wanted to run, but he stayed. This was his town, it was the town where his family had grown, and the town where his youngest daughter had disappeared one morning on her way to church, never to be seen again. One of several women and children to have vanished in the past twenty-five years.

If he ran now, he suspected he'd never learn what had happened to all of them. He wouldn't be able to live with himself.

The preacher broke their silence. Ignoring the growing screech, he began to pray, in a loud voice, his prayer book open in the palms of his hands. Quigley had noticed his wife speaking to him only moments before, probably commanding him to banish the beast.

Quigley suspected that that wouldn't work.

Now they could see the train, a black dot beneath the black cloud. Every eye was glued to it as it approached, every ear filled with its unholy sound roaring in counterpoint to the preacher's booming prayer.

"That don't look like any train I ever saw," the elder of the Lorraine boys said.

"Hell-trains aren't regular trains," Cooper replied grimly.

It consisted of a single black carriage, twice as long as a steam locomotive, but shaped like a bullet. The black shone in the sun and the smoke emerged from both sides of the train. It had no windows.

"Watch out," Cooper said. "Ain't no bump stops here. Not sure if the train will stop at all."

If it didn't, it would slam straight into the buildings behind them. They moved to one side and watched, out of the way of the rails.

It was moving faster than any train Quigley had ever seen, even that time when he'd traveled to Chicago to buy supplies for his store.

A higher-pitched screech added its unpleasant sound to the train's roar, and it began to scrub off speed. As they watched—fascinated, aghast—the black bullet stopped right at the end of the tracks.

"Pray for it to leave!" the preacher's wife shouted. "We can defeat these minions of the devil."

Quigley studied the machine in front of them. While he didn't think it was a human construction, something about it told him that the devil wasn't involved, either. This seemed like something outside of Christian faith, something like the stories they told of African religions. Parker would know, he suspected; everyone knew his servants were more than just servants.

Then he moved back. Heat rolled off the train in waves.

With a crack that hurt the ears, the front of the train opened like the mouth of some obscene serpent and three figures emerged.

A man with skin so dark as to be nearly blue and his face painted white, taller than everyone in the road, a woman whose brown skin was creole-light, and another man, a muscular figure with skin so white as to glow in the sun, with pale grey eyes and curly white hair. All three of them wore nothing but loincloths and bead necklaces. The tall man held a staff in the form of a snake.

"Pray!" the preacher's wife shouted. "These are the servants of the dark one."

Parker fell to his knees. "Sacred loas!" he whispered hoarsely. "I repent my errors."

The tall man stared at him and nodded. "It is good that you do so. You have much to repent. A true man would have protected his niece under his own roof." The man's voice was so deep that it made the ground shake.

"Have you come for me?"

"Not unless you desire it. Your life has been blameless, albeit weak. You should have led this town. You had the knowledge to stop the darkness and you chose to hide from it. Knowing that you could have acted is enough punishment." He looked around. "But this town must be cleansed. It has fallen afoul of dark things."

Cooper had his gun out and pointed it, trembling, at the tall man. "The only dark things here are you. Foul creatures from hell."

The black man gazed impassively at the marshal and gave a rumbling chuckle. "We can be dark, that is true. But there are rules about the darkness. Innocent blood, though valuable, is also sacred. It is not to be taken lightly, never to be spilled without cause. It brings power, but also responsibility."

Quigley felt anger growing in him. "Innocent blood?" he asked, stepping forward. "Like my daughter's? Little Mary is dead?"

"She is."

"All to give this," he spat towards Parker, "this monster power to do evil."

"To give a monster power, but that man isn't a monster; he is just weak."

He and his companions took a step towards the place where the Lorraine boys stood beside the preacher and his wife.

"Stop right there," Cooper commanded. "Not another step."

The trio ignored him and kept going.

A gunshot brought everyone back to their senses, breaking the mesmerizing spell of the three figures. Cooper had fired, and now he fired again. Two bullets aimed at the man's head.

Cooper never missed.

But the tall man simply smiled a broader grin and kept going, completely unmarked, completely unaffected. Three steps sufficed for him to stand facing the quartet. The younger Lorraine boy broke and ran, but the preacher stepped forward.

"I'm not afraid. I'm a man of God. I've lived a life of virtue and have nothing to fear from the denizens of Hell."

The big smile broadened even further. "You are right. We have no issue with you... but mostly because we are not from your Hell. Step aside."

The preached did so, unthinkingly. He either didn't realize he'd left his wife alone to face the loas or had fallen under some spell.

The severe, black-clad woman, so feared by the town, stepped forward. Her hair had somehow escaped from the tight bun she always wore it in and framed her eyes, wild with rage. A large wooden cross appeared in her hand, and she brandished it like a shield.

"Begone, foul creatures! I command it of you in the name of God!"

The tall man raised an eyebrow. "That is not my god. That is not your god."

"I am a woman of the church!" she screamed.

"You are a woman of the spirits, but not the ones from that cross. You know the lore, taught by one of this one's former servants." He nodded toward the kneeling Parker. "You were given the power, but you never showed the respect and never gave as much as you were given. You killed without giving thanks, without sharing the glory. That is why the town sank into evil. And it would have sunk even further had there not been someone stout of heart there to stop you from turning this into a witch's mire, a den of darkness."

The tall man turned from the voiceless wife of the pale, silent preacher and walked to Anna.

She stood her ground, defiant to the last, as if facing a drunk in her house of ill repute.

The tall man put a hand on her. "You are the spirit of light in this town and, though you are not of our spirits, you have our blessing."

As Quigley watched, years seemed to evaporate from Anna's face. Lines she'd earned through long nights, the bags under her eyes from lack of sleep, and even her corset seemed to fit more comfortably, suddenly compressing less sagging flesh.

The preacher's wife broke the moment. "You honor the whore?"

"We honor the woman whose bravery and kind-heartedness saved the town and kept the niece from joining the sister who was her mother. Had you been able to partake of that blood, you would have been too powerful to stop." He paused and grinned impossibly, even wider, showing more teeth than humans should have in their heads. "And you would have been strong enough to resist us. But thanks to her, you aren't."

The preacher's wife screeched and ran toward the big man.

His grin nearly split his head in half.

An explosion rocked the street, sound and black smoke filling the empty space.

When the smoke cleared, the preacher had joined Parker on his knees, the prayer book forgotten in the dirt beside him. The rest stood dazed and pale, all except Anna, who glowed with health and radiance.

The train was disappearing into the distance, the track disappearing in its wake. Where the tracks had ended stood a grotesque statue of the preacher's wife. It was the same woman, but her face was contorted in a rictus of hate, her formerly smooth features lined and wrinkled. It was the preacher's wife as hag. She stood on a cylindrical base, on which were inscribed several words:

This monument marks the place where the Francine Jameson, witch and blasphemer, was taken by her gods to account for her actions. She was the murderer of...

A list followed, headed by the name of Renée Parker.

Quigley walked up to the base and, ignoring the statue and the rest of the lettering, ran his hands over the shape of one name: Mary Quigley.

He felt the tears run down his cheeks and felt thankful. Thankful that he knew, now. He was free to mourn.

And when he felt a hand on his shoulder, he knew without turning that it was Anna's. The gods, the loas, whatever they were, were right. This woman—a woman he'd barely acknowledged as a neighbor, and had often pointedly ignored when they passed on the street—was the soul of the town, the light against the darkness. She should be the town's leading citizen, not him.

Quigley cried into the dirt of Main Street.

***

It was late afternoon, and Quigley was tired and very old. But he wouldn't let that stop him from taking the pilgrimage he'd taken every day for the past forty-five years.

The statue was exactly where the strange visitors had left it. The street was now cobbled, and the horses were slowly being replaced by the new-fangled horseless carriages that were sweeping the nation. A Ford, one of those Ts everyone was buying cheap, narrowly missed him as he tried to cross into the middle of the street.

It wasn't Main Street anymore. Since they couldn't remove the statue or dig it up—not even with dynamite—they'd simply moved Main Street one block over and renamed this one Second Street.

Quigley didn't care. The statue was as crisp and fresh as when it had been erected. No bird ever perched on it; the rain was as powerless to erode it as the dynamite had been in removing it.

No one else remembered when it came. Anna had left a few weeks after the black train, and the people—fathers, siblings, husbands—who'd once come to run their fingers over the names of lost loved ones had stopped coming. Some had died, some had left town, some had simply moved on with their lives.

But Quigley would come every day for as long as he lived. He'd sold the store to Sears years ago, and his children had left town, but he never would, not as long as Mary's name was on the statue. No matter how the town changed, how the world changed, it was his comfort to know that, when he and all his other children were forgotten, Mary's name would live on as long as the statue remained in place.

From what he'd seen, that would be forever.

This time, his tears fell on the cobbles of Second Street.

INNER SKIN
BY
KEVIN M. FOLLIARD

The Devil's Spring Saloon was all but empty thanks to the after-sundown curfew. Yet five card sharps lingered, too brave or too stupid to fear the murders. Clyde was used to tending bar the night of Wild Wilfred's poker game, but never by his lonesome. The players in Wilfred's game rotated, and the cheaters never returned.

Folk suspected that Wilfred had been the one robbing stagecoaches the previous spring, but nobody could prove it. His pals Hoss and Johnny Wolfsong were his likely cohorts. The other two completing the quintet lately had been the Mendez twins, Mitch and Marco—both young, strong rancher's sons whom Clyde had schooled with. Clyde found both brothers equally easy on the eyes: tanned, muscular, with smooth skin and chiseled jaws. He felt like a fly on the wall listening to the game, waxing the bar top.

Any other night, Clyde might feel privileged, if not a little dirty, eying the Mendez brothers in a way that would turn his parents in their early graves. But tonight, the deserted corners of the saloon felt haunted. Dread hung in the air, and a terrible thing—more than just a feeling in his guts—told him that Wilfred's poker game was inviting danger into the saloon.

"You're cheatin', Hoss!" Wilfred's bushy eyebrows arched as he studied his cards. "Can't figure out how, but I know it!"

"Settle down, Wil!" Hoss grumbled. "Just because someone else wins a few hands don't mean they're cheatin'."

The men were so engrossed in their poker game they hadn't bought a drink in an hour. Clyde had wiped the glassware until they glistened like hung diamonds behind the bar. He wanted to tell them to wrap it up, head home if they weren't buying. That's what his friend and mentor Garret would have done. But Garret was dead now.

Clyde had dutifully tended the saloon in the weeks since Garret's corpse turned up in the desert. But there hadn't been a will, and the pit in Clyde's stomach told him that by the law of the West, the bar belonged to Wilfred as much as it did him.

The whole town is supposed to be on lockdown and you five are keeping me in danger. Least you could do is tip. He wished he had the guts to say it.

But Clyde wasn't stupid. There'd be a bullet in his head if he mouthed off. Wilfred was dynamite on a timer. Everyone—even the newly appointed Sheriff Riley—knew Wilfred was fast becoming the real power in town.

Of course, lately, that could change overnight.

Maybe, he hoped, *if I send Wilfred home tipsy, that creature will pick him off, and we'll have one less monster in town.*

"Anyone thirsty?" Clyde offered.

"No." Wilfred anted up. "I like to keep my wits about me."

"Say, kid! I'll take a whiskey!" Hoss held up two calloused fingers.

"Comin' right up!" Clyde poured, then spotted a dark silhouette with a cowboy hat and a rawhide poncho lurking outside the saloon door. Whiskey spilled over his fingers. "Jesus!"

The five poker players turned in surprise, cards clutched against their chests.

"Evenin'," said the man outside.

His smooth timbre and even tone sent Clyde's chest pumping with excitement.

Joe Zhang pushed through the saloon doors into the light. Clyde took in Joe's handsome dark eyes, tan complexion, and stocky, muscular build. Twin revolvers were holstered at his hips. Joe looked exactly the same as he had that night so many months ago, when they lay under the stars together.

Wild Wilfred flattened his cards on the table. He turned his head and spat. "The hell are you doin' here, Chinaman?"

"I was sent for." Joe flashed a debonair grin.

Heat rushed into Clyde's face. He'd written to Joe over a month ago, after the first three killings. Clyde feared Joe had moved, never gotten the letter. At the time, he had hoped Joe's services would not be needed, had figured the killings would stop, or the culprit—a human culprit—would be apprehended.

In truth, he'd summoned Joe more out of a desire to see him again. To be held by him again. But since he'd written the letter, the situation in Devil's Spring had worsened.

"Sent for?" Wilfred stood. His chair scraped wood. "By whom? This town's on lockdown." He gripped the handle of his pistol with one hand. The other four backed away from the table, clearing a path between Wilfred and Joe.

"Easy, Wilfred!" Clyde rushed around the bar and stood between Joe and the card sharps. "I know this man. Fact is, I sent for him. This here's Joseph Zhang. He's a friend of Garret's, a special kind of bounty hunter."

Wilfred sneered. "What kind would that be?"

"I'm a monster hunter, friend." Joe held up his hands in a gesture of peace. "I don't like to shoot men, not if I can help it. So unless you're a monster, maybe repurpose that trigger finger back to your card game?"

A gold tooth glinted in Wilfred's sneer. "Only person who tells me what to do is nobody."

"Please, Wilfred," Clyde said. "Let's not get the sheriff involved."

"The real sheriff is dead," Wilfred said.

"Clyde," Joe whispered. "Step aside."

Clyde backed against the bar.

Wilfred started to raise his pistol.

Quick as lightning, Joe's hand blurred left. A shot rang out. The glass of whiskey shattered. Joe's other gun was now aimed square at Wilfred. "As you can see, friend, that bullet could just as easily have wound up between your eyes. Now I believe men in this country are innocent until proven guilty. I will, however, shoot you in self-defense."

Wilfred's face burned red. The gun quaked in his grip.

"Gentlemen, please!" Clyde said. "We're all friends here, because we're all human. Joe came to help us find... that thing."

"You're a good kid, Clyde, and I like you." Joe said. "But much of what you just said was untrue. Apologies to Garret for the glass. I will pay to replace it, of course."

"Garret is dead, Joe," Clyde said. "I've been running things. A lot of people have died since I sent that letter."

"I understand." Joe's eyes remained trained on the card sharps. "Sadly, your newly appointed Sheriff Riley is dead as well. I went to see him first, proper protocol."

Wild Wilfred grinned. The gun in his hand steadied. "That means there's no law in this town. And that means we don't answer to you, or anybody."

Joe ignored him. "Sheriff Riley is your skin-changer's latest victim. He was pinned down and gutted by something big, with claws sharper and longer than any bear or mountain cat. His throat had been torn out."

Hoss and the Mendez brothers went pale as ghouls.

"Skin-changer?" Wilfred shook his head.

Johnny Wolfsong cocked an eyebrow. "What do you know about skin-changers, Chinaman?"

"Enough," Joe said. "The attack happened within the past few hours. The creature entered the sheriff's office as a man, mauled him as a beast, and left as a man, I suspect. Now, I propose we form a timeline for everyone in this room." Joe holstered his left revolver, then reached into his pocket. He pulled out a glowing, blue arrowhead.

Johnny Wolfsong's jaw dropped. "Is that a moonstone? How did you—"

"A friend loaned it to me, and for those not in the know, this stone glows in the presence of an evil spirit. That means the skin-changer is in this saloon. So again, I ask that we all cooperate, and establish a timeline."

"We've been playing cards for hours," Hoss said. "Clyde'll attest to that, won't you, Clyde?"

"That's true, Joe," Clyde said. "I would say at least three hours. Before that, I saw Johnny Wolfsong tending to horses at the inn."

"Wait a second," Wilfred snapped. "You strut in here and want our life stories because of some parlor trick arrowhead, but none of us have seen a body. If Riley's dead, how do we know you didn't kill him? We don't know a damn thing about you."

"Joe wouldn't do that," Clyde said.

Joe held up a hand to silence him. "I didn't ask for life stories, gentlemen, I want to know about today. But if it puts you at ease, I'll give you the abridged tale of one Joseph Zhang. I only ask that we all move our hands away from our holsters, so we can have an honest to goodness conversation. I assure you, you're all innocent to me... until proven otherwise."

Wilfred relaxed, shrugged, returned his pistol to his holster, and crossed his arms.

"Thank you." Joe removed his hat, revealing a sweep of coarse black hair. With a flick of his wrist, he sent his hat twirling onto the bar top. He spun the revolver in his right hand and holstered it. "My father was a Chinese laborer who died of consumption working on your transcontinental railroad. My mother was Cherokee, but I've learned from many different tribes. The native people have a far deeper connection to this land and the spirits who have been here long before any of us."

"Hooey," Wilfred grumbled.

"I worked for a time with the Pinkertons, so I know the law. I also traveled abroad, and I've seen more than my fair share of the strange and unusual."

Clyde reflected on the first time he'd met Joe. They'd ridden together with their mutual friend, the late saloon proprietor Garret Grant. Joe's campfire tales of adventures in Europe—werewolves, ghosts, and vampires—had drawn Clyde in. The fire glowing in Joe's dark eyes had hooked him.

After Garret had gone to bed, it had been just the two of them. Clyde had been but eighteen at the time, and Joe twenty-eight. Joe tried to discourage the advances, but they both felt an almost supernatural attraction. It had been the first time Clyde had felt such intensity, and he'd never forgotten.

Now here Joe was again, diffusing the tension in the room with his silver tongue. Even Wilfred seemed at least momentarily charmed by the highlights of

Joe's career.

"To make a long story short," Joe continued, "Clyde and Garret wrote to me for information about the creature, and upon reading the details, I made my way here. I didn't know for sure what I was dealing with until I saw Sheriff Riley's body just now. His attacker's bloody footprints changed, you see, from beast to man. Skin-changers are human most of the time. Their dark selves emerge as they please. It's possible that one of you may be this monster without even knowing."

Wilfred spit. "Hogwash and hooey! This half-breed waltzes in and expects us all to believe in his magic stone."

"Call me that again, and I might put one between your eyes, whether or not you're the creature," Joe said, maintaining his cool demeanor. "Truthfully, Wilfred, and all of you, this stone is going to make quick work of our problem, because the skin-changer cannot hold it, even in his human form. He *is* in this room." He clutched the stone tight. "And he's decidedly not me. So, who among you will volunteer to hold this stone?"

Clyde raised his hand. Slowly, reluctantly Wilfred raised his hand, and his poker crew followed suit. Wilfred nodded to Johnny Wolfsong. "Let Johnny step forward. If he passes your little Voodoo test, then Johnny can run down to the sheriff's office and confirm for everyone what you've claimed."

"That's a reasonable request," Joe said. "Step up, Johnny."

Johnny Wolfsong hesitated, then shuffled toward Joe. He wiped his hand on his pants.

"What are you waiting for, Johnny?" Hoss whispered.

"We all volunteered," Johnny whispered. "I know these stories. This guy said it himself. One of us could be the creature and not know it. What happens if..."

"Gentlemen." Joe's face darkened. "Trust me. When I kill the man who has been hijacked by this monster, it will be a mercy. Take the stone."

Johnny's fingers trembled. He reached out and took the glowing arrowhead from Joe. He winced, squeezed it. Opened his eyes. And exhaled. Then he shoved it back into Joe's hand and raced out the door.

"He didn't hold it very long," Hoss said. "What if he's—"

"He's clean," Joe said. "The reaction would happen in an instant. Who's next?"

"Wilfred's next," Marco Mendez said.

Wilfred glared. His hand hovered over his holster. "Why me?"

"Because," Mitch Mendez said, "you insisted Johnny go first. Why wouldn't you go first if you were so sure it wasn't you?"

"Nobody knows it isn't him," Clyde said. "That's why Johnny was so afraid." Clyde's heart pounded as that idea sunk in. *Could it be me? There's no unaccounted time in my day, is there?* He remembered minding the saloon since noon, and he'd seen Sheriff Riley several times outside, hadn't he? Could he have slipped away in the dead of midafternoon? Could the creature be making him remember wrong?

Clyde's palms sweat.

Wilfred marched across the room and got in Joe's face. "I've got nothing to prove to you people. But nothing to fear, neither." He flattened his palm.

Joe's trigger finger twitched on his left hand. With the right, he dropped the arrowhead in Wild Wilfred's palm.

The scoundrel squeezed the arrowhead, turned, and showed everyone. "I told all of you, this is hooey. It proves nothing."

"It'll prove plenty once we've all touched it," Hoss said. "Give it here; let's get this over with."

"Catch!" Wilfred tossed the arrowhead. It glimmered as it flipped through the air. Hoss stepped aside. The pile of poker chips rattled as the arrowhead skidded across the table.

"Pick it up." Joe rested his hand on the butt of his gun.

Wild Wilfred rounded the bar. "Go on, Hoss. It's all Voodoo anyway." He pointed to the whiskey bottle. "Don't mind if I help myself, do you, Clyde?"

"Pour away," Clyde said.

Hoss reached for the glowing stone.

"Sweet Jesus!" Johnny Wolfsong shouted from behind the saloon door. "He's right! Riley's dead! And by the looks of it... I..." Johnny stuttered and stammered. His face had gone pale as paper.

"Get in here and tell us what you saw." Hoss turned his attention away from the arrowhead.

Johnny shook his head and backed away from the saloon doors. "No human did that! No animal, either! You can keep my money on the table, I fold. I'm riding far away from this town. Far as I can get." He darted away. Dust billowed from his footfalls as he crossed the street.

"Well shit." Wilfred slugged whiskey straight for the bottle, then he drew his pistol and aimed it at the table. "Okay, I'm with the Chinaman now. Everybody touch the stone. No sudden movements."

The Mendez Brothers exchanged uneasy looks. Hoss reached with trembling fingers.

Clyde's heart slammed against his ribs.

Hoss scrunched his eyes and grasped the arrowhead. He lifted it, opened one eye, and exhaled relief. "It ain't me." Then he recoiled from the two brothers and backed toward the bar.

"Heck, Hoss!" Mitch Mendez said. "If one of us was going about murdering folk as a skin-changing monster, don't you think the other would have noticed?"

"I haven't ruled out the possibility there's more than one monster," Joe said, twin guns now trained on the brothers. "Hoss, toss the arrowhead to the boys."

Hoss tossed the glowing arrowhead. Marco stepped forward and snatched it out of the air. "See?" He showed it to everyone. "Now lower your guns. It ain't my brother, neither." He grabbed his brother by the wrist and slapped the glowing stone against his palm.

An unholy howl erupted from Mitch Mendez. Smoke seethed from his palm, and he wrenched away.

"Mitchell!" His brother's voice cracked with fear. "This can't be right!" He spun and spread his arms. His brother hunched over. Unearthly snarls rumbled as he clutched his palm.

"Get out of the way, Marco!" Wilfred shouted.

"That's not your brother," Joe said.

Mitch Mendez's form swelled. His vest ripped.

"This is a misunderstanding!" Tears streamed down Marco's face. "I was with him all day! There's no way he killed Riley! Please! Don't shoot my br—"

In a flash, the thing that had been Mitch Mendez snapped upright. Wolfish jaws clamped Marco's neck. Six-inch claws sank into Marco's chest, ripping bloody lines across his shirt. The creature ripped a chunk of flesh the size of a saddle bag from Marco's neck and shoulder. Blood splashed the poker table.

Hoss and Clyde ducked and covered.

Joe and Wilfred opened fire.

Clyde watched from behind a stool as the creature held Marco Mendez's body like a human shield. Bullet wounds popped on Marco's chest. Blood sprayed like crimson fireworks.

The creature's hisses and growls sounded almost like laughter.

Clyde crawled around the other side of the bar, knocking stools over. He peeked around the corner in wide-eyed terror. The creature was slender, covered in spiny black hairs and the tattered remnants of Mitch Mendez's clothes. Huge, clawed feet had burst from his riding boots. He tossed Marco's body and slunk snake-like to one side. Then he pushed over the poker table and used it for cover. Wood splintered as Wilfred and Joe continued to fire.

"Aw, hell!" Hoss screamed and sobbed. "Sweet holy hell!"

Blazing red eyes glowed from behind the table. A serrated smile spread. Clyde stared into those eyes, desperate for any sign of humanity. Any sign that Mitchell Mendez, the handsome cowboy he had admired, might still be in there somewhere.

In one swift movement, the skin-changer hurled the table like a discus right at Joe.

Clyde shouted.

Joe ducked and rolled away. He fired two shots, but the skin-changer was already dashing across the room. Joe cursed and reloaded.

Clyde ducked next to the end of the bar. The beast hurled another cocktail table, revealing Hoss cowering and whimpering. He snatched Hoss by the neck.

Clyde squeezed his eyes shut. Hoss screamed. Liquid splattered the floor.

"Shit!" Wild Wilfred's revolvers clicked and clicked. He was out of bullets.

More gunshots rang out from Joe.

Glassware clattered and bottles spilled. The creature raced right at Clyde. Clyde winced, but the beast leapt over him and thumped across the bar top. Wilfred shouted. Clyde whipped around and shuffled into the corner. He spotted the profile of the creature, pitch as shadow, save for those gleaming eyes and blood-stained teeth.

He was gnawing Wilfred's throat.

Wilfred gurgled and choked. His hands and feet spasmed as the creature hoisted him off the ground. More gunfire rang out. The creature twitched. Blood spurted through his hide. At last, a shot exploded through his eyes.

The creature howled. He dropped Wilfred's slack body to the ground. A red river poured down the scoundrel's chest like a scarlet necktie.

Clyde trembled.

Wilfred reached in his direction, then his arm fell slack. His eyes turned up.

The creature collapsed. Lanky arms hung past his wolfish face. Slowly, the black beast shifted back into Mitch Mendez's naked, bullet-riddled body. His beautiful blue eyes had been blown out.

"Mother of Mercy," Clyde said.

"Clyde," came Joe's steely voice. "It's best you come out now."

Clyde forced himself onto his feet. He walked dream-like toward Joe, past Hoss's bloody remains. Garret's saloon lay in ruin.

Joe stood silent as a sentinel, dark eyes obscured in shadow. Smoke wafted like gray snakes from the barrels of his revolvers.

"Jesus, Joe!" Clyde wanted nothing more than to collapse into Joe's strong arms, just like that night by the campfire. To be held. Protected. He stepped toward him.

Joe's guns snapped to attention. "Hold it, Clyde."

Clyde raised his arms. "Easy, Joe! You got him! Just look at him. He's dead. Shame about these other men. They weren't the best men, but they didn't deserve..."

Joe's lip quivered. Lamplight glinted at the corners of his eyes. Tears.

"What's the matter, Joe? You did good." Clyde's heart pounded.

"Look over there." Joe gestured with his head toward the wall, where Marco

Mendez's ravaged body seeped a lagoon of blood.

"Jesus, Joe, I don't want see it. I...." Then he noticed. On the floor by Marco, the arrowhead was still glowing bright as a star.

"I said there might be two. Heck maybe more by now. And I don't think that one killed the sheriff."

Sweat beaded on Clyde's brow. His muscles burned. "Joe, c'mon. It's me! It's still glowing cuz Mitch's corpse is still right there."

"I'm sorry, kid," Joe sighed. "That's not how it works."

A horrible ache surged through Clyde's jaw. He tried to scream, but only a stifled grunt escaped him. His bones surged with pain. Guts boiled. Fever swelled into his face. All at once, Clyde remembered.

He remembered the ladies walking in the late hours back to Miss Gulliver's house. The smell of their fear. The tang of their blood. How their screams had been like otherworldly music.

He remembered how Garret had locked up the saloon. How he was planning to shut it down until they caught the creature. The creature had hated that. He killed Garret with cruel, surgical precision and dragged him down to the creek in the dark of night. He made Clyde clean up the blood before he slept and forgot.

He remembered just last week when Mitch Mendez had been his final customer, ten sheets to the wind, barely able to stand. The polite thing to do of course would have been to walk him home. But Clyde's blood boiled for the handsome, tipsy gentleman. Sweat beaded on Mitch's exposed, hairy chest.

The creature had bargained with Clyde in a way it hadn't before that night. The skin-changer made him choose whether to kill Mitch or violate him.

He'd chosen to keep Mitch alive, but cursed.

And at last, he remembered locking up in the middle of the afternoon for an hour to visit Sheriff Riley. He'd ripped him apart and painted the jail with his blood.

He always remembered and always forgot that he was the creature's slave, his puppet. He could never be rid of it.

"I want you to know, Clyde, I've thought about that night camping in the mesa, too." Joe aimed his revolver. "A lot."

Clyde's fingers split open. The skin-changer's claws curled out. His unholy howl rattled the walls. His loins burned with a mixture of lust and malice for the man with the gun. The creature wanted this man Joe Zhang to be just like him. To share in his curse forever and ever.

"And I'm sorry. Very sorry."

The skin-changer lunged.

Joe fired shot after shot. He backed toward the saloon doors.

The skin-changer staggered. Pain flared in his shoulder, his thigh, his stomach. Deep down, Clyde tried to plead, to beg Joe to help, not kill him. He wanted so badly for Joe to hold him like he had that night. Run his fingers through his hair. Sing with the crickets.

He wanted to lay beneath those stars one last time.

Finally, a shot exploded between his eyes.

The saloon blurred red.

The creature collapsed.

Clyde's aching bones shifted back to normal. Hot blood raced down his arms.

At last, he did feel Joe's fingers running through his hair, for just a moment, before the shadows swallowed him up.

THE TEARS OF
SCORPIONS
BY
JOHN B. ROSENMAN

Love and compassion came to Dulton, New Mexico, at 2:27 in the afternoon. It was a bright, sunny day, and those in the street saw the girl ride into town on an exhausted bay horse lathered with sweat. The girl was even worse. She was crying, her dress was torn, and she looked as if she would fall from her mount at any moment.

Dulton was dull like its name, but deep down, its citizens possessed a heart and could not resist such misery. Almost at once, half a dozen townspeople roused themselves and responded to the girl's distress. They approached the horse, which had stopped before the Roundup Hotel on Jackson Street.

Simon Wood, the first to reach her, asked, "Miss, are you all right?"

It was a stupid thing to question when anyone could tell that the girl had gone through hell, but it briefly stopped the flood of tears. She turned her face and gazed at them.

"They r-raped me!" she wailed. "All those men, they just wouldn't stop!" She wailed again, clinging to her horse's neck so she wouldn't fall.

The people of Dulton stood stunned. Their visitor's face was dirty, bruised, and swollen, as if someone had repeatedly struck her. It called out for compassion and understanding. In the case of two women whose husbands abused them when they'd had too much to drink, it sparked something more: empathy. They felt as if this girl were a younger sister, a part of their family.

"Please help me," the girl pleaded. "I barely escaped, and I fear my despoilers will come after me." She turned frantically and looked back the way she had come.

The townspeople turned also and gazed back down the road, searching for her despoilers. Though the word was unfamiliar, it sounded bad.

More people arrived, including the town's new doctor. Dr. Everett King had failed to receive a diploma back East, but two months ago, he'd put up a shingle here anyway. At once he took control.

"Let's get her into the hotel," he said. He pointed to two young men. "Ease her down from the horse and carry her gently inside."

They carried the girl into the hotel while Simon Wood saw to it that her horse was cared for at the stable where he worked. The girl's piteous voice tugged at the two young men's hearts and made them feel blessed to be entrusted with her care. "Oh, thank you for your kindness," she said. "You are so wonderful."

They took her to the best room on the ground floor and laid her softly on a bed. A midwife from the town removed her bloody clothes, careful not to tear her skin and reopen any wounds. To Dr. King, the victim already seemed to have recovered a little. Her wasted face and body looked fuller, and her color was better. He stepped in and gently examined her, then took her vitals. To his surprise, he found them all normal and asked her for her name.

The girl's strange eyes met his. "I don't remember."

Amnesia? Well, it was understandable given the terrible ordeal she must have endured, perhaps for many days. King rose and shooed away the women who had pressed their way into the room. "She needs privacy and rest. Come back tomorrow."

The women obeyed, though they left grudgingly, as if they were leaving a part of themselves behind. King closed the door and returned to the bed. As he did, the girl's eyes met his again and seemed to pull him.

He dismissed the impression. Nonsense! Eyes couldn't pull. Yet there was something odd about this girl's eyes. They weren't exactly blue but seemed like a color he'd never seen before, a subtly different hue. He pulled up a chair and sat down by the bed.

The girl reached out and took his hand. Clung to it.

"Will you help me get well?" she pleaded.

He squeezed her hand, suppressing an inner chill. "Yes, my dear, and I promise we will do everything in our power to arrest the men who did this to you and bring them to justice."

***

But they couldn't find the men, no matter how hard they tried. The town sheriff directed that telegraphs be sent as far west as Phoenix and as far east as Dallas, as far south as Tucson and as far North as Denver. Still, nothing turned up. No gang of rapists had preyed upon women, and no girl matching their guest's description had been reported missing. It was as if she had come from the earth itself, from the fertile soil of the plains.

Indeed, their visitor's health continued to improve, and within days, her stricken features ripened into beauty. She had an earthy, natural appearance, and Dulton's schoolmaster said she reminded him of Gaea, the Greek goddess of the Earth. The name seemed right, and they called her that even though she couldn't remember her real name. King thought Gaea fit her perfectly, and he was glad she had come to Dulton for help.

His first doubts rose when he walked into a room one day and found Gaea kissing a woman three times her age.

He retreated before he was seen. Surely, he told himself, it was an innocent kiss, a kiss given by a young girl in appreciation of some kindness the older woman had shown. Still, the experience triggered an all-too-familiar pain in his belly, and he went to sit down. This comes from expecting the worst from people, he thought. You should strive to stay positive.

Shortly after this occasion, King began to notice a change in the townspeople. It was barely perceptible at first. Regardless of age, they all seemed a bit drained or wilted. He told himself it was just his imagination, but he could not dismiss his qualms.

Three days later, he returned from a house call to an aging widow and saw Gaea dancing with some men and women in the town square. She laughed and skipped from one partner to the next, her bare feet skimming the grass and her dark hair waving in the wind. Her previous partners stared after her as if bereaved and regained their spirit only when she rejoined them. Yet King saw the subtle hint of decline deepen in each face.

What was wrong with these people? In the past few days, King had examined over a dozen townsmen, using an excuse about evaluating the community's health. Nothing had seemed different. Their weight, blood pressure, and other signs were normal. Most important, they were cheerful and told him they felt fine. Yet with every hour, he detected an inner wasting, a growing diminishment. Damn it, why couldn't they tell what was happening to them?

King knew he had to help them, save them from whatever sickness they had. Their deterioration seemed to have started the day after Gaea arrived here and he had helped the girl regain her health. Her victimization had been cruel—if she was victimized. He was beginning to have doubts.

Gaea. Had she infected the people in some way, and if so, what was the disease? Or was it simply his imagination? If the people didn't see anything wrong with themselves or each other, who was he to think otherwise?

As he watched, Gaea approached Dulton's pastor in a teasing manner, her body swaying with delight. "Reverend Hightower," Gaea crooned, "will you dance with me?"

Though King had only been in Dulton two months, he knew its pastor was stuffy and self-righteous. He was not the sort to dance and enjoy a good time unless it was in heaven. And he was clearly reluctant now. King saw Gaea take his hand and pull him out onto the grass. Reverend Hightower glanced back at his fat wife, beseeching her help, but she stayed put as if under a spell.

The good pastor surprised his congregation by demonstrating that he was not only a capable dancer but an inspired one. He swung Gaea around and around, laughing and kicking his heels. As they whirled, the townspeople started to sing a familiar, bouncy hymn.

This little light of mine, I'm gonna let it shine.
This little light of mine, I'm gonna let it shine.
Let it shine, let it shine, let it shine.

Round and round they went, Reverend Hightower's thinning hair swinging in the air as he laughed and danced. In the growing circle around them, people sang and clapped their hands.

Won't let Satan blow it out.
I'm gonna let it shine.
Won't let Satan blow it out.
I'm gonna let it shine, let it shine, let it shine, let it shine.

Gaea pulled Hightower close and pressed her body against his. As she did, she stared directly at the parson's wife. Gaea seemed to grin with malignant lust, and King had a strange sensation. He felt that Gaea hated them all and sought vengeance. But that was madness. What wrong could the town have possibly committed against her? They had only met Gaea a week before.

The dance continued. Laughing, Gaea ground her body against Hightower. In return, Hightower pounded his hips against Gaea, emitting screams of pleasure and pain. The community urged them on, singing and clapping.

Everett King felt a terrible foreboding. Something evil was happening, and he himself had helped to unleash it. He didn't know exactly what it was, except that Gaea seemed to have infected the townspeople with a debilitating madness. Perhaps she did it physically, either through a kiss, sex, or a touch. Yet she couldn't kiss, seduce, or touch everyone, could she? No, but those she infected could infect others.

The dance ended, and Gaea permitted Hightower to leave. He returned to his wife, his face pale and stricken.

Gaea swung around, searching for a new partner. With dread, King saw her gaze fall upon him.

"Ah, the good Dr. King. I owe you so much for saving my life." She moved seductively toward him, her hips swaying as she held out her hands. "Brave physician," Gaea said, "won't you dance with me?"

Brave physician. She was mocking and playing with him. King met her eyes and felt his soul quail. He stumbled back.

"Oh, doctor," Gaea said. "Why are you so shy? Come, the people want you to dance with me."

As if on cue, the people started to clap and shout. "Dance with her, dance with her, dance with her!"

King turned and started to leave, only to find a girl of about seven blocking his path. She reached out and pressed her hand against his stomach.

"Dance with her," she shouted. "Dance, dance, dance!"

King tried to remove her hand, only to see the girl's fingers dissolve into powder and blow away. The girl herself didn't notice. "Dance, Dr. King," she said. "Dance, dance, dance!"

King pushed her aside and ran.

***

He went to the stable to rent a horse. The door stood wide, though, and no one was inside, not even Luke Broggins, the owner, who had taught him how to ride and care for a horse. On the wall, a tattered picture showed Jesus raising Lazarus from the dead.

Avoiding Gaea's bay, King saddled up a chestnut mare, then put the halter and bridle on. Born in Boston, he'd had little experience with horses until he'd answered this town's longstanding call for a doctor. The town had been happy to get him, but he knew they might have changed their minds after his display of cowardice.

He snatched an extra blanket for himself from the tack room and led the horse outside. Despite his relative inexperience, he mounted the mare smoothly and guided her in the direction he wanted to go.

He headed west out of town. On the way, he passed Reverend Hightower's church. King gazed at the white steeple, wondering what the parson's next sermon would be. Perhaps he would preach about Satan, and all his—or her—tricks. *Like turning a girl's fingers into powder.*

He rode about five miles, until he felt he was far enough away. Then he dismounted and proceeded to make camp. He put the blanket down but found he had neglected to bring matches. What should he do—rub two sticks together? Gazing in self-disgust across the prairie grasslands, he saw no trees or wood, nothing he could use.

What a failure he was! What an ignorant incompetent! The only thing he'd ever accomplished in his pathetic life besides getting sick was to summon the courage to travel nearly two thousand miles to an insignificant town in New Mexico. And what had it got him except the disgrace he so richly deserved? Before most of the town, he had turned tail and run from a beautiful woman's invitation to dance.

He knew he was being too hard on himself. Yes, he was timid, but there was something unnatural and dangerous about the woman. Besides, he'd had the guts to attend medical school before sickness had made him lose so much weight and forced him to withdraw. And since he'd arrived here, he had helped many people, even though his diploma and shingle were fraudulent.

He doubled up in pain, clutching his stomach. Such agony! Sometimes, when the pain got really bad, he'd imagined he was a woman in childbirth and there would be a glorious reward for such misery. But he was barren and knew his pain would lead only to more pain and imminent death.

As if that were not bad enough, King realized he had acted rashly and neglected to bring his laudanum. More and more, he found the opiate was the only thing that eased his pain. Soon, even it would fail him.

King lay on the blanket until the pain subsided. Then he rose and walked across the prairie grasslands toward the mountains. The West was so vast. A man could lose himself in it and die forgotten, like the animals whose bones he'd seen. Hadn't the Pueblo Indians lived around here? He remembered reading that their culture went back seven thousand years. And there were other tribes, such as the Navajo and the fierce Apache. The wind blew, and he inhaled the land's vast scent. Everything died sooner or later, he thought. You should not be afraid of death.

He returned to his blanket and sat down. Suddenly he stiffened. Was that what he thought it was? He leaned closer. Yes. By God, it was! A scorpion at least four inches long stood just a few feet beyond the blanket, its exoskeleton the same color as the sand and its grasping pincers and poisonous tail ready to strike.

Only he wasn't the target. Its focus was a black beetle that scuttled nearby on the dirt, going about its business, apparently unaware of its camouflaged enemy. The scorpion didn't move, but King had heard they spread their multiple legs on the earth to detect the slightest vibrations. And then they would strike.

Perhaps not, though. Perhaps this time, the scorpion would let its dinner go. Call it a tender mercy. Ah, but there was no mercy in the West. A predator never let its prey go, and scorpions never shed tears for their victims.

He forced himself to watch as the scorpion attacked.

***

King rose early in the morning and rode back into town, thinking of the scorpion. The arachnid had Scorpius, an entire constellation in the southern celestial hemisphere, named after it, and yet look what it did. You would think it would be better behaved.

It was a beautiful day, but his heart was filled with dread. To his surprise,

Reverend Hightower sat on a bench outside his church, evidently enjoying the weather. It was a common practice of his, and King was comforted by this sign of normalcy.

He clucked to the horse and moved closer. "Good morning, Parson," he said.

Hightower didn't respond, nor did he even stir. King hesitated, then dismounted and went to him.

"Parson Hightower?" he said.

Still no response. After a moment, King reached out and touched his shoulder.

It crumbled in his hand and spread inward. He watched half of Hightower's body dissolve in a white powder and blow away in the wind. His head hovered, its patrician features and fine mustache as impressive as ever. Then it went too, vanishing in a puff of dust.

King numbly returned his horse to the stable. As before, the door was open, and it seemed empty except for a few horses. He stepped carefully around piles of white powder, heading toward the back where the owner kept his small office. King's stomach churned with fear. Surely Luke would be back by now.

When he reached the office, he saw that Broggins was sitting behind his desk and smiling, his spectacles perched on his nose as always. King felt dizzy with relief. Thank God! Luke was the closest thing to a friend he had in Dulton. The man had taught him everything he knew about horses.

He entered the office. "Luke, I'm so glad you're all right!"

No response. Broggins continued to smile.

"Luke... have you seen what's happened?"

Broggins remained silent. King hesitated, then rounded the desk and looked down.

Below the waist, there was no Luke Broggins. His legs and manhood had dissolved into a pile of powder on the floor.

King gagged, trying not to vomit. Hightower's fate was terrible, but this... He reached out for Broggins' shoulder, then caught himself. Lurching back, he turned and stumbled out.

What should he do? Dazed and distraught, he considered returning to his room at the hotel but knew there was no escape. In the end, there was only one place he could go.

He headed down Jackson Street, avoiding piles of white powder with clothes mixed in. A hat, a dress, a pair of jeans. A child's toy, its wheels slowly spinning. Soon, he knew, the powder would be gone, dispersed by the winds.

She was waiting for him on a swing in the town square. As he approached, she set it in motion. He watched her rise higher and higher, laughing with delight. To King, she looked like a beautiful, innocent girl of about eighteen. But appearances could be deceiving.

He stopped before her. "They're all gone, Gaea," he said.

The swing came down and stopped cold. No backswing. She stared at him, sitting so still, so silent, she reminded him of the scorpion. He remembered how the scorpion had watched its prey and hadn't moved until it attacked.

Finally, she spoke. "My name's not Gaea, Dr. King. I have no name. I was spawned in this world's rivers and born in its deep dwelling heart. I'm a child of the West, of this vast country you shall never tame."

King nodded. "And you've lived a long, long time."

"Oh, yes," she replied. "Before the Apaches, Pueblos, and Navajos, I was here. For countless centuries I waited for the first hunters and trappers and Indians to appear and inhabit my land."

King sighed, finding he understood though he could not say why. "And you're bored, aren't you? You'll do anything, resort to any measure to fill your endless existence. That's why you pretended to be a helpless girl preyed upon by heartless men. You—the greatest predator of all."

She laughed. "So true. I've played many games to while away my days. At first, I tried to do good. But doing good is boring. It's no fun. So, I changed my tune. Who do you think created half your ghost towns? Or helped the Indians to get smallpox? And don't even ask me about all those earthquakes and wildfires."

King looked around. "And now you've killed everyone in this town."

"All except one," Gaea said. "I've saved you for last."

"Why?"

She smirked. "Don't you know?"

He swallowed. "Tell me."

"Very well. Because for some reason I sense you understand me. And because you refused my invitation to dance."

She rose from the swing and glided around him, weaving a sensuous spell. He tried to resist the deadly lure of her moist lips and swaying hips, her heavenly, intoxicating scent. Her supple hands darted in and touched him in intimate places, reminding him of the scorpion's pincers that had seized the beetle in order to kill it. Part of him wanted to run; the other part wanted to embrace her.

Her hypnotic eyes seemed to see deep into his soul. "Dr. King," she said, "Haven't you ever wanted to know a woman? To possess her body and to be possessed in return?"

King felt stricken. She knew he was a virgin, and she knew his deepest desire! He retreated, but she only followed.

"Will you dance with me now?" she asked.

Do I have a choice? He stepped forward, feeling a familiar pain in his innards. Though he knew it made no difference, he tried to hide it and not show any sign of weakness.

She slipped into his arms like a dream, as if she belonged there. He felt the crown of her head press against his chin. She was five feet six at the most, and they might be dancing at a church social or a town dance. But he knew that nothing here was what it seemed. Whatever this nameless, timeless creature was, she had adopted her current form only to deceive and entrap. Most of all, she did not give a damn how she hurt and destroyed him, as testified by the dwindling piles of white powder on the grass.

Music rose, from where he could not say, and they began to dance. He felt the music's rhythm in his blood, its fierce hunger course through his veins. It was the song of the great West, of its mountains and plains, its rivers and towns, and above all, its rich variety of people. As they moved in liquid grace about the square, King sensed what it was like to rule such a vast realm for millennia, and to have no escape from such a burden. The land had borne her, and the land was a possessive mother.

They stopped dancing, and he felt again the power of her eyes. "Just one kiss," she said. "And you will be with me forever."

King had been a coward all his life, but he found he could not refuse this challenge even if it destroyed him. He accepted her invitation and pressed his lips to hers, thereby plunging himself into the most erotic and fulfilling experience of his life. Compared to it, the few women he had dared to kiss were nothing. She was a goddess, and he felt them both join in an ecstatic union as the world sang about them.

Then it all changed.

Suddenly her lips became a snare and he felt them begin to drain his essence. Moment by moment he emptied into her. He tried to pull away and halt the loss, but her force was irresistible. She sucked him down and down, and he was helpless to fight back. Her arms squeezed him tighter, so tight he could barely breathe. Soon, he knew, he would be only another pile of white powder on the grass.

Then something stirred inside him, and he felt an ally rise to his defense. It entered her and fought back, striking through her walls and defenses and seeking her core. She pulled back, screaming in shock, but he recaptured her and brought her home, draining her just as she had drained him.

Finally, he let her go.

She collapsed and lay shriveled on the grass, her lovely face ruined. She reached up, her hand trembling. "How..."

He gazed down. "I think it's my cancer. It's spread so fast and is so virulent. Back home, the doctors gave me only a few months." He eyed her closely. "It looks like it's even more deadly to you."

Her body convulsed and began to change—changed until he beheld her hideous true form, the unspeakable horror she had concealed for so long. Though his mind teetered, he fought the urge to look away, just as he had with the scorpion.

"I've hated your kind all my days," she said. "Hated your sanctimonious preaching and your joyful copulations. I've wanted to tear you down and make you suffer. Despite all my powers, I could never feel what you did. I could never love or care. And unlike humans, I was always alone."

King remembered his feeling of the day before, when she had seduced and humiliated Reverend Hightower. "I know," he said.

She moaned. "But now I'm free at last," she said. "Thank you, Dr. King for finally lifting my burden." She smiled and like the scorpion, delivered her final sting. "Now *you* can carry it for me."

As he watched, the girl the town had named Gaea dissolved into a pile of white powder.

King stepped back. *Carry it for me?* What did she mean? The creature was dead, and its powers died with her.

Only something was different. He looked down at his body, seeing it fill out before his eyes, regaining the weight it had recently lost. The cancer... He sounded his body, but he could detect not a single trace of it. Granted, he didn't have medical confirmation, but he knew in his core he was completely cured. And that she had done it to him.

Now you *can carry it for me.* In dying, had she transferred her powers and role to him? No, it was impossible. She had lied to him, played a last evil trick for her dying amusement. Yet somehow, he knew she had spoken the truth.

The realization overwhelmed King and he clutched his head. This was madness! He would never accept Gaea's burden and be her replacement. Yet if it was true, would he be doomed to rule the West as she had, like a spoiled and spiteful, destructive child? Would he bring only pain and death to people whose lives were already so miserable? Or could he be different? Like the doctor he had strived to be, could he help where she had harmed, give life where she had taken it away? Show compassion where she had been only cruel?

King staggered across the grass, wanting to flee this devastating responsibility. He stopped before a pile of white powder near the swings, thinking it might once have been a child.

Help or harm? Build up or tear down? Resurrect or ruin? He thought of the picture of Jesus and Lazarus in the stable and knew there was only one way for him to test the limits of his new powers.

Trembling, Everett King raised his hand above the powder. "*Rise*," he said.

BAD DAY AT PROSPECT RIDGE
BY
STUART CROSKELL

When Annie Lightning and me returned to the relative comfort of the Buckhorn Saloon, I experienced what you might call a freezing of any useful brain function. Like a character in a dime novel confronted with significant awfulness, my jaw dropped. Try as I might, I just couldn't get a handle on what I beheld. Judging by the sudden tightness in Annie's breathing, she was struggling, too. So dreadful was the scene, we halted, dead in our tracks, unable—for a while at least—to take another step forward.

The tableau presented made no sense, was bereft of meaning, and all my poor mind could do was make a kind of inventory, listing parts of the whole, one discrete aspect at a time.

So, for example, Annie's barkeep, Jim Turner, in his quiet, unobtrusive way, yet tended—though his face was a little paler than usual, and a sheen of sweat speckled his bald pate. Then to our right, five gentlemen—strangers—were seated at one of the trestles, nursing the Buckhorn's five-cent beer. One of the men bolted the door behind us.

The man who stood at the bar I recognized.

Captain Cracker Styles. A bilious-looking, cadaverous fellow, the Captain had the appearance of a man rehearsing his own death.

The Captain was one of the first-ever recipients of the newly minted Medal of Honor. Back in the day, old Cracker was a hero. Recently, his stock had fallen somewhat. Being a murdering son of a bitch will do that.

Now to the thing that was giving me brain-ache. Next to Styles' glass of beer, all in a row, nice and neat-like, facing Annie and me, were three severed human heads. Sheriff Ames was one of them; recently deputized Ricky Dawson, too. The third belonged to Hank Monk.

Styles smiled. "Evening, sir. Ma'am." He tipped the brim of his hat toward Annie, but his narrow blue eyes stayed on me. "I know you?" he said, weighing me up in the way that men do, wondering if I might pose a threat.

Annie's hand found mine, held it tight.

Somehow, I managed a reply. "Gettysburg. After the defense of Culp's Hill. I was there when you marched back what was left of your men."

"Ah, yes. You shook my hand."

"That I did, sir." I was impressed with Styles' memory feat.

Culp's Hill. The Confederates had flanked us good and proper. But Cracker Styles, he'd rallied the troops. Against overwhelming odds, he and his remaining men had prevailed.

"Ah." Styles took a massive swig of his beer, wiping his mouth with the back of his hand. "And you?"

"Sixty-Ninth New York Infantry."

"The Irish brigade."

"*Faugh a Ballaugh*," I said proudly, my voice firm.

"*Clear the Way*, indeed," Styles said. "And you, soldier, you have something sergeant-like about you."

"In fact, Sergeant *Major*."

He looked me up and down. It was a curious feeling, like I was on parade once more and that my uniform, my brass buttons, had been found wanting. I had a terrible urge to come to attention.

"And you came home," he said. "Lived to tell the tale."

"I did," I said. "Many didn't."

"No, they did not." Styles nodded toward the heads. "Just like these fellas."

Styles stared at the heads, seemingly fascinated, as if he'd just become aware of their unholy presence. Still holding onto Annie's hand, I turned to where his men sat. They variously sported a mix of remnant Reb and Union uniforms. It happened a lot after the war—men from both sides finally finding concordance in their mutual inability to go back home, unable to let go of the freedom. Vicious gangs formed from their old Bushwacker units, forever restless, addicted to the comradeship. It was unusual to see them this far north.

I'd known fellows like Styles. Damaged, killing for the sake of it. In war, some men developed certain behaviors and were reluctant to give them up. Cracker and his ilk, they relinquished their humanity gladly, giddy with the latitude to do what they liked. In a way, he was worse than many such—the Captain, he'd come from a good family back east. I'd read about him in the papers. He'd been up at Yale, too, out Connecticut way, had all the advantages. There was no reason for him to turn out the way he did.

Addressing me, Styles said, "However, first things first. Our horses require stabling. They've had a hard few days."

I looked toward Annie.

Placing her hands on her hips, she stepped forward. "Out back," she said to Styles. "Help yourself. There's hay and water. You can settle up later."

Re-evaluating Annie, Styles tapped the brim of his hat with his forefinger. "Yes, ma'am." He affected a broad smile, though his eyes didn't join in with the effort. He gestured toward his men, and two of them moved swiftly toward the entrance, unbolted the door, and silently exited the Buckhorn.

Annie let me guide her to the other end of the bar, the furthest we could get from the heads without leaving the premises. "I have to ask, Captain," I said, pointing at the remains of my dead friends. "What is the significance of this?"

"This, Sergeant Major, is what you might call a three-head problem."

***

Earlier I'd stood with Annie at the western edge of Prospect Ridge's town limits, both of us gazing out over the vast empty plains.

Like her, I couldn't fail to notice the sky's peculiar sickly tint.

Our part of Colorado had a language all her own. Drawing down the wind, the land spoke by way of the trees, the tall grasses, through whispers, sighs. And while not as fluent in the lingo as Annie, I understood some of it, enough to sense the menace. It was there in the susurration of dust and dirt as it blew down Main Street, the far off rumble of thunder circling in the lowering yellow-black clouds. You could hear the plains' voice in the animals, too: horses snorting and blowing as if readying for a fight; jittery cattle—even gentle milkers—bellowing truculently; dogs howling.

"What is it, Annie?" I asked.

"Dust storm on the way," she said. "Be here real soon."

"Sure. But what's it bringing with it?"

"Nothing good."

"Are we talking about Hank here?" Hank Monk was the bachelor stock tender who ran the stagecoach swing station twelve miles northwest of us. Yesterday, while the mail coach rested its horses, its driver informed the sheriff that Hank had vanished. The driver had searched the small cabin and corral, but: no outward indications of violence, no upturned chairs. No blood. Just an open door, an unfinished meal on the table. Like Hank, he had left in a hurry.

"Hank's dead," Annie said, more to herself than me.

Sherriff Jack Ames and Deputy Ricky had immediately headed out to Hank's place. See if they could shed some light on the mystery. Last night, they'd failed to return.

"What about the sheriff?" I asked. "And Rick?"

Annie shrugged. I did the math. Four or five hours there and back. They should've easy returned by now.

The wind picked up, building on what it had already established. Annie's braids lifted, exposing her slender neck. On the distant horizon, a solid, red wall of dust and debris rising thousands of feet into the air rolled toward us.

"Maybe the storm caught 'em by surprise," I said, "and they're riding it out at Hank's." It was a fair stab at an explanation for the men's no-show.

"*Dimbibishus asaakwasi*," Annie whispered, easily slipping into the Shoshone tongue.

I turned to her. "Evil dirt?" I hazarded a guess.

"Sand devil," she corrected, chuckling. For some reason, it amused the hell out of her, me trying to get to grips with her mother's language. Unfortunately, while I was a quick study in many things, philology was not one of them.

"Nah," I said. "Just a regular windstorm."

"If you say."

I sought her hand and found it, clasping it in mine; she squeezed back. Annie.

I was as smitten as a schoolboy since she'd come into my life. It surprised the hell out of me, but I loved her. As for Miss Lightning, I suspected our relationship was more about pragmatism. Winter nights on the frontier were cold and lonesome, and for all my shortcomings, heat-wise, I was more efficacious than a copper bedpan. Those were her calculations, I fancied.

Orphaned at an early age, Annie had been taken in by a childless couple, wheat farmers. It was not hard to see why. Who could resist the emerald green eyes that shone so fiercely out her high-cheeked, olive-skinned face?

Though I never enquired too deep of Annie's history—how she came to Prospect—I knew some of it. Shoshone mother. Irish father. A Cork man who'd been killed by Union Red Legs down on the Missouri-Kansas border on account of his alleged affiliation with the anti-abolitionists. Heartbroken, her mama had gone to glory soon after. Her shaky origins notwithstanding, when Annie fetched up in Prospect, she'd the wherewithal to purchase its only saloon.

"We should get back," she said, about-turning and walking away from me, swaying her slim hips, knowing damn well I was watching. I hurried to catch up with her. Everywhere was deserted; the townsfolk had bolted their doors, shuttered their windows. Battened down the hatches, so to speak.

Steam rose from the flanks of the six saddled horses tied to the hitching rail outside the saloon. They'd been ridden hard.

***

Appraising the three heads lining the top of the bar, Styles said, "I'm guessing you're familiar with these former citizens?"

Nodding numbly, I told Styles who they were, *had* been.

"Hmm," he said, rubbing his chin as if deep in thought. "A station master, and a sheriff and his deputy. At least the latter two *passed* together, had each other's back. Not that it did them any good. Sometimes you just don't know what's coming at you until it's too late." He looked at me. "Last coupla days, we've lost four men in the same way. Picking us off, one by one. Leaving the heads. Never any bodies."

Styles was playing with us—I was sure of it. He and his men had killed the sheriff. And Hank and Rick. For the hell of it. There was only one end to this. Annie, me, Jim: dead. All of us.

"So, ah, what happened at the station?" I asked, buying time.

"Empty, abandoned. We found your people in the back yard, heads sitting in a row. Like they are now. Like with our fellas, no bodies. Nothing. Heads tore off."

He was lying again. The heads on the bar, they'd been lopped, clean cuts. I knew the difference. Styles' heavy cavalry saber snug in its iron scabbard lay against his left leg—three and a half feet of lethal-edged steel. Separate a man from his head like cutting through cheese.

I glanced at Jim. Imperceptibly, he nodded. I knew he'd have the shotgun under the bar trained on Styles' midriff, but that still left his several riders.

"Something's been following you," Annie said, "ever since you left the mountains."

"Now, how the hell would you know we've come from the mountains?"

"*Tsawhawbitts,*" Annie said, something close to awe in her voice.

"*Shawbits?* Hell's *shawbits?*" Styles demanded.

Annie paid him no heed; instead, she was staring at the Buckhorn's westward-facing shuttered windows as if she could see through and beyond them.

Styles looked to me. "Is she drunk?"

"*Shawbits.* It's Shoshone," I said.

"For what?"

"Not sure, Cap." I turned toward Annie. But she was still peering out toward the mountains, lost in her own world.

I racked my memory. The word was familiar. I was sure Annie had told me the story of *shawbits.* A midwinter kind of tale. The kind you told while the wind howled into the dark of night.

"I'm waiting, Sergeant."

I could tell that Styles was at the limits of his civility and that the monster inside him was once more rising. Annie, Jim, and me, we were all skating on very thin ice. His eyes glittered like an animal's caught in the firelight. Feral, unforgiving.

And then I had it. "*Shawbits,*" I said. "It's from a story. A *creature* of some kind."

"Some *kind?*"

I shrugged.

Styles laughed. "A creature, you say?" He laughed some more. I noticed his men remained silent. "Maybe you have it right. For surely, we are all creatures, and wretched with it."

"Why would someone take against you so, Cap? Seems pretty extreme."

He rubbed his chin. "I have to confess that some unpleasantness occurred. In the mountains. We were only defending ourselves, you understand, but some *individual* has taken offense at our robust methods of self-preservation."

Annie shifted her attention from the window, facing Styles. "There was no one left alive? On the opposing side?"

"That is correct, ma'am. And therein lies the mystery."

"*Shawbits*," Annie whispered.

I didn't want to think about what Styles and his men had done in the mountains. Whatever it was, it looked like they'd bitten off a plug bigger than they could chew.

"The thing is, folks," Styles said. "Is that whoever's following us, killing us, we've brought them to your door. I am very much sorry for that."

"So what happens now, Cap?" I asked.

Old Cracker, he needs us for something.

"We've got to make a stand, soldier. Just like in the old days. Understand?"

I nodded. But this wasn't the old days. Everyone knew that Styles and his mob had been murdering and pillaging like old-timey Vikings, from the Rio Grande to the Oklahoma panhandle.

Styles looked at Jim. "How about you, my friend? You with us?"

Jim nodded. "I served. I know how it goes." I wondered if Styles knew about the shotgun trained on his belly. If he did, he acted as if he didn't.

"Good man. If we're to survive tonight, we must organize."

Styles said to Annie, "So, you're the queenpin here?" He looked around the Buckhorn. "Mistress of all you survey?"

"Does that trouble you, mister?" Annie said sharply.

He grinned. "No, ma'am. I just like to get a sense of my surroundings, that's all. You know, appreciate the furnishings, the *fittings*." His eyes lingered on her.

As a distraction, I nodded at what was left of my friends. "You going to let them sit there like that, Cap? Seems kind of disrespectful."

Tearing his gaze from Annie, Styles considered me, and I wondered if I'd gone too far. With a strange glint in his eye, he put his hand on my shoulder, shaking his head. "Lordy, Lordy, what is the goddamn matter with me? Excuse me while I retrieve my manners." Expecting to be shot right there and then, I was surprised when, instead, he picked up the kitbag by his feet and placed it on the bar. And carefully, one at a time, he stowed away the three heads. Once the deed was done, Jim whipped his tender's cloth off his shoulder and wiped away the blood and general gruesomeness as if he was dabbing away at spilled beer.

Styles carried the bag over to his men and lowered it to the floor so that it rested against one of the trestles.

"There," he said, rubbing his hands. "All tickety-boo."

At that moment, one of the two men Styles sent out to stable the horses returned. When he finished bolting the door, he scanned the room. "Where's Bobby?"

"I might ask you the same question, Zeke," Styles said reasonably.

"I was only behind him by a minute or so," Zeke said. "*Shit.*"

"Yeah, *shit,*" agreed Styles.

Shaken, the man called Zeke resumed his seat next to his pals, nervously glancing toward the entrance.

I harrumphed gently into the conversational hiatus. "Has Bobby—"

"Now you see what we're up against, Sergeant Major," Styles said grimly, interrupting me.

I guessed it was Styles' need of us that was keeping us alive. If falling back into military rhythms and appellations kept me breathing, so be it. "So, Captain, how can we assist?"

Ignoring my offer of help, he said, "Whoever's been following us, they're good at it."

"You think it's *one* man?"

"Yeah, it's one, all right."

"Shoshone?" I said, glancing at Annie. For her part, she shook her head slowly, gazing at me, unblinking.

Noticing the silent messaging between Annie and me, Styles said, "She's right. Not Shoshone. They don't sneak around in the dark butchering men in their sleep. It's not their way."

Yeah, that's yours, I thought. "So, who?"

Styles winced as if in pain. "Hate to say it, but likely one of our own."

"A soldier? A militia veteran?"

"Could be. His strategy, it's guerrilla tactics. He's using our own capers against us, anticipating our every move. Only comes at night. Takes the watchman. So t'other eve, we posted *two* watchkeepers. Damned if he got them, too. Like a goddamn ghost. Me and the boys, we slept right through. He coulda finished all of us off in our sleep. Wonder why he didn't?"

Without thinking, I said, "He's playing with you, Cap." *Just like you're playing with us.*

"Yeah," Styles said. "That sounds about right."

"And you think he's—"

"Close," Styles whispered as if he thought whoever was out there could hear him over the wind's eerie whistle. "Closer than I like. In here, I think we're safe." He thumbed toward the back of the bar. "Are the rear of the premises secure?"

"Jim?" Annie asked.

"Always lock the backdoors at sundown," Jim said, swallowing hard. "Never liked the idea of anyone sneaking up behind."

"Well, that's all to the good, Jim," Styles said. "I don't take to being caught unawares either. It's unsettling." He turned to me. "Tell me, Sergeant. What iron are you carrying under that coat of yours?"

I lifted my jacket hem away from the side of my pants, revealing my holstered pistol.

"Ah, a forty-five."

"Makes all men equal, Cap," I said.

"That she does, Sergeant," Styles said. He had dropped the "Major," mockingly. "That she does."

He faced Annie. "And I dare say you can handle a firearm, miss."

From behind the bar, Jim pulled out another Colt, this one a six-shot revolving carbine. He shoved it gently toward Annie across the counter as if it was a holy artifact. She held it easily in her arms, cradling it comfortably as if it were a small child.

Again, I wondered what it was that Styles and his men had done in the mountains to incur such wrathful fury. Whatever this was about, it was personal.

The storm was hitting us good and proper now, flinging grit and sand against the Buckhorn's walls.

"Nobody's gonna be out in that," said Jim.

"Something is," whispered Annie.

"So, what's the plan, Cap?" I asked.

"Well, Sergeant, this is where *you* get to take the initiative." As one, his remaining four men trained their weapons on Annie and me. It wasn't a flashy move on their part, merely a subtle realigning of several gun barrels in our general direction. A fellow less sensitive to the presence of firearms might not have noticed. "Now," Styles continued, "to my thinking, what we need to do is draw our friend out into the open. Create an opportunity. The best way to do that, soldier, is if you take a stroll. I know it's not the best conditions out there to indulge in an evening perambulation, but you'd be doing my men and me a considerable favor, if you were to oblige."

"You want me to draw him out?"

"That would be the preferred outcome."

"Like *bait*?"

"That's a tad dramatic, Sarge, don't you think?"

"And you fellas, what're you gonna be doing while I'm out there getting killed?"

"We'll be on the sidewalk entrance, covering you. There's nothing to worry about. My boys, they're all sharpshooters."

"And where exactly do you think I should ply my wares?"

"Oh, anywhere out on Main. Just, you know, walk around, up and down, left to right. Long as we can see you, you'll be fine."

The man called Zeke lifted one of the Buckhorn's oil lamps from its hook, bringing it to me.

"So we can see where you are," Styles said.

"Like, easier to get a bead on what's coming at me, you mean?"

"Yeah. That, too."

"Can I take my forty-five?"

"Just be careful not to wave it our way."

"I'm going with him," Annie said to Styles. It wasn't a request—she was telling him.

Careful, Annie, careful. "No, Annie," I said.

"If you like, miss." Styles said. "As they say, the more, the merrier."

"*No*, Annie," I said. "God*dammit*, for once, can't you do what I say?"

"We are *not* in parley," she said. "I'm coming, and that's that." She had the *look*; the one with which I was all too familiar. The one that said, *You see if you can stop me.*

Zeke gave Annie a lamp, too.

All the better to see us with.

"You want us to go *now*, Cap?"

"Good a time as any, Sergeant." Styles nodded toward the entrance. "Mind you both keep in view, if we start to lose you to the storm, it'd be all too easy to mistake you for the enemy. And Jim here, he's kind of relying on you to do the right thing—if you get my drift."

"Sure, Captain," I said. "Whatever you say."

Annie by my side, I moved over to the doors and unbolted one half of them. We slipped outside, immediately buffeted by wind and near blinded by dust. The combination of dusk and storm made for sketchy visibility.

Behind us—true to his word on one thing, at least—Styles and men stood outside the Buckhorn, their ordnance aimed at our approximate whereabouts.

"You okay?" I shouted at Annie.

She nodded, squeezing my arm briefly.

"Back to back," I said. "Stay real close."

"I'm not stupid," she said.

Exercising maximal caution, we made our way down Main; so close were we, we were like one entity. The wind, when it gusted, carried a weird gamey smell, cloying and intense. I looked back toward the Buckhorn. Styles and his men were still silhouetted against the saloon's exterior doors, their weapons at high port. Alert, hopefully. Annie's back was literally at mine, and like me, she, too, was waving her lamp around with her free arm. We both knew that someone was close by.

Or some*thing*, if Annie was right. Something from Shoshone legend.

Whatever way you looked at it, we were being watched. And not just by Styles and his crew.

And then we heard it. A heavy person walking nearby, their footsteps dulled by the roar of the wind. As if aware of our attention, the footsteps stopped.

Annie started talking loudly in her native language, too quickly for me to get a handle on what she was saying.

It sounded like a prayer. I hoped someone was listening.

And then whatever, whoever, had been trailing Styles' gang, he charged out of the storm, barging through Annie and me, knocking us flat to the dirt. For a moment, the gamey animal smell was overwhelming. Seconds later, shots rang out, cutting through the night. Men shouted, and some screamed. Bullets whined past our heads like angry bees. I grabbed hold of Annie and pulled her to me, putting my body in front of hers, keeping her down. More shots, more screams. And then silence. Except, of course, for the wind.

"Annie?" I hissed. "You okay?"

"I think so," she hissed back.

We lay like that for what seemed like hours. Damned if I didn't almost nod off. I always was prone to a perplexing energy-depleting enervation while in the grip of sheer terror.

I shook my head, tried to knuckle some of the dirt out of my eyes. "I'm going to take a peek," I said. "See what's going on." I was about to tell her to stay put, but she was already up and trotting toward her saloon. I leaped up and tried to catch her.

"Dammit, Annie!"

She stopped at the saloon's entrance, and I caught up with her, breathing hard. The outside doors hung off their hinges, banging disconsolately in the wind. The sidewalk was slippery with blood. One of Styles' men lay on the ground, headless, his chest ripped open.

"Annie!" I hissed. "We gotta get away from here, fucking *now*."

But she twisted out of my grasp and strode into the Buckhorn.

"It's my bar," she said as if her statement made all the sense in the world.

"*Chrissakes*, Annie," I screeched, yet following her to what I was sure was my doom.

And for the second time that day, my brain went off-ranch, leaving no hint as to when it might return. Hauling up against Annie, I leaned on her, beside her, trying to tease some explication, some goddam *gist*, out of what lay before us.

In the middle of the floor, sat on the wooden planking, were three bodies, the remainder of Styles' men, back to back—all headless.

Leaning with *his* back to the bar, resting on both elbows, was Captain Cracker

Styles. He, too, was sans head. His body, tired of defying gravity, crumpled to the floor.

"Jim?" Annie whispered.

Like the great white whale Moby-Dick surfacing for air, Jim's bald pate slowly rose above the bar.

"Jim?" Annie repeated.

Wide-eyed, lower lip trembling, Jim nodded to my right.

At one of the tables, set in the gloom, a pipe-bowl of tobacco lit up orange.

Another stranger.

Pipe wedged into the corner of his mouth, he stood up and stepped out of the shadows, raising his hands slowly in surrender. A wide-brimmed hat obscured the lower half of his face, while his linseed-oil cloth duster reached down to his ankles. He was easily over seven feet tall.

"*Tsawhawbitts*," Annie whispered.

For my part, I remained speechless.

The huge man, if such he was, had eyes only for Annie. Truth be told, I was getting mighty tired of all and sundry making sheep's eyes at my girl. He said, "You are Sho-shone?" He stuck to single syllables, his voice a loud whisper, a raspy *sotto voce*, like his vocal cords weren't built for talking.

Annie just stared at him, mouth open. To be sure, it was a day for jaws to be dropped.

Several things happened fast. At any rate, too quick for me to react. First, Annie raised her big old carbine, pointing toward the tall fella. At the same time, he whipped out his pistol, aiming it at Annie. I closed my eyes and waited to die.

Reopening my eyes, the big fella still had *his* firearm on Annie, while she returned the favor with *hers*.

"Annie," I said, real slow. "Stand down, *please*."

But she remained stubbornly at the ready. I looked at the other guy, managed to catch his eye, and something passed between us, an understanding, like he'd caught my thoughts. He nodded, slowly lowering his gun, shoving it in its holster. It was an old Colt Paterson, the one with the long barrel and no trigger guard. With his thick fingers, I guessed, the big man would find guards a problem. It was a substantial weapon, but in his hand, it was severely diminished.

"*Tsawhawbitts*," she said again.

"On-ly part," the big man said.

Annie lowered her carbine. "Not *Tsawhawbitts*?"

"Fa-ther on-ly."

"And your mother?"

"Like you," the man said to Annie.

"Shoshone?"

The man nodded.

"I'll be damned," Annie whispered.

The man turned to me, said, "I am Ed-ward Saw." He nodded toward the headless gang members sat on the floor. "Bad men. Did bad things," he said. "Bet-ter dead."

"Drink?" Annie said.

Edward Saw nodded, returning to his seat, the chair ominously creaking as he lowered his massive self into it. "Old Crow, if you have it," Edward Saw said in that laborious, whispery way of his.

"What he's having," I said, pulling a chair up to Saw's table. I was sure that whatever Edward Saw was, he had a hell of a story to tell. And I was determined to hear it. The wind blowing out there like it was, it was a night for stories.

"You come out here, too, Jim," Annie said, sitting next to me, her eyes bright with wonderment at Mr. Saw's presence. "May as well bring the bottle."

None of us had the heart to ask Ed Saw what he'd done with the heads. And I really didn't want to deal with the bodies that littered the Buckhorn and her environs. Not right then, anyhow.

That stuff could wait till later.

Funny, how after a few shots of Crow, you kinda got used to Mr. Edward Saw's diabolical stench.

Kinda.

SHOWDOWN IN THE PANHANDLE
BY
MATIAS TRAVIESO - DIAZ

"If I owned Texas and Hell, I would rent out Texas and live in Hell."
~ General Philip Henry Sheridan

In the spring of 1890, Harry Gunnach was forcibly booted out of the Nicolett Hotel in Lubbock for cheating at card games. He was accused of having some way of figuring out other players' hands and using his skill to swindle hundreds of dollars from the merchants and cattle ranchers of the town.

Soon, a mob of dispossessed gamblers assembled and began chasing after Harry, seeking to recover the moneys he had stolen. He ran for his life and barely escaped his pursuers by purloining a pony from a stable on the outskirts of town. After a three-day forced march, Harry covered the hundred miles between Lubbock and the new town of Oneida (which was later to become Amarillo), and made a stop.

Oneida's original location had been in a low-lying area prone to flooding and, after the disastrous 1889 rainy season, had just been moved to higher ground. The move had led to an influx of merchants, cattle buyers, and settlers, whose business had spurred the opening of the 66 Saloon next to the Crescent Hotel. Harry had heard about the 66 from another card sharp in Lubbock, who claimed it was already the roughest new bar in Texas and the easiest place to get killed outside of Mason County. Harry had been intrigued by the implicit challenge in the description; its memory drew him to gallop towards Oneida as the citizens of Lubbock organized a posse to lynch him.

Harry hated the West. He was originally from Philadelphia, but had learned early in life that the City of Brotherly Love had no affection for him. After leaving Philadelphia, he had been forced to relocate scores of times, moving from one Eastern town to another in search of places where he could pass unnoticed. The vast emptiness of Texas had lured him in, but soon the big cities like Houston and San Antonio had become inhospitable. He continued to search for a place where he could thrive in obscurity as a card sharp, and at last discovered the northern corner of the state and chose it as the area most likely to fit his needs.

He had several hundred dollars left from his last games in Lubbock. He got himself a room at the Crescent and paid a visit to the town barber for a haircut and a shave. Then, dressed in his business suit, he walked the few steps over to the 66, which was a crude wooden shack squat on the yellow dirt of the panhandle. He entered the saloon at sunset and sat at a side table, ordered a whiskey, and nursed his drink, waiting for a card game to get going.

It did not take long. Six men had already gathered around the long table next to the bar; two seats remained empty. Harry watched for a few minutes, concentrating on the emotional and physical signatures emitted by the players. He concluded that four of them were amateurs, cattle ranch hands come to gamble away their pay. Another player, a giant of a bearded man named Karl, seemed to be an experienced player, for he took few risks and displayed no feelings on his stolid face. The sixth player was another big fellow called Lucius, who said little and sprouted a white goatee on his square jaw. Lucius' emotions seemed shrouded by a veil that Harry's probing could not penetrate. Harry concluded that the man was some sort of a card sharp, like himself.

They were playing Five Card Draw, a version of poker that had become increasingly popular since the war between the States. Harry liked that variation of the game, since each player immediately saw the hand he was dealt and couldn't stop broadcasting his feelings about it. For someone like Harry, able to read other people's emotions, no bluffs could disguise weak holdings. He did not need to know the exact nature of the hand held by each player to be aware of who held losers and which had good prospects, although that information would become more evident as the betting progressed.

There was a break as the players got their liquor refills and two of them went outside to relieve themselves. Harry sidled over to the gamblers' table and asked whether he could join the game in progress. Karl, the man who Harry pegged as the experienced player, seemed to be in charge of the game and nodded his assent as Harry took one of the empty chairs, two seats to the left of him.

The players' reaction to the hands they were dealt by Lucius was revelatory. After nickel antes were deposited, each player received five cards, one at a time, all face down. The remainder of the deck was placed aside, secured under Lucius' half-empty whiskey glass. The players picked up their cards and held them in their hands, being careful to keep them concealed.

Harry closed his eyes and cast his mind around the table. Two of the amateur players were unhappy with their hands. One inadvertently sighed in resignation; the fourth's mood had become upbeat. Karl only registered a subtle feeling of disquiet. Lucius's mind was blank.

A first round of betting began. One of the ranch hands immediately dropped out. The rest, starting with the one to the left of the Lucius, placed bets that either raised or met the existing high bet. By the end of the round, another of the ranch hands had dropped out.

Each of the remaining players then specified how many of the cards in his hand he wanted replaced and received fresh cards from the deck in place of the ones discarded. There was more for Harry to learn then: one of the ranch hands asked for two cards, though he seemed unhappy with what he held previously and remained so after he was dealt replacement cards. Harry concluded he was getting ready to bluff. The other, which had previously seemed in a good mood, remained somewhat upbeat, though no more so than before the cards he had discarded were replaced with fresh ones. Harry knew he held at most a two pair. Karl had asked for two cards and had registered just a smidgen of satisfaction with the new hand he had gotten. Lucius drew only one card for himself and had remained aloof after the exchange. Harry had asked for three cards and had given only a casual glance at them. He did not expect to win this hand.

There was a second of betting, after which Harry could predict the personalities and likely behaviors of most of the players for the rest of the night. Three of the cattle ranch hands were transparent: they would immediately telegraph the quality of their cards. The other one would try to bluff and pretend his hand was better than it actually was. Karl proved hard to read, except if he held a very good or very poor hand. Lucius remained a mystery.

Play continued for over two hours, through over a dozen games. At the end, all four cattle ranch hands had lost everything and had gone home or remained around the table as spectators. Karl was losing moderately. Lucius was ahead by about twenty dollars. Harry had won about forty.

Karl then proposed: "Let this be the last round. I'm getting tired and have a lot of work ahead of me tomorrow." Harry and Lucius agreed.

Lucius then suggested: "How about a twenty-dollar ante for the last game?" They all agreed. Karl opened the bidding with a five-dollar bet. Harry raised ten; Lucius and Karl checked.

Karl asked for a three-card replacement. After seeing his new cards, his eyes gleamed for just one second on the otherwise stony face. Harry sensed that Karl's pulse had quickened. Lucius discarded one card, but again, Harry could not detect any emotions. Harry asked for three cards, and a quick look at his new hand showed a full house, sevens and queens.

Now the second round of betting started. Karl bet twenty, and Harry raised twenty on him. Lucius folded. Karl then raised two hundred, and Harry glanced at him briefly. The hopeful gleam in Karl's eye was there, but then dimmed; at the end, his pulse had quickened and his heart was beating a bit faster. Harry realized he was bluffing. He felt like raising again, but it was not wise to be too greedy on his first night out: there would be more money to be made tomorrow. He called Karl's bet, and they went into the showdown. Karl only had three kings. Harry's full house won, and he readied to take the pot.

"Not so fast," growled Karl. "You've been cheating. You are a damn card sharp!"

"Why do you say that?" replied Harry. "What have I done?"

"Somehow you knew my hand," countered Karl. "I initially had a couple of kings, but when I drew the three cards, I saw another king and momentarily mistook a jack for a king, so I thought I had four kings. Then I raised two hundred and stared at the cards again. I immediately saw my error, but nothing could be done about it. Normally I would have expected you to hesitate for a moment or two, wondering what to do. You didn't, but jumped on my bid right away. And your hand was good, but not good enough to be so confident. Somehow you knew I had goofed."

"That's hogwash," said Harry, getting to his feet.

"Cheater!" screamed Karl, getting up himself, seizing Harry by the waist and forcibly throwing him on the table, scattering cards, money, and glasses in the process.

"Let me go!" demanded Harry, but he was a small man and no match for the irate Karl.

Lucius, who had remained silent since dropping out of the game, cleared his throat. "I spent years in Japan training in *mushin no shin*, a form of mind control. From my training, I can play cards automatically, letting my brain simply plow through, while still well conscious of my surroundings. I noticed the same thing Karl said, but saw no signs of card sharping as such. I reckon this man won the games fair and square."

Karl let go of Harry and turned his rage onto Lucius. "What makes you such an expert on cheating? Are you in cahoots with this bastard?"

"No, sir" replied Lucius icily. "I am a marshal sent from Austin by the Governor to investigate the spate of recent killings in this town. Right now, I'm going to take this man into custody for questioning. Please step aside." He got up and took Harry by the arm and led him out of the saloon.

"Now, you better come clean. What's your real game?" Lucius demanded of Harry in a tone that left no room for prevarication.

"I do have a special gift," answered Harry. "Somehow, I'm able to tune into the emotions of others around me. With time and practice, I have learned to profit from this talent. But there is nothing criminal about my gift. A good listener is almost as talented as I am, as my father used to say." Harry shuddered apologetically.

"Come on, there has to be more to your story. You're a Cryptid, aren't you?"

Harry gave a deep sigh. "How did you know?"

"Back in Austin, Cryptids are getting to be common despite the city's efforts to get rid of them. You can tell them apart because they are sort of scrawny and pale, like you are. But their main giveaway is their necks, because the glands around their necks are swollen up and they try to cover them by wearing scarves or bandanas, the way you do. Those glands send something into the air that helps them figure out what decent folks are thinking so they can take advantage. That's how they beat regular folks at card games, and cheat them in business and get rich at their expense."

Harry reacted violently to the accusation. "I'm no damned Cryptid like Bigfoot or the Goatman and the monsters of popular legends. I'm only a regular man trying to make a living the best way I know how."

"That's not the whole story, is it? You better come clean, or I'm arresting you." He seized Harry by the arm and started to pull him away.

Harry pressed his lips tightly, as if he were unwilling to say more, but at the end relented. "Word among us is that our breed comes from the backcountry in Appalachia, where a knot of Scottish families had settled. There was a lot of inbreeding, and soon newborns started to show what we call empathy. At first, we didn't think much of it other than it was nice that our kids didn't to get into fights because they understood each other so well. But then, sometime in the 1750s, we were driven out of our lands by the government and forced to spread into the towns and cities of the South.

"Once our peculiarity started to be noticed we became outcasts. Not only were we visibly different from the general population, but we had a perceived advantage over the rest of the people. Our kids were resented because they did better academically, so in some towns they were barred from schools and had to be taught at home by their relatives. As we grew more numerous, our people worked hard and succeeded in all areas where human interaction is a factor. We are good teachers, doctors, lawyers and judges, preachers, merchants and salesmen, politicians, and even card players like me.

"But that success has come at a heavy cost. We live in fear and have to hide what we are, because if we are recognized, we are fired from our jobs, roughed up, arrested without cause, expelled from some towns, and imprisoned. There have been a number of unprovoked riots resulting in some of our people being put to death.

"So, yes, I have chosen to make a living playing cards. I'm pretty good at it, and the stupidity of my opponents allows me to win most of the time and cut my losses when the cards turn against me. Arrest me if you will, but I do nothing that any ordinary citizen wouldn't do if he could."

Lucius let go of Harry's arm. "All of what you say may be true, but it doesn't excuse you. You and your kind may think you are victims, but you still use your gift, if that's what it is, for your benefit at the expense of normal folks. If I were not here on a law enforcement mission, I would be tempted to put a bullet through your skull, but I don't want to add another dead scoundrel to this town's tally." After a moment of reflection, he added: "I reckon it'll be enough to run you out of Oneida, but the word will get around these parts, so you might as well get out of the state. Go to the Territories to ply your trade. Maybe you'll have better luck with them rubes in New Mexico or Oklahoma than here. And maybe you should change your line of business. Remember the '84 election? That preacher George Ball who almost cost Grover Cleveland the presidency was a Cryptid like you.

"Do whatever you like, but don't come back to Texas or I'll put you away!"

Harry went back to the Crescent and climbed on his horse, tired but eager to skip town. He was last seen galloping away in a cloud of dust.

Later that day, three men from the Lubbock posse arrived in Oneida, looking for Harry and the money he had stolen. They left after an hour, chasing after a fugitive they would never catch: Harry had crossed into New Mexico.

Harry settled in the Taos area, changed his name to Gunn, and became an influential local politician during the Rio Hondo gold fever period. He discovered, as other Cryptids had, that more money can be made in public life than in saloon card games, with much less risk of getting shot.

STORE OF VALUE
BY
CHARLES WILKINSON

Big Nose Nerys-Bess used the gold she extracted from a small claim outside the town to crown her patients' teeth. Most days she did the mining in the mornings and the dentistry in the afternoons. When the pain in the streets was high and mighty, she'd work on till late at night. She'd no consulting room; no fancy receptionist. Though it was real hard, she carried her equipment with her and set up wherever she could: sometimes by the railroad or round the back of the hut where the Greeks sold kebabs. B. Herford wouldn't let her work in the Old Harp Saloon. She'd no paperwork saying she'd a right to set up in the dentistry trade and no real estate in the town to rent or call her own. A no-diploma-and-no-walls kind of dentist was what she was. Not one to go to if you couldn't take a little discomfort. But her prices were low, and her gold was pure.

***

After sixty miles slow traveling on his mobility scooter, Dorgan reached the town at dusk. The blue street lighting was on, but the shops were closed: the corrugated shutters pulled down on the jewellers and cash converters; chairs on the cafe tables; the working day's dust swept into a corner. The quiet time before the bars opened and yellow light leaked onto the sidewalks from behind the batwing doors.

He kept to the centre of the road; not swerving, except to avoid a pothole, a flag flying from the mast attached to the rear of his scooter, his eyes fixed straight ahead, never glancing at the men staring down from the balconies. Just another stranger riding in from the plains: that was how they saw him. Dorgan thought of nothing but the ache in his mouth and finding a place to stay. When they asked him later, he told them why he was in town. A conversation with a doctor who advised him to go to a place in Wales—or maybe Wyoming:

"That town has everything a man needs: gold and dentists."

"And what about women?"

"Yes, it's got them, too. As long as they're dentists."

Dorgan told himself he was there to find a wife who'd fix a few of his teeth and maybe cook a little, just soft solids and appropriate liquids. But every night when the stars picked white holes in deep space, he knew he'd come to escape Stringer.

He chained his mobility scooter to the post outside the petrol station. No sound, apart from the breeze-sigh in the dust on the sidewalk; the shuffle of dry leaves over baked earth. Then the distant yet unmistakeable high note of a drill drifted in from the outskirts: a dentist working al fresco and late. Dorgan tapped his pocket and felt reassured: the diamonds shifting in the red velvet purse.

There was a room free, and just habitable, in Herford's Old Harp Saloon. He took it. Nobody asked for his back story, which was just as well, for why all he could recollect was the trouble with his teeth, a conversation with a doctor—and Stringer.

Whichever town Dorgan found himself in, Stringer would be there. It seemed the man was pursuing him, but then he'd discover Stringer had arrived before him, checked into the finest hotel, and had his Elite Travel, three-wheeled mobility scooter repaired by the best mechanic in the only garage. Who was doing the following? Dorgan couldn't say. All he knew was they had come a long way: over high moorland speckled with sheep, across good cattle country, past a lake that held the white mountain's reflection, through coal-mining towns and round remote ranches. One day they lunched in Llandudno; the next they dined in Laramie. But so far, he'd not seen Stringer on this trip.

***

On Sundays, after her praying was done, Nerys-Bess worked on the claim. Her prices were low, and her gold was pure. That summer she dug herself a brand-new shaft, right down to where the veins were bright with ore. She was proud of her box set timbering. In the afternoons, she liked to put down her shovel and do a little panning in the stream at the bottom of the hill. Nothing soothed her like an hour above ground, sifting the gold dust from the gravel. And no sound, except for the water-rustle on reeds, the soft lapping round stone: not the scrape of a spade on rock, nor the screech of the drill's descent where whiteness rots.

***

Thirty thousand head of cattle being driven down Main Street woke Dorgan at eight o'clock in the morning. For a second, he was no longer in pain; then his nerves lit up, one after another, until the bottom of his mouth was a horseshoe of agony. He took a pull of whiskey, straight from the bottle, and went over to the window to watch the steers, not one with known orthodontic needs, moving through a storm of unsettled dry earth. Then as the last beast galloped out of town, he saw, in the wake of the dust-plume, a mobility scooter, more brightly painted than his own, its flag flickering like black lightning in winds funnelled from the mountain valleys. The figure at the wheel had long silver-grey hair; a pinched and narrow face: Stringer.

Dorgan went downstairs. At the end of the corridor there was a room with a brass plate saying HERFORD'S OLD HARP SALOON AND INVESTMENT AGENCY, and in smaller letters underneath: *B. Herford, Financial Services Manager and Purveyor of Liquor, Fine Ales, Milk, Butter, Cheese and Cream.* In the saloon, the windows were closed against the dirt; the top panes trapped squares of a blue morning. Overturned tables had been righted; the spent cartridges and broken glass from the evening's revelry swept away. Demure waitresses in black and white, dressed as for a traditional tearoom, took orders and poured tea from gigantic silver urns. The bar was shut, but that wasn't preventing Stringer from leaning against it. He must have tethered his scooter outside. Part gunslinger and part drover, he wore the flat cap and tweed jacket of a hill farmer; the chaps and spurs of a rancher. He was holding a shepherd's crook painted white.

"Feigning another disability now, Dai Stringer?"

"I prefer Daffyd. As you know very well."

"This time I really thought I might be rid of you."

"You'll not last long here, Dorgan."

"Strange you should mention that. Fact of the matter is I'm thinking it's time to settle down. And this place looks as good as any other. Better, perhaps."

Stringer took off his cap, placed it on the bar. Meeting his gaze, Dorgan felt the shock of seeing that something long known to be bad was now worse: one pupil still a dot; the other a black twist in the eye, but shiny like the blood-darkened blade of an axe.

"I was thinking of you when I went shopping," said Stringer, the lilt still on his tongue.

"Really?"

"Yes. I've bought you something with which I hope you'll become acquainted."

Dorgan tried out a dismissive laugh. "And what could that possibly be?"

"A rope."

***

Her prices were low, and her gold was pure. But once she'd dug it up there was the question of where to store it. Most nights, Big Nose Nerys-Bess slept near the entrance to the claim, the nuggets nesting on the straw inside a hempen sack, a hard, rough pillow. When trade was poor, Herford would let her have a room in the Old Harp Saloon, so long as she didn't do no drilling or disturb the other guests: the bus conductor with the broken jaw from Pontypridd; the fur trapper who spoke French; the gambler with the slippery dice; the sheriff who'd lost his badge, the longbow men in the lounge bar, who drifted in from a different century; the cowpokes and the rustlers companionably playing cards—faro, poker and bray; the Methodist minister with a bottle of gin in a hollow Bible. There were men staying there who needed bridge work, root canal treatments and crowns; women trailing reluctant children with mouths filled with metal. A maverick orthodontist rented a lean-to by the outhouse until Herford found him receiving patients. The one-time Big Nose Nerys-Bess took her gold with her to the saloon, a gang from Boulder rode across the border and cleaned out Herford's safe. Since then, she'd acted counter-intuitively: hiding her gold in her gold mine.

***

The diamonds had gone. The red velvet purse, its drawstring loose, lay on Dorgan's bed like an open mouth. Not one sparkling tooth remained. Dorgan did nothing except cancel his appointments. He couldn't afford a man with paperwork. He'd have to look around for other practitioners, the street dentists and part-time tooth pullers who lounged around town.

***

The next evening, Stringer was in the bar. His tooth decay had always been ten months behind Dorgan's, but now his smile was regular, broad, and white. He had the look of man accustoming himself to fresh dentition; a man adjusting to the joys of an even bite; a man enjoying the freedoms that America gives to hunt down a brother.

Dorgan said nothing. Just chewed a lump out of his tongue while trying to eat a steak. A martyr to malocclusions.

There was no way forward except through talking to Herford. All Dorgan wanted was revenge and affordable dentistry. He had a few dollars left. When those were gone, he was just a man with a gun and a mobility scooter.

Dorgan found B. Herford out on the back yard. The man was dressed in a suit of black and white hide. His face was broad with large brown eyes set far apart. His heavy shoulders led down to a lean white belly and thin legs that ended in neat small shoes as hard as horn. He was chewing tobacco, ruminatively. Dorgan spoke first and B. Herford listened, his eyes unblinking, as if he were watching something he couldn't identify approach from way over the plains of grass.

"Way I see it," said Herford, "is you got to fix those teeth first. A man in pain never shot straight in this state or any other."

"So you will help."

B. Herford's eyes revealed little but the shine of speculation. "It's like this. I'm an investor in people. If I end up helping someone, why, that's all to the good. But what I aim to do is find myself a store of value."

"Sorry? I'm not quite sure what it is you are proposing, Mr. Herford."

"Are you a Chapel man, Dorgan?"

"No, not really."

"Well, there are some folk who like to store a few good deeds. And me? I'm a saver, too. There ain't nothing that's certain in this town, and a wise man always puts something by. But I like an asset you can retrieve this side of the grave."

"And so... precisely?"

"On behalf of Herford's Old Harp Saloon and Investment Agency I say we are prepared to take a stake in you. We'll pay for bullets to put in your gun— and cover your dental fees."

"And how and when do I repay you?"

B. Herford's smile was broad, deceptively bovine. "You don't need to worry yet... not for a long time. Let's just say we're real happy to look after you. We take a growing interest as time goes by." He flicked away the flies that buzzed about his eyes.

***

The night they ran out of novocaine, Big Nose Nerys-Bess could hardly sleep for the pain that crept up from the town past the foothills till it sang high and mighty in the claim. The lost ghost of Jacques LaRamie howled in the pass. Mary Morgan was hanged again and again.

The next morning, the mountains and valleys moved around in her exhaustion, one peak from Wyoming peering down at the Rhondda; in the meadows and the cattle country the Indian Paint brushes mingled with the daffodils; sagebrush and prickly cacti grew alongside bog rosemary and Snowdon lilies. But a patient in a mobility scooter was waiting for her down by the water mill. She could see him parked amongst the mallards. He was holding his jaw. She picked up her forceps, a mirror, a prop, and the low-high speed drill with the foot pump attached.

"You come highly recommended by Mr B. Herford," the man said. He told her his name was Stranger.

"My prices are low, and my gold is pure," she replied.

Then she took him out of his scooter and tied him to a tree stump. For an hour she drilled and pulled; she finished with a song and a little burnishing.

"That's more than amalgam," she told him; "that's an investment."

***

Dorgan couldn't remember a time when Dai Stringer wasn't around. No sooner had he climbed out of his high chair than Stringer was in it, spreading his baby-self about, assuming a rightful inheritance; already assured in his plotting; banging his spoon as he stared down at Dorgan. When Dorgan took his first few steps across the drawing-room carpet, bought one rainy afternoon in Wrexham, he heard a sound behind him: Stringer trying to crawl past him on an invisible inside lane, eager to steal parental applause. At school, with only ten months age difference, Stringer won promotion to the same form. His hand was always up fastest. At college and in the city where Dorgan had his first job, Stringer was never far away: living in the next residence block or working in a different department for the same firm. All of Dorgan's friends were friends of Stringer.

Now, the brothers were fifteen metres apart in the middle of Main Street; mobility scooter faced mobility scooter, each blocking the other's way.

Noon.

No backing off.

The showdown crook-armed shadows of dead gunslingers waited by the saloon doors; whores in dresses like froth watched from the balcony of The Old Harp Saloon; the lawman asleep in the County Jail; white chrysanthemums for sale in the schizophrenia friendly florists (why can't the mad love flowers, too?); the old men on verandas nursing whiskeys and toothache; no singing in Bethesda Chapel; the coal mine closed; a sheep dog circling his flock on a distant green hill; Wales and Wyoming blending blue skies above the long sidewalks hazy in the baking heat. Silence. The street empty except for two old men in mobility scooters. Dorgan remembering how he changed his name to Stranger by deed poll and walked through a lake in the hope of finding America, but whichever state he was in, he knew Wales and Stringer were there, too.

A cigar in Stringer's mouth—he exhaled, presaging gun smoke. His rope was ready to string up the corpse for target practice.

"However hard you've tried to be a cripple," he said, flicking the stub away like a spent cartridge. "I'll always be a better class of cripple than you."

Dorgan was calm. Now the pain in his mouth had gone, he'd be the first to the draw. His hand hovered over his holster.

Neither man saw B. Herford, his shotgun hoof-held, the Deputy Marshall's badge a burning star on his hide, one horn sticking through his broad black hat, as he came shouldering, barrels blazing, through the batwing doors.

***

The mountain range above Big Nose Nerys-Bess, its line once sharp against high miles of mid-continental blue, began to blur; peaks vanished behind grey-brush weather and flags of cloud; alchemic sunrise melling with the density of morning mist thick as hodden. Mizzle from midday to dusk. The borders were no longer straight. She had a sense of living in ancient, contested territory, her hours somehow ambiguous, too close to the coast. The nights were inscrutable black. Then came the rumour: Colorado was about to cut all ties. Already she'd noticed a difference in the veins: Wyoming ore found only in the most difficult, inaccessible places. Welsh gold was rare; rose-coloured when blent with copper. She closed her claim before her prices were high and her gold impure.

Big Nose Nerys-Bess took herself down from the mountain. She'd just her drill and some dental tools in a bag. At noon, she heard shotgun cracks and thought B. Herford must be shooting bears. On the outskirt of the town, she admitted there was no way of her making a living without a mine and amalgam.

It was B. Herford who had her retrained as a commodities analyst with special responsibility for global pasteurisation.

***

Dorgan knew he was behind the door of the back room with the brass plaque. He was immobile but seated upright. The armrests were familiar. Big-Nose Nerys-Bess had found a new use for her old dental chair. There were no windows, only a skylight that some days showed unmistakably American cloud formations; on others a lowering grey mass, which could only be Welsh. B. Herford and Big Nose Nerys-Bess came in and out of the room. Often they were both present, working on computers. During coffee breaks they conversed: Big Nose Nerys-Bess saying her dreams had gone macroeconomic since she joined the firm; B. Herford telling her he was on the verge of cornering the global cheese market; soon he'd consolidate all production into three brands, none with national associations.

With his perceptions reduced to a well-regulated continuum, Dorgan Stranger was no longer in any pain. He could move his tongue. The proximity of Big Nose Nerys-Bess was a reminder of his *en plein air* appointment. His molars fixed whilst the mallards clucked around his feet; the singing of blackbirds; the essential rurality of the dying art of old-fashioned, country-style dentistry. In the town, the last independent practices were closing. Treatment was standardised; the loss was a lack of individuality in the amalgam.

No one was following Dorgan, and he wasn't in a position to follow anyone else.

Stringer was dead, his teeth asset stripped by an interloper; one mobility scooter, pockmarked with bullet holes, waited for the crusher. Sibling rivalry was no hedge against markets falling: For Stringer and Stranger, brotherly pursuit and escape were over.

Energy driven by revenge was uneconomical. In the back room of the Old Harp Saloon, B. Herford had sold his bonds and was trading in the physical: rare coins, Brie futures, fine Bordeaux and Krugerands. But there were bandits to watch out for. Susceptible to high explosives, the traditional safe had fallen out of fashion.

Dorgan ran his tongue over his teeth of gold. He could see the needles strapped to his arm; the drips, the tubes feeding him intravenously. He was a one-mouth deposit box, a store of value, fungible, his glittering treasure accessible after a simple medical procedure; he was heavily invested in, his lips surgically sown, wire-locked; a safe-in himself, waiting for a world-wide bull market in precious metals.

A DRINK WITH THE DEVIL
BY
JONATHON MAST

Full moon.

I hated full moons. They meant I could be tracked, even at night. I'd done everything I could to hide my trail, but it might not matter much. Not tonight.

Full moons also meant the weird stuff came out.

I just wanted to get home. I'd followed all the signs back to Hidden Creek; through the Superstition Mountains, keeping to Darren's Trail until I sighted the turnoff, through several dry creeks, over a few spurs of the mountains.

The saguaro loomed over me, staring as I rode past. Jacob, my horse, didn't seem to mind. Nothing much bothered him unless someone was shooting at us. That tended to bother both of us.

Right now, though, it was us, the moon, and the saguaro. His hooves thudded into the rocky ground. It had been a long ride. One last rocky outcropping to turn past, I'd be sight. My heart ached.

Home.

We turned past the stones. The moon shone down on what should have been Main Street. There should have been Bennet's General Store and the saloon and the schoolhouse and all the other buildings. Especially the little house just past the saloon. This late, everyone should have been in bed, except maybe Bennet counting his change and Harold in the saloon, and maybe a certain woman waiting up for me, but Hidden Creek wasn't so small that the buildings went away at night.

At least, it wasn't last time I was here.

There were no buildings. No sign of human habitation. Instead, saguaros stood in a circle, like some sort of witch's hoop. They pointed up to the sky, their arms all turned to the center of the circle. Inside, bare shale and the sand of the desert floor shone white in the moon's light, like fresh-fallen snow.

Jacob stopped at the edge of the circle. He refused to move forward, flicking his ears and not moving a hoof.

I crossed myself and unholstered my pistol. My breath was too loud in the silence of the night. Where were the buildings? Where were the people?

Where was my Bess?

Even if something happened and everyone had to run, there should still be buildings. And Bess would leave some sort of message for me. She'd want me to find her.

I dismounted, my eyes scanning the cold-lit hills. More saguaros. Sagebrush. Nothing moved. I stepped to the edge of the circle and crouched, reaching out my hand to touch the ground within. The sand of the desert could shine white, but this seemed to glow.

What I felt wasn't the grit of sand. It was soft as flower petals.

No. It *was* flower petals.

"You're late, my fine fellow."

My pistol aimed at the voice faster than I could think. It may have fired a few times, too, but you couldn't tell by the person leaning against a saguaro like it was the corner of the post office. He wore black. Black denim pants, black boots, black shirt, black hat. The white light of the moon seemed to vanish in his clothing.

His skin, though, was the bright white of the sand inside the circle. He took a drag off a cigarette as he straightened. "You have arrived. I have awaited you. I find that you were not part of the bargain I struck, and I do so desire the complete set." He threw the cigarette down and ground it into the sand—flower petals— whatever—inside the circle.

I didn't move my pistol from him. "Buddy, I don't know what you're talking about. I'm just trying to get home."

"I presume you reside in Hidden Creek?"

"Yeah."

"It is no longer here, as you can see. I won it, just tonight. A card game with the mayor. I have yet to ponder what I will do with this gathering of hovels you call home, but I am positive I can discover something to amuse me with. I've been distracting myself with a few of the residents, of course." Dark eyes flicked to me. "But I desire the complete set. Everyone who resides here. I want them all to belong to me."

I stood my ground. "You've got to the count of now to tell me what the hell you're talking about."

The man's smile sprouted on his face like some sort of weed. "Your mayor was quite the betting man. He liked high stakes. Blackjack was his game of choice. He bet the town." He shrugged. "And now it's mine."

I glanced around, never taking my eyes off him for more than a second. "No. No way. I've heard of some fellows that won businesses in betting games, but that don't make the business disappear."

He shrugged again. "I suppose when you're human it works that way. Now, would you like your city back? I do so enjoy games, you see, and I can be a fair sport. If you'd like, we can make a little wager. If you win, you get your city back, and even all the people in it. But if I win, well, I get my complete set." That grin grew wider. "I get you."

"Why don't I just shoot you and take the city back?"

He laughed. The sucker laughed at me. And then that smile again. "Well played, sir. Perhaps you should. Perhaps it would be proper for you to seek revenge and slay me with your, ahem, mighty weapon. But perhaps you might consider how you already shot me three times, and all you have done is damage my wardrobe." He pointed to three holes in his shirt. "Surely you wounded this body, but I am not knit together as you are. So, yes, sir, you may shoot me all you wish. And then we may make our wagers, if you are willing. Or you may ride from here, never to see your beautiful city that you have sacrificed so much for. Oh yes, Malcolm Sidwell, I can scent the blood on your soul, like my mistress's pies in the evening. But come, sir, a wager?"

He knew my name. This bastard knew my name somehow. And he stole the town. But my eyes landed on the holes in his shirt. I'd met plenty of men with bullet holes in their clothes, but those men tended to wear shirts they'd stripped from the dead. I spied black holes in the flesh beneath.

This was no man, whatever he was.

But this is where Hidden Creek was supposed to be. This was my home. This is where Bess waited for me. And all that was left was a circle of saguaros.

Hell. I'd already lost my soul long ago. What's one more game with the devil? Bess was worth it.

Get your head in the game. Don't think about her. Just focus on this, just like when you're on a job. Just do the job and get paid, like anything else.

Just this time, you're getting paid with your home.

And if you lose, you're just as dead as in any other job.

"A wager, you say."

"Indeed, sir." He tilted his head. "Choose your game. I find that it adds excitement when I don't choose."

I rolled the thought around my head a moment. "I'm only good at two things: Killing and drinking. And you already showed me I can't kill you. That leaves drinking."

That slow smile again. And he nodded. "A fine competition to select. Do you have a drink of choice? I'm afraid my usual favorite might prove strong for your simple palate."

I raised an eyebrow. Now, I'd been in cities where they served smooth sake and good port, but they'd never much appealed to me. Give me a good beer or a good whiskey and I was happy. But challenge me, say that something was too strong for me? That rubbed me the wrong way. "And what do you usually drink?"

He shrugged. "I imbibe deeply of fermented nightmares. A finely aged concoction of losing one's teeth and centipede legs simply makes me giddy. But, alas, such distilled spirits cannot exist on this plane."

I ran my tongue over my chompers. I hated those nightmares. "All right. Whiskey then. Straight up. Whoever can hold their liquor best wins."

The man in black gave a slight nod. "Agreed."

I held out my hand.

He stared at it, his nose wrinkling just a little. "Why do you humans insist on corporeal touch to seal agreements made in good faith?"

"I don't agree to nothing with a man that don't shake on it. Can't trust a man like that."

"And can I trust a man like you, Malcolm Sidwell?" His eyes shifted from my hand and up to my eyes. "A man who shoots his prey in the back? Your scent sings treason. I can smell symphonies of it. The brave hunter, returning to his town with resources to share for his woman. What would she think if she knew who you were, I wonder?"

"I protect my own. That's all that matters. Now shake on it, or I ride out of here. Maybe shoot you a few more times before I go."

He sighed. "I must complete my collection." And he put his hand in mine. His skin was soft like a banker's.

Never liked bankers. They're always thinking about numbers instead of people.

We shook.

"Now. I suppose I must conjure some of your whiskey." He raised one of his banker-hands and indicated the space behind me. I turned to look.

There the saloon stood, right where it ought to be. Oil lamp light flickered through the wax-paper windows.

My eyes raked the landscape around it. No other buildings. Bennet's was still missing. No houses. Not even one where a woman should be waiting for me. Just a circle of saguaros. Just a full moon.

Just a saloon.

"Come, come. I do have other obligations to attend to before the Silver Gates close." The man in black led the way through the swinging door.

I took a deep breath. Jacob still stood outside the saguaro circle. I didn't blame him.

But I'd shook on it. Even to a banker I'd keep my word.

I wonder how much a devil can drink. Probably more than me. But at least I could still shoot him, even if I couldn't kill him. Maybe it would make me feel better when I lost.

Wait. *I could still shoot him.*

I smiled. Yeah, maybe there was a way out of this yet.

I marched into the saloon. And then I stopped.

Before the bar stood Harold. He wore his red flannel shirt like always, no matter how hot it got. He had his stupid mustache, that little thing that made him look like he might have just started puberty. His eyes were as bloodshot as always. His shirt lay open, and instead of nipples he had two taps. And as I took him in, my eyes fell on his boots. Well, where his boots should be. He didn't have any feet. His legs grew together somewhere halfway down his shins until what rooted into the ground was a saguaro.

"Mal?" His glazed eyes passed over me. "Are you home? I thought there were just girls here. Girls." He smiled.

The man in black strode behind the bar and plucked up a mug, returning to the bartender. "I desire a repast." He turned on one of the taps sticking out of Harold's chest.

Thick blood oozed out of him. He groaned, at first as if a girl were pleasuring him, and then as if he were a saguaro bending in a dust storm. His knees knit together until he was more saguaro below the waist than man.

"I win, everyone goes back to normal?" I asked.

The devil turned to me, taking a deep glug of blood. He sighed. "Should you be the victor of our wager, you may do what you wish with your people. The town shall come to you, what is the term, 'as-is?' Ah. So much better than any of your so-called liquor." He licked his lips.

I eyed Harold. "Is everyone like this?"

"Oh, no. The owner of your general store has scorpion tails instead of fingers. He is currently trying to make love to his wife, who of course greatly fears him. Meanwhile she is slowly melting, making it rather difficult for her to run away. Her legs keep bending in awkward ways. It is quite a comical turn, if I do say so myself. And there is a woman who wears a blue dress that is slowly becoming younger and younger. She knows she is growing younger. She knows she is forgetting her life, minute by minute, hour by hour. Oh, I do believe she has forgotten you now. She knows she has lost something of great value, but can't fathom what it could be. I wonder how much younger she will be before we complete our wager?"

I growled, pacing back to the bar. I grabbed out two handfuls of shot glasses and a bottle of whiskey, slamming them on the bar. "Come here. I need to make this right."

"If you say so. Or perhaps I will win." He smiled. "I believe I will hold my drink better than you will."

I set my pistol on the bar and poured the first shots. "Drink."

We slammed back those first drinks. The heat coated my throat. Harold never had good whiskey, but I was used to bad stuff.

The man in black grimaced. "How barbaric. Pour another."

A second.

"Poor Bennet. Your general store owner has caught his wife, but his scorpion fingers have pushed right through her skin. Her scream sounds like she's eaten too much pudding, but it's just her vocal cords melting. Delightful."

A third.

I felt my brain slide ever so slightly in my skull. It was that good feeling of not caring. The man in black blinked at me.

Harold groaned again. "The girls, Mal. The girls." Needles grew from his upper lip instead of hair.

The man held up his fourth shot. "Oh, look at that. I guess she's not a woman anymore. Just a girl. Pity. I guess she could still be waiting for you, but she'd have to call you her father now."

I growled and slammed back my fourth drink.

He slipped his back. "She's crying. Trying to write down everything she remembers, but it's flowing past her so fast. Faster than a man's blood pours out of him when you shoot him."

We took our fifth shots. The room was spinning ever so slightly.

He raised an eyebrow. "Care to call it quits? It would terrible if you blacked out before I could have any fun with you." He paused. "Oh, it's so hard to hold a pencil in fingers that are that little, isn't it? Poor girl. Have you ever seen someone age themselves back before birth? It's a horrid sight. Very slippery."

I slammed back a sixth. He shrugged and answered in kind.

Harold held his hands up as if they were saguaro arms. The walls of the saloon writhed with spiders. The moon was too bright.

A seventh. Black danced at the edges of my vision.

"I do believe you fight a losing battle, my friend. I have won this wager."

I held up an eighth shot in my left hand. "Like hell. Let's make this better. You win, you don't just get me, but I'll hunt down whoever else you might want." The words sloshed in my mouth and in my mind. I had to get this right. "I'm a good hunter. You know it."

"I could use another agent for when the Silver Gates are closed." He considered.

I pressed on. "But I win? Everyone goes back to normal. Just like that. From before the mayor got stupid."

"Your mayor has never been blessed with intelligence."

"Before he made that bet."

He nodded. "For your boldness, and your hopelessness, I will accept this addition to our wager."

I plucked up my pistol and shot him right in the gut.

He rolled his eyes. "You cannot harm me."

"Maybe not, but I just won."

He raised an eyebrow. "I am not inebriated in the least."

"Maybe not, but you ain't holding your liquor." I pointed at the hole in his stomach.

Whiskey flowed from it.

His eyes narrowed. "Clever." He looked up at the moon, now just above the horizon. "And the Silver Gates close. You have won yourself a town. In one month, when the Silver Gates open again, I request a rematch."

The ground seemed to pitch up around me. One too many drinks, I'm sure. "Sure, buddy. Just make everything right again."

"Done."

And with that, the man in black vanished, and I passed out.

WHAT HATH GOD WROUGHT?
BY
ALISTAIR REY

2 December 1846

Arrived in Houston last Monday, from where I was able to arrange transport to Austin and on to San Antonio. The territory, only recently annexed to our great union, looks nothing as one would be led to believe. The cities—should one be so inclined to consider them such—bear little resemblance to the bustling streets and gabled houses of New England. Here everything is flat, dusty, vulgar. The people have a peculiar character. They speak in long drawls and manifest a fiery republican spirit at odds with the decorum of respectable New England life. In the mornings, you can see boys escorting herds of longhorns across the plains and covered wagons bound west dotting the horizon. The region is not without its rustic charms and should provide an abundance of local color for the reports I am to send back to Boston by courier.

In Austin, the streets are unpaved and stony. Mud and dirt abound, and it is not uncommon to see horses parked in the middle of the road drinking from stagnant puddles. The low laying houses have an ominous character, tilting and slanting at such angles as though they were constructed from nothing more than mud and twigs. The phrase made popular by Mr. Morse—*What hath God wrought?*—persistently enters my thoughts as I meander about the grubby main thoroughfare where the old governor's house sits, grey and dreary, on its perch along the hills. I have to wonder whether Morse had Texas in mind when considering his communiqué. What hath God wrought, indeed?

The proprietor of the bordering house in which I am to spend the night—a certain Window Saunders—is a voluble woman. Upon entering her establishment, she cordially invited me to a glass of sherry and a hot meal consisting of meat steeped in red lentils. While I ate, she provided me with a concise history of the area, enlightening me on the Spanish missions and the recent war of independence that remains fresh in everyone's mind. Her husband gave his life for the cause, she told me with pride. When I informed her I was heading to Coahuila y Tejas to cover the current struggle, her expression darkened. She preferred not to speak of the events occurring along the Rio Grande and remained silent while I hastily finished my meal. I had the impression I offended her in some manner, although it is difficult to read the people here. A constant air of melancholy appears to linger over them, inscrutable yet present all the same.

7 December 1846

In the morning, I met my contact, Mr. Wicker, who arranged my travel to Ciudad de los Santos. When my driver learned I was a reporter working for an Eastern journal, his face lit up. During the three-day trek, he talked incessantly, informing me about the war and the bandit brigades running arms through the area. He mentioned the bodies strung from trees with a macabre grin and related how during his previous return from Ciudad de los Santos he had come across one such unfortunate individual hanging from a huisache tree. The body had been distended and encrusted with flies. Checking the corpse for any valuables, he discovered the man had been eviscerated, a common tactic used by the local gangs. These are the grisly details of the secret war ravaging the region, a war outside the battles waged by Taylor and Santa Anna on the front, a war that will, no doubt, be lost to history.

I abided my companion, laughing at his crude jokes and colloquialisms. When the conversation lulled, I sat atop the wagon recording my impressions of the desolate towns and farmsteads we passed along route.

Ciudad de los Santos is a dreary garrison town. Pulling in, one first sees the hovels on the settlement outskirts occupied by Tejanos. Military men in dirty uniforms mill about the streets, heckling prostitutes and arguing with local business vendors. On our approach, a crowd of reserves called out to us in broken Spanish and made gestures in the air with their hands. The horses kicked up clouds of dust, drawing angry looks from pedestrians.

Parking his cart before a small, clapboard building on the far end of the settlement, the driver flashed a smile. This is where I am to reside. Despite its squalid appearance, the structure is newly built and in much better condition than the other buildings we passed on our way in. To the east, an expanse of flat, parched terrain extends as far as the eye can see, emitting shimmering waves of heat. Descending, I noticed little puddles of mud dotting the earth, the remnants of last week's rain I was later told. A hundred yards out, a rotting animal carcass lay face-down in the fetid water, attracting vultures.

The station chief is a burly Ohioan named McAllen. He greeted me politely, showed me to my quarters, and introduced me to the main garrison commanders. Next, he gave me a tour of the barracks where half-dressed soldiers sat about playing cards and cleaning rifles. They cast furtive glances in our direction as we toured the grounds and McAllen gave me the lay of the land.

"They can be a bit suspicious when it comes to civilians," McAllen explained after we returned to his quarters. "Don't take it personally."

He authorized me to conduct interviews with the men if needed but urged me to avoid political topics in my discourse. He did not want Whig politics eroding morale, he stated candidly. I assured him he had nothing to worry about. Journalistic integrity and objective reporting were my stock-and-trade. This remark seemed to please him.

8 December 1846

Ciudad de los Santos is situated over one hundred miles from the front. It occipies a key position in the supply lines, serving as a transport hub for men and weapons destined for Buena Vista and San Gabriel. When I was told I was being dispatched to Coahuila y Tejas, I never expected to see combat. However, it is evident that even these garrison towns are not immune to the violence and destruction raging further west.

On my first morning, I awoke in good spirits. Taking my morning coffee by the window, I noticed a small Spanish mission on the horizon toward the northeast. The building is plain, earth-colored, and adorned with a bell tower that juts up into the sky. I have been told that it is derelict, which explains the building's egregious state of disrepair. The Spanish missionaries have long abandoned these parts. The building remains shrouded in silence, sitting on the horizon like an abscess growing out of the earth.

When the war first began, the garrison commanders used the mission as a stable to keep the horses. According to some of the men, the horses never grew accustomed to the confinement. They would whinny and run about during the night, creating a ruckus that kept the men awake. The horses are now sheltered in the barn with the food provisions, leaving the mission to moulder in the dust.

I was studying this structure from my window when I heard the first gunshots. I immediately ran to the courtyard to seize a rifle, fearing we were under attack. Entering the courtyard, I saw a body spawled on the ground. A pool of crimson streaked the dirt, spreading out like an oil stain.

Men in uniform stood about the courtyard in a semicircle. Butch Crommer, the garrison sous-lieutenant, was looking over his work with a grin. To his left stood a line of slovenly-dressed men, their wrists bound in twine. The fear on their faces was legible, having just watched Crommer execute one of their companions.

I asked the recruit immediately adject to me what was occurring.

"Brigands," he whispered, his eyes fixed on the prisoners. "Found them in the hills a quarter-mile from here."

"Were they surveying the garrison?" I whispered back.

"Most likely."

"And so he'll execute them?"

"Most likely." His expression was unflinching and expectant, giving the impression this was a regular occurrence.

Crommer began circling the line of prisoners like a vulture cutting a gyre, a Colt Walker clutched in his fist. He smiled and spat in the dirt. Some of the prisoners were visibly upset. A few retained their composure, head held high, resigned to their fate.

"Tejanos aren't exactly welcome here," Crommer was saying, training the barrel of the gun on the men. "'Specially those intent on stealin' from us."

Some of troops grumbled their agreement, and Crommer's mean grin widened.

Settling on a man at random, he pressed the barrel to his forehead. A shot rang out and the man collapsed into the dust like a ragdoll. The troops cheered, and one of the prisoners began to wail.

Crommer went down the line, executing all five. I was powerless to intervene, although I wondered whether McAllen had authorized these killings or whether I was witnessing an injustice. When Crommer was finished, he looked down admiringly at his work and spit.

"Don't bother burying 'em," Crommer said as his men began clearing the bodies and dragging them through the dirt.

I later learned that there is a defunct well on the premises that is being used as an informal mortuary. A column extending into the bowels of the earth filled with corpses; the idea is ghastly.

"Welcome to the City of Saints," one of the men said to me as the crowd dispersed. He did not bother to hide the irony in his voice.

I have been here less than twenty-four hours and I have already borne witness to the sickening atrocities of war. I dare not speculate on what is yet to come.

Now, as I sit in the yard observing the night constellations and recording my impression, the image of those men continues to haunt my thoughts. I see them quivering and collapsing in the dirt, their bodies spasming like insects. A dark pool marks the killing grounds, the earth saturated with the blood of the fallen.

11 December 1846

The mornings here are still. I rise close to dawn and watch the sun cresting over the flat horizon. Its light is warm and radiant, bathing the landscape in fiery hues. Out here, the colors are extraordinary and vibrant, unlike anything I have ever seen.

The men take their breakfast in the yard, mumbling in low voices. I can feel their eyes directed at me as I pass. They have little trust for Yankees, especially one assigned by a newspaper. I am sceptical whether I will be able to assuage their suspicions and establish confidence among them.

Yesterday, McAllen requested to see me in his office. Upon entering, he lit a pipe and gestured for me to take a seat. He looked out the window with a plaintive gaze, blowing coils of smoke into the air. His eyes were fixed on the site of the previous day's atrocities. He lectured me on the grim realities of war and the need to keep up morale among the men, adding that such details may be difficult for a civilian like myself to comprehend. War was "existential," in his opinion. He asked me if I understood what he meant. I replied that I did, and he nodded.

"Do you think of the future?" McAllen then asked, drawing his pipe from his lips.

I did not know how to respond, but it appeared he expected no answer.

"I do," he continued. "It is filled with farms and towns spreading out across this savage land, of God-fearing men fulfilling a noble mission which does not belong to them alone, but to providence."

He fixed me with a cold stare.

I was under no illusions he intended me to quote this in one of the reports I will send back to Boston. Summary executions and wells packed with corpses have no place in this august narrative of manifest destiny. They are simply the grisly means to a more righteous end. The minutiae eclipsed by a far vaster plan.

I spent the afternoon conducting interviews with those troops willing to confide in me. They are amiable for the most part and excited to speak with a reporter. They constantly make certain that I have spelled their names correctly in my notes: Bosworthe with an *E*. Jesppson with a *double* P. All recounted stories of hardship and privation, of courage and sacrifice. Yet they are not reticent when it comes to speaking of the melancholy and horrors that afflict the average soldier, either. The brutality, the nightmares that plague their sleep. The toll of war runs deeper than the blood-drenched slaughter that wreaks havoc across this land. It is manifest in the weary faces and gritted teeth, the agonizing screams that pierce the stillness of the night as men cry out in their sleep, fists clenched, begging for absolution. I recorded these impressions in my notebook with an equanimous face.

In the later afternoon, I was walking along the outskirts of the garrison when I heard calls of "Newsman! Newsman!"

Looking about, I discerned no one in sight until my eye drift upward to a tall observation tower positioned against the fort wall. A sentry was waving his arms frantically in an effort to get my attention.

"I got a story for ya, too," he called down, beckoning me to join him in his roost.

Climbing the rickety ladder to the top, I was greeted by a view of the vistas and bluffs extending out into infinity. Flat, open space dotted by the occasional homestead as far as the eye could see.

The guard let out a soft whistle. "Think of all that empty space out there," he said, noting my gaze.

From our position, I could clearly make out the old Spanish mission. It looked small and diminished in the distance, like a warped dollhouse. Crimson light bled across the plains, and as my eyes scanned the landscape, I perceived a small precession making its way along the rocks and dirt to the east. The line was composed of five women. They walked in slow, measured steps, their colorful shawls flowing behind them in the evening wind. Each carried a basket in their arms.

I pointed to the line and asked who they were.

"The widows," the guard explained, his voice sober and inflectionless. "They are bringing flowers for the dead, most likely."

"The mission is still in operation?" I asked.

The guard shook his head. "Old habits die hard."

I wondered if they knew that their husband's bodies were interred only two hundred yards to the west, left to rot in the shaft of a neglected well. Would they have dared to leave the flowers there at the final resting place of their beloveds? I watched as they ambled through the dust and entered the crumbling building, the procession mournful and with unspoken purpose.

Eventually the guard broke the silence. "That gonna make it into one of your stories?" he asked with a malicious chuckle.

I feel as though I am on a very tight leash here.

That night, I sat up in bed thinking of the women trekking along the mission trail. Before extinguishing my lamp, I turned my eyes out the window. A soft glow emanated from within the mission. I imagined the women placing candles around the courtyard and strewing the paving stones with dried flowers. Each widow stood in silhouette, solemn in the flickering light. In turn, each drew a rosary from their calico shawl and lay it on the earth. "*Tierra de los santos,*" they whispered. "*Nunca olvidamos.*"

Suddenly, a loud shriek cut through the night. I heard the shuffle of feet and murmurous voices coming from the barracks. "'S all right. We're here," the voices uttered. "They can't git ya here."

I listened to them soothe their restless companion, and eventually quiet consumed the barracks. For all their talk of courage, these are broken men, worn down by the hostilities and evil cultivated within this war-ravaged land. The City of Saints is populated with ruins and debris. There are no spoils to be had.

12 December 1846

Curiosity got the best of me. In the morning, I set out across the plain for the mission. The building is more dilapidated than I first assumed. At a distance, it appears somber and dignified, juxtaposed against the expansive landscape. Up close, it is a pathetic shell of crumbling stone and spotted plaster. Parts of the tiled roof have collapsed. The main entrance is a gaping black hole where a door once stood. Inside, the floor is littered with debris and stagnant pools of water. Ribbons of light cut through the holes in the ceiling, casting skeletal shadows along the walls. As I entered, I could hear animals scurrying in the darkness.

In the chapel beyond the foyer, I found a large, conical pit where the floor has caved in completely. Remnants of tallow candles were scattered throughout the room. A single woven palm basket sat on the floor, emptied of its contents. The fibers were moist. Further down the crevice of the pit sat a mutilated cattle skull, decomposing in the heat and gathering flies. I shivered. *Old habits die hard*, I recalled the guard remarking.

I refrained from mentioning my discovery to McAllen or the other men. I know not what I would say aside from giving a descriptive account of my wanderings. Even this seems obscure to me. I work with words, and yet words now fail me.

14 December 1846

On Wednesday, a convoy passed through Ciudad de los Santos carrying a platoon of troops. They were returning from Santa Fe where they endured heavy losses against the Mexican *permanentes*. All I could think was how tired their faces looked. They stood about in their dirty uniforms, smoking tobacco and discussing reports of the strange malady that has recently afflicted many of the officers and recruits on the front. From their accounts, it appears chronic somnambulation and melancholy are a routine occurrence. One man noted an entire subdivision at Valverde seized by what one can only describe as madness. He described men walking about at night in a daze, muttering incomprehensible words.

"I seen it," he told me, pipe clenched between his teeth. "At Santa Rita, an entire regiment decimated in an unnatural way."

I informed him of recent medical studies documenting the phenomenon of mass mania and hallucinations. Under extreme forms of trauma, it is believed that the mind can be stricken with severe apoplexy, resulting in hysteria. The man nodded and smoked in a meditative silence as I spoke. "Perhaps," was all he offered when I finished.

As the wagon receded into the distance, I thought about his remark: *in an unnatural way.* I am under no illusions that the natural world conceals the most arcane and beguiling secrets. Its study daily reveals such mysteries which man is yet to comprehend. *Unnatural* is merely a synonym for our profound ignorance. We cannot fathom what God designs. Nature is only what God allows us to see and scrutinize.

15 December 1846

I have taken to making daily excursions to the abandoned mission. I detect signs of visitation, although I have yet to see anyone enter the desolate construction. Small figurines carved from obsidian and melted candles are strewn across the floor like strange votive offerings. The cattle skull has vanished, and the aperture at the center of the pit appears to have widened. The diameter is now approximately three feet across, a hole big enough for a man. The soil is dry and friable, explaining the cause of such rapid erosion. Here, everything eventually turns to brittle dust.

Peering into the cavity, I could only discern an inky blackness without end. I tossed a pebble into the hollow, waiting for the sound as it hit the bottom. None came. I assume the earth below is covered in moss or some variety of undergrowth. All the same, it felt like tossing a stone into a cavernous void, the echo consumed by obscure nothingness.

I cannot say precisely what draws my fascination to this forlorn place. From my window, I keep close watch over the slumbering construction, anticipating the approach of the women to replenish the candles or leave additional tokens of mourning at the edge of the crater. Yet they have not returned. The mission slumbers in the thick evening shadows.

17 December 1846

Dinner in the officer mess this evening. McAllen appeared laconic, sitting at the table with a troubled expression on his face. He continually tapped the tines of his fork on the tablecloth, a peculiar tic that drew looks from the other officers.

After a few glasses of wine, Butch Crommer began to converse on the behavior of certain men housed in the barracks.

"They're calling it *Mexican fever*," he said with a sardonic laugh. "They say it's a psychological disorder incurred by intense heat on the brain."

"But it's not an *actual* fever," one of the officers interjected, leaning back in his chair. "The reports from Santa Fe detail somnambulism and incoherence. Nothing that would derive from miasmic properties."

"A swelling of the brain, according to Dr. Percival," another offered. "The product of this abnormal environment."

McAllen grimaced. "Which is exactly why this land should be cleared and made habitable."

"Godliness *and* cleanliness," Crommer reminded with a smirk.

"Not that again," replied a young officer with a scowl. "These people aren't heathens. We're not in Africa!"

"You follow what the French have done in Algeria?" Crommer asked, leaning forward across the table. "They're building roads, schools, doing what the savages can't. In a decade, Algiers will resemble Paris!"

"We're not fighting Muhammadans here!"

"We're fighting something worse," Crommer bellowed. "We're fighting wild dogs and jackals that refuse to be domesticated."

"I don't see what this has to do with this so-called *fever*," said one the officers at the end of the table, clearly weary of the conversation. "I have twenty men in my company who can't sleep and wake up at night hollering to the high heavens, and you want to prattle on about the French killing Muhammadans in Africa!"

McAllen bit his lip and looked at me for the first time.

"Funny how none of this Mexican fever business has been reported in the newspapers," he said. "One might assume it's nothing more than gossip."

The table fell silent and the rest of the meal passed in polite, labored conversation.

The meal concluded, I returned to my quarters. On the way, I decided to pass by the infirmary to satisfy my own curiosities. At the entrance, a cluster of medical orderlies stood about talking in sibilant voices. A dejected wail came from an open window, punctuating the stillness of the night. It was difficult to discern their visages in the moonlight, but I could feel the cold stares of the orderlies as I continued in the direction of my quarters without a word.

18 December 1846

As I set out along the trail in the early afternoon, the sentry posted in the observation tower began whistling.

"I'm beginning to think you might have a cache of whiskey hidden out there," he called down.

"A what?"

"I won't tell no'ne," he promised, adding: "though, *if* it is whiskey you got, a man can get mighty thirsty up here. Keep it in mind."

I assured him I would as I continued along the path winding through the ocotillo and mesquite. Walking, I had the impression of following a trail of accumulated footsteps across ages, a line scored in the dirt by an ancient human traffic of men and women in search of God's salvation.

Inside the chapel, I found signs of recent activity: fresh candles, tracks in the dust, an abundance of stone figurines scattered across the broken tiles. The pit in the center of the floor was wider, extending over three-fourths of the chamber like a gaping maw ready to swallow the sky. Squatting by the edge of the carter, I thought I could discern faint voices emanating from the depths. My mind conjured up images of rotting corpses piled atop one another, forming a column of tangled and malformed bodies. Their jaws clacked together, trying to speak, trying to tell their story. Slurred words conflated in the darkness, echoing across an immeasurable void filled with grief and suffering. Closing my eyes, I saw lines etched in light stretching out across a plain of darkness. They shimmered like constellations fallen to the earth, and I instinctively felt that these clusters of light were pulsating with human life and energy. Moiling like some strange species of luminescent insect, they combined to trace the outlines of towering buildings, centers of commerce, and thoroughfares limned in white radiance.

I cringed as the distant cry of a bird drew me from these macabre reveries. I blinked into the ribbons of pale sunlight, wondering whether I had been dreaming or seeing into some nameless future that had yet to be written in the annals of this cursed land.

19 December 1846

Morning light has now begun to bleed across the land, and yet even in the clarity of the coming day I am still uncertain of the phenomenon which I have witnessed. I cannot remember when I first became cognizant of the low, puling sound coming across the night. It emerged slowly, a faint apian buzz gradually thickening into a plangent cry. Even as I became conscious of the noise, I had the curious impression that it had always been there, present, waiting for me to discover it. By the time I rose from bed to ascertain the source of the commotion, the wailing had saturated the air, subsuming the crickets and restless wind through the acacia trees.

Gazing out upon the starlit landscape, I saw stretching before me a column of half-dressed men trickling out of the barrack gates into the sprawling night. Their movements were spasmodic and juddering, like puppets being dragged along invisible threads. As my eyes drifted to the head of the formation, I immediately understood. The mission was bathed in a flickering glow and the men were marching toward it like insects attracted to a lamp.

Rushing into the night, I merged with the crowd, following its trajectory. With each step, the howling grew louder. I imagined a wounded animal crying out in pain. As my eyes drifted over the throng, I spotted Butch Crommer, his eyes wide and glassy. I waved and called to him, but his gaze remained fixed straight ahead as the column snaked toward the mission in silence. Sprinting ahead, I jostled against the men filing through the doorway and there beheld a sight that will forever remain imprinted on my memory.

The howling became deafening as I lurched into the chapel and filled my lungs with a foul, miasmic air. The screaming was coming from the cavity in the center of the floor, its perimeter now lined with concentric rows of teeth. The walls of the pit throbbed with each shriek, emitting an abominable stench. To my horror, I watched as the column of men entered the chamber one by one and without hesitation marched to the edge of the precipice and hurled themselves into its abysmal depths.

I wanted to shout, to raise my voice above the thunderous scream, but I remained paralyzed, watching as each in turn approached the gaping mouth and strode obliviously over the edge. As this gruesome procession continued, I saw McAllen advancing toward the lip of the chasm. I cried out, begging him to stop, but my words were inaudible. Yet as he teetered on the brink, I am convinced our eyes locked for a moment. His mouth appeared to open, and his lips formed a rictus on the verge of speech. And then, without a word, he lilted forward, his body spiraling into the cavernous abyss.

THE HEXMAN
WHO CAME FOR DINNER
BY
GREGG CHAMBERLAIN

"**I** reckon I met a hexman once," old Mose said. "Not that anyone'd know to see him."

The taproom at the Lone Pine went awful quiet just then. Some of the boys had been jawin' for a spell about miracles an' curses and that led right off to stories about conjures and hexmen.

Now Mose used to be a stage driver his own self. That was a'fore he lost his right hand during a run-in with bandits. Nowadays he works relief barman at the Lone Pine and does 'bout as well with one hand as most of us do with two.

Mose took a long pull at his mug. He don't talk much and that pause to wet his throat was a sure sign that whatever he had to say was goin' to take a while sayin'.

"I was driving the run along the Tully Road from Fairchild up to Aaron's Ford," Mose said, wiping the foam from his mouth with an arm. "Coming up on to Gallow's Crossing I see this fellow step out from between the trees onto the road and wave for the stage to stop."

***

Now [says Mose], no driver with any sense stops to pick up strangers along the road in the middle of nowhere. Though it's a good way to meet up with robbers, if'n that's what you've got in mind. But stoppin's just what I go and do. Find myself hauling back on the reins, going "Whoooooaaa there!", and bringin' the team to a halt.

"Are you going to Aaron's Ford?" the stranger says, smiling and looking up at me.

"This is the Aaron's Ford stage," I says back to him, "and I'm the driver so, yes, I'm going to Aaron's Ford."

I'm a bit sharp with him, it may be true, but then I am still some puzzled and peeved with myself for stopping the coach when I knew I shouldn't have. I could also hear a couple of the passengers inside calling out, asking what was the holdup.

The stranger don't seem to mind me being rude, though. Just asks if he can ride with me to Aaron's Ford and how much for the ride. I calculate maybe two bits, at most, since we're at the Crossing and it ain't like he got on at Fairchild after all.

"But you'll have to ride up here with me," I tell him. "Because I already got a full load of folks inside."

"That's fine," the stranger answers back, still smiling away. "I much prefer being out in the air." He clambers up beside me on the bench, hands over his two bits, and so away we go again.

There ain't a whole lot to see along Tully Road 'round near the Crossing. Lots of trees, yeah, and an occasional clearing where a creek runs under the road or mebbe where the ground is too spongy for much besides bulrush or brush willow to grow. It's kinda nice to have company for a change up on the bench while driving along. After awhile, me n' the stranger get to talkin'. His name is Arvid and he's headed on to Aaron's Ford on business.

"Profitable business, I hope." I look alongside at him while still watching the road. He's dressed well enough, but his clothes do look a mite worn besides havin' some dried spatters of mud along the bottom of his coat.

He just smiles and says he hopes so. Kind of ordinary lookin', he is. Not big n'er small. Nobody you'd look twice at, really. Hang me, though, if he ain't the smilingest fellow I'd ever met. He could teach a raccoon to grin.

After a while he asks where and when the nearest stop was, sayin' he could do with a bite to eat.

"Next stop is The Red Rooster," I tells him. "But you won't get much of anything to eat there."

"Food no good?"

"Food's fine, I 'spect. You just won't get to eat it is all."

Then I up and start tellin' him all about The Red Rooster. Red Robber or Robber's Roost, I calls it, but only to myself most times. It's a nice enough-lookin' little inn set up along the Tully Road but the owner there is a shady, tricksy sort. Whenever the stage arrives, the meal for the passengers is never quite ready in time. So ever'body waits around while the horses are fed and watered, the post collected and stowed away, and any letters, freight and whatnot dropped off. Comes the time when the landlord calls ever'one to pay their coin an' set down an' eat is always just before the coach has to leave. Nobody ever has time for more than a mouthful or two, if even that much, because they don't want to lose their seat on the coach or be left behind.

That's the way it always was 'round about then and there was nothing to be done about it. The Roost was a fixed stop on the Tully Road and the owner paid the stage line good money for the privilege. If any passengers ever complained to the line about The Roost, I never heard tell of it.

Arvid listens and clucks his tongue when I get through explaining. "Well, well, quite the rogue of an innkeep," he says, all formal-like. "Still, I think that I might be able to get a proper meal out of him."

I shook my head. "Only if you stay behind when the coach leaves. You've already paid two bits for the pleasure of riding on the driver's seat to Aaron's Ford. Best just wait until we get to the next stop after. That's Camden and you'll get a good feed there."

Arvid just smiles and says, "I'll bet you that two bits that I not only get to eat my fill at The Red Rooster but I also still end up riding to Aaron's Ford on this stage."

Well, I just laugh and tell him it's a fool's bet and I'll just keep what he's already paid me now to take him to Aaron's Ford. He don't say anything more. Just keeps smiling away.

We arrive a while after at The Roost and it's like I'd said. The owner come outside and he's all sorry but the lunch for the passengers ain't quite ready just yet. So ever'body has to wait. I had a couple strips of dried beef to chew on, just in case, y'understand. I offer one to Arvid, but he says, no, thank you, he'll wait for lunch to be served.

I shrug and go on about giving the team some oats, then climb back up on the stage and toss down a sack of cloth goods for the inn, before unhitching the horses and leading 'em over to the watering trough. Right about as I'm leadin' the horses back, the landlord comes out and announces that lunch is ready. He stands there at the door and collects from each of the passengers for the meal before he allows them to go inside.

I finish hitching the team back up, take a look around to see if there was anybody new waiting to get on, then amble on over to the inn door, stick my head in and holler that it's time to go.

Ever'one who'd been riding inside the stage comes a'rushin' out to claim their seats again. I don't see Arvid, so I look back inside the inn. There he is, setting at a table, knife and fork in hand, getting ready to eat.

"What are you doin'?" I says to him. "Stage is all ready to go."

He smiles and says he's goin' to have lunch.

I blink. "Didn't you hear me? I said the stage is ready to go. Now."

"And I am ready to eat now," he says to me, still smiling.

"I cain't wait for you," I says.

"And I do not expect you to," he answers back.

I watch him stab a slice of beef off a platter onto his plate and then reach for a basket of rolls. I just shake my head, turn around, and head on over to the stage and climb up on to the seat. I look back once at the inn door. Don't see Arvid there so I pick up the reins, call to the team, and away we go, down the road again, leavin' The Roost behind.

We're prob'ly a good half hour or so's drive down the road when I hear what sounds like someone yelling from way behind. I look back over my shoulder and see a rider on horseback chasing after us.

Now I got a schedule to keep and I already made one unscheduled stop and I ain't inclined for another. So I just keep on a'drivin' and watchin' that rider try and catch up.

Which he does after a bit and I see it's the owner of The Roost and he is fit to be tied.

"Turn back!" he yells at me. "Stop the stage and bring it back to the inn!"

He makes a grab for the reins. Which is a fool thing to do since we're both moving along at a pretty good clip. Damn near pitches himself off his horse. When he gets himself pulled back into the saddle again, he yells again to turn back.

"Why?" I ask. "I've got a schedule and I'm losin' time already."

"One of your passengers is a thief!" he yells back, loud enough I s'pect for everyone inside to hear. "My good silverware's gone and one of them done took it. You turn back now, or I'll get me some friends and we'll bring you back later."

Well, there ain't much else to do. He's bound an' determined to find whoever it is took his good silver. So it's bring the team to a walk until we come to a clearing along the road, then turn the stage off the track and around and head on back to The Roost. I hear grumbling from inside but ain't anything I can do about the sitch'ation.

What I'm gonna tell you now is what one'a the stablehands told me the next time I stopped at the station. When the stage left The Roost, you remember that Arvid was about to dig into the lunch prepared for all the passengers.

After I left the front door, the innkeeper come into the room from the kitchen door in back. He's surprised to find Arvid still sitting at the table, forking a piece of meat off his plate and into his mouth.

"Say there, you'll miss your stage," the innkeeper says.

Arvid shrugs and goes right on eating. "I paid for lunch and I intend to get a full lunch and maybe then some."

Innkeeper shakes his head like he never heard tell of such a thing and goes on back into the kitchen. After a while he hears Arvid calling for him. He comes back into the main room and there's Arvid, still at the table, putting a last piece of bread and gravy in his mouth. The plate sitting in front of him is wiped clean. Innkeeper looks about and sees that every one of the other half dozen plates set out for the other passengers who never got the lunch they paid for is also wiped clean. Along with the platter that had a small roast settin' on it, and ever one of the bowls what held the potatoes, the peas, and the gravy. Weren't even a roll n'er slice of bread to be seen neither.

"Would you be so kind as to bring me a bowl of milk and bread?" Arvid asks him. "And a spoon, too, so that I may eat it."

"Spoon?" says the innkeeper. "Why, I set out spoons and knives and forks for ever'body who come in here off the stage."

"Yes, I'm sure you did," Arvid says to him. "But since they all had to leave before getting to eat any of the lunch they paid for, well, you really couldn't blame anyone who might want something for the trouble."

Well, the innkeeper starts in to swearing about how that's his good silverware and damned if he'll lose it to some grab n' go thief. Next thing he's out the door, saddlin' up a horse, and ridin' on down the road after the stage. Which he catches up to, and so there I am, driving back to The Roost.

Arvid is standing outside the inn when we all arrived back. He ambles over as the team comes to a halt, humming to himself and rubbing his hands together. He stops and whispers somethin' in the ears of the horses while stroking a hand down the chest of each one. Then he steps around and sets a foot onto a front wheel, ready to hoist himself up. Right then here comes the innkeeper and demands Arvid point out who took the silverware.

Arvid looks surprised. "Why, no one took your silverware, my dear sir," he says, as nice as could be. "It's all right where you left it, sitting on the table."

"That's a lie!" yells the innkeeper. "You told me one of the passengers on this here stage stole my good silver."

"I said no such thing," Arvid answers back. This time, I notices somethin' different about him. He ain't smilin'. There's this frown on his face, too, what makes me think of a little dark storm cloud.

The innkeeper, he keeps on yelling and swearing about Arvid telling him that someone took the silverware and he's gonna have it back and see that whoever took it loses a few fingers at least or know the reason why. By this time, I'm down off the seat. All my passengers are standin' outside, too, wondering just what is going on and when is the stage gonna get back on the road.

Arvid goes over to the innkeeper and holds up a hand in front of the man's face. Who right then n' there quits turning the air blue with his cursing and shuts up. Arvid beckons and walks over to the inn. All of us follow.

We go inside. Arvid points. There on the table, in plain sight of everyone, are all the plates and the cups and the bowls set out for the lunch that nobody but Arvid got to eat. And beside each plate is a clean n' shiny knife, fork, and spoon.

The innkeeper just stands there, staring, his mouth hanging open wide enough to stick both his feet in and still have room for a hand or two.

"A good innkeeper knows where he keeps his silverware," says Arvid. "An honest one also knows how to treat his guests." He looks the innkeeper right in the eye. "Try to be both in the future."

With that, Arvid goes on back outside and the rest of us follow, leaving the innkeeper still staring at his "stolen" silverware. Everyone gets back on the stage and we leave The Roost behind. Again.

***

Now here's the funny part about the whole thing [says Mose, holding out his mug to the potboy for another refill]. What with me stoppin' to pick up Arvid to begin with and then makin' that return trip to The Roost and all, thanks to that idjit of an innkeeper, I reckoned we'd be more than an hour late gittin' on to Camden. But we still arrived there on schedule an' with time to spare. Once I give the horses their head, they set to gallopin' without slowin' down once.

I remark on that out loud while giving the team their feed bags at the Camden stop. Arvid smiles and suggests I might want to give them a double portion. Then he reaches into a pocket of his coat, pulls out a little roll o' bread an' roast beef an' takes a bite of it.

I look at Arvid. "And I 'spect you had yourself a pretty decent feed too over at The Roost." He looks back at me an' smiles an' swallows what he's got in his mouth.

"Yes," he says, nodding, "and it looks like I will be riding with you to Aaron's Ford."

"Like you said."

He nods again. "Indeed, it's just as well you declined my offer of a wager." Still smiling he then says, "I imagine that fellow who owns The Roost will be a little more careful about his silverware from now on."

I allow that may be possible, though I don't 'spect him to change much in any other way. That dark little frown shows up again on Arvid's face.

"If not," he says, "then I just might find myself visiting his establishment again." Then the frown vanishes and he's smiling again. "Maybe next time," Arvid says, giving me a wink, "he'll find his plates missing, too."

He ambles off then towards the water trough to wash his hands, leavin' me to spec'late on what all else he might have stuffed inside that coat pocket.

***

There was a long quiet spell all around the taproom of the Lone Pine after Mose finished his yarn. Then Des spoke up. "So, what happened next?"

Mose gave him a *what do you think?* look. "Finished the run to Aaron's Ford. Everyone got off. I spent the night at the station and then did the early-morning freight run back to Fairchild."

"What about that fellow, Arvid?" asked Esra. "Was he a hexman or weren't he?"

Mose drained off his mug before answering. "He never said, an' I never asked. He got off at Aaron's Ford with ever'one else and went on about his business, whatever it might have been. Never saw him again." Mose paused. "Though I recollect about a month later havin' to deliver a load of new plates and silverware and a complete set of cooking pots and pans and such to The Roost."

With that, Mose heaved himself up and said he said he needed to go "pay his respects" to a tree outside.

There was a bit of talk after he left about whether or not Mose was telling the true word or just yarning for the fun of it. But there was general agreement all round on one thing.

It don't pay to rile a hexman.

THE GHOST SHIRT
BY
DWAIN CAMPBELL

"How is the noggin, MacNabb? Nothing like the business end of a crowbar to dent the skull bone."

"Head is fit as a fiddle, sir." A blatant lie, but in this age of calamity, the North-West Mounted Police was terribly under-manned and strained to the hilt. Constable MacNabb felt obliged to get back on the Thin Red Line *tout suite*.

"Good lad," said Inspector Manfred. Tired, careworn, the old warhorse allowed himself to resume his leather-padded seat. "Damned business, all this. You heard we let the fellow who clocked you—Tatvinko? Ratinko?—out of the gaol and onto last Wednesday's refugee train, Vancouver bound?"

"Can't blame you, sir." And MacNabb didn't blame Krakinko, a Ukrainian settler who scarcely had one crop when the American chaos flooded over the border, necessitating a precautionary evacuation of the Prairies. No wonder he was irate enough to swing iron at the law.

Manfred absently tapped a notebook on his gleaming maple wood desk. It sat beside an 1891 calendar with a fanciful lithograph of Edward, Prince of Wales, on the jacket. "Right. A thousand items on my docket today, so to this summons. I'm detaching you for an assignment, one of a diplomatic nature." Suddenly restless, the inspector shot to his feet and nearly knocked over the flag stand bearing the Dominion's Red Ensign. He called for tea, and an unseen orderly in the annex without scrambled in response.

"Doubtless you have heard of White Fox, perhaps the most militant of the Ghost magicians?"

MacNabb nodded warily. "After the second massacre of the Seventh Cavalry at Wounded Knee, he rose to prominence within the Sioux Confederacy, albeit he is on the young side."

"Just a stripling," Manfred agreed. He added, "Also reputed to be the instigator of this Great Drought that is killing our agriculture, and medicine chief of several thousand phantasmal warriors from the Beyond, as per this Ghost

Dance nonsense." Nonetheless, I noted he superstitiously brushed fingers on the family Bible that held a place of honor on his desk.

MacNabb withheld comment on nonsense. The Indian insurrection was all too real, and hysterical reports from the south of ghost armies lead by vengeful living, breathing Prophets were too numerous to discount. Armies that could kill but not be killed. The Americans had started their pell-mell retreat from the Plains several months before. Only now was the Canadian government following suit, trying to get ahead of the crisis before it blew up like Krakatoa.

Tea arrived, and the constable nearly fell over when Mandred fortified each cup with Irish whiskey. Indeed, the world was coming to an end.

"A Cree informant tells us White Fox and his band are moving north. Apparently, his destination is a noted medicine circle at the confluence of Caton Creek and Frenchman River. Ottawa assumes his purpose is to extend the conflict by having our own tribes join the Ghost Dance cause. In short, the blighters wish to formally make war on the British Empire."

MacNabb neglected to say they were at war already, in all but name. Canadian Permanent Army and militia regiments patrolled the 49th Parallel, and in their rear the North-West police faced unrest with the Blackfoot, Cree, and Assiniboine, primarily in the form of countless fires set to tinder dry prairie grass and sickly wheat fields. No raids or open bloodshed as of yet.

MacNabb coughed pointedly. "My role in this, sir?" Lowly constables do not get involved in high history.

"Right, to the nub. You are to ride out, intercept White Fox's village, and read him the riot act. He is to be keep out of the Queen's domain, no trespassing."

MacNabb's jaw dropped. Perhaps unwisely, he blurted, "That's like sending out a drummer boy to stop Napoleon at Waterloo!"

Manfred responded with a wane grin. "Not altogether a Forlorn Hope, on two counts. You see, White Fox was scarce out of nappies when his family accompanied Sitting Bull north after the Little Big Horn bruhaha. Then, a single redcoat policeman did ride out to read the riot act, and the great chief complied. Hopefully, that scene impressed the very young White Fox, and he will be influenced by like audacity." MacNabb gathered from his tone that Manfred thought the stratagem a thin reed. As did he.

"Point two, sir?"

"You speak for the Dominion of Canada and the North-West Mounted. However, you will be accompanied by a nabob, an honest to goodness earl from Great Britain. He represents Great White Mother Victoria, and he will promise the wrath of the Empire should these Prophets eye her territory, which in my mind is their certain design."

He added a liberal dollop of whiskey to MacNabb's empty cup. Not welcome, for this would only acerbate the fierce headache MacNabb suffered since the head injury.

The meeting came to a close. Inspector Manfred imparted one more bit of intelligence: The aristocrat stays at the Assiniboia Club. "Our earl wants to see the medicine wheel before confronting White Fox. This circle is heap big medicine, Constable. Do not interfere with it and excite the natives. Treat it like Westminster Abbey. That's all." Manfred opened his to-do notebook with a sigh. Dismissed, MacNabb saw no recourse but to get on with the job.

On exiting the officer's barracks, MacNabb marveled at a blazing scarlet sunrise, made all the more vivid by a thick haze of grass-smoke hugging the eastern horizon. The medicine wheel was a fair ride south-west, but if the earl were keen, they could cover miles before day's end.

MacNabb first visited the quartermaster to be issued a MK II Enfield revolver to complement his Winchester Carbine. Add new Strathcona boots, seeing how Manfred offered him carte blanche. With said favor, the young constable imperiously asked the stablemaster for Saskatoon Pete, a lively but utterly dependable bay. Though supply ran short, Pete received several bags of grain ration, on account of the prairie grass being sun seared to a brittle serge brown.

While at the stable, a police corporal led in a bedraggled and hard-worn troop of militia cavalry. From insignia, MacNabb made them for the Princess Louise's New Brunswick Hussars, a Maritime outfit. They had been bloodied, for two wounded troopers moaned on travois.

"How goes the battle, Mac?" greeted the corporal, an old salt who started with the original mounted police way back in '73. The fellow blew dust cakes from his nose.

"Better than your lot, it seems. Indians?"

"Nope," cut in the troop lieutenant. He wore a mishmash of uniform and gentleman's clothes, typical of a hastily raised unit. "Ne'er do well outlaws, crossed over from Montana and didn't like our challenge. We bagged one." He indicated a wide-eyed, scarecrow-thin kid who looked more farmer than outlaw. Perhaps the boy knew shooting troops during martial law was a hanging offence, for he regarded the stable rafters nervously.

Corp followed his worried gaze. "Don't fret, kid. I'd say it's ten years in the hoosegow and a kick in the arse back into Montana."

That got a reaction. Eyebrows rose sky high over hazel orbs wide as teacup saucers. "Don't send me back. Black devils ride the Yellowstone River. Even the flesh n' blood ones ya can't shoot, not if they got a damned Ghost Shirt on." He shuddered, sweat tracing grimy runnels on his dusty brow. "The dead ones is worse. They take into ya like wolves. No outrunnin' them; they just don't quit."

The Ghost Dancers and the Army of the Dead, called to harry the White Man into the sea. This boy bought the malarky hook, line, and sinker.

Corp dismounted the kid and frog-marched him to jail, there to rot pending trial. The Hussars hustled wounded off to the infirmary, while a weary few unsaddled worse-for-wear steeds and rubbed them down. Acting opposite, I gathered my kit, saddled Pete, and trotted into Regina proper and the Assiniboia Club. Great lords didn't rise too early, so I took my sweet time. Imagine my consternation on seeing a well-heeled oldster planted by the front club gate, impatiently studying his gargantuan silver pocket watch and giving me a piercing death stare.

"Goodness gracious, sprog. It is 6:45 a.m.; the day is half done. Did you have a mattress glued on your back?" Not a plummy voice. More that of general steadying the line against Crimean Cossacks.

MacNabb squashed irritation. "Sorry, sir. Had to wait on docs for morning rounds, to get sprung from the infirmary. Then Inspector Manfred." He dismounted and saluted. "Constable Daniel MacNabb, southern Ontario originally. Of late, the North-West Mounted Police."

Daniel MacNabb studied the lord. Though appearing elderly with deeply wrinkled skin and iron-gray Father Christmas beard, he stood ramrod straight and projected uncommon vigor. His eyes, a disconcerting lake-blue, were separated by a Roman nose that Tiberius might envy. Indeed, his commanding presence would suit a Legion legate, which goes with being in Westminster's House of Lords, most like. He wore a Norfolk jacket of brown herringbone tweed, knickers of the same material, and black as coal riding boots. On his head he sported a flat salt n' pepper hat. Fine wear for a day grouse hunting in Scotland, but it might not serve here in the Northwest. Still, one does not argue with the Earl of...

"Antonius Merle, Earl of Glaston, estate straddling Somerset and Devon," the fellow offered, remembering his manners. "You are my knight errant and guide."

MacNabb didn't really like being told who he was. "Guide, anyhow. But I have a charge to give White Fox. I'm to tell him to mind Ps and Qs and turn back."

Lord Glaston barked a hard laugh. "That's like a mouse telling an owl to stay up in its tree." He stepped back to appraise the policeman. "No mouse though. I expect Lancelot would envy your shoulders. What are your dimensions, boy?"

"Six feet, six inches. Two hundred and eighty pounds."

"Ate your mother out of house and home, most like. Well, such bulk befits a gendarme." He gestured me to follow him, so I led Pete out back of the Assiniboia Club. There, waiting contently, stood a swayback gray-dappled stallion harnessed to a dogcart painted violent red. It belonged to the earl, for he rummaged in the back and fished out a weighty bundle. He let it furl out with a metallic jingle. A coat of chainmail, by God.

"I thought you were joking about the knight business," said MacNabb, covering surprise with lame levity.

"Not entirely," Earl Glaston admitted. "I mean to give White Fox a taste of his own medicine, fight fire with fire." He held the coat to MacNabb's chest and whistled softly. "It will barely do. I do not wish you ill, but hopefully you will lose a pound or two in our mad dash to this magic wheel."

"Medicine wheel," MacNabb corrected automatically as Glaston returned the shirt to his load of gear. "And you're going nowhere fast with that nag pulling an overloaded cart."

Numberless merry wrinkles gathered about the old man's bright eyes. "Granted, Enbarr is far past his prime, but once he was warhorse to Manannan mac Lir." MacNabb didn't have a clue about mac Lir, likely a Scottish laird. "Daniel, your only worry is if your own mount can keep up."

Constable Danny MacNabb guffawed. An hour later he stopped that, for Enbarr struck a rapid trot and refused to lag. The earl lit a cherrywood pipe, and as the cart rattled at speed it resembled a Canadian National locomotive trailing coal smoke. Poor Pete did well to range ahead as MacNabb followed a route southwest out of Regina. They passed abandoned homesteads, many no better than first year sod houses built of earth and grass by newly arrived Pole and Ukrainian dirt busters. Darn shame, the way they had been scared off by the Indian Wars to the south.

The prairie grew emptier, and flatland turned to undulating hills of brown. MacNabb hoped to bag a deer or buffalo, for his rations were meager. Game proved as scarce as people, so that night they camped in a depression to conceal a cheerless cookfire that did no more than melt cheese on bread.

No stars in the sky, Stygian dark. No night sounds, not even cicadas, much less coyotes. Bloody eerie, and MacNabb kept both Winchester and revolver to hand. Thus armed, he walked to a rise to answer nature, and did a double take at the top. "Earl Glaston, up here, quickly."

For an ancient, Glaston took the slope with nary a breath lost.

Far to the south, crimson fire glow limned the horizon. Blazing tendrils writhed into the night.

"Hmmm... hmmm... Our side of the Parallel, or within environs of our Yankee Doodle Dandy cousins?"

MacNabb pursed lips. "Hard to reckon, but I'm guessing our side."

Then, on a hillcrest about a mile off, a file of riders became silhouetted in the far-off flame. Constable and Earl unconsciously lowered to one knee. By the cut of their jib—exotic headdresses and war lances trailing eagle feathers—the riders were Plains Indians.

Now, dull but heavy, the men heard ominous tom-tom beating of drums. Rather like far off, muted thunder, thought MacNabb.

"That answers our question," whispered Glaston. "White Fox's outriders. Dead or alive, I cannot tell. Methinks we had best make that medicine wheel tomorrow. I wish to deny the magician access to such power."

Unable to believe his ears, MacNabb blurted, "You take this hoodoo Ghost Dance magic seriously?"

"Most assuredly. And we best stop it, for if not, the Chinese or Africans or Sikhs might also devise magical systems to render our bullets impotent. Albion cannot realize her imperial destiny if she is pushed about."

As hair stood on the nape of his neck, MacNabb watched the endless file of warriors. Outriders? More like a horde.

Another concern. "We're a helluva stretch away from the medicine wheel. We'll not make it tomorrow."

"We shall." By God, the codger believed it.

Next morning. they set out, Constable MacNabb carefully scouting the countryside. No immediate evidence of a large war party, but hours later, as a fierce sun scorched the prairies, they happened upon a burned-out cabin. Beside the smoking ruin was a cottonwood pole sporting three bloody scalps, a torn Stars and Stripes flag, and a charred guidon from Princess Louise's New Brunswick Hussars.

"I do not think our military border cordons fared well," observed Antonius Merle, Earl of Glaston.

MacNabb rubbed the back of his sweaty hand over cracked lips. "Bloody savages!"

"You think so?" asked Merle conversationally, tamping vile tobacco in his pipe with a gnarled thumb. "I have seen men drawn and quartered in the Tower. Others burned alive at the stake. When in a mood, Christians outdo primitives. Cruelty comes naturally to men, whatever their creed or degree of civilization."

In no mood for philosophy, MacNabb led on. By and by, his poor night's sleep and the merciless sun conspired to have him nod off in the saddle. In a dream that could not have lasted a minute, Saskatoon Pete and Enbarr sprouted wings like Pegasus and took to the air. Hills of amber, dull orange, and ugly brown fell away beneath them, and behind. Fleet as eagles, they crossed rivers and sloughs, as well as sun-tortured stands of poplar and maple trees. Seemingly, in seconds, a circle of stones roughly one hundred yards in diameter hove in view. Various rock lines formed spokes in the wheel, though four were most prominent. MacNabb realized the figure in a hazy, mesmerized fashion, then...

... he snapped awake near the joining of two waterways. His face felt strangely waxen, while his mouth was parched as sand.

"You are awake," Earl Glaston announced, as if making it so. "You dozed in the saddle all day. We have arrived at our destination, with hours to spare. Fortunate, for much is to be done. First, we must water these beasts." Sprightly as an elf, Antonius Merle jumped off his garishly painted cart and unhitched ol' Enbarr in sixty seconds flat. Abashed, for every mounted officer makes his mount a priority, MacNabb groggily unsaddled Pete, removed his bridle in favor of a rope halter, and led him to the drought-depleted river for a much needed drink. As per trail routine, the constable filled his canteens, all the while being watchful. Coming fully awake, he remembered the war band in the previous night's vision.

The earl eschewed such mundane matters. With the strength of a gorilla, he wrestled a large, unwieldy object off his cart. He flipped off a canvas covering to reveal a plough.

A wooden device, with but one ploughshare!

"Carved of best English oak, off my own estate. Trees that were seedlings when William the Conqueror arrived."

"No time to start farming, Lord Glaston." Some English aristocrats were barely sane.

Merle emphatically shook his head. "I mean to emulate Romulus, who ploughed a margin around the seven hills of Rome to mark its sacred boundary. As I plough a furrow to contain this circle, you will trail behind dribbling a line of sea salt and herb mixture. Special blend. This will keep White Fox out until we deal with him."

MacNabb warily regarded the medicine wheel. "Do... do you reckon there are evil spirits here?"

"Here? Now? No. This is a place of power, where much healing has been done. The tribes use this space to synchronize with the cycles of life. Stones, circles and the heavens; I know such places well." He removed his hat and scratched a head well gifted with a mane of steel-gray hair. "But, as a place of power, White Fox can use it to summon an army of dead warriors from northern tribes. That we must prevent at all costs."

"For the glory of England?" MacNabb hefted the salt sack and found it hellish heavy.

"And this new Dominion, a cub of the English lion." He commenced ploughing and raised a thick turf of powder dry soil. Staggering behind, MacNabb traced an unbroken line of salt and herbs within the cut. An hour later MacNabb was done in, but not the lord.

As the constable caught his wind and guzzled water, the Earl raised a tourney pavilion. Perhaps he figured Ivanhoe might drop by and take on White Fox? Not entirely to MacNabb's surprise, the eccentric Englishman doffed his trail-stained duds and threw on a light wool cloak clasped at the throat with a jade oakleaf. He then brough over the chainmail coverlet for MacNabb.

"What good will that do?" Mind, it might stop arrows and war lances.

"Two can play the Ghost Shirt game."

If one wanted to advance in the North-West Mounted, ticking off a Mad Hatter British lord was no way to do it. Reluctantly, MacNabb shrugged into the godawful heavy shirt to humor Merle. However, that was not the end of it. First came a garland of acorns, then another of bright orange berries from last year's wigan trees—anathema to witches, Glaston offered. Next, in black paint, Merle ruined the coat's metallic gleam by brushing on runic symbols. All the while he muttered nonsensical prayers in Gaelic, or so MacNabb supposed. Finally, the earl stepped by to admire his handiwork.

"A tad small on you, but the whole effect will serve. Ghostly warriors cannot harm you with arrow or spear."

"How about a tomahawk?" MacNabb joked weakly.

"Thank you for bringing up weaponry." The earl reached into his inexhaustible cart and brought out a long bundle wrapped in oil cloth. "Behold, the gem of Britain's arsenal."

MacNabb regarded the broadsword. "A British Museum antique showpiece?"

"You have the antique part correct. Not in tip-top condition, I apologize, but it has been in the keeping of a Lady who is no armorer." The old man reverently handed the blade to MacNabb, who found it curiously light in his hand. "With this you can smite White Fox. Your Winchester and Birmingham bullets are no good in this magical clash of civilizations."

Constable MacNabb felt damned silly. His broad face flushed red as a raspberry. "Hell, I feel like a kid dressed up as St. George for a Christmas play. Damn it all, I'm confronting White Fox in my red serge tunic, as Inspector Manfred means me to. As Ottawa means me to."

"Do that, and spectral braves will riddle you with arrows, lift your hair, take your eyes, and much worse if reports are true. Vengeance roils in their souls. Yet, if I have my incantations correct, your dress-up, as you put it, mirrors the aboriginal Ghost Shirt magic. They cannot hurt you, but wielding that talisman blade, you may hurt them. Perhaps end this dangerous young mage."

The constable sharply turned his head. Faintly, out of the south, a steady drumbeat sounded. A visceral, serrated vibration, one to grate bone and make blood run cold. By now the sun set rapidly, casting odd shadows in the half-light that seemed to dance away from MacNabb's peripheral vision. He felt like an interloper in this sacred place. Maybe this country wasn't Victoria's claim. Maybe the owners wanted it back.

"Saddle your destrier, young MacNabb. A cosmic joust is about to begin, and you are knight on the chessboard."

"If I'm a darned knight, what are you?" MacNabb realized he was blathering out of sheer nervousness. However, he carefully rested the sword on the cart seat and did as he was told.

"Why, a bishop. Terrible irony in that. Bishops wanted my heathen guts for garters, in days of yore."

Hurriedly, Glaston sorted himself. He saddled Enbarr and fetched himself a gnarled staff from his cart. In these minutes, the drumming became palpable. Brittle grass flamed east and west, as if to fence them on the flanks. Southward, about a quarter of a mile off, a lone rider astride a magnificent palomino appeared atop a knoll. A score of native families followed, enough to constitute a village. MacNabb ignored these adherents, knowing they were but an entourage to the great shaman who now surveyed the paltry force between him and his goal.

Could he sense the barrier Antonius Merle ploughed? In thinking that, MacNabb unconsciously slipped into the Great Game of Magicians. No longer a doubter, he accepted the otherworldly forces in play.

"Do your duty, Constable MacNabb. Approach yon sorcerer and say your two cents. Just don't get killed and sully my *tour de force*."

Saskatoon Pete reluctantly answered MacNabb's heel. Not good, for police mounts are trained to shoulder into riots without a thought. His horse sensed evil in the fetid, dry breeze that carried drum beats to them. Could be his imagination, but the sword pommel in MacNabb's hand felt hot.

In response, White Fox urged his golden mount into a slow advance. In age, he was no older than MacNabb, and rather more lithe than muscular. His regal, handsome face bore bright yellow and white war paint, and a precious gem, a ruby perhaps, dangled from behind his left ear. A racoon cap trailed several fox tails. Powerful medicine radiated from him, largely due to the Ghost Shirt he wore.

The garment, elk skin bleached snow white, was elaborately fringed with rawhide. Painted on it were designs of bison, turtles, bears, and a stylized bird unknown to MacNabb. Eagle feathers dangled from cuffs of wolf fur. MacNabb wondered if this shirt was worn at Wounded Knee last December when cavalry fired into the Ghost Dancers, to no result. The world changed then.

Perhaps tonight it would change again.

MacNabb stopped within hailing distance. "White Fox, you are now within the borders of the Dominion of Canada. You and yours are ordered by the government to turn about and..."

A loud thrumming, like the hum of a gigantic beehive, sounded from over the hill. Then the darkness above thickened, seemed to waver and ripple.

Before MacNabb fully comprehended, black war arrows struck the earth, sticking up like quills on a porcupine. A score harmlessly passed through him and Pete both. Then the quivering lot melted full away like slush on a hot rock.

Two can play the Ghost Shirt game.

Stunned by the attack, MacNabb missed the sorcerer charge him. Like a lancer from Napoleon's army, White Fox unerringly thrust his weapon at MacNabb's heart. Perhaps charmed, it did not pass through him, but neither did it pierce chain mail. The force cartwheeled MacNabb off ol' Pete and he hit the dusty earth like a sack of rocks. White Fox galloped on for the medicine wheel, and a wild hunt followed.

Shadowy warriors steamed past, many mounted but more sprinting on naked feet. They had strange green-black skin that sparkled with starlight—though no stars shone—and faces and hands painted bright scarlet. All matter of regalia suggested Sioux, Cheyenne, Blackfoot... all the tribes of the West.

So far, Constable Daniel MacNabb had not covered himself with glory. He flailed about, searching for the darned old sword. A beckoning gleam in the grass led him to it.

Antonious Merle, Earl of Glaston, now wisely inside his ploughed perimeter, sat unperturbed as a throng of ghost warriors surged widdershins about him. A primal howl filled the night, as though every hellhound from Tartarus had found voice.

With the advent of ghost warriors, Saskatoon Pete sensibly crossed the Frenchman River. MacNabb fought the panicky impulse to follow. He could not leave the old man to be massacred. Sword on shoulder, he ran toward the action. But what to do?

A shrill bone whistle stopped the circling. White Fox now directly faced Antonius Merle, with his war band surrounding the impenetrable furrow.

With no little showmanship, Antonius Merle lowered his staff to the ploughed circle. He cried a word, and the air thundered.

"Ouroboros!"

Before Daniel MacNabb's bulging eyes, a fleshy mass gelled within the ploughed furrow. It rose like leavened bread, but instead of crust, dark scales formed. In the yards separating Merle and White Fox, great crocodile jaws firmly clasped a narrowing tail. A wingless worm, devouring itself, had coalesced in the dirt grove.

OK, thought MacNabb, that is a *tour de force*, by God.

The worm's toothy jaws opened wide and defiantly hissed at White Fox. A warning, but in that momentary aggression the barrier broke. From horseback,

White Fox defiantly hurled his lance, and it pierced the worm's viper eye. The cosmic reptile erupted into emerald balefire. An outward blast worthy of Vesuvius rippled over the Prairie. Thousands of warrior wraiths burned in the light and flew off, like wind-driven flinders from a bonfire. No lightweight, MacNabb was knocked of his feet into a pell-mell somersault that nearly broke his neck.

Through it all, White Fox remained ahorse. The Ghost Shirt, potent medicine, allowed the terrible explosion to pass through him. This could not be said for Antonius Merle, who in the convulsion had gone down over Enbarr's head. He lay insensible on charred grass, smoking staff thirty feet away. Most seriously, the ploughed furrow, now devoid of enchantment, proved no impediment. White Fox dismounted and unsheathed a hunting knife nearly as long as a Roman gladius.

After slaying Earle Glaston, the Indian Magician would have the Medicine Circle. *That we must prevent at all costs.*

Fighting to his feet, MacNabb roared, "We're not done, Medicine Man."

Whatever he was, the magician was no coward. He ran at the constable and leapt like a hungry wolf, twisting at the last second to avoid MacNabb's lusty but clumsy swing of the broadsword. The knife cut Daniel's forearm. Perhaps the Ghost Shirts cancelled each other. The two circled, policemen jabbing with the long blade, Sioux dancing away as though he were an air sprite. In this activity, blood droplets fell on the broadsword.

The metal grew red hot. White Fox eyed it warily.

Red hot, and light as a feather. With a skill not his to claim, Daniel charged, blade flashing.

The broadsword cut the Sioux Ghost Shirt. Sliced it several inches. Blood splashed from White Fox's arm.

With that the earth heaved, and MacNabb fell into a dead swoon.

He awoke next morning with Antonius Merle wiping his face with a wet cloth. "Wakey, wakey, Corporal MacNabb. You'll sleep the day away. We must get back to Regina, by and by."

"I'm not a Corporal," MacNabb muttered thickly. His brain felt like day old porridge.

"You will be," Glaston assured him. "Why, you warned off that White Fox fellow in fine style. Put the run to him. Inspector Manfred will be pleased as punch. Crisis averted; order will be restored."

"I... I... Was there a giant snake here last night? It came from that magic trench you ploughed in the ground."

The earl marveled at such lunacy. "Bad dreams. Moldy cheese for supper. We did dig around the Medicine Circle, looking for artifacts. And did we find a doozy." He held up an ornately decorated elk hide shirt, marred by a large bloody tear on one arm. "This shall find a home in a British Museum."

MacNabb greedily drained a canteen. As he did so, a rain droplet cooled his upturned forehead. Overcast sky; perhaps the Great Drought was breaking. "No... swords?"

"I did lend you a butter knife to slather your bread. Did you lose it?"

"Must have." Dazed, MacNabb hobbled to Saskatoon Pete. He examined a bandaged cut on his arm. With these aches and injuries, he must have fallen off his horse.

"No... magic?"

"Tons, old boy. In fact, I have another trick to show you. I packed up my cart, but if I can find that deck of cards, I shall create magic to amaze the world."

Deep inside his soul, Constable MacNabb of the North-West Mounted Police did not doubt that.

PONY EXPRESS
BY
VONNIE WINSLOW CRIST

The antlers caught Drucilla's eye. Backlit by the last rays of the sun, the silhouette looked like a man seated upon a horse. Which was a common sight in the Nebraska Territory. But deer antlers sprouting from a rider's head were not.

Maybe it's a Cheyenne or Arapaho headdress, she mused. It seemed plausible—even though she'd never seen or heard about one of the local tribes wearing antlers.

When she galloped closer, the figure melted into the shadows. Instead of being comforted by the disappearance of the deer man, Dru felt uneasy.

She'd made good time from Kearney Station to Fort Kearny on the little chestnut mare galloping beneath her. With only seven miles between the two stops, Fort Kearny wasn't even a swing station. Like usual, she'd stayed aboard her horse as a soldier slipped another correspondence into the mochila slung across her saddle. After the letter was secured, she'd given the soldier a wave. Eager to get to Platte's Station, Dru had urged the mare to a trot, then a canter, and finally, to a gallop.

"He's probably nothing to worry about," she said.

The chestnut's ears twitched.

Perhaps spurned on by fear of the deer man, Dru and the mare galloped the rest of the distance to Platte's. They even arrived a little early.

The station keeper at Platte's had a piebald filly waiting for Dru to ride. The mochila and Dru quickly transferred to the piebald's saddle. With a nod of his head, the station keeper sent the pair off to Garden Station.

The first half of the leg between Platte's and Garden went smoothly. They'd just started the second half when a screeching owl swooped down and flew alongside Dru and the piebald. The bird refused to leave. It kept sailing past, circling back, then flying next to them.

Nonetheless, the determined filly galloped on.

Suddenly, the piebald stumbled. Dru gasped. She leaned back and pulled on the reins. The half-mustang quickly recovered, then settled into a smooth canter. Though rutted from prairie schooners headed to Oregon and California, this stretch of the trail was relatively flat. Dru ought to know. She'd ridden the fourteen miles between Platte's Station and Garden Station during daylight hours several times a week for the past four months. But this was her first night ride.

Darkness, much less being followed by an owl, made even the familiar frightening. Dru supposed that was one explanation for her pounding heart. Of course, it could be the deer man she'd seen when she left Fort Kearny.

Dru tried not to think about the fireside stories Gramps told. In the evening after dinner, her grandfather often spoke of magical creatures from across the ocean. "People like to think fairies, goblins, old gods, forest spirits, and the like stayed behind. But they didn't," he'd begin. Next, a yarn of magic would unwind. Frequently, the tales were funny. Occasionally, they were sad. But sometimes, the stories were terrifying accounts of an encounter with a dark being.

"Nothing to worry about," she told the piebald cantering beneath her. "They're just make-believe."

Dru knew a gallop *was* the preferred gait. But at this point, the moon was obscured by clouds, and the pony was exhausted. Riding at a canter seemed prudent.

"Better to get to Garden than not," she said. The pony snorted. "We're almost there," she assured the tired horse as she spotted the lantern hung outside the Central Overland California & Pike's Peak Express Company's Garden Station.

Such a mouthful of words, thought Dru. *No wonder folks call it the Pony Express. It's easier to say, and to remember.*

Seeing her next mount saddled and waiting for her, Dru slowed the piebald. Once the filly stopped, she lifted the mochila and handed it to Biddleman.

"On time, Dru," said the station keeper as he placed the mail bag on the saddle of Dru's next mount—a buckskin. "Careful on the rest of your run. Heard Cheyenne and Arapaho have chased a few of the boys."

"Thanks for the warning," responded Drucilla before gulping down the cup of water offered to her by the station keeper.

Like every other rider, station keeper, and stable hand, Biddleman thought her a young man. Had any of them known she was Drucilla Blosser from Doby Town, Nebraska, she'd have been fired. Dru, like dozens of other teens, had been lured into applying for a position with the Central Overland California & Pike's Peak Express Company by the promise of fifty dollars per month starting pay. Plus, she had to admit, carrying mail for the Pony Express seemed an exciting adventure to embark upon.

"Do the Cheyenne or Arapaho wear deer antler headdresses?" she asked Biddleman. She handed him back the now empty cup.

"Not that I heard of." The station keeper shrugged his shoulders. "But another rider asked me the same question last night. Now, get going."

"See you on my return trip," said Dru as her pony started to trot.

She nudged the buckskin to a faster gait with her heels. Moments later as they began to gallop, she recalled the first time she saw the Pony Express poster. It had been tacked on the wall of the Doby Town boarding house where she'd worked. The poster announced: "*Wanted: Young, skinny fellows, unmarried. Must be expert riders, willing to risk death daily. $50 per month pay plus board.*" Then, she'd noticed scrawled in ink below the official requirements the words, "*Orphans preferred.*" Whether the additional phrase was the result of someone's attempt at gallows humor or a real requirement, it didn't matter. Dru fit the bill.

Except for one detail, she mused as her mount galloped westward toward the Plum Creek Station. *But a haircut and a change of clothes fixed that.*

The fifteen mile leg to Plum Creek should be uneventful. The even-tempered buckskin beneath her was named Dusty. Like most of the Pony Express's mounts, Dusty stood about 14.2 hands.

Dru yawned. She'd set aside thoughts of deer men and settled into a comfortable position leaning over the horse's neck. All of a sudden, she heard howls.

"Better be coyotes, and not wolves," she muttered.

Dusty's ears flicked.

Hidden by darkness, Drucilla knew on either side of the trail were countless items discarded by pioneers, fortune-seekers, and miners. Sadly, broken equipment and boxes of heavy, useless goods weren't the only things littering the trail. Sick and dying oxen, mules, horses, and other livestock were left behind as well. They became easy meals for predators. In the daylight, their scattered bones told a cruel tale.

"But we're not going to be dinner for a hungry pack," said Dru.

Dusty never broke stride. The thumping of the buckskin's hooves offered her rider some comfort as the howling continued.

"I don't think they are any closer." She spoke out loud to boost her morale more than to comfort her mount. Loud howls behind them seemed to challenge her statement. "But I could be wrong," she added.

Moments later, she heard the pack closing in. Drucilla considered pulling her pistol from its holster. She'd have to be judicious with her shots. Weight, always a factor in the equipment allotted a rider, dictated she carry only a dozen extra bullets. A fair shot when standing still, Dru had no idea if she'd be able to hit a coyote or wolf while riding at breakneck speed across the prairie.

The moon slipped out from behind the clouds. Near full, the bright orb illuminated the terrain both before and behind Dru. She saw the pack that followed.

"Two wolves." She squinted. "Or at least I think they're wolves." Dru exhaled the lung full of breath she'd been holding. Still dangerous, two wolves were less likely to take down a horse and rider than a larger pack. She squinted again. There was a third figure pursuing them. It appeared larger. Then, she spotted the antlers.

She faced forward again. Dusty might know this section of the trail, but the parade of people, animals, and wagons heading west left unexpected obstacles daily. With the wolf pair and the deer man so close, there was no room for mistakes.

Suddenly, an ox appeared before them. The beast struggled to stand but seemed unable to do so. It bellowed pitifully.

A slight tug of the reins, and Dusty swerved a little closer to the Platte River. *Good pony*, thought Dru as they avoided the injured bovine and raced on.

Drucilla didn't glance back as she heard the wolves attacking the ox. The dying creature's cries were soon drowned out by the growls and barks of the hungry predators. She hoped the antlered man had stayed with his wolves.

In the months she'd been riding for the Pony Express, Dru had been in other dangerous situations. But just like tonight, her horse had been steady, and luck had been on her side. Still, any close call made her reconsider her present employment.

In the spring, she'd been living three miles west of Fort Kearny with her grandfather in Doby Town. Good with horses, Gramps worked for the stagecoach company. It had only been the two of them for the last nine years. In the first half dozen years of her life, one by one, Dru's parents, younger brother, and Grammy had succumbed to disease. It didn't matter if they'd been taken by the ague, smallpox, or scarlet fever. Gone was gone.

"Let's not add Dusty and me to that list." She patted Dusty's neck with her right hand. The horse was lathered. She wiped the buckskin's sweat off on her pants. With this fifteen-mile leg of the trip almost complete, it made sense the pony was sweating.

"Hal will cool you down," she promised, "once we get to Plum Creek."

The words had hardly left her mouth when Drucilla saw the light from eight or nine campfires. She shook her head as she slowed Dusty to a canter. Stories of Cheyenne and Arapaho had no doubt caused the wagons to spend the night at the relay station under the false notion it offered protection. She knew the smaller stations were attacked regularly. Provisions and corrals of ponies were an irresistible lure for the tribes of the Nebraska Territory.

She supposed one of these pioneers was the owner of the fallen ox. Unfortunately, the owner's fate might be no different than his bovine's end. This group of settlers was late. In all likelihood, they wouldn't make it over the Rockies before snowfall.

"Whoa!" shouted Hal Halloway as Dru slowed Dusty to a trot, then a walk.

"Don't go galloping by, son."

"Not to worry," replied Dru as she handed the station keeper the mochila. "Dusty is spent. I don't think she'd let me pass by food, water, and a day's rest."

"She's one of my best," said Hal as he held the reins of both Dusty and a wall-eyed skewbald. "But Patches here is a fine horse, too."

Dru considered telling Hal about the antlered man and his wolves. But he was sure to dismiss her fears as nothing more than an overactive imagination. Then he'd share the tale with the other riders.

No, keeping quiet about the deer man is best, she decided.

Nearly as quick as a rattlesnake strike, Dru was on the skewbald's back. She double-checked the mail pouch, gave the station keeper a nod, and urged her mount into a canter. Soon, the brown and white pony broke into a gallop.

"Next stop, Willow Island," she told Patches. Though Dru was certain the skewbald heard her, the horse didn't move her ears.

As her mount galloped away the miles, Dru relaxed.

She heard no owl screeches or howls. She saw no wolves or antlered men. The only thing bothering her was her grandfather's stories. He'd told tales of antlered huntsmen. She couldn't recall all the names, though Herne and Wodan popped into her mind. Old gods, they rode with their hounds hunting the unwary. Sometimes, their prey was forced to join a forever hunt. Other times, they were slain.

"Pay attention to the trail," she reminded herself.

Though the skewbald must have heard her rider talking, Patches again gave no sign of it. Instead, the steadfast pony ran like the wind. Without incident, she trotted to a stop at Willow Island.

Bud Cozad, the station keep, stood outside the large log cabin that served as the Willow Island Station. Per usual, there were ranch hands from several spreads playing cards and drinking inside the cabin. Their cow ponies were tied up in front of the station.

"On time," said Bud as he grabbed the skewbald's bridle.

"Yes, sir." Dru slid off Patches, flung the mochila over the saddle of a waiting gray, then climbed aboard the near-white horse.

"This here's Misty." Bud patted the gray's shoulder. "She used to run between Gilman's Station and Cottonwood Springs. But she's with us now."

"She's a beauty," said Dru as the pale filly and she trotted west toward Midway.

Only fifteen more miles to go, she thought. Midway was a home station. As long as her replacement was there, Dru was done with her part of tonight's ride.

Moonlight silvered the landscape as Misty began to gallop. The gray's hooves thumping like a heartbeat, and Dru felt her shoulders relax.

Suddenly, an owl flew by them. Then, the howls from earlier in the evening returned. Dru knew it was the antlered huntsman and his wolves. This time, it was unlikely an injured ox would save her.

"Run, girl," she urged the gray. She held tight and leaned forward.

Pony Express horses were kept in excellent condition. They had to be, to outrun the mounts of Cheyenne, Arapaho, and outlaws. Now, Dru hoped her pony could outrace an old god—for her future rested on Misty's churning legs.

The wolves howled again. Dru glanced back. Thundering behind her was the antlered god astride a huge ebony horse. On either side of him raced a wolf as black as a nightmare. The eyes of the horse and wolves burned crimson. As for the Huntsman, his eyes glowed green.

Dru faced forward once more. She scanned the trail ahead by looking between Misty's white ears. That's when she saw hundreds of spectral oxen, horses, dogs, mules, hogs, men, and women had gathered on either side of the trail.

Dru remembered one of Gramps' sayings: "If you stare between the ears of a white horse, you can see the dead."

"Save us," screamed Dru to the throng of wraiths.

The phantoms studied Dru and her pursers. Then, they floated near and surrounded Misty. Like a nearly forgotten dream, the spirits hovered around horse and rider in a ghostly fog. Dru felt their manes, muzzles, paws, and hands touch her. She saw the kind expressions on their translucent faces. After several miles, the ghosts groaned a terrible moan. Then, the otherworldly horde dropped behind Dru and her horse. To catch them, the Huntsman and his hounds would have to deal with the dead.

Ignoring the hair-raising screams, bellows, howls, and roars behind her, Dru clung to Misty and prayed. Though it seemed like hours, within minutes the gray and her rider trotted into Midway Station.

"You two look spent," commented Harry Shuggs, the station keeper. "Good thing, Slim is taking the next lap."

Harry grabbed the mochila. He transferred it to the saddle of the bay Slim was riding, then slapped the horse's rump. Off trotted Slim and the bay.

Dru slid down from Misty. She pressed her forehead against the gray.

"Thank you," she whispered. "And thank the dead."

The almost white horse lowered her head. She gazed at Dru with knowing eyes. Then, Misty nuzzled her rider as if to say, "You're safe with me."

"We outran the Huntsman this time," Dru told the gray. "But I think *this* rider is ready to return to Doby Town for good."

As Dru walked the gray pony toward the corral, she added, "Better a quiet life, than no life at all."

Misty stopped, pressed her pale cheek against Dru's face, and sighed.

THE BALLAD OF BILLIE LEE
BY
STEVE GLADWIN

Prologue

There is something you need to remember about stories. By the time they reach you, they've already passed through many other hands, other voices, other places.

In each one of these they have changed—even if it's just a mite.

There may be some who have made the story worse. More often, someone has tried to improve it.

Some stories, mind, need to be changed. Specially if the ending just don't sit right. This is one of them kind.

One: He Keeps on Coming

Joe

A hail of dust kicks up as the wagon moves off. The pale face of a woman peers from behind the grimy curtain, and then is gone. Is it she? I surely ain't about to recognize her now. How long has it been?

I move back into the battered saloon with its even more battered barkeep. His creaky stool, the only sound in the whole deserted mausoleum of entertainments.

He has the shot ready for me—just like he always does—and as always, I swig it down in one, and nod my thanks. He is no respecter of tidiness, this man, let alone cleanliness. Always the smell of horseshit about him. Always the black and broken fingernails, bitten to the quick.

"Marshal will be in soon." His line.

"I'll wait, then." And mine.

It's scarcely worth the argument. He's long gone by now and won't see another spring owing to the state of his liver. Barman's curse, they call it!

Jethro Whitlock—that's his name—shines one glass after another, putting more care into any of that than he ever does into personal or public hygiene. The only thing that can make things worse is the cloth he uses, as there's more germs and opportunities for casual death in that than in any of the rotgut he peddles day after day. Day after day! It isn't as if anyone comes in here no more. Not even Sam Walsh, the marshal they call Black Sam, due to his sunbaked complexion as much as his sunny temperament. Sam, like all people, knows better. The only time he turns up is to collect any takings from the bar and tables. That's all there is now. Nothing more to be had now in a place short on entertainment, friendliness and hope.

It used to be different. When this place swung, the whole town swung with it. The Pale Horse was the epicenter of culture, opportunity, music, food, and showgirls. And yes, they sure were them kinda girls. Show girl, see, because the name was all for show, unlike what you paid her to show it.

Billie Lee was her name. The girl I was looking for here. She used to do this act with a gun that needed some quite special acrobatics. She used to use a snake, but the snake—perhaps possessing more taste than its audience—had up and died rather than ever have to perform in this shithole burg again. Billie Lee was heartbroken. Said the snake was the closest to a friend she'd ever had. As for the gun, well it wasn't just for the new act—Billie, as I say, being in all ways what you might call "flexible." Many of her clients, especially ones full of rye, could become more of a handful than she was prepared to tolerate. Well, dontcha know her mother was a school mistress, and Billie took after her in the manner of speech department. "Gennelmen," she would say, when stuff got out of hand. "Sir. I pray that you might desist, should you not wish to end up with an ass full of buckshot." I doubt if the "ass" bit was ever part of Ma Lee's teaching, but you got to hand it to Billie Lee. She had style as well as sass.

But time's moving on, and the next stage is due. This time, Jethro hardly looks as I park my coin on the bar. I whistle as I toss a silver dollar from one hand to the other. The next one, maybe.

Sam

The horses kick up the dust. Our driver is just this scrawny twisted kid—lowest of the crop—who ain't picked too often, in any case, depending on how particular the client. Say there might be some rich banker or rancher and his daughter moving on to pastures new, where the streets ain't exactly paved with gold, but he's convinced he can dig it out anyway. Being rich and particular, he's more likely to hire help to do it for him rather than get his hands dirty, before he sticks his hands in the bucket of stinking riverbank to fish out the little nuggets—this being all his hired men have managed after months of tearing their nails off and their palms open.

The scrawny kid—I think they call him Ethan—reaches back and throws me my hat. I'm already halfway to the bar when I catch Billie Lee's smile. She's adjusting her blouse and skirt like there like nothing's been going on. By her tight little smile, you'd never guess at the commerce which has just taken place. But truth is, she's a mite sweet on me, and I've gotten kinda fond of her—outside of the workplace, you might say. Maybe this is why they use the kid when Billie Lee is part of the service. I used to hear tales of a snake, although that just might have been bar room dirty minds—which, there being an abundance of—might hardly be a lie. Nowadays she keeps a perky little handgun in one stocking and the money in the other. And in case you fancy trying something on, she knows which one is which.

But Billie Lee and me have got a fine thing that's part of our very special arrangement. Special coach, special time, always the same service. Or variations—plenty of them. The kid Ethan is smart for all his damn fool ugliness. He knows that this one is free of charge, and he ain't bothered long as he can bring back his share. Sides, if a man cain't have negotiations quietly with his business partner—no matter how fine she might be—and there's still time left to seal the deal, so be it. Normally the kid would be plenty old enough to think he could get some kinda favors for himself, but due to him having a face like a smashed-in stove we ain't had no problems yet.

So, I puts back up at The Pale Horse, which lately was the center of wickedness and still nightly plays the devil's tune, even if the strings have gone out a bit. That's where Billie did her stuff in her heyday, when there was that trick with a snake, if it ain't just gossip. This is where it happened—all of it.

Billie Lee

I sure as hell have a thirst on tonight, and this old joint is jumping. The Porker's got another rush on, and as our arrangement is of a particularly specific variety, I have to step in now and then when it's quiet, serving the customers in one way, before switching to another kind of commercial exchange later. It's that keeps the crowd coming—the thought of coming back for the other thing when they've got the coin, or the nuggets (there's less of them!), or just 'cos it's the end of the week.

Could be this will be one of them bar and back doubles. He ain't told me if it is. Slaving away behind the bar with scarcely a stop for a piss, and the other half on my back to all and happy sundry. Woo woo! Climb on board the good stage Billie, boys, as long as you have the coin. For The Porker will send me the filthy and smelly, the crook-backed and the lame and the cursed and cruel—which twos often come together. Not that I'm without a resource or two, which—it being put into operation—could result in the loss of a vital part or two.

Now, such words of wit, as you might guess, are the sort of graveyard humor designed purely for my profession, where the only constants are the weekly visits of the clap-doctor and the regular soreness down below. How often do I wish I'd kept covered and away from the site and touch of evil men—done what my saintly momma advised.

"My, but what rare commodity we can make of you, Billie Lee," the dark face with the gold tooth and the twinkle had said.

"There's gold to be had between them thar thighs," cackled the far, sweaty pig other. Momma warned me not to grow up to soon and I—teenage rebel—chose to ignore her, and look where it got me. Twenty years and long since a veteran.

People assume that I'm the property of the corpulent mine host of The Pale Horse, and it is true that there does exist some kind of arrangement. It is one, however, that suits only the single party, the lady as ever, having little say if she wishes to keep her teeth in her pretty mouth and a brand from scarring her delicate skin permanent.

But the good Porker merely shares me. Shares me in the sense of being able to take the money from me, rather than the goods, which he knows I will surely sick up over him rather than give up. He's wise enough not to press it and has no desire for the gun pointing at his lame brain pecker to ever go off. And besides, he knows his business partner Sam is a little bit soft on me.

Even got down on his knee once to ask me, but I allowed him he was drunk when he said it. Ask me again in a month, I told him. But that month never came, because just like that, Sam was gone one day, without any hope of that month ever reoccurring. They say there was land left for him back east by his folks. It's nearly a year gone, and he's probably gone and married his childhood sweetheart by now.

Being only twenty, mind, my education in gennelman's pleasures having, as I said, begun early, there is another role I am obliged to play which is more pleasurable, and for which I have recently persuaded the barman pig to give me a little coin in the way of assurance. For I am, you might say, by way of being some kind of mother hen to a brood of six more bruised little chickadees. You thought I carried the weight of the town's menfolk on just my back? I would have been worn out and dead by eighteen.

There are six girls, and—

But I'm coming over faint with the heat. I can hardly breathe. I needs must have me a lie down.

"Mollie, I'm feeling a little down. Could you bide a while here while I take a nap? And no, sir, that ain't no invitation. And you, Bill, a bit less of that if you expect I should jerk your rod to attention this time. Well, 'scuse me for my words, but he ain't here and for now he's left me in charge, which means I can delegate. Which means I can go and lie down a spell until I feel better. Which means, as you're of a complaining and ornery nature about now, you can take your pick later of 'em that ain't me.

"Oh, go on with you. I didn't take anything by it. And you, Seth. Did you bring me those fine stockings I asked for? I'll try them, for sure, but not now. There's a good boy.

"Oh! There it is again. That buzzing. Got to get me a rest. I'm having the strangest feeling—as if I ain't really here. Best send me up a nip as well, Mollie."

Two: Porker's Playtime

There he goes—Black Sam, All a rush and never in time. He'll never reach her in time. There she lies. Exhausted Billie Lee, who feels mighty strange, but ain't a clue why. This broken-down bed can be a sanctuary sometimes, too. Just a little shut eye and then hope the only reason she has to come back to it tonight will be to sleep.

As he rides into town, Sam remembers all he used to be and them who's got in his way, while Billie Lee dreams the dreams and feather comfort of the just, and of her schoolroom home with the dusty floors and the cracked old slates. Momma was never what you might call comforting, but she would often block the way between Pappa and the strap. And Momma didn't get roaring drunk and know only the way of her fists to put the world to rights. So, right here and now, Billie Lee sucks her thumb as she sleeps and maybe, just maybe, she tastes a sweet taste like maple syrup.

***

Only Ephraim Cole, he ain't gone away at all. That bad Porker of a man has only been shuffling around in his sty and looking into the cracked mirror at his sweating pink face with its sprouting hairs. What he can't have willing, he's going to get by sheer force of his personality. From his greasy little den, he's watched as Billie climbs up the stairs and up into the barn, which is the bedroom of her and her brood.

Ephraim is rubbing away at something in his mind. He could have done it long ago, but he's finally taking his chances. Billie Lee never takes time off, and that gun of hers—which she can use, you can be sure—is always there close to her. But sly little Mollie now having fixed it all for him—both the gun and the other thing—it will be some kind of revenge for the looks of disgust she gave him. Not to mention that time when she laughed. Aye, he'll grant that squealing Jezebel his own special brand of dispensation and forgiveness. It'll be a shame after all this time, but there h'aint no going back after. He'll soon be needing a new hen for his clucking brood. Luckily, he's got Mollie lined up. Girl would do anything and betray anyone for more money to buy her flounces and fineries.

***

Sam rides hard and desperate, but here and now and forever he'll get there too late. Here and now there's no extra time left, and Ephraim is already wheezing up them stairs, pulling at his belt as he is about to take the favors of the little lady muck-muck who's been tormenting him so long. And Sam—hasn't been seen for near a year. Some say he fell in with prospectors and tried to cheat them from half their nuggets, until a few clouts of the spade stove his head in. Others say he's shaved off so much hair on head and beard that he's become an outlaw that no-one can recognize, leading the law a merry old leaping dance on the black devil who matches him in temperament, speed and low-down cunning.

No-one seems to know the truth, which isn't anything near the tale, or quite as exciting. The sick mother, and the battles with his father. A long illness and an even longer settling of the estate. Sam is now a rich rancher, which means the throwing in of his badge, for the sheriff—being of an old-school and kindly disposition—had elected to keep the position dependent on his return. More important, with his folks gone, who he was so long estranged from, he sees it finally as the time to settle back down. That's why he's come back for Billie Lee, to make an honest woman of her. Imagine her face when he tells her it weren't no drunken joke after all.

***

Imagine that great straw covered place where seven pallets are stretched for weary bodies—four at one end and three across. Ephraim has made sure there's work for all his girls tonight—just in case one should show and get in the way. No chance of that with Mollie, of course—little pecker tease turncoat. Perhaps he'll have her squirm in another way for her sins. 'Case she should think of coming on high and mighty. Maybe he'll remind her. Ephraim sweats and feels the pull in his groin.

Billie Lee is sleeping. The colorless powder was bitter, but hardly noticeable in Billie Lee's drink. The washed glass will be used again—but never again to such delightful effect.

Ah, the sweet little thing has got her thumb in her mouth. You wait there while I give you something better to replace it.

Billie Lee's eyes snap open. Instinct and a terrible dread flood her brain. She sees her death in one picture. The Porker. Belt swinging, gut already escaping, and her so woozy that her skirt is far away on the chair. Could she make it in time—for she's never seen any speed on the pig. Only half a move and then.

"This what you're looking for?"

***

Over the way, The Pale Horse is full up with custom, and the night-time girls are powdering and smoothed. Many of them are nipping gin or sniffing something else just to get them through, special snuff brought in from Paris. One to clear the head and the other to fog the memory.

Doc Gutteridge is leaning on the bar. Even at such an early hour he is partways gone, more to add to his whiskey fire breath and his broken-veined nose. They say he has even performed certain procedures for ladies in such a state, and there are a few as shudder to recall it. But like most everybody, he is bought and sold, bought and sold by a man missing these eleven months, and the pig who represents him. The pig whose patience—never one of his finer qualities—has gone and run out on him.

He knows plenty of stuff about Ephraim Cole, but he's also wise enough to keep his trap shut. He's a looser mouth with drink than most, has our friend the doc, and his hands shake like danger most of the time. A scrawny fly of a man like him, the good Porker could knock him on his ass before pummeling him until he's dead, and he knows it. It's a crying shame that he's such a coward that would put his own reputation before a showgirl down on her luck. Doc Gutteridge has known Billie Lee since she was a baby catching her first wind, and he's been known to her on a professional basis too many times to count. That's what you might call a conflict of interests, so there'll be no hope from that quarter.

He also knows that one particular secret of The Porker's he'd never dare to let slip. Such as the fact that there's parts of the man that no matter how much service they're offered—willing or no—there ain't no winch in the whole of the state going to get him a raise.

Doc Gutteridge would know that, were he to see the man taking out his belt as he climbs the stairs of the barn next door where the girls sleep, and where lies a Billie Lee drugged with the particular concoction he's provided. The girl is as helpless as any lamb, and the shepherd a'waiting to attend on her does a fine and varied line in cruelty that none would call refined.

When the screaming starts—and then goes on and on, the roar of the bar and the mood of the weekend cowboys, ranchers and good-time girls, drowns out the rest.

The next day Ephraim Cole acts as shaken as anyone, and of course ma'am, sir, he's in full co-operation with our friend the sheriff to get the snake who did this thing to our Billie.

Three: The Barman's Tale

The horseman rides on and doesn't stop. How many years has it been? How many coaches checked and bars scoured? How many shots and how much road? Throat full of dust and knuckles flexed into iron.

Thing is, this whole thing happened long ago and—as you might say—all the participants are dead. So, what's in it for him, this dark-cloaked man with the sort of face you can never quite make out?

But there are some folk whose tale can never be quite told. And yes, there are even a few who can't take no for answer. They may be dead, but they won't lie down.

Black Sam, however, well, he's one of the more restless variety, due to having one whole heap of guilts piled on him. He hadn't been there to prevent Billie's awful death at the hands of an out-of-control Porker. Instead of planning to marry her now, he should have done so long ago and taken her away with him. His proposal weren't no joke, so why hadn't he told her? He should never have left her to the ministrations of a bastard, who had the sign of the devil all over him. If, that was, the devil was really some fat, sweaty pig.

And Ephraim Cole never did get his. Instead, he drank his liver out of being and him with it, but it took another twenty years. Ain't nowhere near enough misery for the likes of him, and Sam had been too much of a coward to ride all the way back from his fine ranch and take him down. What's a fine gentleman to do, having a past that won't quite lie down? Ask Miss Billie Lee.

***

Billie ain't in the same crowd as Sam anymore, as they kinda got separated on the way out. Seems it's on account of Billie's God-fearing mother that she don't have to take the plunge downwards, but rests in the quiet white garden with the Christian folk.

Were she not being so polite, she might say that she'd have more in common with those on the descent the other way, but her old lover Sam notwithstanding, she wouldn't particularly take to the idea of a pitchfork up her ass. Ephraim Cole, mind? Chances are he's in for a whole bunch of that! Be a shame if he weren't.

***

Joe Turner thinks he has the whole story down now—going to be the first thing in the paper with his by-line. He's not sure that Mr. Henry is going to take to his style, but he thinks it's got a certain buzz. 'Sides, how can you go wrong with such a story? It's got everything! Black Sam himself! The brute everyone called the Porker behind his back. Then there's poor, sad Billie Lee, who was someone for all the good reasons in her youth, and later for all the wrong ones.

Joe settles down, re-reads.

A hail of dust kicks up as the wagon moves off. The pale face of a woman peers from behind the grimy curtain, and then is gone. Is it she? I surely ain't about to recognize her now. How long has it been?

I move back into the battered saloon with its even more battered barkeep. His creaky stool, the only sound in the whole deserted mausoleum of entertainments.

He has the shot ready for me—just like he always does—and as always, I swig it down in one, and nod my thanks. He is no respecter of tidiness, this man, let alone cleanliness. Always the smell of horseshit about him. Always the black and broken fingernails, bitten to the quick.

"Marshal will be in soon." His line.

"I'll wait then." And mine.

Joe puts down his pen, pleased at the way it reads. His practiced eye scans through the rest, stopping every once in a while to frown over this, or question that. There isn't much time. Maybe he should reconsider the cuss words. No point in offending. He removes two of them and tones down a couple more.

As the door slams, the dark figure looms over him, someone who seems impossibly tall, and he has the odd sense that time is way out of line. He'd have looked at his watch if he had been given the time. But the gleaming knife, as it gutted him like a fish, made the decision for him, and as he writhed and unsuccessfully strangled his screams, the last black blood came roaring up right the way into his throat, such was the force. His feet kicked, like a hangman's last dance, and Joe's career at the *Southern Star* was dead as fast as he was.

His assailant kicked him aside and wiped the blood from his knife on the dead man's shirt, its pristine white forever compromised by death. Then he kicked at the chair and sat himself down on it, one flailing elbow knocking off the story Joe had worked on for so long and was about to set his career on, scattered and useless.

And Sam reached into his pocket, unrolling the band of a good cigar, and set it to his teeth. He wouldn't smoke it! Not until this was good and done. He set up the typewriter with practiced skill, inserted a new pristine sheet. He wasn't even sure that it would come—what had spent so long boiling and cooling in his brain, but he knew this had to be his last chance.

A title first. *The Ballad of Billie Lee?* Why? This wasn't any kind of song. Maybe something else? Something more of style and refinement, then! Or something more in keeping with his long overdue revenge.

He bit down hard on the cigar. That was it. His fingers tapped.

The Barman's Tale

His digits sharp, he tapped away until the job was done, and blue-grey smoke drifted over the fresh pile of pages.

Long after The Porker had met his deserved and timely end, and Sam and Billie—good church-abiding folk now—being now long settled with their three children on the family ranch, The Pale Horse had undergone somewhat of a revival customer wise. Had you asked any of the regular folks then their answer was unequivocal. "It's because of the tale."

"What tale is that?"

"Why, the barman's tale. Hain't you heard?"

"Well go in there and have a look see."

These gentlemen (and it was always gentlemen!) would—on making the enquiry—be shown the curious, but somehow familiar, brown wrinkled object kept in a glass pickle jar over the bar. Seeing it, and surmising what he surmised, he'd find himself in no hurry to examine the thing any further.

"So, you've seen the tail. Now maybe you want to hear it." (This clearly being the current occupant mine-host and part-time history guide's party piece.)

"Well, see, the marshal they call Black Sam, on account of how he used to often hide his face, was in partnership with this, my long-ago predecessor Ephraim, who was called by all The Porker, due to his size and dirty habits.

"Now, Sam was sweet on a good time show girl name of Billie Lee, who did tricks on and off the stage. But he made the mistake of leaving Billie in the hands of his working partner The Porker. Now he was a cruel man, and he was wanting a piece of Billie's soft lily-white flesh for some time—only on account of a regular mechanical failure in the area that matters, he was left a little short, which made him mad. So, while Black Sam was way over the other side of the country a' visiting with his folks, Ephraim got drunk and took his chances. He drugged poor Billie, and if Sam hadn't come riding back in time... If he'd taken the stage instead as he'd intended..."

"What happened? Did Sam kill him?"

"Well, The Porker lived another twenty years until his liver shut out, but he sure wasn't the man he started. And there's many like me who'd call it some kind of poetic justice."

"And Billie Lee? Was she okay?"

"Fine and dandy on their ranch, the both of them, and with three pretty children to their name. All long gone, of course."

"That's good."

"So, here's to the barman's tale. Will you be wanting another shot?"

The stooping black figure all but purred his satisfaction. This was an ending he much preferred!

Then he stood for a while, knowing it was all done at last. The longer he stood, the more of it—which had never been quite real, anyway—faded away, or crumbled, or, once or twice, even both. Until it was his turn. He heard Billie Lee singing softly behind him.

Now!

And then there was her perfume and her arms around him, and life—even here in death—came flooding back.

STATE OF THE ART
BY
JOHN B. ROSENMAN

Johnny Graves rode into Abilene, knowing he could die at any time. Half the town would like to shoot him in the back and collect the $5,000 reward on his head. Ever since he'd entered the place, he'd been watchful, his senses on a hair trigger as he searched the wooden buildings on both sides of the street. The false fronts were as deceptive as a boomtown floozy's painted face, a lie you could never trust. Abilene in 1882 was smoky and smelly, a dirty railroad cattle town.

His horse trembled and hung his head, tired from the long ride. Graves licked his dry lips, his gun hand ready for action.

He passed a dry goods store, a feed store, a land office, and then entered the seamier part of town where bawdy houses, dance halls, and saloons ruled. The Alamo, his destination, was the main watering hole. He felt he'd been in this town and others like it a hundred times, ridden down the same dusty road and swilled whiskey in saloons as long as he could remember. The Alamo he found more impressive than most. It had a long room with three double glass doors at the west entrance. Having visited countless such establishments, Graves no longer looked forward to their crude attractions. He was weary, tired of killing men and of constantly looking over his shoulder for the next punk seeking to make himself a big reputation. His wild, roaring days were long gone, and he wanted only one thing.

Tracy.

Turning toward the saloon, he dismounted and hitched the reins around the rail. He hesitated, searching the buildings' facades. On the second floor landing of a hotel across the street, several men watched him, and Graves's spine crawled. Did they recognize him? If they did, everybody would soon know, and gunnies would come running.

Ah, hell. They'd know soon enough anyway.

Seeing a sleek red Chrysler with tail fins, he froze. What the hell was a car doing here? It didn't fit. And how did he know what it was?

Come to think of it, hadn't this type of thing happened more and more lately? Strange objects appearing where they had no right to be.

Rubbing his eyes, he saw the Chrysler turn into an old buckboard with a grizzled farmer.

Ah, that was better. He'd had a long ride, and his eyes must have been playing tricks on him.

He turned and entered the Alamo.

The forty-foot-long room was fancier and more elaborate than most. A bar ran along one side with polished brass fixtures and rails. In the large mirror behind it, Graves could see bottles of liquor waiting. The walls featured huge paintings of naked women done by Renaissance masters. They smiled down at the gaming tables, which were busy even in the noonday heat.

As soon as he entered, the room fell silent. Card dealers stopped dealing and conversation died as if chopped by a knife.

At one time, such attention would have flattered him. Now it bored and sickened him beyond words. Scanning the room for a likely challenger, he saw with relief that all of them looked away.

He went to the bar, his spurs jingling. "Whiskey," he said.

The bartender turned, and his face lit up with a smile. "Johnny Graves! It's good to see you!"

He tossed a coin on the bar. "Just give me whiskey."

"Sure, sure." The bartender produced a glass and bottle, then poured. Graves noticed his hair was neatly divided in the middle and combed with meticulous precision to both sides. He wore a prissy vest with a string tie and exuded a faint perfume smell.

Graves raised the glass and drank as the bartender continued to grin. "Don't you recognize me, Johnny?"

He thumbed back his hat. "Can't say I do."

"I worked at the Longhorn in Dodge City, and you used to come in with Frank Martin." His eyes gleamed with hero worship.

"Sure, I remember," Graves lied.

The man laughed in delight. "Those were great times, weren't they? The best." He slid the coin back across the bar. "It's on the house. You can have whatever you want, Johnny. Would you like a steak?"

Graves spat in a nearby cuspidor. "What I'd like is some information. Does Tracy Marshall still live in town?"

The bartender started to respond then gasped as a shiny object with a fancy dial appeared on his wrist. "What the hell? Where did that come from?" Timidly, he touched it with his finger. "W-What the devil is it?"

"It's a smartwatch," Graves said, wondering how he knew.

"A *smartwatch*?" The man's eyes bulged as if it were a bomb.

The other's shock was humorous, but to Graves, the situation seemed wrong. It was as if something was meddling with reality.

He tried asking again. "Does Tracy Marshall still live in town?"

"Turn around, mister, and do it slow."

Graves stiffened, then obeyed.

"I've been waiting a long time to meet you," a naked stranger said. He wore guns on both metal hips, and his metal face grinned. "And now I finally have."

***

The Designer froze the Life Slice and turned to the Director. "Sir, this is going too far. I can't put a smartwatch and a robot in a nineteenth-century frontier town."

His superior peered into the display. "Why not?"

"They're anachronisms. The red Chrysler is bad enough, but they just didn't have smartwatches and thinking robots in 1882. And other details are wrong, too."

The Director patted his fat stomach. "The Old Wild West is three hundred years dead, son. The masses are asses and don't know anachronisms from alfalfa. We just give them what they want, what our polls and focus groups indicate is trendy and popular. Such as flashy cars circa 1950s, smartwatches, and futuristic robots."

"And mix it all in?" the Designer asked. "Like a chuckwagon stew?"

A careless shrug. "What's the harm? Our job is to give people what they want. We cater to their tastes, whatever they may be."

The Designer was not only a gifted young man but a frustrated purist with scruples. "Sir, I believe we do run the risk of causing harm."

"How so?"

He pointed at Johnny Graves who faced a metal gunman in an Abilene bar. "I've programmed some nits to be more sentient than others. Most possess only a rudimentary intelligence, but the main character here is deeper and more complicated."

"Nonsense. Our experts all agree they're superficial. They possess the ability to respond to cues and perform mechanical acts. That's all."

"With respect, sir, I believe the state of the art has gone further." He gazed into the tri-vid display, feeling he could walk right into the saloon. "Some nits may even approach full consciousness, and I'm worried that they'll start to suspect their lives and realities are being tampered with. They might notice inconsistencies, elements which don't fit."

A long silence. "Son, you will continue to write code according to the specifications we give you. Is that clear?"

The Designer sighed. If he didn't need this job so much, he'd tell the schmuck off. "Yes, sir," he said, and reactivated the scene.

***

Graves couldn't recall seeing a metal man before, let alone one who was completely naked. Metal head, metal chest, metal... everything.

The stranger spread his legs and tensed, his hands just inches from his holsters. "Slap leather, hombre."

Slap leather, hombre. Who spoke like that? It didn't fit, but then, what things did lately?

"Look," he said, "we don't have to do this."

Smiles appeared on a few faces, and he knew what it meant. They were beginning to think he was yellow, and that would never do.

"What's the matter?" Metal Man sneered. "Don't you have the guts?"

How did you shoot a metal guy anyway? *Where* did you shoot him? Graves knew the code of the West dictated that you let the other draw first, but for the first time he realized it made no sense.

Graves smiled. "On the count of three, hombre?"

Sharp metal teeth flashed. "Fine with me."

"Good." He drew and shot the bastard six times, emptying his gun. Bullets ricocheted off the man's chest and stomach, striking walls and floor. But one slug drilled him right between the eyes, making a nice, neat hole. He fell to the floor with a loud clank and lay still.

Graves spun his pistol in his hand and did a few flashy tricks. As they all gaped, he slid it back into his holster with lightning ease.

"Glad that's over," he said. "He was starting to annoy me."

***

As ordered, the Designer paused the display. "Sir, I know Johnny wasn't supposed to shoot first."

The Director scowled. "The hero waits for the bad guy and draws *second*. It's the way it's always been. It's the *hero's* way."

He shouldn't contradict his boss, but he couldn't help himself. "Not always, sir. There's been revisionist westerns before."

"Not lately! And you called him *Johnny*. It seems to me you identify too closely with your nit and are personally involved."

Uh-oh. While the Designer knew he was talented and the Company valued his services, he also knew his job was hanging by a thread. It would be wise to treat this fat fool with respect.

"I'll correct the scene," he said. He straightened his Stetson, which he wore for inspiration.

"See that you do! And remove that silly cowboy hat."

The Designer obeyed and tapped a button to rewind the scene. Only it didn't respond. Funny, not only did Johnny seem to be resisting him lately, but now the program was as well. Could he be losing control of it?

"What's wrong?" The Director's voice was heavy with menace.

He tried to suppress his alarm. "Just a glitch, sir. I'll have it right as rain in no time."

***

The saloon seemed to flutter and fade, and a current ran through Graves. In the flickering light, the saloon changed. The dead gunman vanished, and a small, winged machine buzzed by, delivering drinks to the tables. Soon he heard weird music. A frantic beat filled the air, and a man chanted, "Want ya, baby, want ya so bad!" The cowboys looked different, dressed in three-piece suits with tight, prim ties. They shouted in alarm when they discovered their new clothes.

Graves closed his eyes and resisted the change, fought it down. When he opened them, the old room was back and the gunman lay on the floor again, leaking oil.

He heard a roar outside and ran to the door just in time to watch the red Chrysler he'd seen before race down the street, blaring its horn and almost smashing into a stagecoach, which swerved to avoid it. The bright cherry vehicle had four wheels and two doors with windows. Not to mention those sweeping tail fins.

How did he know they were called tail fins? And how could the damned thing go so fast? Seeing a man inside, Graves realized he was driving it somehow, steering it where he wanted it to go.

How did he know this? What in hell was happening?

He glanced at the dead man. "Don't you think someone should go get the sheriff?" he asked the men.

"W-hat?" a cowboy said.

"Get *the freakin' sheriff!*" he said. *Freakin'*? Where did that come from?

"Oh yes, Mr. Graves. Right away!" The cowboy turned and rushed out.

Graves went to the bartender, whose smartwatch vanished as he approached. "Whiskey. And leave the bottle."

The man complied, as happy as ever. No, happier, because he'd just seen Johnny Graves do what he was supposed to—beat someone to the draw and kill him. Matter of fact, scanning the room, Graves saw that the customers were beginning to liven up and enjoy the excitement. Nothing like a little shootout to perk up a dull day and give folks something to gab about.

The sheriff came in as he was finishing his second shot of rye. To Graves, he looked like a stereotype, someone's hackneyed, simple-minded idea of what a sheriff was supposed to be. For the first time, he realized that many of the folks he'd encountered had seemed the same way.

Take the bartender for instance. Wasn't he another one-dimensional stereotype, right down to his string tie and fancy vest? Yup, he sure was.

And what about himself? Was he any different? Was he even real? He glanced at his hands and felt his body, half-expecting himself to change, like so much else these days.

Such strange, troubling thoughts he was having!

As the sheriff approached him, Graves gripped his glass and tried to be positive. Maybe a standard issue sheriff with no surprises was exactly what he needed. He felt reassured by the square chin, broad chest, jeans, and flannel shirt. And of course, the tin star and holstered gun, which was fine as long as the sheriff didn't try to use it.

"I'm Sheriff Royce, Mr. Graves." He glanced at the dead man. "Seems there's been some trouble here."

Why wasn't the sheriff surprised the dead man was naked and made of steel? "He forced my hand," he said, looking to the townsmen for support.

"Mr. Graves had no choice," one said. "Hank was about to draw."

"That's right," others chorused.

The sheriff shrugged. "In that case, there's no foul." He smiled. "Mr. Graves, since there's no warrant for you here, I only ask you to be careful." His gaze dropped to Graves's gun. "I don't suppose you'd comply if I asked for your firearm? We do have an ordinance."

Graves nodded at the dead man. "Apparently, Hank didn't observe it. If I'd been unarmed, I'd be lying there instead of him."

"Point taken," the sheriff said. They watched the undertaker enter with his assistant. The undertaker examined the corpse and then the assistant picked it up, slung it over his shoulder and trudged out.

"No muss, no fuss," the sheriff said. "Oh, by the way, Mr. Graves, someone you know wants to see you."

"Someone I know? Who?"

"Tracy Marshall."

Tracy Marshall? It was the girl he'd come to see, the sweetheart he'd left behind in his foolish, wild youth to become an outlaw and make a name for himself. The girl he loved and could never forget no matter how far he roamed. How many women had he loved and left in a vain effort to forget her? How often had he thought of her, wondering if she'd found someone else, if she was married?

At last, unable to resist, he'd returned to their hometown, hoping to see her. Sweet Tracy with the peach blossom cheeks. Was she as lovely as he remembered?

He tried to speak. "Where?"

The sheriff poked a thumb over his shoulder. "Right outside. Shall I..."

"Please."

Royce went and opened the door. "Tracy."

Graves's heart pounded. His hands tingled with expectation. Tracy had loved him, begged him not to go. If she wanted to see him, she must still care. Maybe they could go away someplace where no one knew him, start a new life together. Maybe his life could still be saved.

A figure appeared in the doorway. The lighting was poor, though, and at first he couldn't see very well. He took a step forward, shading his eyes.

"Tracy?" he called.

"Johnny?" a deep male voice responded. A moment later, Graves saw a broad-shouldered man with a heavy beard. He was three inches taller than himself.

The man spread his arms. "Oh, Johnny," he cried. Before Graves could think, the man ran forward and embraced him in his brawny arms.

***

"Excellent! Outstanding!" the Director said, kissing the Designer's cheek. "While we discourage the use of personal initiative, you've tapped into a key demographic here. The LGBTQ community has grown to forty-five percent of the population, but our entertainment division has lagged behind. Giving Graves a male lover is a definite step in correcting the balance. It's brilliant!"

The Designer stared at the screen. He was as surprised and horrified as Graves by Tracy Marshall's transformation.

"Sir," he whispered, "I didn't do this."

"Heh?"

"I didn't do this! I didn't redesign Tracy."

"Then how..."

In the Life Slice, Tracy Marshall had actually raised Graves half a foot from the floor in a crushing bear hug.

"I think," the Designer said, "the system has evolved."

"What do you mean?"

"It's alive. Don't you get it? It's friggin' alive. It's taken over!"

***

Graves finally overcame his shock. Summoning all his strength, he pushed the huge creature away. The man stared at him, his hairy face filled with hurt and disbelief.

Graves pointed at him with a trembling hand. "*You're* Tracy Marshall?"

"Johnny, dear, what's wrong?" a deep baritone replied. "Don't you want me?"

It was either a nightmare or he'd gone insane. "Want you?" He eyed the man's thick, muscular body. "You must have fifty pounds on me."

The man held out his hands. "Don't you remember how we danced together? How you used to tease me and say, 'Don't mess your dressy, Tracy,' when we played as children?"

Mad or not, he couldn't stand it. The red Chrysler... the smartwatch... the naked metal gunman... now this, the worst of all. It was the latest in a series of mad events he had barely noticed but which today had reached a crisis. He felt like the plaything of fate, as if God were toying with him. His whole body burned, about to boil over.

Suddenly he snapped and drew his gun. Though it was empty, he put three bullets in Tracy's manly chest. The man clutched it, gazed at him with an expression of boundless betrayal, and collapsed.

"Get out!" Graves screamed. "All of you!"

Soon he was alone, obeyed even by the sheriff. Clutching his head, he tried to understand. Everything else he might explain, but not his childhood sweetheart turning into a brute.

What was happening? What had changed reality? Even more important, what was doing this to him, and why? For God's sake, who and what was he? He felt he was waking up, but he didn't know to what.

Sobbing, he spotted a hole in the mirror behind the bar. It grew until he could see a face, then two faces. Both were watching him.

The hole continued to grow. Now he could see another room. He raised his gun and aimed.

***

"What the fuck?" the Director exploded.

"Run for the hills!" the Designer answered. He rose and flung himself toward the studio door. He didn't quite make it.

In the saloon, Graves gripped his pistol. "Damn," he said. "Never thought I'd live to shoot someone in the back." He moved toward the hole, determined to get answers.

SUNSET COWBOY
BY
JOHN A. FROCHIO

In the fading light of sunset, I lazily watched shooting stars from the porch outside the sheriff's office. I sat up quickly when something else caught my eye.

In the distance, against a fiery red mountain sunset, a tall and ominous figure ambled slow and steady toward our quiet little town on an unnaturally large horse.

My heart pounded in my chest like a buffalo stampede. I held my breath. I was unaccustomed to any confrontation that might end in conflict. Of course, as sheriff, I should be able to handle suspicious strangers; but the truth is, we don't get many strangers around these parts. On top of that, I was staring at my forties and moving a mite slower.

From the stoop, I studied the stranger. What dark secrets or malicious intentions lay in the heart of this mysterious rider from the West, this sunset cowboy, haunter of dark dreams?

The closer he got, the more peculiar his appearance, which of course made me even more anxious. Not the usual dusty coveralls, corduroy, plaids, and suspenders. No, this character was dressed all in black, a striking contrast against the bright red sunset. His silhouette reminded me of a sharp-dressed city slicker, a teacher or government official.

With that last image in my mind, I burst out laughing. Nothing to fear here.

His beast looked less like a horse the closer he got. Big and ugly, it trailed gray puffs from its mouth like a steam locomotive. Its face looked more like a lizard's. Bulkier than a draft horse, it was thickly covered with long black strands of hair.

I moseyed out to greet him. We stopped a few feet apart. I couldn't see his eyes beneath the dark rim of his Stetson.

"Howdy," I said in my most cordial tone.

He nodded. At least I think he did. His head sort of bobbed like a robin.

I went on, "What brings you to our little town, mister? Business or passing through?"

The next thing I knew I was talking to empty air. Now where did he get to so fast?

I spotted him at Mack's Saloon, sliding off his horse thing and striding into the place. I decided I better keep an eye on him, so I hurried to follow him. I scooted way out around the ugly beast, since I noticed he hadn't tied it to the post. I didn't like the way its eyes followed me.

When I stepped inside, I breathed a sigh of relief. The stranger stood at the bar talking quietly with the barkeep, Jake. I sidled up to the bar a few stools down and caught the tail end of their conversation.

Jake said, "Some strange goings-on at the Brewster Ranch, if that's what you mean. The Brewster boys should be in later if you want to talk to them about it."

The stranger turned away and strode toward an empty corner table.

When Jake came over to me, I said, "What business does he have with the Brewsters?"

"He'd heard about some strange things happening around these parts. I told him about the Brewster Ranch."

"You don't believe all those stories, do you?"

"Well, Sheriff Ray, people been saying there's evil spirits out there or something. Who knows?"

"Old wives' tales, that's what they are. Why was he interested?"

"Didn't say."

"Seems funny. So why does he talk to you and not me?"

Jake shrugged. "Everyone talks to the bartender."

He poured me my usual and moved on.

I sipped on my beer and waited for the Brewsters to show up. I didn't have to wait long.

The three Brewster boys burst into the saloon, shouting out their drink orders and cheerfully greeted everyone in the place. They carried on, whooping and hollering as they usually do on a Friday night, hanging out at the bar and laughing at their own jokes and droll stories.

When they eventually noticed the stranger sitting alone in the dark corner, who stared right at them, they instantly became real quiet. They spoke in low whispers after that, finished their drinks in record time, then announced they were turning in for the evening.

I stood up. "Mighty early evening for you boys, ain't it?"

Jonah, the oldest, said, "Tiring day, Sheriff Ray. Early day tomorrow."

"I thought all your days were early on the ranch."

Joey, the youngest, said, "That's right, Sheriff." His voice was shaky. He looked at the stranger and back at me.

Jimmy, the middle Brewster boy, said, "Let's get goin'."

They left without another word.

I glanced at Jake. He shrugged.

Not long after, the stranger got up and spoke to Jake, then walked out of the saloon.

I asked, "What'd he say?"

"He wanted to know where he could stay for the night. I told him about Lou's Place."

I peeked outside and watched the stranger mount his beast and ride down the dusty street. The full moon cast an eerie glow over them. Wisps of steam trailed behind them in looping swirls.

Later, with that haunting image stuck in my brain, I had a restless night's sleep.

***

The next day, on my way past Lou's Place, I spotted the stranger's beast outside munching on some weeds. I slumped half-dozing on the wooden chair on my stoop. The morning and afternoon were quiet. I had my deputy Rodney check on the stranger from time to time.

Late in the afternoon, he came running and said, "He's gone."

I stood up, my knees complaining, and said, "Where'd he go?"

"Lou said he asked how to get to the Brewster Ranch."

"Rodney, saddle up our horses. We have to get out to the Brewster's."

"You worried about Jessica, boss?"

I threw my hat at him. "Get moving, buster."

Rodney knew I fancied the Brewster's only girl. Jessica was shy, pretty, polite, and strong-willed. She had to be with three big brothers. My heart skipped a beat any time I was around her. She had long black hair the color of midnight and narrow piercing green eyes.

They lost their parents a long time ago, so only the four of them ran the ranch. No one knew exactly how their parents had passed away. They never wanted to talk about it, which led to a lot of whispered gossip around town.

Jessica told me a little about it once. I had run into her at the general store and could tell she was feeling a bit lowdown.

When I asked her what was wrong, she said, "All the ladies in town... Why— why do they turn away from me?"

I knew why. They considered Jessica an odd bird. The way she looked and acted, like some kind of foreigner or an angel or something out of a dream. Of course, I never saw that. I saw a lovely, coy girl who made my heart pound like a war drum.

I didn't know what to say. "Sometimes people can be heartless and cruel. They prejudge others who might seem... uh, different?" I began to regret opening my mouth. "Uh... They don't give people a chance. It's unfair, I know. If they only knew the sweet girl I know, I'm sure they would act differently."

That brought a small smile to her face.

"Anyway, it doesn't matter how other people act and think. What matters is how you feel about yourself."

I felt relieved about my quick recovery.

She dropped her eyes. "But I don't know how I feel about myself. My mother once told me about a stranger who came to town long ago, before I was born, a charming man. She spent time with him. My father never knew. Not long after the stranger went away, I came along. I always felt treated different. Not just because I was the only girl. That's what I used to think. But over the years, I came to realize I truly was different. Oh, Sheriff Ray, I don't know who I am."

She wept in my arms. I was caught off guard but managed to hold onto her.

She continued through her sobs, "When I was ten, not long after my mother's confession, I awoke to find my father dead in his sleep and my mother gone. We never saw her again. My brothers decided we'd say they both died in some tragic accident.

"Oh, please don't tell anyone."

"Of course."

That was the most she ever opened up to me.

Naturally, I've heard all the stories about the strange things happening out on their ranch. Some were just plain crazy, like cows floating in the air or sick animals healing overnight or crops growing faster than possible. The Brewster boys laughed in your face if you asked them about it. And Jessica would blush and say nothing.

Yeah, I was worried about Jessica. Another stranger in her life. That bothered me.

We saddled up and rode.

The sun slid toward the west. A few sparse clouds lingered in the sky, wrapping up another day without rain. Over two weeks without rain had hurt the farms and ranches.

We stopped on a hill overlooking the Brewster Ranch. From our vantage point, everything looked perfectly fine, yet too quiet. No one out and about was odd for early evening. I said nothing to Rodney about my concerns.

We trotted down the hillside and approached the ranch cautiously. When we arrived, we dismounted and tied our horses to the hitching posts in front of the ranch house. No one acknowledged our presence.

We were on the front porch when we heard the commotion coming from the barn out back. Howling sounds, shouting, and noises like animals fighting. A chill raced up my spine.

Rodney rushed to the barn, his gun drawn, and I hurried after him, my stomach clenching. That's when things started to get weird.

We were a dozen feet away when the barn doors flew open, tearing off their hinges and rolling away like tumbleweeds, like something blew up inside. But there wasn't any explosion.

Rodney and I jumped back like scared rabbits.

Next came a torrent of hay, strewn about like dust in a windstorm, followed by the Brewster boys scampering like spooked antelope or chickens with their heads cut off. They flew past us so close we could see the bloodshot in their bulging eyes.

Then came the stranger plodding out of the barn, carrying Jessica Brewster's limp body in his outstretched arms.

My stomach clenched. My heart raced. Beautiful Jessica, sweet Jessica, a little bit crazy Jessica! Was she dead? Did the stranger kill her?

No, I saw her arms lift weakly, her head try to move.

Behind the stranger marched the beast, huffing and puffing.

I drew my gun. Rodney backed away from the unreal spectacle until he stood next to me. He whispered, "What the hell, Ray? What the hell?"

I spoke aloud, trying like the devil to remain calm, "Hold it right there, mister. What are you doing with the girl?"

He stopped. We stared at one another for several moments. Then he gently lowered Jessica to the ground. She sat up unsteadily, looking up at the stranger with something like awe or fear.

The stranger tossed his hat away, then peeled open his dark suit and tossed it aside. Rodney and I gasped. I couldn't believe my eyes. Beneath his clothing he was covered from top to bottom in a metallic skin, like a suit of armor, except it was smooth and tightly contoured to his body. The metal skin reflected the setting sun like a silvery moon.

He spoke in a gravelly voice that I didn't expect. "My master has sent me to claim his own."

I took a deep breath and said, "Who is your master?"

"He is called Varr."

"And she belongs to this Varr character?"

"She is his own."

Jessica stood up shakily. "He says he's my real father."

I said, "She was raised here. This is her home."

"He said it was time."

I looked at Jessica. "Do you want to go?"

She dropped her head. "I—I don't know. I asked him about my mother. He said she's gone to a higher kingdom. I don't know what that means."

"Where will you take her? Where is Varr's home?"

She pointed toward the setting sun. "Far from here, he said. Beyond the sunset."

I could see the fear in her eyes, hear the tremble in her voice. How could I stop this man of metal and his ugly beast from whisking her away to who knew where?

I stalled for time.

"Why didn't Varr come himself to claim his daughter? Why send a servant to do his bidding? Wasn't this important enough? And why isn't he gracious enough to give her a choice, whether to stay or go?"

"My Master sent me to claim his own."

"I know, I know. You sound like a stuck phonograph."

The metal-covered stranger climbed back onto his beast and held out his hand to Jessica. She lifted a hand hesitantly. I wondered if he had hypnotized her.

I cried out, "Wait! Tell Varr she's no longer his, for I have claimed her as *my own*."

Jessica stared at me. I wished I could've read her expression, but it was too jumbled up. I didn't know if my ruse would work or not, but I had run out of ideas. I suspected a gun battle with that metal fellow wouldn't end well.

Of course, my worst fear was Jessica would choose to go with him instead.

The stranger said, "You claim the woman?"

I spoke firmly. "Yes."

"Then Varr must challenge you."

He dropped down from his beast and stepped several paces away. The beast reared back on its hind legs and let loose a mighty roar, an unearthly sound, like nothing I've ever heard from man or beast. Instinctively, Rodney, Jessica, and I covered our ears.

Now this next part is hard to describe.

Before our astonished eyes, the beast began to change. Its body twitched and trembled, shook and spasmed, bulged and squeezed, until it changed into a whole new form, man-like, tall and regal, rugged, gritty. Its face turned from an ugly lizard face to an attractive youth with golden locks, a stark contrast to the bulky, muscular body it bore beneath. Covered from head to toe with golden fur, its eyes burned like hot coals, and it stood tall like royalty.

I turned to say something to Rodney, but he went missing.

The voice of the man-thing boomed, "I am Varr. You challenge my claim to what is mine?"

The man-thing towered at least twelve feet over me.

Still stunned, I managed to croak, "Yes. She may have been yours once, but I claim her now as mine."

I took several steps forward and reached out to Jessica. She took my hand, her face expressionless.

I craned my neck upwards. The man-thing looked down on me as though I were an annoying bug.

He growled, "Then we must do battle."

I didn't like the odds.

Jessica grabbed my shoulders and looked deep into my eyes. "Save yourself, Ray. Run. You can't win against him."

I looked back at her, into her sad eyes. "You belong here, Jessica. This is your home."

She backed away from me. "I don't want anyone hurt."

A bitter howl made us look up at Varr. The giant man-thing spat a fireball at me. I leaped out of its path and hit the ground hard. I watched it hit the farmhouse, which instantly burst into flames.

I scrambled to my feet and pulled out my gun. I fired two shots, hitting him square in the chest. He didn't flinch.

Now I began to worry.

At this point, things got even stranger.

He sprouted full, colorful wings and arose straight up into the air. He circled high overhead, stalking us like a buzzard.

Before I could come up with a new game plan, Rodney, Jimmy, Jonah, and Joey came running out of the burning house, whoopin' and a-hollerin' and choking, dragging smoke trails behind them. When they saw the metal man and flying man-thing, they froze. I think they considered running back into the burning building.

Jessica ran to me and wrapped her arms around me.

She said, "He won't throw a fireball at you as long as I'm close by."

I hoped she was right.

The metal man started stomping toward us.

I shouted to the boys, "See about distracting that metal man. I'll deal with the flying one."

They threw rocks at the metal man, jumping back frequently like a bunch of scaredy-cat kids listening to ghost stories around a campfire. At least that slowed it down some.

I studied my flying adversary. With my rifle, I could drop a quail from thirty yards. Still, this was no quail, and it appeared to eat bullets for lunch.

Jessica held onto me tightly, which made it tough to concentrate on the task at hand.

While Rodney kept the metal man occupied, the Brewster boys ran to the well and filled buckets with water to put out the fire. That's when an idea hit me.

"Listen, it spits fire like a dragon, right? Maybe I can douse its flame with water. Get me a bucket and meet me at the well. I'll keep him distracted."

She ran off.

As I expected, the flying man-thing dove right for me. I bolted, weaving back and forth like a crazy person, and worked my way to the well. I'm not usually a praying man, but I fired out silent prayers like I was catching up with all the church services I'd missed.

I reached the well just as Jimmy left with a bucketful of water and Jessica showed up with an empty one. She stood close by while I filled the bucket. Varr circled ominously.

"Now get away. I need him to come close."

She touched my arm. "Be careful."

She stepped away. I lugged the full bucket out into the open, where I became an easy target.

I shouted, "Come down here. Face me man to man. I defend my claim."

It lunged, a clear red flame igniting in its throat. I tensed. The next seconds were a blur. I waited until the last possible moment. Just before it was upon me, I heaved the bucket of water straight at its gaping, flaming mouth and leaped out of the way, rolling as I hit the ground.

A cloud of hissing steam burst from the man-thing as it hit the ground. For several nerve-wracking seconds, I lost it behind a wall of steam.

As the haze cleared, I saw it struggling to get to its feet. Without thinking, I threw myself on top of it. I pulled out my Bowie knife and thrust it deep into the base of its neck, where the skin seemed most exposed.

The man-thing shuddered violently, then grew suddenly still.

I staggered to my feet and backed away. Bewildered, I stared at the hulking body sprawled out mere yards from me. A deathly silence and an awful stench overwhelmed me. I wondered if this bizarre nightmare was finally over.

The Brewster boys were now hurrying to carry buckets of water to their burning home. The fire seemed a bit smaller, more contained.

The stranger in metal stood unmoving. Rodney stared wide-eyed at the dead man-thing. Jessica ran to me. She took my arm and we stared in silence at the lifeless creature.

The man of metal came toward us.

She held up her hand and said, "Stop."

He stopped.

She pointed toward the setting sun. "Go home."

He turned and walked toward the sunset.

I stared for a moment at Jessica. She shrugged. "My father could control him. Figured I could do it, too."

I said, "What a strange evening it's been. Sorry about your father."

"I never knew him."

Rodney came running over and said, "You got more buckets?"

She said, "In the barn, to the left."

He retrieved a bucket and began helping the Brewster boys put out the fire.

I said, "We should help, too. Some rain would be nice about now." I knew that was unlikely, since we'd been in a two-week drought and there wasn't a cloud in the sky.

Jessica looked up at the sky. A few moments later, dark clouds formed rapidly above us. Soon rain poured down from the sky. Rodney and the Brewster boys scurried into the barn.

Jessica smiled a gentle smile as water poured down our faces in streams. Again, she shrugged.

"I believe you do have a little bit of your father in you. In a good way, of course."

A moment later she said, "So you've claimed me as yours?"

I blushed. She giggled and hugged me.

In the dimming light of sunset, I thought I spotted a shooting star. Shooting upward. I wasn't surprised.

THE SHOW MUST GO ON
BY
LAWRENCE DAGSTINE

Our names, mine and hers, were on the programs whenever there were programs. Otherwise, they were on those A-frame signs in front of the theaters, the windows of one too many backwater saloons—many of which I wouldn't dare a retired Union desperado to take a piss in—or on the mirror of small town drugstores, written in soap. First time we saw our billing it was on the oak billboard of a Joe's Eats, where we sat with our elbows on the counter, admiring the curlicued white letters like finger-painted cake frosting on the wood grain: THE SPECTACULAR TURCOTT AND ROSS.

Forget Buffalo Bill Cody, never mind Annie Oakley, or that short-lived no-talent hack, Bill Hickok. Sure, he might have been an exceptional poker player, but all it got him in the end was a bullet to the back of the brain. I'm talking about real showmen, the kind of thespians you don't encounter every day, the kind that are different and play in some of the mangiest and rowdiest locales. It was James Turcott and Ginger Ross on the breadbasket route through Iowa and Indiana and Illinois and Nebraska, even the harsher parts of the Dakotas. Bad weather? No problem. Mudslide? We got you covered. We were a small troupe, but we'd somehow find a way to nickel and dime and get our wagon train through.

Long after the war—and even before the tensions that faced North and South—we traveled to every uncharted frontier pit stop and watering hole we could, Southern States included. Texas was for Texans, and if you hadn't paid your dues, or weren't a class act, or you weren't related to a ranger, there was no securing a show there. Still, we rode through interesting little towns like Willow Creek and Galloping Gulch and Don't Blink and Sunrise Valley. Surprisingly, many of the inhabitants welcomed us and had a penchant for outside entertainment. It was Turcott and Ross in the small settlements of the mid to late 1800s, but also the small theaters of some of the big cities as we worked our way west—Chicago, Cincinnati, Des Moines—some locations poorly funded and composed of drafty made-over stables and granaries called the Apex or the Palace or the Bird Pit or the Jewel, the farthest thing from a "palace" or a "jewel."

Of course, the places we did play weren't too respectable back then, with vaudeville a new concept and still moving out of the stage halls and into the family houses. Sure, we played some serious dives, but we never played the dime museums with the freaks; I remember those dress patterns they used to give out to prove the show was clean enough for the ladies. And don't get me started on those oddities, even though Ginger was a bit of an oddity herself.

It was Turcott and Ross, yes sirree, usually number three on the bill in the wake 'em up slot, mostly on before a singer and after a comic, six days a week, four and five and often six times a day, with one night camping out with the cacti, making the jump between The Ideal and The Imperial, between The Royal and The Right, all small-time boardinghouses for actors only, special rates, animals allowed. It was Turcott and Ross, in the number three slot as usual, on the night—I'll never forget—she wore that red dress.

Those first few years of our act she wore her own dresses onstage, dresses she'd made from human skin patterns, girlish styles with puffed sleeves and ruffles and smocking, but with scared faces embedded into the seams. These were expressions the likes I had never seen. I always wondered how she managed to sew them that way, take a morbid approach to dressmaking where the audience would have no choice but to not take their eyes off her. She looked so very young and small in them, standing next to the long guns, that the comics backstage used to say to her, "Well, baby, you up past your bedtime?" and it wasn't long before she didn't like it, and it wasn't long before a comic just upped and disappeared and wasn't playing that house anymore.

Whatever theater we played, she'd stand in the wings watching the women— the singers and strutters who'd played the honky-tonks—somewhat envious. They looked hard-faced to me, those cookies, but she studied them with a hushed sort of longing. I remember how her face lit up that evening when one of those women sidled over to her backstage: Maisie Partridge—so she styled herself—half of a singing sister act called Doll n' Dame. She was wearing a gown of acid-green satin, tight, cut low; her lips were painted into a red pout like some monstrous strawberry, and her hair was caught up with a large waxen rose on a comb. I could find nothing in the least charming about her, but the way Ginger gazed, I knew she found Maisie Partridge exquisite. Ginger's sexual preferences never bothered me, and I can still hear the click-click of those long oval nails on the barrel of her Winchester.

"Well," said Maisie, throaty-voiced and seductive, "aren't you the little honeybunch. Innocence is your number, hmm? Innocence and guns. Real small time." Click-click.

Ginger ducked her head, stung, and moved off with me to the dressing rooms. For the rest of that evening she was quiet, and for the rest of that week she stayed up sewing human faces at night after I was asleep. Five days later, when we opened at another theater, she had another costume. This one was more disturbing. I'll never forget how she looked, walking out of that dressing room just before our call, no time to change, in that new red gown.

Here was Ginger, swathed, sheathed, draped in satin the color of blood, slinking down the hall, her shoulders and the curve of her breasts bared to the light. Here she came, her hair swept up on her head, her rouged lips smiling; Ginger posing, pirouetting before me, one hand on her hip, one hand on her rifle.

For a moment, she thought I'd been struck dumb by this vamp she'd revealed in herself. An instant later she saw the horror in my eyes. Finally, I started to laugh, unable to help myself.

"I like it," she hissed.

"They'll hate it," I whispered back, and then we were on.

At first, they whistled, those drunk middle-aged men who always made up the first few rows. Then they went silent. She made shot after shot, but they were just sitting on their hands, the air in the house chilled, suspicious. The silence held whenever she took a shot, but we alternated every pair and whenever it came my turn, the men cheered raucously for me: "Git her, whup her good, mister," or, "Dang nab it, put them Colts to use, would ya."

The jeering started to spoil her concentration, and she took a miss, then another. Then she had a shot lying back over a chair to hit a disk I tossed into the air. The way she looked draped over that chair in that gown—I have to admit, it dented my own concentration and inspired such renewed catcalls from the house that she missed that shot as well. It was like watching a succubus at home on the range, while her man was off to play and looking for quail. As soon as the act was over, she stalked off into the wings, not saying a word.

That night I found her out in the theater alley, perched on a barrel, her face wiped clean, a shawl over her shoulders. She looked up, her eyes angry but not, I saw, at me. "Said I wouldn't ever let you down, now look," she said. "Bet I got us canceled."

"It wouldn't be the first time," I said.

"Gee, thanks." She crossed her arms.

"I'm kidding, I'm kidding. Maybe you just had a lot of stuff on your mind."

The theater manager appeared in the doorway, a burly German named Weismueller, with brick-dust hair and a nose like a spoon, shaking his head at us. "You said you vas sharpshooters."

"The crowd threw her."

"Nah, she threw the crowd. I give you one more chance, but nix on the costume." He turned to Ginger. "Sweeties, you can't outshoot the fellers and give 'em the hots same time; it won't play."

"But I can't go onstage without my wardrobe," Ginger argued. "I'll malfunction."

"You already malfunction," the manager pointed out.

"He's right," I added. "And those dresses give me the creeps."

"But I don't want to look like a kid anymore," she said with something like a wail in her voice.

"I'll say it plain. With what you got, you don't look like a kid." He dropped his cigar in the sand bucket by the door and went inside.

She stood there amazed for an instant. Then we both burst out laughing. That week she started making new dresses, slim-sleeved and stripped of ruffles, less the human faces. But somehow after all that, she still couldn't throw out that red gown.

***

Those were Ginger's early years, mind you, but now and then I'd sense something troubled, something withheld—certain weeping dreams she'd never discuss. Not too often, and it was little I heeded it. Not of age when she married me, what could she have to hide? She seemed such a snippet of a girl, sitting across from me in the back of all those wagons and horse-drawn carriages, her shoes scarcely skimming the floor. Yet at the same time there was an irregularity about her, as if she was running away from something. Her parents? Who knows. Just five feet tall, she was light as a child. Her head never quite reached my shoulder; I could always see the hole in the part in her hair.

It seemed to me that I was the one, much older, who'd been out in the world committing the sins, me and my cavalrymen pals, my partners in crime. Bootleggers. When acting didn't adequately pay us, large quantities of distilled liquor did. We'd paste it to the bottom of our wagons so the Pinkertons wouldn't find it. And we got searched often. What fine men of the world we thought ourselves, too.

As a bride, Ginger had come on the road with me and a man named Bart, putting up with his high talk and, toward her, his courteous suspicion. He thought her odd.

"Where did she learn to tailor clothes like that?" he asked me one day.

"Heck if I know," I said. "Maybe her mother taught her."

"Have you ever met her parents? What's her father like? What does he do?"

"You know, now that I think about it, I never met her old man. Matter of fact, she's never once brought him up."

"Don't you find that suspicious?" Bart asked.

I didn't answer.

Here was this shy little girl who liked guns more than we did, shooting with us in the clubs and galleries wherever we went. Quiet, contained, she watched the act from the wings and tried to finish her schooling between times. I remember her reading in the dressing room, sitting on the floor, her long hair screening her in with a McGuffey Reader. Reading was important to her. Knowledge in general was important to her.

She was studying like that the day Bart collapsed with fever before our first well-paying gig in Mississippi. I remember the somberness of her face, the light in her eyes. She couldn't hide it. She knew, even as I called a doctor for my friend, that Bart was moving on from this world.

She sat in the back of the empty theater while I fixed it with the manager, an hour till show time, the house dark, the curtain raised. In front of the stage the piano player sat in shadow, picking out the tune to "My Darling Clementine." Around him the place still felt hushed, not yet smelling of ale and smoke.

I slid into the seat next to her. She was hunched there, knees drawn to chin, fingers like ice. We sat without speaking, her hand pressed into mine. After a while there was a sputter from the balcony as the gas lantern spotlight was lit. We looked at each other. It was time to go load the guns.

Standing in the wings an hour later, she didn't seem to hear the opening swell of music. "Come on," I whispered. "We got to do this. For Bart."

Her lips were moving, though not in prayer. She was going over the act in her mind, step by step, the way she'd seen it done so many times. "Left-turn-left," she was whispering, "turn-cross-right." She stood dead still in the back curtains while Floatsie the Man-Fish played a trombone in a tank of water and Aoife & Patrick followed with their Gaelic number.

There was a loud groan from the house, a pelting of boos. There were some mean hombres in the back, and the cowpokes who actually footed admission seemed restless. "Amateur night!" some yelled. "Not on my money," came a bearded gentleman with an empty jug of whiskey. Ginger flashed me a look of desperation. What could we say? There was no more time; they were pushing us on. We only squeezed hands tight, and then she followed me out into that thin bright silence.

It was so quiet, my first two shots, I could hear the spent shells hitting the stage. Then it was her turn. I'll always remember how she looked, stepping forward in her green-sprigged summer dress with its stiff under-petticoats, a Winchester .22 in her hand. In the light I could see the damp shine of her face, the small silver drops at her ears leaping like sparks. She jerked her head, tossing her hair back over her shoulder, and walked to her mark.

The mark was near but not so near it would be easy. She cocked the rifle and waited, hands steady, eyes level on me. Right there, like a magician, I made the dime appear between my fingers. As my hand rose, her arm rose, the rifle snug in her shoulder: glint-aim-pull—and a sweet ping. In the air a glittering arc, dropping into the darkness, finally rolling off into a well of clapping hands.

Before the clapping stopped, she had turned, crossed the stage, taken the shotgun. More difficult now, more danger. I was her conjurer. I had set five glass balls dancing on the air, globes of light circling my head. She was moving with them. The gun was her shoulder and the length of her arm, and now-and-now-and-three-now-five she hit the center of each spinning crystal. She turned it into sea spray floating off into the lights, turned it into her laughter and mine, into the explosion of applause from the stomping cheering dark.

Faster then, she had them. It was cracking; it was right. This girl was not only a natural showman, but if she chose fit, she could be a natural born killer too. We put over the act five times like that with only one miss apiece. Before we knew it, the curtain was jerking shut. We stood there, center stage, both of us breathless and grinning, and the audience, as inebriated as they were, brought us back three times. The fourth time I sent her out alone and whispered, "Told you you wouldn't need your red dress."

As soon as she got offstage, I lost my dignity and picked her up. She kissed me full on the mouth—all of this against theater rules, of course—but the stagehands just smiled, and the house manager just pounded us on the back and said, "Kids, kids! No spooning in public, keep everything like it is. You killed 'em!" We made Bart proud. I was sure of it. After five shows, a little supper and hot coffee, we were nowhere near to calming down. We stayed up most of that night in the Imperial boardinghouse.

I can still remember that room we had. Rattling iron bedstead. Wobbly pine bureau, old programs lining the drawers. No sleeping amongst the rattlesnakes this starry night. We earned our keep. I can't think now what made that room so fine, all those years ago. I suppose it only had a glory to it because of that night, because of us. We were sitting up with beer and sandwiches at three in the morning and we kept talking at once. We were talking through new stunts. I could see so many grand things to try out with her.

There she was, sitting cross-legged next to me on the bed, in her chemise and drawers, her hair up in a knot on her head and an orange streak of makeup still on her jaw. There she was, my wife, my girl, face flushed, soul afire that night, telling me how it felt being out there.

Out there. The feeling she put into those two words. She said them in just that way only when she was talking about two places: out onstage or out in the fields.

"Before I ever saw a theater," she said, "I used to sit on this one fence out there in the fields. Just longing to see something different. Something fine, big. This one time, I remember, a flock of wild pigeons came over—birds wing to wing, maybe a mile across, they went on like that for hours. Just around sunset their feathers got to looking like they'd turned gold. Like some magical creatures in a story. I just sat there and watched, wanting them to go on and on and never stop."

"What are you trying to say?" I asked, as I took a sip of my beer.

"Out there tonight, you know, I thought of that. But this time I wasn't just sitting, watching. And I don't want this feeling inside me to stop."

The things we talked about that night, the plans we made. We drew stage blocking on laundry paper, we scanned maps and circled towns and timetables. One off-day, I was reading advertisements to her from the smaller papers—"*Wanted: boy-girl team/novelty act/fast pace*"—and she was laying out her dress patterns, thinking of costumes, this one but shorter, that one but looser, and what did I think. The bed came to be afloat with paper, the whole of the quilt sweetly crackling. Then her face sobered.

"James," she said, her name for me sounding clear and grave in the quiet room. "I keep remembering. There we are, shooting at each other. Some people, they'd say we're fools. Well, I know the danger. I've seen the gents with the missing fingers. And worse. But so many times, watching you. I wanted to be out there with you. Just the two of us." She took my hand. "Never said how bad I wanted it, for fear you'd say no. And now it's happened. I promise you, James, I won't take it too light." She paused briefly. "I guess what I'm trying to say is you don't need to make a wish to use me in your traveling act."

"Our traveling act," I said, and smiled.

"What I meant to say is I'll take care of you. I swear, each shot." Her face brightened again. "You know, out there—it was like we were mind readers. I want it to be that way always. I don't ever want you to be sorry you let me try."

I touched her cheek. "I won't be, Ginger," I said. "You know, I keep promising you someday I'll buy you a house, a big—"

"No," she cut in sharp. "Told you I don't want that. Don't need that. I'm made of something different, so I don't require those things. Let's not talk about it. I like the moving, the different places, never one week the same. Houses—they don't always bring good. Especially for people like me." Her voice had shifted, her face turned away. "Houses are like bottles. Tight spaces. I know how they can be sometimes. I used to believe in houses. Bottles, too. Not anymore." For an instant her eyes, clouded, looked out beyond my shoulder at nothing I could see. Then they came back to me. She shrugged off whatever it was, and I shrugged it off with her, paying it no more heed.

**

The next few weeks we traveled from one small town to the next, the kind you couldn't find on any conventional map. We mostly found ourselves in whistle-stops with populations of less than a hundred and saloons crude and unbecoming of Ginger's talent and looks. But they had decent-sized stages, big enough to perform our act, and they offered free room and board and paid in real money. That's all that mattered.

During our travels I needed to make sense of the things Ginger told me, and what more she'd be telling me. It was as if I was learning something new about her each and every day. I needed to set it against what I'd always knew of her and make it fit somehow. Even when we did score a room, long after we'd put out the light, her existence racketed about my mind. No parents. No identification. No memory of her past. There came a point where I figured her for an orphan. I just found her out in the wilderness; I had even come up with her last name.

So many nights I'd roll over and ask her questions. I'd feel her leave the bed as if in alarm, see her in the lamplight with her embroidery hoop at three in the morning. For an instant, feeling my gaze, her eyes wide, those gray eyes, so clear they seemed to have their own weather. She always had a questioning look, as a teenager might, awakened in the night. She'd stare at me ominously, then go back to what she did best—sewing people's faces onto dresses.

Now, occasionally, I'm the one awake in the nights.

First time I noticed something seriously wrong was in a small coal mining settlement called Wilmington, and we were playing a dump called The Big Show. The place had been a barn before they put in the seats and put up some kerosene lanterns and the letters VARIETY THEATER. It still smelled faintly of cows and horse manure. I remember that smell, and I clearly remember the cabbage. Potatoes, too.

I remember her standing in Ratner's grocery on Main Street, holding in her hand a perfect head of cabbage and being embarrassed by the attentions of the grandfatherly clerk. She looked so girlish then, dark hair down loose, that smocked yellow dress. The clerk mistook her for a bride buying fixings for her first home-cooked meal. She planned to take them down the street and shoot them to pieces in front of five or six hundred people.

The clerk asked if she was maybe making a nice pot roast.

Coleslaw, she told him finally.

It was our last night at The Big Show, and the last night was always when we tried out new stunts. We were on after a midget number, and the groceries made a mess onstage but a grand show in the air. Ordinarily, she would have wondered if the clerk from Ratner's had seen his produce slawed and scrambled. She would have asked if I'd seen him out and about, if she suddenly hadn't realized someone else she knew was sitting right over the footlights.

At the time all I noticed was that she seemed to freeze for an instant, just after we put some .22s through a spread of cards and tossed them into the audience as souvenirs. That was when she first saw him, but thought she was imagining. The man with the strange looking bottle. She put it from her mind and went on through the setups, the shots, and the last turn. It wasn't until we were coming downstage for our bows that she seemed to freeze again. Her hand tightened on mine when she saw the man had removed the lid on the bottle. For a moment there was a kind of wince on her face, as if she'd just stepped on something sharp. I never really knew till now what she saw.

Someone else knew. Someone she used to know.

Someone she had known once.

She spins it different ways, as if trying to get close to some truth she can't bring herself to speak. Even to this day, she's still unable to tell me his name.

I like the moving, the different places, never one week the same. Houses— they don't always bring good. Especially for people like me.

She had leaned forward, curtsying into the applause, looking for the grocery clerk. Instead, someone else was there, just across the footlights and now standing rather than sitting, front row left. His sun-bronzed face was lifted toward her. For an instant it seemed to float above his collar. The curtain was closing, the lights dimming out. But there in the shadows was this man, cradling this bottle.

"You don't look so hot," I whispered.

No answer.

"Hey, I'm talking to you. You all right?" My voice fell on deaf ears.

She was so flustered she didn't remember coming offstage, didn't remember me saying I was getting our supper. She edged close to the place where the stage manager often stood to count the house. Maybe she'd seen wrong after all. But she couldn't see well enough from there to be certain.

She went out into the hall that ran the length of the theater and turned left to a closed door that opened onto the shed a yard or so beyond the footlights. She waited there for the other lights to come up after the next act finished. With the lights up, it wouldn't be so noticeable when she opened the door. She would be able to see him plainly, once and for all.

A moment later he was there. Someone she'd hoped never to see again. She knew the slope of his shoulders, that aging cherub's face. For a moment she was unable to move, even as he looked toward the door and saw her. He rooted there with the open bottle, as if he still had power over her. He started edging down the row, saying her name, the old name. She saw it forming on his mouth. Then she broke away.

"Come back to me, Jinn. Return to whence you came."

She ran down a flight of stairs, rounded the landing, ran down the dim hall snaking out ahead of her. She passed doors and doors and then she was pushing one open and pitching into our dressing room. Only then did she look back.

The dressing room was empty and very still. The trunk was there. The gun rack was there, our names stamped on the glass. She stared at the words, at her reflection above them. Her face, wild-eyed, startled her. A homicidal genie's face—dark, distorted, tainted. Now a woman's face, with makeup and a hat.

Houses are like bottles. Tight spaces. I know how they can be sometimes. I used to believe in houses. Bottles, too. Not anymore.

When I came in a few minutes later she was trembling as if from a chill, and so white it scared me. Onstage she always wore her wedding ring on a chain around her neck to keep it from catching in the guns. Now she had both ring and chain clamped so hard in her fist they'd made a deep mark in her palm.

After that, when we played towns west of the Mississippi, she would awaken before dawn and look ill before performances. Her sickness always passed as soon as she went on. It only happened in these places. She told me that was because they were close to her former owner and someone who knew her power could sense it. Her former master didn't approve; I knew that.

So Ginger told me, those first few years we were on the road, that she was a genie. So she has told me all these years. I don't think she intended to be evil, and I don't think she set out to deceive me. I think she was trying to be creative and see the good in herself because of the shame of killing, because of the pain. The change started right then in those vaudeville days, in those early years when she was first wearing her new name.

I loved her dearly and accepted her for who she was. I've always loved her, ever since the day I found her draped in rags in that pine forest.

***

I can see her now through our hotel room door, cupped in the porcelain tub. Her head tipped back in the bath, a square of towel behind it. Her hair up with combs. Her face moist and shining, eyes closed. As always, I am stirred by the sight of her. But I'm not used to seeing her lie still for so long. In all our travels, all those tents and trains and carriage rides, we'd mark off the ground and walk through the act, the turns, the jumps, swinging with the guns empty-chambered till it was sharp, till it was right.

We've come a long way. To be honest, I'm glad she's burned that red dress. Now she dons a cute little cowgirl outfit whenever she performs. We've shared feelings so long, passing them back and forth through the air, I can't help but breathe easier. Let the past sleep now, I think. It will always be here with us, a little, but now I know what it is.

After all, the show must go on.

ALL THE STARS IN SOUTH R'YLEH
BY
Q PARKER

Jana tried to scream. Her ravaged throat couldn't make more than a pathetic, wet gurgle. Even then, this sound came from the freshly-torn hole in her neck, not her mouth. She gasped as best she could, her body tuned to fight or flight—knowing she only really had one option left—her mind clinging to a few phrases as if reminding her of its need to survive. *Keep breathing. Pressure on the wound. Losing blood. Get to the sheriff's house.*

Didn't matter.

The shadow loomed over her, with the waning moon doing little to reveal a face or even physique. That cruel white sickle above seemed to make it worse, seemed far too eager to descend upon her, waiting for her ragged breathing to finally stop. Jana kicked at the shadow, her hand jostling, letting out another crimson spray that stained the dirt and dust. Her boot connected, slid past its leg, catching it with its spurs, but the figure didn't flinch. Something assaulted her nose; she didn't recognize the scent. Horse shit, cheap booze, and the copper sting of her own blood mixed with something wholly different, an odor that Jana couldn't place, but it made her body shudder—a recognition deep inside like a warning carved into her bones.

She could still feel every second of what, at this point, she knew was her final moment alive. A cool breeze blowing, a firefly swarm of brilliant stars overhead, the crunch of dry earth beneath her heel. She'd stayed too long at Mari's, and maybe her husband would be upset, but not angry. Never angry. Only worried.

"You never know who's out there with you," he'd admonish, but she'd walked her town's streets this late dozens of times over, possibly hundreds, without issue. Nobody so much as whistled at her. This night, like every other, she stood with her back straight and a smile on her face, taking in the night, a scene just for her, cool and empty and quiet.

This night, like every other, she had enjoyed herself without hesitation or regret.

Right until the one additional crunch of a footstep behind her. Before she could turn, hands grabbed Jana's shoulders, pulling her back. She didn't have time for so much as a hello before teeth sank into her throat and ripped the whole damn thing out.

Now, the shadow stepped closer. She couldn't tell why it hadn't outright killed her. Maybe it didn't understand what blood was. Maybe it wanted to play with its food. Maybe it needed her drained first, then it could go through with its plans. Still, carefree as Jana might've been, she knew a thing or two.

Slicking a finger with her own blood, she turned, scribbling in the dirt. This set the figure off. Seeing her react, it let out one shrill shriek, tensing, leaning back on its haunches, ready to lunge. It should've killed her sooner. She finished the sigil in record time, except this time, having used blood instead of ink, it actually did what it needed to. The blood flashed, letting out a blinding white that sent the shadow reeling, letting Jana turn away from the illumination to see one quick glimpse of mottled flesh, horrible and drooping, covered in scars and stitching, before the protective barrier cast it away from her.

Jana had used the small version, a tiny one, without any additional empowerment runes, as quick, dirty, and cheap as any of the saloon girls, but like fucking hell was one of those freaks about to get her soul. Her life? Sure. It got the jump on her. The moment it bit, she knew she had seconds left. But her soul? Absolutely not.

Collapsing onto her back, she smiled up at the stars, as safe as one could be while bleeding to death in the street, and let out a slight, victorious chuckle. It came out as a couple of sodden chortles, but hey, that would be enough, for now.

Her eyes started drifting shut, but she forced them open to go through with one final thought. With the very last of her strength—and, she assumed, her blood—she wet her fingers once more, writing *DEAD* in the dirt. Then the darkness took her.

***

A few days later...

Carri snuck out of bed, as she always did. She moved as quietly as a tombstone, with the reverence of a pallbearer, not daring to disturb Sierra, who still faintly snored beneath the covers. Once extricated, Carri tucked the sheets around her wife, kissing a finger and touching it gently to her, then slinked across the room to grab her clothing. Judging by the ambient light creeping past the pulled curtains, it must've been mid-afternoon.

Sierra gently caught her hand.

"Don't shoot first," she whispered, eyes shut. Still sleeping.

Her hand fell. Carri nodded and left the room, appreciating these little warnings where they came. They were always helpful.

The hotel they'd settled in for the night had its share of amenities, like any other hotel. The amenities here, though, far outclassed the other places they'd been to in the past year. While many had little more than a washbasin, if that, the South R'lyeh Inn had a basin *and* two buckets that would refill themselves with fresh water, one hot and one cold. The windows blocked all street level view—they'd checked. Even with the curtains wide open, you couldn't see inside, the windows only displaying a murky black that didn't even betray their lights being lit. A candle, once lit, could only burn itself, unable to ignite anything else, and wouldn't be extinguished without the permission of the one who lit it.

According to Sierra, the mirror also let her wipe the bags from under her eyes with one sweep of the thumb, but it didn't seem to help Carri's complexion at all. She did take a glance into it before heading out. Her faintly milky eyes stared back at her, irises gray where they'd once been... blue? Green? She had trouble remembering. At least they matched her skin, which was marred by scars. She fixed her bangs to hide the big one: the round indentation in her forehead, looking like a third eye yet always feeling like a bullseye. Being the way she was drew enough stares without the literal target on her forehead. Still, she loved her nickname.

Carri fixed herself, dressing quietly, not rushed but not wanting to linger, clasping her belt into place so she could affix her holster. Well, and her pants. She had trouble finding clothing that fit someone with barely any muscle or body fat, yet loathed the thought of seeing a tailor every time she bought something new. A belt did the job just fine, letting her keep her gun on her hip and a grimoire tucked into the pocket of her canvas trousers.

Once dressed in her usual pants, work shirt, and vest, she stepped out into the hotel proper, a finely furnished place with only a few instances of floating obelisks or non-Euclidean geometry to suit the town's motif. That's the key, really. Don't beat your patrons over the head with the whole "you are nothing" cosmic grandiosity. Just give them a *dash* of the Old Ones, then let them fill in the rest. A teensy little test of your customers' sanity that wouldn't impede them from being repeat customers.

She passed a beaming young straight couple, the man all doe-eyed for his missis, with her barely able to take her eyes off her ring. Wasn't clear if just married or just engaged, but they only spared a fleeting glance toward her as she passed. She gave a little wave, said congrats, they said thanks, and all but fell into their room.

A curved staircase wrapped lazily through a grand foyer, so she perched atop the rail and slid down, enjoying the gradual sweep of her view as she went.

Hopping off at the bottom, she approached the receptionist, an aged man with a kind smile and weathered skin, wearing a tailored suit and breezy confidence that seemed to charm the whole room with a little mirth. His name plate read *Alzi*.

"Ah, good afternoon..." Despite his confidence, his smile faltered just a little as he seemed to mill over the right mode of address. She got this a lot: people not quite able to tell if they should say sir or madam. "...my friend," he finished with the breezy confidence of a customer service veteran. His voice had the same warmth as his smile and eyes, welcoming and genuine—a campfire on a cool night, offering its heat to any who drew near.

"Thanks," Carri replied, acutely aware of the contrast in their timbers. Where he spoke with the gentle embrace of a life well lived, hers creaked and rasped, caught between the rusty hinge of an iron gate and trees shuddering from autumnal wind, knowing that winter drew near.

"How may I assist you today? And are the accommodations to your liking?" He actually, truly wanted to know, unlike the dozens of other places they'd stayed that just wanted their payments without complaint.

"Oh, absolutely!" She assured him. Carri really did like the place. "Especially the water system. H and C, for Hellfire and Cocytus, I assume?"

Alzi let out an open, hearty laugh, though not too loud and hidden behind his hand, tempered as it was by the decorum of his position.

"That's a new one! Always nice to meet patrons with a sense of humor. The heat does make some so terribly agitated."

"Aw, thanks. Heat never bothers me, though. I run cold." She gestured to her face with her slender hands, thin as they were from lack of fat, with their deadened nails giving her a permanent and admittedly fashionable purple-black hue.

They exchanged a few more pleasantries before Carri got around to her actual point: she needed work. Not a lot, not really, but she had more than enough time on her hands, so she liked to keep busy. He gave her a few pointers, as well as the names of some people to talk to at local establishments, before hesitating.

"There was a rather strange murder just a few days ago, at the western edge of town," he explained. "Along with a few disappearances before that. Possibly related. You may find some people... wary. Do be careful."

Carri crinkled her eyebrows, thanked him, and set off into the late afternoon sun. Probably a scorcher, but true to her word, she didn't feel it. Besides, he'd left her with a lot to think about. Didn't take much to whip a bunch of cautious people into a frenzied mob. Nothin' much out there could hurt Carri, but Sierra was a flesh-and-blood mortal human, despite her supernatural talents.

South R'lyeh didn't seem like all that dangerous a place. If anything, one could say it were a bustling up-and-coming town, far larger in size than a lot of the places she and Jessica had stumbled across recently. The buildings still had most, often all, of their shutters, with their exteriors well maintained. Streets were wide and somehow clean, as if the town hired someone to follow the horses around, constantly cleaning to keep shit off your shoes. No tumbleweeds distracted from the idyllic view, a fair portion of the cacti were flowering, and the green obelisks, floating as they did while basked in a sourceless green light, frequently complimented the city planning. Humans built this place *with* the Eldritch structures, not despite them. The only traces of negativity seemed limited to an occasional HEED THE ANTI-BELLUM or THE SOUTH STATE CULLING WAS A WARNING signs, which could more be seen as a reminder—or perhaps a warning—of what happened the last time humans summoned one of the Old Gods.

Well, that and the people who turned to stare. Carri grew used to that years ago. Perhaps the influence of the Ancient Ones had become commonplace—in fact, just a hundred yards south, some kids were shrieking with joy as they climbed up a tentacle-covered statue of yet another nameless horror as if it were a strange tree—but people who weren't strictly human were still relatively rare. Those like her were exceedingly so. Plus, even in death, she liked to think she was pretty cute, and despite her wraith-thin frame, she still retained *some* semblance of curves, courtesy of her bone structure. Her organs atrophied long ago, most of her muscle had wasted, and she didn't need life-preserving fat, so she cinched in at the waist pretty nicely. Didn't feel like that's why people stared today, though.

She soon confirmed this. Hadn't even made it to the first stop on her list before someone called out to her, politely explaining the situation.

"Hey, you fuckin' zombie," a sunburned man in his late twenties said, eyes on Carri, puffing up his chest. "You back for more?"

"Back? I just got here. Rode into town with my darlin' around midnight, been sleepin' like the dead since then. Guess I always do, though."

He snorted, a bull ready to charge, smirk fixed in place, thinking she had nowhere to run. The man shifted his weight around, almost reaching for his gun, but not quite. Rubbernecks craned around, staring, not daring to approach or intervene.

"Yeah, sure you did. A lady gets eaten right on the main drag, and you got the nerve to stroll your zombie ass around these parts in broad daylight like we don't know you did it?" He spat at the ground in front of her feet. A huge amount, too, with pinpoint accuracy, barely any trace of splatter, and not a drop actually on her. She might've been impressed if she weren't busy wondering why his mouth was so wet.

"I'm not a zombie," she corrected, calmly, albeit tired of this conversation. "I'm a lich. Zombies are more of a Louisiana thing, you know? And even then, it's a cultural situation that most people aren't practicing after the Anti-bellum. I'm from New York."

"You a long way from home. Got run off for eating your family or something, zombie?"

All right, this wasn't going anywhere. Just another self-important Lone Ranger type looking for trouble. Between her gun and her grimoire, she could easily give it to him, but this wasn't worth the time or effort.

"This was fun, kid, but I'm here for work, and you're holding that up, so I'm just gonna go. See you around." She needed to meet people. Survey the area. Something felt off about this place, and not in the usual way.

Carri turned to leave, figuring she could head back the way she came and circle the block, when the hammer of a revolver slowly clicked behind her. She sighed, rolled her eyes, and turned around to see the muzzle aimed directly at her forehead. Still nothing worth her attention.

"Not letting you eat anyone else, freak." The stranger growled, teeth clenched.

"You're a special kind of stupid, aren't you, boy?" she said, shaking her head.

His brow furrowed, glancing between her and his gun. Probably thought this overcompensation would intimidate her the way it did for living beings, or maybe still believed that old rumor that zombies were highly susceptible to headshots, which only makes sense if you destroy their hindbrain since that's the part that has life sustaining functions and motor control. Doesn't work so well if you destroy the frontal lobe, which is for complex thought, and was also where he decided to aim.

"I'm gonna shoot you, bitch."

"I'm sure."

"You think I won't?"

"No, it's pretty clear you will." She tapped her foot, checking an imaginary watch.

"Gotta protect my town," he said, gun arm shaking, just a little bit, the resolve on his face beginning to look a little less certain.

"My name is Carri. I'm a lich. I'm a fully sentient no-longer-human who doesn't eat people. But you're not listening to me anyway, so I don't know why I'm talking."

"Shut up, zombie!"

Footsteps crunched through the dirt behind her, coming up quickly. The man's eyes darted over, keeping track of whomever approached, but Carri's Wife Sense started going off. She smiled automatically, always glad to be in her wife's presence.

"Hi, Sierra," Carri called over her shoulder, not taking her eyes off the gunman. "What's got you awake before sundown?"

The steps came to a stop a little ways back. Carri couldn't die, but Sierra still could, so she usually kept out of the riskier situations. Sierra was tough as a railroad spike and twice as sharp, but that didn't mean much compared to Carri's magick-induced non-death status.

"Hi, hon. The proprietor came to wake me up. Said you were in trouble." Sierra's tone came cool and steady, a desert wind in the darkest hour of night, but that little spark of warmth that filled Carri's chest whenever she spoke was the only warmth she'd felt in years.

"Wait," the man said, getting a little more confused, then curling his lips into an eagerly malicious snarl. "This your darlin' you mentioned?"

Carri looked back over her shoulder, smiling. Sierra stood, as ever, wrapped in an aura of mystery, her dark skin belied by the dark in her eyes, which were always just a tiny bit out of focus. Seeing the past, present, and future at the same time, she didn't, sometimes couldn't, see all of her immediate situation at once. But then she looked over to Carri, her eyes snapping to attention, gaze clearly focusing, as Sierra smiled back.

"She sure is," Carri nodded, not forgetting about his gun.

"My beloved," Sierra said, "now and always."

The man chuckled, and if Carri's blood could run any colder, it would've. She knew that tone, too. Knew that one too well.

"Figures. Freak. Not only are you a dyke, but you're a..." he paused, searching for the most offensive word possible. "You're a couple'a cross-breeders."

"First off," Carri snapped, "I'm *dead*. My skin is *gray*. How do you even know what race I was? Not that it matters, because our bedroom's not your business!"

She drew her own gun, which had a faint green glow to it despite the blazing high noon sun. The hilt bore sigils and a finely inscribed incantation, but the only way the average person would see them up close is if it was already too late.

Carri stepped between herself and her wife, holding the gun aloft in her left hand.

"You *really* don't want me to kill you with this," Carri said. "I don't eat *flesh*, but your soul? That'll be just fine, assuming I don't just destroy it instead."

"Oh, you're a lefty, too?" he chuckled. "All right, zombie, have it your way. If it's a duel you want, it's a duel you get. Gonna put you back in the dirt."

A faint snort drew their attention. An older man with faint stubble and dry, well-tanned skin glared at them. The stranger wore clothes a little too nice to be a commoner. Carri smelled blood in the air. Held his gaze a little too long. His eyes were the wrong type of dark.

"I'm the mayor here, and I'll count you in," he growled. "Let's put the corpse back in the ground."

The gunslinging stranger chuckled, as if that somehow meant he'd win the duel, but Carri's focus lay elsewhere. They turned, back to each other. They took ten paces, as you do. She played along, thinking over her next move, because there weren't many things that could kill what was already dead, but her old body had new wounds from the last time she crossed the wrong beast and wasn't ready.

Faintly, in the background of her consciousness, she could hear the "mayor" counting them in. Normally, she'd ask Sierra for advice. Normally, Sierra wouldn't have been standing fifteen feet from the damn thing. She laid her free hand on her grimoire, mentally turning the pages, frantically trying to remember which incantation did what. The fact that she *had* a spell book didn't exactly mean she used it all that routinely, and the dumbass trait of hers to not fucking use every tool in her arsenal wasn't nearly as charming as Sierra made it out to be.

She muttered a few syllables, hearing the call for them to shoot, and turned around. If she got the spell wrong, she'd die here. Maybe they all would. If her judgment was wrong and this wasn't playing out the way she thought it would, then she'd spend the rest of her... well, ever, probably, rotting in prison.

Whatever-his-name-was fired first, bullet hitting her square in the chest and punching out the back, probably moving through a lung along the way. Didn't matter. Not like she was using them.

Carri spoke the last few syllables and literally fired.

The flame round struck home, igniting their so-called mayor, his outfit going up in a flash. He did his best to imitate a human scream, but even the most gullible observer would've been able to tell there wasn't any real fear in it. These things wore human forms like armor, protecting them from harm.

What he couldn't protect from was that now, all the townsfolk could see the stitching crossing along his body. Not wholly unlike Carri's scars, but his were freshly sewn, mottled gray-black, as if torn open and closed over and over. The heat began singing away the seams of his flesh as the crowd began to shout.

"What's wrong with him?"

"What are those—the mayor? Is he okay? Is he sick?"

"Looks like a Frankenstein to me!"

The damage had been done, its disguise tarnished. Carri kept muttering, hoping to oblivion and back she'd even picked the right spell because she'd had to start over twice already. At least Sierra backed away from the burning hybrid.

Seeing his fate otherwise sealed, the monster shuddered and began to change. The stitching tore fully away in a burst of blood, revealing a legion of gnashing mouths with crooked yellow teeth.

The man who'd been so eager to defend his town by killing Carri took one look before fainting. He never hit the ground. Tongues lashed out, far too long, extending from some unknown hell inside the thing to draw the man in and quarter him one bite at a time.

But Carri got it right, finishing her second spell to paint her vision a swampy green, obscuring the human realm but letting her get a good look at the black heart pulsating where a human stomach would be, pumping eldritch sludge through what passed for his veins. It hadn't fully shifted, too smart to let its guard drop that way, but the mouth in its chest would work fine.

All the huntress had to do was time her shot. She took aim, letting the creature pull the gunslinger closer until its many jaws unhinged, with half the crowd fleeing or fainting, but none daring to help. Good. It bent double, leaning in to shred the man, leaning just far enough that its chest-mouth provided easy access to its rotten heart.

She let the hammer drop.

The mayor's body nearly split in two at the middle, with mouth after mouth gaping open in shock, unable and unwilling to scream. Its arms contorted, trying to bear its claws, swinging frantically, trying to tear into its last meal. Even through the Ancient Vision, she could see blood staining its claws, and when it screamed, the sound carried the voices of all the people it had consumed, all the souls it stole away, alongside its own guttural roar. It collapsed dead to the dirt, part way through transforming back to its original otherworldly state, a creature born of two worlds yet belonging to neither.

A few people managed to stay calm enough to draw weapons during this, and the man who shot Carri collapsed to the ground in a sweaty, panicked mess, but when the creature stopped moving, so did everyone else.

She walked over to the body, gun drawn, knowing damn well a second bullet wouldn't do much of anything if the first one hadn't done the trick. The haze of Ancient Vision made its twisted anatomy all too clear, and she still couldn't see half of it. No doubt at all this was the killer behind whatever-his-name-was had been talking about. A mostly rotted creature of stained teeth and broken bones who, at its most altered form, would've probably left anyone who saw it with a lifetime of screaming at the sight of their own shadow.

But, thank her stars, the damn thing was dead. Confirmed. The telltale wisp rose from its chest, too solid, too lit with unearthly green light, to be mistaken. Same green as her gun, of course. The smoke trailed its way back into the barrel of her gun like time played out in reverse. The sigils on its hilt took on a sickly blood red.

Carri spoke a few words, quick, quiet, and smooth, their cadence etched into her brain. One of the only spells she'd memorized, and one she'd not dare forget. A weight lifted from her hand as smoke again rose from the barrel. This time, wretched and black.

She lifted it to her lips and blew the remnants of the creature's soul away. She *could* harvest them, add their power to her own, but evil humans were pretty low-key targets. Mostly just misguided spell slingers. Even if she distilled out the evil, absorbing something like this? Absorbing something that powerful? That ancient? ...Once had been enough.

Carri turned to face the crowd, wondering what they'd do. Revolt? Cheer? Actually fuckin' pay her for once? No, of course not. Silence. She turned to the people she'd saved and faced the unblinking stillness of people too scared, too confused, to process what happened here today. Didn't matter, in the end. She had enough money. Besides, she'd grown used to this.

"You're gonna need a team to cut this up," she called out, loud enough that even the furthest bystanders in the crowd would hear. "Don't bury it all in one place. Ride at least ten miles out in each compass direction, then bury the pieces ten feet deep. Don't leave any record of where, so they can't be found easily later. And, uh, hold an election, I guess, for a new mayor. Or don't. I'm leaving town. Doesn't mean a damn to me either way."

She walked over to Sierra, offering her hand, as she always did. It mattered that her beloved always accepted—always took her hand. That ask-and-answer, the dance they danced after each of these tousles, set Carri's head right, even if it would take a few hours for the damned spell to wear off and give her regular sight back.

"Why'd you tell them all that about cutting up the body?" Sierra asked. "No, wait, let me guess." She put her other hand to her forehead, squinted at Carri, and did her goofiest impression of Carri's casket-raspy voice. "They insulted us. They shot me. Then, they didn't even pay me. Damn city slickers can do their own legwork or leg it out of my way, but I'm not fixin' to tolerate that a moment longer."

They busted up laughing. They always did.

"I don't talk like that!" Carri protested.

"I know," Sierra smiled.

They arrived back at the hotel and explained to the proprietor that they were leaving town. He nodded in quiet understanding, and they had all two of their bags packed with enough time to fool around a little without worrying about the sun setting. Not that it mattered. Sierra didn't know how to ride a horse unless she found herself saddled up behind an experienced rider, and Carri couldn't see worth a damn right now anyway, so Sierra blindfolded her and... that's another story.

Somehow, they managed to get out of bed and back on their horse, Horsecraft, before night completely fell.

"Which way we headin'?" Carri smiled lazily.

"Hm..." Sierra squinted again, taking in the world around her in a way only a few privileged Seers could. "Northwest. I'll tell you when to turn. Trouble about fifty miles out. Kids going missing. Feels like a human culprit this time around."

Carri nodded. Sierra wrapped her arms around her wife's waist, and Horsecraft began trotting off to the edge of town. A long way to go, but they had a setting sun at their backs and a cool wind rushing coming in, blowing the heat away to welcome the huntresses into the cool, familiar darkness.

PARTNERS
BY
PETER PRELLWITZ

"There she is."

The wind was coming down harsh from the craggy mountains surrounding us, turning a cool summer evening into a cold one. Our two mules were already of poor disposition, and the bite of wind didn't improve their nature. I held onto both sets of reins while the old man waited.

"She" was a cabin built against a cliff face that stretched up hundreds of feet. The Rocky Mountains did nothing by half-measure, and here in the San Juan Mountains of southwestern Colorado, size was doubled down.

"Where can we put these two?" I asked. "And where's the mine?" I wasn't fond of cold. I was fond of gold, however, which accounted for my being here.

"This way," he replied and waved an arm. "The cabin has a stable." He walked uphill to the building. Everything in this Godforsaken place was uphill. Even downhill was uphill, just not as steep. He went along the cabin's side and pulled a section of loose wall open. It was on leather hinges that creaked in protest. He went in and I followed with the mules, who seemed inclined to think it would be warmer inside.

They were right. Larger than I expected, there were two stalls and a tack area with scraps of tackle and trimmings. A saddle blanket covered the stone face making up the back of the stable on our right. I nodded with approval.

"Nice. Warmer than I'd thought it would be," I said. "We'll need to store any hay we cut outside, though. How far to the mine?"

He gave me a knowing grin and a dry chuckle.

"Already covered that bet," he replied and pulled back the hanging saddle blanket. "Welcome to our mine, partner."

Instead of a wall face, there was a tunnel cut six feet high and three feet wide. Lighting a lantern from the stable, the old man led me inside to a hollowed-out area fifteen feet around and eight feet high. Some looked like a natural falling of stone, but much had been taken out by hand. A small cut only four feet high and ten feet deep stretched into the base of the cliff.

"I been comin' up here for goin' on three years. I found this cabin abandoned and forgotten. I found the stable and decided to stay for a couple weeks an' look for gold.

"After some months pannin' the stream out yonder, I took out a bit of dust, but not much and nary a nugget. I figgered to beat the cold and snow, I packed up Bitsy and was headin' out when she backed up against the blanket an' it come down. That's how I found the shaft. I had to leave so as not to get trapped here, so I set the blanket and left.

"Next coupla years I came back and fixed the place up and cut a mess of hay further up the canyon, so nobody would notice and anticipate my hopes. I worked the shaft at night but was just too tuckered to get anywhere. I was sixty when I found this place, and I'm sixty-three now. I just ain't got the giddyap any more for this to be a one-man job. I needed me a partner."

"And now we're partners, bound by oath an' honor," I said cheerfully and clapped him on the back. "Old man, you done right by me, and I'm gonna do right by you. You got the smarts an' plannin', and I got the youth an' strength. And by spring, we'll both have the gold!"

"Reckon we'll both do well," he agreed with a chuckle. "You get Bitsy an' Betsy set up, while I get the cabin fit for livin'. Then we'll get to minin'! This shaft ain't gonna dig itself!"

***

The days melted into weeks and the weeks into months. Every day was the same: Rise at dawn, get the mules pastured, then breakfast for us and then into the shaft. I did the diggin'; the old man did the haulin', taking the stone out by the stable door for me to bust up every afternoon. He tended the cabin, the mules, and the hayfield. Every evening after dinner I cut wood whilst the old man set the night's fire in the hearth and made bread for the next morning. It was a good time for us. I picked up more than a share of new muscle, an' the old man seemed to enjoy himself.

But I only got stronger, an' my partner only got older. Neither of us got any richer.

The stone looked good for gold, but there was only ever a tease of a vein. We inspected the day's rock every night. Only rarely an' faintly did the gleam of gold set our hearts to gladness. So, the days went to weeks and the weeks to months. Summer faded to autumn.

And then, two days after the first heavy snow, we hit gold.

More like, the gold almost hit us. The shaft had doubled in length and width, with two side tunnels. It was in the tunnel I'd started on the day before. I was pickin' away. He was muckin', shoveling what I'd cut into a barrel on a cart we'd rigged to carry out the ore. Suddenly, he straightened.

"Get out," he said quietly as he set the shovel against the stone face. I stopped in mid-swing.

"What?" I asked.

"Get out," he repeated in a voice that bespoke of deathly danger. "Get out now." He was backing away slowly. I weren't no fool: The old man had a sense about minin' and such things. I just set my axe down and we left on as light of footsteps as we could muster.

Not two minutes later, the ceiling caved in just where we'd been working. We waited at the mine entrance in the stable, calming Bitsy and Betsy who took none to the rumble and dust. I pulled the wall blanket over the opening to keep the dust in to settle a mite.

An hour later, the old man pulled back the blanket an' we went back in with lit lanterns an' made our way back to the cave-in. The dust was mostly settled but left some fine mist of earth in the air, giving a glow to all about in the lantern light.

We reached the site. Ceiling rock lay all busted up everywhere. Our pick and shovel were still leanin' against the stone, but the barrel cart was all wrecked. You couldn't see half of it for all the fallen rock. There musta been ten or fifteen tons of it. Above us, the ceiling was now twelve feet high where it had been only eight.

"Rotten quartz," he said like he knew about mining, which he did.

"Does this dash our intentions?" I asked, like I didn't know about mining, which I didn't.

"I reckon it does if you was intendin' on digging more," he replied and gave a huge grin. "But if you was intendin' for gold, you can stop lookin'." He raised his lantern.

The pile of dross an' rubble glittered and gleamed like the road to the gates of St. Peter.

"Rotten quartz can kill you like any other stone," he said, giving me a huge schoolboy grin. "Only you die like a king, with gold all about."

***

The only thing darker than a mine shaft, I decided, was a new moon sky on a cold mountain night. The stars were sparklin', but they only seemed to make it darker and colder. It was a strange thing to behold.

I had spent the day tryin' to locate the ghost of a trail we'd come up on but gave it up as a waste of strength and hope. The snow was far too deep. I didn't get even a mile from the cabin. I didn't need to. The ground sloped off in a rush, and by late afternoon's light I could see the pass down to Durango was completely blocked. We were trapped here for the winter. *Trapped with our gold,*

I reminded myself with a grin. There were worse things. Best get back to the cabin. At least I could follow the trail I'd tramped through the snow. I turned and headed back to the cabin on the dark mountain, my only companions being the frozen stars. And shamefully poor company, they.

An hour later I banged the latch to break the ice that had formed and went inside, an armful of wood I'd gathered to toss onto the fire. The old man looked up from the workbench and looked at me over his spectacles. Quartz pounded to bits and dust covered the bench except for one corner where sat a scale and a cloth bag.

"All full up with snow, I reckon," he said.

"You reckon right," I replied as I put the wood on the fire and stirred it up. "We ain't gettin' out for another three, four months." I nodded at the scale. "We any richer since I left?"

He chuckled.

"I reckon that, too," he replied as he set down the four-pound hammer, then stood and stretched. "I banged out another twenty-three ounces of nuggets and gold dust. That brings us to three hundred and sixty-seven ounces. Close on to 23 pounds."

"Shouldn't be too hard, makin' ends meet once we get back to town," I said. I swung the pot arm over the flames to set the beans to heating. "Feel like beans tonight?" I called out behind me.

"Don't see why not, since that's mostly what we got."

"You are a wise man," I laughed and stood up. "We'll finish this pot tonight, so I'll put on a new batch for tomorrow."

"Fetch out some more flour and salt and yeast," he said. "I'll make some bread once I finish these last pounds." He banged a fist-sized piece of quartz with the hammer, then smiled at me as he picked up a gold nugget from the rubble.

"Maybe I'll toss in a little gold for a richer flavor."

I laughed again and went into our storeroom. It was cold outside, and we were snowed in for the duration, but gold bought a lot of patience.

***

"Last can of peaches," I said as I exited our storeroom. It had been four months since the world had shrunk down to our tiny snow-filled valley.

"Seems only fittin'," my partner said as he cut up a piece of meat. "This is the last of Bitsy." He shook his head sadly. "Too bad. I really liked that mule."

"My condolences and thanks to the deceased," I mumbled as I banged the can on the now tidied workbench and picked up the can opener. "I'll head out again an' try to scare up some game."

He nodded and scraped the final chunks of Bitsy into the pot, added more water and some beans an' potatoes, and swung it over the fire. Some carrots would have been nice, but they was gone, too. He looked over at me and mustered a tired smile.

"I appreciate you goin' out huntin'," he said with a gratitude that warmed the room as much as the fire. "The times set upon us have been worrisome, but you've given yourself over as a good partner and a good friend."

"My thanks back, partner," I said as I picked up the rifle and opened the door. Outside was deep, white snow and a full, white sky. "See you and the stew come dark, hopefully with fewer bullets and more meat."

I worked this day up the hill toward our small hayfield. I'd shot a deer up yonder two months back, that last thing I'd seen worth shootin'. With the snow nearly waist-high in some places, it was a hard go. Nonetheless, hope and hunger lent me determination in my purpose, and I achieved the edge of the hayfield and the trees beyond it in an hour.

Three hours later I was headin' down the hill in the now dismal weather. The snow had started up again as night threatened its arrival. Nothin'. Not a critter, not a shot, not a chance. They was either stayin' safe in their homes or there just weren't any at all. My day meal had been naught but a full servin' of disappointment to chew on.

I reached the cabin and gathered up some extra firewood. We had enough of that, at least. 'Course, we'd reckoned on ample supplies of food, and that was comin' up short. I banged around the door with the rifle butt to jar the ice from the jamb, - opened the latch and went in.

The old man turned to me from the fire where he'd been stirrin' the stew. His eyes were bright with anticipation but settled down to proper understandin'. He nodded and picked up a bowl and spoon and ladled some Bitsy Stew into it. He passed it over to me as I sat close to the fire to chase the day's cold from my extremities.

"You'll get somethin' tomorrow," he said quietly, then filled his own bowl halfway and sat in the other chair.

I nodded my thanks and began eating. And thinking.

We weren't gonna make it.

The amount of time up here and the supplies we brung was all backwards. Too much time; too little supplies. Now we'd et first Betsy and now Bitsy. I stood up in a sense of worrisome bother.

"This ain't goin' well," I declared, pacing about. He glanced at me, then returned to his soup. He swallowed a spoonful or two before speaking.

"You just wait it out, partner," he said quietly and kindly. "We'll be hungry when the snow melts, but we'll be alive. Now that we're not diggin' and workin' hard, we don't need to eat as much. Once the pass clears, we'll head to town and get another couple of mules. Then we'll head back up and haul out our gold."

He went back to slurping his soup, calm as could be. I picked up the four-pound hammer and walked behind him.

"We're not gonna make it, partner," I said and swung with all my strength. "But I will."

He turned toward me just as the hammer hit him full in his face. His body was heaved back off the chair and hit the floor with a thud. I think he moaned, but I gave him a couple more thumpins and he quieted down.

His face and most of his head was all stove in and there was blood comin' out of more than a few places. I dropped the hammer and grabbed the old man by the collar. I opened the door and tossed him outside beside the cabin wall. He landed face down, his feet just clear of the doorway, so there weren't no need to situate him further. It was snowin', and it melted on his body a bit, but that would change as he cooled down and froze up. Satisfied, I closed the door and helped myself to some more Bitsy Stew. I now had all the food.

I was into my third bowl when it came to me that I now had all the gold, too.

***

The next morning was bright and sunny. I got up from my cot and stretched, feeling better than I had in days. The fire had burned down for the most part, but there was still some coals which I stirred into flames with some added wood.

I took a whiff for the bread the old man made every mornin', then saw the blood spilled on the floor. Oh, yeah. I should probably clean that. I sure would miss his bread, though.

I heated and ate up the rest of the Bitsy Stew, then grabbed up the rifle. Maybe today was the day I'd get a deer or somethin'.

It had snowed through the night before clearin' up come daybreak, so when I looked at the old man, he was just a mound of white, as though it weren't no more than a bed of flowers. The soles of his shoes stuck out a bit but weren't no bother. The door opened inwards, so they wouldn't get in the way.

I headed uphill again, following in my tracks from yesterday. That made it an easier trip, though the new snow slowed me down some. Maybe today was my day.

***

It was late afternoon when I headed back down to the cabin. The day had clouded up and the cold was comin' down with the snow. That made me no never mind, though; I had me a deer over my shoulders to keep me warm. It was a youngin' of a doe. Prob'ly her first winter. Last, too. She didn't have a lot of meat, but I was thankful for what there was. An' if I could find one deer, I could...

From down the hill near the cabin, a mule brayed.

I stopped in my tracks. Someone was at the cabin! I crouched in the snow and studied the landscape in the quiet of the fallin' snow. I couldn't see no movement, but one thing I knew for sure was I was plumb out of mules.

An hour passed for dark to come full on an' it was safe to get closer. I heard the mule bray a few more times, so whoever was down there wasn't leaving. I left the deer in the snow to better handle my rifle an' crept down cautious like to the cabin.

I looked about for tracks but didn't see any. The moon was up and plenty bright, so there weren't any to be seen. Figurin' the mule was probably in the stable, I snuck around there. There had to be tracks of a mule and a man over there.

Only there weren't.

Scared someone had gotten up here and found the old man, I dashed around to the front. But the snow mound was still there. I couldn't even see his shoes now, from all the snow.

I looked at the door. It always had ice on it when the snow would melt from the heat inside, then freeze up around the cracks. It was frozen up, meaning the cabin was empty. Still, being a wary soul, I banged the ice off, then pushed the door open, standing to one side, next to the old man. Nobody shot at me and nobody rushed out, so I went inside.

It was dark and cold. I lit a lantern and checked around. I went first to the stable, but the only thing in there was what was left of Bitsy and Betsy, which was mostly bones and some inedibles. I took a look-see behind the blanket that covered our mine, but it only held dark and cold.

A bit disturbed but satisfied I had the cabin to myself, I started up the fire until it was crackling and brightly chasing away the dark and cold. I spent the evening enjoying the last of the stew and a hot potato before turning in for the night.

***

I opened my eyes. Something had woken me. The fire had died down to embers and the cabin was in deep shadow. I lay still, cursing myself for not having my pistol near me. After months of seeing nobody but the old man, I'd gotten careless.

There it was again! A small sound. As though somethin' like sand or sugar was spillin' onto the floor in a slight trickle. The rifle was at the foot of the cot. Could I grab it, cock it, and bring it to bear before whoever it was shot me?

Another tricklin' sound. It was near the workbench... the gold! Someone was takin' my gold! Instantly, I heaved myself and grabbed the rifle. I worked the lever and spun around, ready to fire. There! A pair of eyes! I began to squeeze the trigger...

Nothing.

I took one hand off the rifle and threw some wood on the fire, watching the workbench and ready to fire if anything moved. The embers heated the wood and began licking it with flames that grew and cast light on parts of the room and deeper dark in other parts.

I was alone. I checked closer and saw a small pile of gold dust on the floor. On the workbench above, a bag of gold dust had tipped over, starting the mound and the noise. Breathing a deep sigh of relief, I swept up the gold dust, returned it to the bag and tied it tightly. I stoked up the flames a little more, retrieved my pistol, and went back to bed.

It was an hour before I fell asleep.

***

Where was that deer?

It was colder than yesterday, and it was snowing again. My trail down from the hill was no more than a depression in the snow, but I was sure of where I'd set it down. I even found the larger depression where I'd laid it down. But it was gone. My first thought was a wolf had gotten it, but no, there were no tracks and no signs of draggin' or feedin'. I cast around further to see if there were tracks of any kind.

An' I found 'em.

They started in the middle of a large patch of settled snow, as though the feller had stood still there for hours while the snow fell all about. Someone was watching! Except... the boot prints were sharp, made only a little while ago, and headed down to the cabin door.

I lifted my rifle and followed them. He made no turns or stops. Just made a straight line down the hill. It weren't less than two minutes before I reached the cabin and the tracks ended at the front door.

Only they wasn't facing the door. They was facin' the feet of the old man, lying in his blanket of snow, his boots only just showin'.

Fear come over me, chokin' my throat so's I couldn't breathe. I dropped the rifle, then scooped it right up and fired six times into the snow. If that old man was still alive, he wasn't when I finished shooting.

Terrified but resolute, I brushed the snow off his corpse and had a look-see.

Oh, I'd hit him with the bullets, all right. I could see the holes in his clothes and body. One still smoldered a bit. But they was wasted on him; he was rock hard froze and his face an' head was all caved in such that life couldn't exist in this mortal shell. I brushed some snow over him—tellin' myself I was doin' it out of respect an' not fear—reloaded the rifle, and went inside.

**

I slept in the cave that night, under the collapsed shaft ceiling that had dropped the tons of quartz and two hundred pounds of gold that had made us— made me—rich. After moving my cot in, I started a small fire to light and warm the area, then turned in.

When I awoke hours later, the fire was down to embers and the cave was cold and dark. A freezing sweat come over me. Something had awoken me. I tried to turn my head toward the cave entrance, but fear stiffened my neck. There it was! A sound like quartz gravel scraping softly on the cave floor. I gripped my pistol under the covers and finally forced myself to turn my head.

A slight glow come from the fireplace in the cabin. Part ways blockin' it was the soft outline of a man. He was already in the cave and walkin' slowly toward me in a purposeful manner. As he moved, his steps brushed aside the quartz gravel, causing the sound.

I tried to bring my gun up, but my arm was stiff and motionless, as though from a statue. I wanted to sit up. I wanted to scream. I wanted to run away. But I could do nothing.

The shape moved into the small cavern. In the dim light of the embers, I could see it was a man. But there was something wrong about his head. He paused only ten feet from me, then turned to the cavern wall. He lightly touched the pick an' shovel leanin' there. Then he began climbin', but not like a climber or human. Instead, moving and clinging to it like a spider as he scurried up the wall. I could only stare in horror.

The wall curved into the ceiling of the collapse and he continued over it until he was directly above me. The embers of the fire popped and hissed, then caught a bit of wood and flared up.

The creature above, its back to me as it clung to the ceiling, flinched, then slowly turned its head. It kept turning until completely around, the coal sockets of its eyes reflecting the embers of the fire. Blood dripped down from the flattened and ruined head and face. The *thap, thap, thap* of the drops landing on my blankets made my heart seize and cramp. A drop—icy cold and bitter— landed in my mouth. I bolted up, screaming...

And woke up. I was in my cot in the cabin. A nightmare! I wept in terror and relief as I struggled to sit up. It was so real! I looked about the room. Everything as normal. I looked up to the rafters. Nothing. I looked on my blankets for drops of blood. None there...

On the floor beside the cot—at the end where I laid my head—was a single black drop.

Screamin', I scrambled from my bed, my pistol up and ready. Shootin' at the darkest places in the room, I soon emptied the gun. I dashed to the fire and heaped on all the wood I could find. It soon flared up and lit up the cabin. My spirits went up and my fears abated along with the darkness.

The cabin door. I just had to look. Rifle in hand, I walked to the door, ready to bang the door with the butt to break the ice around the jamb an' latch. I stopped short, suddenly scared I didn't need to. I lifted the latch and pulled.

It opened.

I was crying now, warm tears coming down my cold face. No turning back, though I desperately wanted to. I eased halfway out the door and looked at the old man. He was still buried in the snow. I sobbed in relief.

Then I noticed the fresh scuff marks at his exposed feet. As I watched, the mound of snow shifted and settled over his body.

***

The cabin's covered now with snow, and shelves of food are bare. The howling winds have not stopped in weeks. The nightmare is the same every night, but the drops of black blood continue to mark time, one drop per day.

I stoked the fire, but it was to a ghost of hope. It hadn't been warm for the life of my memory. The pistol was empty; all the rounds discharged in weak attempts to kill that which was already dead. I had never seen him, except as he lay in the snow. But the drops of blood... they told an accusative truth that I could not escape.

I walked to the cave with the last sack of gold and placed it beside my cot. I laid a fire on the stone floor and chipped it to life with my flint. The flames licked to life and set the cavern to glittering in quartz and gold. *Right beautiful,* I thought. *I reckon I missed the honest wealth that was here.*

I lay down on the cot and stared at the cavern ceiling, hoping it would have one more collapse and bury me with my terror. But it held firm, a last tease of Satan to exact the full price. And now Satan was comin' for my soul. Or maybe the old man, lookin' for his gold.

I was still awake hours later in the dying light of the fire when I heard the cabin door latch bang and the door creak open.

THE TOMBSTONE AFFAIR:
A NORTH POLE SECURITY
HISTORICAL TALE
BY
J.B. DANE

Arizona Territory, December 20, 1881, 2:00 a.m.
Alhambra Saloon, Allen Street, Tombstone.

T welve days ago, I got the shock of my life.

It was an ordinary day. Sun shining fit to blind a fella, and a hell of a lot warmer than it ever got back home at the North Pole. I think I complained about the chill up there from the day I was born. Got the hell away the first opportunity that offered, too.

"Mornin', marshal," one the tradesmen setting his wares out greeted that fateful morn and offered me his hand. Just like he did other times I moseyed by. But that day the moment our palms met I knew he wasn't the honest man I'd thought him.

He was on the Naughty List and high ranking on it, too. Seems he'd tinkered with his scales and overcharged customers every time he weighed something.

Why it was a shock to me was not that he was passing himself off as 110 percent honest, but that *I'd* got the tingle and the message by shaking his hand. That wasn't supposed to happen. I was old Kris Kringle's third son, and only Pa and his immediate heir, my older brother Nicholai, should know what list a man or woman or child was on via the slightest touch.

Which meant that things back home had gone wrong. Not only might Pa have succumbed to something, but one of my older brothers as well. It had to be two unexpected deaths to move me up the roster to List knowledge. It also meant that my sojourn away from the Pole was at an end. Whoever was left ahead of me was on sleigh duty. I would be stuck dealing with elves and those damn Lists.

I'd been testing the tingle since that morning, making skin-to-skin contact with any citizen I encountered, hoping the sensation would go away. It hadn't, so I expected there'd be a visitation soon from an elf in a sleigh pulled by flying venison. Their mission would be to yank me from my chosen lifestyle and shove me into the ancestral one back at the top of the world.

But the visitor that came looking for me that night had nothing to do with things happening in the Claus family. It was a local.

A damn fine looking local, too. I'd spotted her a time or two on the street. She wasn't the type of woman I usually sought out. She favored clothes that covered her up. I preferred to gaze at the dipping necklines of the outfits saloon gals wore.

I'd already been at the table at the Alhambra for quite a few hours when a miner I knew in passing stumbled in the door. I had my back to an interior wall 'cause a man who lived by his gun took a lesson from the late Bill Hickok, and I don't mean that he should fold a hand with aces and eights, which I did anyway rather than tempt fate. I had a clear view of the front door, though there wasn't much foot traffic amblin' in at two a.m.

I'd offered my hand all around before sitting down. Well, except for the dove. I kissed her neck. My unwanted new talent told me the men all had dandy spots on the Naughty List. Oddly enough, the satin-clad honey with the delectable bared shoulders currently sitting on the lap of the man across from me had registered as Nice list, despite her profession. Could be the List had its own criteria for rankin' folks.

The newly arrived drunk steadied himself by leaning a hand on the back of another player's chair. "Lady outside lookin' fer ya, Frank," he slurred.

"A lady." I said it flat 'cause *ladies* weren't in the habit of seeking me out.

The drunk's nod was more of a bounce. "Yup. A proper one considerin' the words she used." Which probably just meant she didn't drop her Gs or swear when she accosted him.

The fact that she was standing outside the saloon in the middle of the night rather than come inside indicated the warmth exuded at the Alhambra wasn't to her likin'. We might be in the desert, and we might have warmer temperatures than the North Pole, but it was still damn cold this late at night in December.

"She say she was looking for Frank North or for a marshal?" I asked. I doubted my real name, Fritz Claus, would have been bandied because I never used it, but it had been a day of unwelcome surprises already.

I wasn't a lawman normally. By profession, if you want to call it that, I'm a gambler, though temporarily filling in as one of the town deputy marshals. Not a position everyone rushed to take considering what had gone down at the fireworks the Earps and Clantons had slung at each other in October. I'd only taken it on as a favor to Virgil Earp, the territorial Deputy Marshal. He'd sought me out because I'd out drawn a sore loser. He hadn't asked whether I could hit the side of barn when aiming at it.

"Said the whole shebang," the drunken messenger avowed. "Marshal Frank North."

The man across the table from me had dealt the next hand and was already perusing his cards. Flicked up the edges on the ones he'd tossed me. Two pair of royals. The red suits. What else would a Claus get on the cusp of Christmas?

I let the cards be, scooped up the winnings before me, and pushed back from the table. "Sorry, boys. You'll have to excuse me while I find out what this female requires. I'll be right back if it's nothing serious."

"We'll save yer seat fer ya, Frank," one of them assured.

Outside, it was quiet on Allen Street even though business at my usual stops was still rollicking. Across the way there were lights still glowing in the foyer of the Grand Hotel where I rented a room. To my right, it sounded like a fight might have been in progress down at Hafford's Saloon. To the left, just across Fifth Street on the corner, someone was singing to rather poor accompaniment on a fiddle at the Oriental Saloon, and the hoots and catcalls they received hadn't discouraged them enough to shut the hell up. Further down that way, on the opposite side of the street past the Wells Fargo Office, things were relatively quiet where the Bird Cage Theater was still planning its Grand Opening on Christmas Eve. I'd been looking forward to that. Now I wondered if I'd still be in town that night.

The woman was off to the side, her back pressed to the building but away from the street facing windows. It put her in deep shadow. When she stepped out of it, the glow from inside was enough to show me she was a neat package. She'd pushed her broad brimmed felt hat back on her head, but there were enough strands of dark hair that had come loose during her ride into town that long tendrils dangled about her face, running like rills over her shoulders and down her front. She was togged out as I'd seen her in the past, dressed for life on the range though wearing a split riding skirt rather than trousers. Spurs rang at her boot heels. Her hands were covered in working gloves and cradled the pistol she'd already pulled from the gun belt hugging womanly hips.

"Evenin', ma'am," I murmured. Had pushed my frock coat back so she could see the badge on my vest. Hoped that would keep her from shootin' me. "Frank North at yer service."

She took her finger off the trigger, though didn't drop the shooter back in the holster. A careful filly this one was.

"I realize this is an inconvenient time to seek you out, but I need your help, marshal." She had a pleasant voice. Not too high pitched and not sultry like some of the doves pitched theirs, but somewhere in between and all business.

I leaned a hip against the hitching post before the Alhambra's doors and took out a cigarillo. Lit it, drawing the taste of tobacco smoke into my lungs before exhaling it in a cloud that a desert breeze tore apart. "Go on," I urged.

She looked around five and twenty to me, but whether she was married or a spinster, I'd no idea. We'd never been introduced so I hadn't a name to go with the face. I had seen her with a man a few years her senior. He wasn't with her now, so she could be a recent widow, too.

She'd seen my eyes drop to the pistol she was packin'. A soft sigh of disgust escaped her, but she dropped it back in the holster. I didn't blame her for carryin'. You can't survive in a mining town without always being prepared for trouble.

And she was trouble.

"My brother Abel Proctor's been missing for three days," she said. "We've got a spread a bit out of town but not a prosperous one by any means. He often drifts home late—" Her nose wrinkled as though when he did turn up, he smelt of too much bad whiskey or of feathered out filly's cheap perfume— "but he's never been gone this long before. I waited a full day before searching for him myself, but there's a lot of land to cover out there."

And it was Apache territory at that.

"You suspect warriors on the run from the Army?" Not that things had been heated in this neck of the desert. Most of the confrontations had been in New Mexico Territory or further north of us. That didn't mean we lacked stray renegades in the area that would have no qualms about killing an isolated rancher or miner. It was why our town was dubbed Tombstone, after all.

"I won't rule them out, marshal, but I'm more concerned that Abel has been making friends with Clanton partisans."

Partisans. Well, she was a nicely educated lass as well as confident with that six-shooter. An odd, yet intriguing woman all around.

"You suspect foul play, then?"

"I don't know what to think," she admitted. "But it is unlike him to leave me on my own for long."

I nodded sagely. "We can't ride out to look for him until the sun's up, Miss Proctor. Do you have a place to stay here in town?"

"No, but a chair in a hotel lobby if there aren't any available rooms will suffice."

"Come with me," I ordered, gesturing her toward the Grand where I stayed across the way. She made no argument but kept pace with me.

The night clerk was drowsing behind his counter but roused quick enough. Fortunately for Miss Proctor, there was a room available. I let him check her in and escort her to her temporary quarters while I returned to the Alhambra.

"That was quick," the card player with the saloon girl on his lap said.

"Quick is the best way to move a good woman along. Slow and thorough is the speed when spending time with Miss Sadie there," I replied as I resettled at the table and waited for the next hand to be dealt.

The gal on his lap, Sadie, grinned an invite at me. One I'd sadly have to turn down. She wouldn't get a slow and thorough from the fellow serving as her chair.

He'd leave the table both broke and drunk, so not only incapable of paying for her time but incapable of giving a noteworthy performance.

I occupied myself arranging the coins and greenbacks I was willing to lose and casually dropped what I'd returned to the table to discover. "Any of you fellas know Abel Proctor?"

"Proctor?" The man to my left squinted. Whether it was to better view the pips on his cards or because he was thinking was a close call. "Sounds familiar, but..." He let the sentence drift into obscurity.

"Ain't he the Eastern dude who bought out Hempleman when he came down with that allergy to Apaches?" another player suggested.

"Eastern dude! He was from Texas!" a third snapped.

"That's east of here," the suggester insisted.

"You playin' cards here or just wastin' my time?" the current dealer demanded.

"Foldin'," the first man said. Only one appeared to think Lady Luck was breathin' in his ear. He called. And lost to the dealer.

"He ever visit you, Sadie?" I asked.

She shrugged. "Not every man is polite enough to introduce himself by name, Frank. You're nearly an exception to the rule."

I played a few hands but couldn't shake any further information from any of them, so within thirty minutes I pocketed my winnings, made the rounds of the other tables asking about Proctor, and came away with nothin'. When I hit the Oriental, my night picked up. Not only did I double my funds at play but found a couple men who knew Proctor. They hadn't anything good to say of him.

"Probably off rustlin' cattle. Saw him talkin' ta Ike Clanton a time 'er two," the first man I cornered admitted.

"He deep in with The Cowboys then?" I asked. The shootout at the O.K. Corral hadn't ended things between the Earps and Old Man Clanton's men, after all. It had merely lit the fuse of the war between the factions. The Earps might be wearing the badges, but The Cowboys had quite a list of supporters in town, all more than willing to take out anyone with a badge pinned to their vest.

"Not 'xactly," my informant cautioned. "More like he wanted ta be one of 'em, but hadn't passed muster so far."

"A hopeful man, hmm?"

The fellow shrugged. "You might ask Zwing Hunt about him, but Zwing ain't all that law abidin', either. My guess is he'd say he didn't know Proctor."

Which wasn't going to get me anywhere. By the time I ran out of men to question, two hours remained before the sun edged over the horizon. *That's* when the expected visitor from the Pole arrived.

***

I'd just hung my holster and six-gun over the bedpost, yanked my boots off and stretched out on the bed fully clothed, commencing to catch some shut eye when I heard the displacement in the air. I didn't bother lifting either eyelid to see who they'd sent. My money was on it being one of the older elves, and not all of them were comfortable with sleigh flight.

"Fritz," a voice growled. It was Handler, the head stock tender. He wasn't afraid of getting in a sleigh hitched to a team of flying reindeer.

"Frank," I growled back at him, not opening my eyes. "I haven't answered to Fritz in twenty years."

"It's time to fulfill your destiny," the crotchety elf snarled. Even with my eyes closed I knew the oil lamp on the table had flared to life, the flame magicked into existence via a snap of his fingers.

"Third son. No destiny," I countered.

"Well, destiny took a fancy to you, boy," Handler said. "Christophe and Nicholai were killed in a fire at the opera in Vienna—"

I opened one eye to glare at him. "When?"

"Evening of the eighth. You should have known because—"

"The Lists tingle." I let my eyelid close again and sighed. "What the hell were they both doing at the opera?"

"Don't ask me," Handler spat. "I just know there was a fire and hundreds of humans didn't make it out. The boys—" who were both much older than me, and I was staring down the barrel of forty— "had seats near the front. Christophe's wife was supposed to go with him but didn't feel well, so Nicholai went instead."

Hell, it was worse than I thought.

"Neither Nick nor Chris had a son? Is that why I'm the new runner up?"

"Both childless, and you're not taking Nicholai's job. *You're* Santa."

Not only did I open my eyes at the news, I sat bolt upright in bed. "I'm *what*?"

"Your old man collapsed when he heard the boys were lost. I left to retrieve you two minutes after he died."

Which, if I remembered flying reindeer speed, meant about an hour ago. Yeah, they beat any steam powered transportation to hell and then some.

"I need to run you through the training before full dark in Samoa on the twenty-fourth," he said, apparently not noticing that I was still gawking at him. "You do remember when that is based on local time here?"

If you'd asked me two weeks ago, I wouldn't have had an answer. One tripped out now like I hadn't had to calculate it at all. "Yeah, sunset is at eight p.m. in Samoa on the twenty-fourth when it is just five a.m. on the twenty-third here in the territory."

"Which means you've got maybe three days to learn the route, get acquainted with the team, and learn the technical elements of entry and exit through chimneys," Handler said. "We need to leave now."

I swung my legs over the side of the bed again. Rested my elbows on my knees and ran my fingers back through my hair in frustration. "Can't be done."

"Can be. It just hasn't been done this fast in the past," he soothed. "But you're a Claus, boy. *You're Santa.* You can do it. Besides—"

"'The team knows the way to carry the sleigh,'" I groaned, quoting Moore's poem. "I've got a man to find. I'm legally bound to go search him out before his sister pulls her pistol on me for failing to do my sworn duty. I'm a damn marshal in this town, you know." To make it clearer, I thumbed my vest forward so the badge caught the dim glow of the oil lamp on the bedside.

"He Naughty or Nice listed?" the elf asked.

"Is he what?"

"You've got an easy solution to the problem, Fritz."

"Frank."

Handler sighed. "Frank," he conceded. "A month ago, you were just human and would have had to do a lot more work to find him. Now you not only have the Lists ready to spit whatever you need to know, you're Santa, and that means..."

He waited for me to find the answer like he was a schoolmaster, and I was an unruly schoolboy. "Means nothin' to me, Handler. Third son, remember? Never supposed to need to know any of this."

"It means you concentrate on his name and where he falls on the list and you'll know exactly where he is at any time," the elf snarled.

Have to admit, I stared at him, totally stunned. Boy, did the Claus family and elven employees ever keep things from a third son! Not that I'd wanted the trouble that came with the job of being Santa. Around the world in twenty-one hours on one hell of a long delivery route every Christmas Eve? We won't even mention all that jolly part. I was not looking forward to any of it. But I also knew I was stuck. I was the only Claus in the direct inheritance line from the first man to ever shout *Dash away* to those magically enhanced flying ruminants.

"Still can't seek him out until after dawn. I hope you've got the team and sleigh hidden where no one will stumble over them." It wasn't like reindeer or snow sleds were things found in the Sonoran Desert.

"All invisible but at hand to get you where you need to go faster than any nag," he said.

I hoped no one would run into the invisible Pole transport before we needed it. Which was not going to be as quickly as Handler thought.

"Not taking the sled on marshal business," I insisted. "It sort of ruins the whole secrecy thing in regards to the Pole, doesn't it?" I might have skipped over becoming the Claus in charge of keeping the magical settlement at the top of the world a secret, but I'd heard my own father grouch about the heir's job enough times before he became Santa. Which was when my oldest brother Nicholai picked up the gripe where Pa left off.

"We're using horses, and *you* aren't comin' along. It'll be just Miss Proctor and me." Mostly because I doubted there would be any volunteers to go with us. Well, ones that wouldn't plug us—or at least me!—rather than let us find Proctor if he was with any of The Cowboys.

Handler huffed loudly but didn't argue. Instead, he stole the blanket from the bed, curled up in a corner by the dresser and was snoring thirty seconds later. I blew the lamp out then laid back down, but it was just to stare at the ceiling in an effort to come to terms with the way Lady Luck had turned her back on me. *Santa! Hell!*

***

"I asked around at the saloons about your brother last night after you settled in at the hotel," I told Miss Proctor as we headed for Dexter's Livery Stable on Toughnut Street between Third and Fourth to retrieve our horses. "Seems your brother might have involved himself in rustling."

"Which indicates that he is riding with Mr. Clanton's family and associates," she said. "You don't have to sugar coat things with me, marshal. I realize that you may have to arrest Abel."

I'd been thinking I'd probably have to shoot him, at least hobble him with a bullet in his leg considering few men were willing to come peaceably.

She hadn't tugged on her leather riding gloves yet. I could see her hands were rough from the work she did around the ranch, though she still sounded like a woman who'd done time in a finishing school when a girl. They wouldn't have taught her to bake, scrub, or help brand cattle—all things I figured she'd been doing since arriving in Arizona Territory.

Because her hands were no longer covered, I wanted to know where she landed on the Lists. "Just so there's no misunderstanding between us, Miss Proctor, I'd like you to shake on this. For me, this is a promise to find your brother. For you, it's acceptance that if there is gun play, that he might not survive the outcome, be it a fatal wound or a post-trial hanging."

She considered a moment, then stopped and offered her right hand. "Agreed, Marshal North."

"Frank," I told her. "And you're...?"

"Miriam."

I enfolded her hand in mine and concentrated on the name Miriam Proctor. Skin to skin. I'd soon know more about her than she'd want me to know and then...

But I got nothin'. She wasn't on the Naughty List, but her name wasn't registering for the Nice List either. What the hell?

"Do we have a destination?" she asked. "A direction that one of the men you talked to last night might have suggested?"

"A general direction," I said, though we'd be heading in a straight line directly to where Abel Proctor was snugged down with his new Cowboy friends. Less than ten minutes later, we'd ridden out of town.

It still took close to two hours to reach the camp where Proctor and his pals had settled. I knew we'd reached it when the dirt kicked up a few feet in front of my horse and was followed by the echo of a rifle shot a half second later. The horse pulled up of his own accord then danced sideways. Miss Proctor's gelding reared, but she leaned forward and calmed the beast with a pat on its neck and soothing words in its ears.

"Whadda ya want?" a gruff voice yelled from cover. It sounded like he was off to our right, which meant the sun would be in our eyes as we faced him.

"I'm looking for my brother," Miriam called in answer. "Abel Proctor. He hasn't been home in days and I wish to know if whatever business took him away is nearly completed."

"What's the badge man doing with you?" the disembodied voice demanded.

When she glanced over at me, I gestured that she should do the talking.

"I hired him to protect me from men like you!" she shouted. "Now, is my brother with you, or isn't he? If he isn't, we need to move on."

"Yeah, he's with us. Hey, Proctor. Yer sister wants a word."

But it wasn't just Proctor who stalked angrily from the brush. Three men I knew were Clanton's men or sympathizers fanned out behind him. None of them was looking at Miss Proctor. All but Proctor had either pistols or a rifle in their hands. He had a branding iron that looked rather fresh from the fire.

"Go on home, Miriam," he snarled at her. "I don't need a woman trailing behind me."

"You need to be tending our herd, or did you steal our cattle from other ranchers and lie to me about purchasing them?" she snapped. "I'm not stupid, Abel. You're altering brands out here."

"Shut up, Miriam," he spat, "or we'll plug you as well as the marshal there and let the buzzards deal with you after."

I nudged my horse a step closer to them. "Sounds like a confession of guilt to me. Which means you're all under arrest, boys. Put the weapons down nice and slow, then kick 'em this way."

"I think we'd all rather shoot ya dead, marshal," the man who fired the warning shot at us drawled.

Which is when things went as I'd expected them to go. Pistols came up, though whether they were pointed only at me or at Miss Proctor as well, was hard to tell. "Run," I yelled at her as I grabbed my shooter.

Not that she paid me the least bit of attention. Her own weapon was drawn. After that, I was too busy to keep an eye on her.

The air was redolent with the sound of gunfire and the scent of burnt powder as smoke drifted from the guns.

In case you wondered, I can do more than hit the side of a barn when I draw. I targeted their gun hands, and soon had everyone but Proctor disarmed. Turned out, Miriam was a neat hand with a pistol herself. She winged her brother in the arm, forcing him to drop the brandin' iron.

"On the ground," I told the passel of them. "Hands behind your backs. If you don't, I'm sure my partner will be happy to wing you again."

"Indeed," Miss Proctor said succinctly. When she turned the muzzle of her smoking gun their way, every man Jack of them kowtowed.

Her brother was moaning, holding his arm and rockin' back and forth where he sat in the dust. I swung out of the saddle and grabbed the coil of rope draped over the saddle pommel. I'd just finished hog-tying Proctor's friends together when Abel left off moanin' and dived for one of the discarded guns.

I'd holstered my weapon while binding my catch. One of them tried to head butt me, but I flinched away, not only reaching for my gun but mentally running though how many shots I'd fired to down The Cowboys. If my count was off, all chambers were empty, and it would be a very poor Christmas for folks around the world when Proctor killed me.

"Your turn ta die, marshal," he snarled, then the shot rang out.

I waited for the pain, for my blood to drip into the hard packed desert floor. For Miriam Proctor's face to be the last thing I saw in life.

None of it happened. Instead, Abel Proctor stared in stunned surprise at his sister as she dropped from the saddle and sank to her knees. Her pistol tumbled from her hand. Then Proctor fell over at an unnatural angle, the six-shooter still in his hand.

The bound Cowboys gapped at her. "Ya kilt yer own brother," one croaked in disbelief.

"I was aiming for his shoulder," she whispered faintly. Then her eyes turned from Abel's contorted body to me. There was horror in them over what she'd just done.

"You missed," I said. The shot had taken him right in the heart.

One of the trussed men tried to struggle to his feet. I kicked the back of his knee, sending him face first into his bound friends. "Where the hell do you think you're going?" I snapped.

"You gonna let her kill us, too?" another whined.

"Tempted," I said, "but instead I'll let someone in town know where to find you."

"You leavin' us here with a dead man?"

"No," Miriam Proctor said, rising back to her feet. She retrieved her pistol and dropped it back in her holster. "If you don't mind, Mr. North, I'll ride with you and Abel's body can be carried on my horse." She was back in control, no emotion surfacing in her voice.

And she still wasn't turning up on the Naughty, which meant she hadn't lied about the shot that killed her brother. And still a mystery.

We were nearly back to town when I broke the silence between us. It felt good—right—to have her in the saddle before me. "What will you do now?" I asked quietly in her ear.

"I don't know," she admitted. "But I won't be staying here."

"Come home with me," I suggested. "It's a place far from here with arctic temperatures and ice."

"And what would I do there?" Miriam asked.

It was a snap decision on my part, but I'm a gamble and this felt right. Felt like a better destiny than being Santa.

"Marry me," I said.

UNPUBLISHED COMMENTARY
ON MY
EARLIER WESTERN TRAVELS
BY
STEFAN MARKOS

Once again, I have looked at one of the museum exhibitions of works from my early Western travels, the paintings which made me famous and cemented my reputation. As to how I got into this field of endeavor, I did it with reasonably pure intentions. I wished to chronicle the great American West in its pristine state, before it all got swept away by the advance of civilization.

I am credited as the artist, of course, but there are two other men without whom it never could have happened, and they cannot ever receive public recognition.

The first was a certain well-heeled English nobleman with extremely risqué, even unnatural tastes in art. The second was a scientist of completely unknown nationality. In fact, he undoubtedly was not even of this world.

At any rate, the first gentleman funded my project, albeit indirectly. I was tasked with creating a work for him that seemed all but impossible to achieve, yet which would be highly remunerative if accomplished.

The second gentleman gave me the means to accomplish the seemingly impossible through a work of science, which I cannot even pretend to understand.

To put this all in proper order, I must begin early in my painting career, after I returned from my first journey up the Missouri River and its tributaries.

While I was only too willing to travel, labor and sacrifice for the cause of depicting the unspoiled West, there was the practical matter of funding, without which I could not continue my work. I had long since given up my law practice and was no longer able to devote much time to painting portraits for pay. Charging admission to my exhibitions brought in a small amount of funds, but not nearly enough to support the endeavor.

As luck would have it, I met the man who was to become my patron while touring England with my paintings, i.e., Lord Humpingham. He approached me toward closing time one evening and told me how much he admired my painting of a buffalo herd. But his remarks were tempered by criticism.

"I say, young sir," he remarked, "Such a huge number of magnificent beasts, yet none of them are mating!"

"Well, sir, the time is not exactly opportune," I replied. "They are, after all, being pursued by a party of Indian hunters."

He adjusted his spectacles and took another look.

"Hm-m-m. None of the hunters are mating, either," he noted.

"That may take place later," I said. "Right now, they are concentrating on providing for themselves and their families."

"Aha. So they *do* mate," he leered. "We can assume that it might be possible to catch them in the act, then."

I cleared my throat.

"Sir, some of these tribes are rather open about the practice, and some not so."

"Fascinating. Might we discuss this further?"

There followed an exchange of introductions, after which Lord Humpingham invited me to dinner at his estate.

Apparently, His Lordship was of an age to be a veteran of the Napoleonic Wars, as well as being a libertine after the style of the last century. He was intensely interested in commissioning a mural. The mural, of course was to reflect his interests (perhaps I should say his obsessions).

He said that it was to be called "Panorama of Procreation," and would depict a compendium of the wild creatures of North America, as well as the Western peoples, in the act of mating. The old boy was especially excited by the knowledge that each of the depictions was to be sketched and then painted from life. It was all to be displayed against the broad sweep of a Western landscape.

The whole thing was to be around sixty feet long by some fifteen feet high, it being intended to cover one wall of the Great Hall of Humpingham Manor. The viewer would enter the hall and begin by seeing the smallest creatures of the North American wilderness, that is, animalcules, then insects, then field mice, then rabbits, wolves, deer, et cetera, all in blissful copulation. The succession was to go all way up to buffalo, then grizzly bears, then after that to larger creatures yet, of which only skeletons have been found.

I was to be paid a shockingly large sum for the project, more than enough to support my primary endeavor. However difficult the results would be of attainment; this was my best hope. Fortunately, my patron was willing to grant me two or three years to finish the project. Hopefully, he would live that long, despite his advanced age and dissolute habits. And so, I set to work on the preliminary planning.

There were, of course, a few difficulties in executing the project and explaining the problems to His Lordship. In the matter of the animalcules, for instance, I had to consult with a scientific fellow at Cambridge to view the little creatures through a microscope and to catch them in the act of reproducing. The scientist pointed out that they multiplied by splitting themselves in two, not by copulating.

But, Humpingham approved my sketch. I proposed to include it in the mural by the device of showing it through the lens of a magnifying glass. So much for the problem of depicting the smallest creature.

Now, for the largest. There were Western buffalo herds aplenty in those days, so it would simply be a matter of patience to catch two of them in the act. Grizzly bears would be somewhat more difficult, since I should have to find a mating couple and sketch them without getting mauled. Humpingham was absolutely adamant on including the grizzlies.

He was just as stubborn on the matter of the truly gigantic skeletons that had been found, those of the mammoths. How was I to paint them mating, when I could not even find them walking about? It was no good trying to paint something imaginary. Even as befuddled as the old boy was, he would be able to tell the difference. If any problem could halt the project, it was this. But, I was committed.

***

Then, it was on my third trip up the Missouri the following year that finally, I could see myself able to complete my magnum opus (his words) for Lord Humpingham. It was early autumn, and I was still anxiously trying to locate the most elusive of my subjects.

As I have already mentioned, it was late in the season, and I needed not only prepare to return to St. Louis, but to proceed from there to New York, thence to England.

It happened that I climbed to the top of a ridge to reconnoiter. My horse Chauncey tossed his head and whinnied a bit, his usual reaction to other creatures that made him uneasy. I looked at the prairie below and spotted two four-legged forms. I brought up my spyglass. Just as I thought: two buffaloes, a bull and a cow.

I leaned over toward the pack horse and retrieved my sketch book and pencils. My spirits lifted a bit. This side trip might not be a total waste after all. I took myself and the horses closer to the animals. I needed to get close enough to get a good sketch of the action, but not so much that I would startle them. I edged in a little more, then halted abruptly.

There was something not quite right about what was going on. The bull pawed the earth and bellowed and snorted as he approached the cow. When the bull began his approach, she stopped, and instead of looking back at the bull, turned completely around to look at him. Then, she reversed herself again and stood as if bracing herself for the bull's onslaught.

The bull's mounting and thrusting were everything I could hope for. The final painting would convey all the force and motion of the event I was witnessing. But the cow's reaction was, somehow, a disappointment. She simply stood there and allowed it to happen. Could I add something to her response in the painting? Perhaps, but the painting would be more compelling if I sketched authentic detail. And it was authenticity for which my client was paying top money.

The bull didn't seem concerned. He went at it furiously. This was a very large and energetic bull. Then, it looked as if the cow's front legs started to give, yet they almost seemed to bend the wrong way. She suddenly righted herself. A second later, the bull let out a huge bellow, as if in pain, dismounted instantly, turned tail, and ran.

The cow stood stock still. It was positively eerie, as if she had died and rigor mortis had instantly set in. Then—was it actually happening?—her side opened in the manner of a trap door, and a figure tumbled out onto the grass.

I moved in closer and got a better look at the individual on the ground. He was a rather short man of unknown race and nationality, somewhat slender of build and below average height. The clothes were totally unfamiliar in their style and fabric, being some sort of one-piece combination shirt and trousers. The fabric was smooth and lustrous, yet did not appear to be silk.

He had a rather pronounced bump on his forehead, but appeared to be breathing. I reached into my valise and pulled out my medicine case. Then, I dismounted and walked over to the stranger.

I knelt and pulled a vial of smelling salts out of the case, uncorked it, and passed it under the man's nose. The results were almost instantaneous. His eyes opened, seemingly almost to the point of popping out of their sockets. The man gasped, sat up, then moaned and felt of his forehead. I produced a flask of medicinal brandy and offered it to the stranger. The man took a reluctant sip, paused, then took a deep draught.

He said something almost, but not quite intelligible. Was it Dutch? He seemed to note my puzzlement, then spoke again.

"I say, that bull gave me quite a start. Didn't expect as much exuberance." He looked at the brandy flask, smiled, reached for it, and said, "May I?"

I nodded and handed him the flask. The stranger took his pull and handed it back. He smiled faintly.

"I am much better, sir, although I still feel a bit odd from banging my head against the controls."

"Controls?" I asked. "Perhaps your buffalo is an automaton of sorts?" I definitely wanted to know more. It occurred to me that I had a second flask of brandy in my valise, and more back at camp. I offered the flask again.

The stranger grinned and eagerly accepted.

"You see, sir," he said, his voice slurring a bit, "I am a scientist here to study the life of this region, to record as much data and as many images as possible in the time that I have. The buffalo enables me to travel incognito and undisturbed, at least most of the time. I had to give that bull a little bit of electricity, I'm afraid, in a very sensitive area."

My head was spinning, and not just from the brandy. Data? Images? In a way, the stranger was doing what I myself was doing, except with very different implements. Was he competition, or were his purposes different enough from my own that he posed no problem? The fact that he could apply the mysterious force of electricity lent credence to his claims of being a scientist. I wanted to get better acquainted.

"I'm afraid I did not catch your name, sir," I said, extending my hand. "I am Jordan Cartlin."

The stranger looked at my hand for a moment, as if trying to figure out what to do, then took it.

"My name is Zarrek. I am not sure that my title would mean that much to you."

Most definitely a foreigner, I thought.

"I am from Pennsylvania," I replied, "and I am here in the West taking notes and making sketches for my paintings."

I again handed Zarrek the flask and waited while he took a swallow from it.

"Very interesting," said Zarrek. "I am doing much the same, except that I have devices that make the images and notes for me. As to where I am from, I doubt that you've heard of it."

I chuckled and took another sip of brandy.

"Try me, Mr. Zarrek. I am a well-travelled man. You are from some remote corner of the British Isles? Perhaps central or eastern Europe?"

"Oh, much further away than that, in more ways than one. And I suppose I shall be returning there soon."

I hoped that my relief didn't show. It looked as if Zarrek's work, if it were displayed at all, would be exhibited somewhere very far away. But, of what were these images?

"Would it be possible to see some of your work?"

"Why, certainly. But we must go to my camp. Let me get back into my buffalo for a moment."

He got up and went over to the statue-like beast and climbed back inside. He emerged a few moments later, shaking his head.

"It is no good," he said. "I shall need another tool, which is back at my camp."

"You can ride double with me," I offered. He looked apprehensive, but he accepted.

Zarrek showed an interest in what I was doing, so I spent the ride telling him. I also mentioned the most difficult problems of locating the mating grizzlies and the extinct elephants. Why I told him, I do not know. Did I think that he might have chanced upon some surviving mammoths?

***

His "camp" would have been better described as a dwelling. Externally, it resembled a small mound in the grassland. Zarrek dismounted, walked over to the edge of it, and fiddled with a pair of stones on the ground. An aperture opened in the side, and we entered.

The whole place was lit by some unknown source. Phosphorescence? There were tables, chairs, cabinets, and things I could not identify. He reached into one of the cabinets, smiled, and pulled out a mysterious implement.

He turned back to me.

"Now, could I bother you for a ride back to the buffalo? When we return, I can show you some of my work, and possibly show you an answer or two to your problems."

It did not take him long to repair his buffalo automaton. We returned to his camp, the buffalo leading the way. It was able to fit within the dwelling, but we decided it would be best to tether Chauncey and the pack horse outside, for obvious reasons.

Zarrek produced a device that resembled nothing so much as a flat, tin box with rounded edges and corners, except that it was not of tin. It was accompanied by a head-sized band of the same material. He placed the band on his head, ran his fingers over the box, closed his eyes, and smiled.

He handed me the band, and said, "Put it on, Mr. Cartlin. You'll see your mating bears."

And so I did. I gasped. It was a transparency of sorts. I could see a mountain landscape, and yes, a grizzly boar and sow in the act of mating. When I closed my eyes, they became solid, real!

I opened my eyes and turned to Zarrek, who was working with yet another box device and headband.

"Zarrek! I must go outside and get my art supplies! Will the bears still be there?"

He nodded, smiled, and said, "They will, indeed. Meanwhile, I am looking for your mammoths."

Once I finished my sketches, I rolled them up to store them in tin cylinders. The actual paintings would be done from these once I went home for the winter. Before the day was out, I had all the sketches I needed to complete the wildlife segments of His Lordship's mural.

***

I accepted Zarrek's invitation to return the next day. I noticed that he had several of the metal devices laid out on the table. I asked him just exactly what they were and how they worked. My best guess was that they involved some natural force such as electricity or magnetism. Perhaps the scientists and inventors of his country were not very communicative with the rest of the world.

He smiled his strange smile, and replied, "I shall try to explain. Of the people I have met here, you are the most likely to understand. You have an aptitude for the use of the instrument, and not even all of my people have that."

"All of your people? Who *are* your people?"

"Let us just say that we live elsewhere. Our visits must be discreet, lest we change things in ways that we should not. I have visited this camp several times over the years, and doubtless will be back several more. Things have happened here that have a definite bearing upon our success."

I shook my head, and replied, "Zarrek, I am afraid that you have raised more questions than you have answered. Success at what? What things have happened? What things might you change?"

His brow furrowed. He stared at the floor, then looked back at me.

"Let us say that we wish to make a better world. In fact, several better worlds. We need to study pristine wilderness and the workings of nature. We need to study the entry of human beings into the picture. And we need to study these over a long period of time. We cannot expose the people of this time and this world to our knowledge, or we will alter the course of your development."

How grandiose, I thought. His nation, whatever or wherever it is, does not think that the rest of the world deserves to share in its discoveries.

What I said was, "You've shared these things with *me*, Zarrek."

He chuckled, and said, "Perhaps I feel that I owe you something for rescuing me. And perhaps I feel a certain kinship with someone else who is trying to depict this wilderness before it is all transformed. At any rate, you are an artist, a person of creativity. You are also a traveler, exposed to many exotic things and strange stories. People will consider this when they listen to you. You will improve the cultural life of your society, you will edify and entertain, but you will not drastically alter the direction of your world or of the human population here."

I had to satisfy myself with that explanation, because after that, Zarrek was not forthcoming. At least, not until the next evening.

Zarrek seemed very eager to examine the recreation and amusements available in these parts, and it occurred to me that perhaps I could oblige him and achieve my object at the same time.

"Well," I replied, "the people at the trading fort put on amateur athletic contests and dances. They also have horse races and gamble a lot."

He seemed to fain polite interest.

"But, for the most fulfilling experience, I would suggest a certain establishment adjacent to the fort. There, we can find the best quality beverages available in these parts, more refined games, and very engaging feminine companionship."

At this, Zarrek perked up. He actually smiled when he answered.

"That, I believe, would be a bit more to my liking."

"I thought so, sir. Please, do me the honor of being my guest."

As I suspected would be the case, he took one of several of the devices with him. We mounted up and rode to the establishment.

I had taken the liberty of making arrangements with the proprietor, Miss Fanny, earlier in the day so that my guest could immediately commence the evening's activities once we arrived. Fanny handed him a drink as soon as he was introduced, and he downed it with gusto. She handed him another and placed an arm about his shoulders.

It was not long before they both laughed and headed to one of the back rooms. At length, Fanny appeared at the door, smiled, and nodded. I entered the room and found Zarrek there, face down on the bed. I rolled him over and found his single-piece garment underneath him. A quick search through the pockets, and there was the device. I dropped it into my haversack until such time as I could take it to my hiding place.

With the help of one of Fanny's employees, I got the fellow out to the waiting horses and we slung him over his saddle, still snoring away. We made it back to camp without incident, except that Zarrek partially regained consciousness once or twice and made some rather curious remarks.

I packed up and departed the next morning, visiting the hiding place of the device before heading downriver.

***

Lord Humpingham was very pleased indeed when the mural was finally installed. He lingered for an exceptionally long time over the depiction of Zarrek cavorting with Miss Fanny.

"I say, Cartlin, how did you ever get to stay in the bedchamber with them while all this was going on?"

It had occurred to me that I might be able to secure yet more commissions from his Lordship with the proper enticement. The old gentleman seemed especially mellow and amenable to persuasion at the moment, having just had a clyster, so I decided to expose him to an experience with the device. I took the box and the band out of my coat pocket. I put the band on my head for a moment, until I was sure that I had the right setting.

"Let me introduce you to Miss Fanny, Milord. Here, let me position this device on you."

I adjusted it to the proper setting and activated it. Humpingham jumped.

"Egad, man, it's as if I'm *there*!"

"Yes, Milord. And, if you'll look at that man closely, if you'll concentrate on *being* him, you truly will be there!"

He followed the instructions, and was soon rewarded. I shall refrain from describing what followed. Suffice it to say that when he got back up off the floor, he appeared exhausted and fully sated.

After a while, he recovered, and went back to his booth to get another clyster. He emerged wreathed in smiles.

"Cartlin, can you provide other such experiences? And then paint them? I have visions of turning the whole west wing of this place into an art gallery!"

This might have been a lucrative although time-consuming arrangement, but tragedy soon struck.

It would appear that Lord Humpingham was starting to enter something very like the final throes of dipsomania. How could this be possible, you say, if no one within living memory had ever seen him take a drink?

The key to the situation was in the clysters I have mentioned. It seemed that, in his libertine youth, he was in a position to be included in the will of a well-heeled but abstemious uncle. The only way the uncle would include him would be if he would sign a solemn pledge never to drink intoxicating liquors again.

This he did, to everyone's surprise. The agreement was very legal and very binding. If he had ever been seen to drink so much as a sip of wine on a social occasion, he would have lost every penny. But, there is another avenue for alcohol to enter the body, as a somewhat dissolute physician explained to him. That is through the anus, by means of an enema, or clyster. So, he got to have it both ways, gaining his inheritance and keeping his cherished vice.

***

When, at last, the installation of the mural was announced, it was celebrated in the grand manner. Everyone who was anyone in the county was invited. Since Humpingham had been generous in his philanthropy and was expected to be so in the future (especially in his will), everyone was eager to attend, or at least to make a pretense of it. The Vicar, for example, put in an appearance, but seemed a bit discomfited by the whole thing.

The wine flowed freely, but not to Humpingham. Instead, he had very frequent recourse to the curtained booth behind his chair. The conversation and the chamber music almost drowned out the sounds of the gin clysters being administered by His Lordship's faithful retainer.

The Zarrek device seems to reach into the brain and do things. I do not pretend to understand all the workings of the device, or what unknown effects it may have on a brain pickled by alcohol. I do know that advanced dipsomaniacs are often prone to illusions and hallucinations. The explanation for what happened next may probably be found in that body of facts.

The kitchen staff brought forth the main course—a huge roast pig, complete with an apple in its mouth. As they sat it on the table, Humpingham's eyes became glassy. His respiration was notably faster.

"Oh, Fanny," he murmured, "you've come back to me!"

With that, he repeated his previous actions when actually connected with the device, except that he was on the dining table before the elite of local society. When he finished, the main course of the banquet did not appear in the least appetizing, and His Lordship lay very quietly, face down on the table. Everyone sat in stunned silence for several moments, then Humpingham's personal physician came forward, checked his pulse, then looked into his eyes.

"I regret to inform you that His Lordship has passed on," he announced.

The place was in quite a turmoil for a few moments, but the butler and household staff took over and restored order. Everyone withdrew to the other end of the great hall until Lord Humpingham's remains could be disengaged from the remains of the roast pig. The Vicar said a prayer for his soul, and most present said "Amen" at the end.

The doctor confided that Humpingham was not too much to be pitied.

"You know, Cartlin, he always told me that the way he wanted to leave this world was in the arms of a beautiful woman. In his mind, that must have been where he was. And he did get to see the completion of," he glanced at the mural, "the, uh, artwork."

***

Some twenty years have passed since my encounter with Zarrek and my introduction to the device. It has enabled me to paint truly lifelike representations of grizzly bears, Indian ceremonies totally forbidden to outsiders, extinct creatures such as mammoths, and even dinosaurs, as those ancient reptiles have come to be called. My works reside in great museums and illustrate learned books. I am successful beyond my wildest dreams.

Still, something is missing from life. I believe it is the struggle, the thrill of the hunt. As my brain has become more attuned to the device, and it to my brain, I only have to make a mental request for a subject that I wish to visualize. If I have taken the device to the place where the subject actually existed, I will see its image. Somehow, though, there is not the satisfaction that I felt in the old days when I first came upon a subject out in the wild.

Then, too, there is the problem of the true ownership of the device. Certainly, I convinced myself that Zarrek owed me something for having rescued him. And I saw for myself that it was a spare, one of several in his baggage.

Finally, there was the action he took when he realized that he would be unable to find it. He announced that, it being lost, he was required to destroy it by sending some sort of electrical signals through the air which gave it the order to melt itself into slag. Officially, it no longer existed, but I presume that these signals are blocked by metal; I dropped the device down the bore of an old six-pounder cannon parked behind the fort, then recovered it later.

I could no longer live with these rationales. I still remember how to get to the camp, as well as how to gain entrance. I also remember that Zarrek indicated that he would return from time to time.

I have made up my mind. I will return the device to Zarrek's quarters, along with a note of explanation. In my note I will mention the increased stores of knowledge it seems to contain due to my use of it during my travels.

I have also been dwelling of late on my feelings of boredom and general discontent. During his night of debauchery, Zarrek mentioned that his organization sometimes recruits people from the places (worlds?) that they visit. He said it in a way that suggested that I might be a potential consideration.

I have travelled the world since those early days, painting vanishing ways of life on several continents, and assembling yet other acclaimed exhibitions. Even this has not been a remedy for my ennui. My conclusion is that this world is no longer enough for me.

I have just reached into my coat pocket and checked my supply of calling cards. I shall leave one with my letter, and hopefully, Zarrek will wish to get in touch.

CANYON CITY CHUCKLE
BY
L.L. HILL

Heston's glass eyes rolled as black flies buzzed inside the green sapphire orbs. A fly landed to drink in the mucous that drained down his porcelain cheek. He blinked, feather lashes fluttering as he tried to focus. Chestnut hairs of his horsehair wig quivered.

A chuckle rasped from Emil the innkeeper's belly and out of whiskered jowls. "Flies is bad this year." He stated the obvious and scratched a sweat stained armpit.

Gwendolyn's North Sea grey green eyes scanned from Heston to Emil. That chuckle had the nervous but determined timbre of single men met in Egypt, Persia, India, Thailand, Japan, and home in England. Behind a façade of kindness, what they wanted was neither moral nor legal to any but themselves.

Heston's joints squeaked as he shuffled his boots. Basalt and clay cliffs dropped sheer to a placid beaver pond, held across the breadth of the Yukon River by dams built of trees and boughs by mammoth resident beaver. Water cascaded over a nitro blown break in the lower dam.

The giant beaver, as long as her brother Merrell was tall and much wider, was not the reason she opted not to bath in the pond. "If she wanted water, she'd have to haul it," Emil had gloated, eyes on her bust. Gwendolyn preferred to be unbathed and was still cleaner than the dirty lout.

"Give me a minute, Heston," she said squeezing a rubber bulb as she opened a vent behind the curves of a china ear. What Merrell had done with an abacus, gear wheels, steam motor, rubber and clay astounded her every day. She released the bulb and felt vibrations as flies sucked in. "One more."

Heston grunted and flexed his rubber fingers. Just like she had taught him to relax, intake of air with extended fingers, regularized compression with curled fingers to exhaust a puff of steam from his nostrils.

Gwendolyn squeezed the bulb to blast the flies out. No point in robbing the local population of bats or birds of their dinner, she thought as she stepped to place Heston between her and the smelly bulk of Emil.

Whiskers twitching, a beaver peered over the tooth scarred cottonwood of the lower dam near the break. He disappeared and returned, long teeth around a tree trunk. With a flip and twist the beam lodged in place and the flow reduced to a trickle.

Gwendolyn smiled, her russet curls ruffled by a gust. Determination and ingenuity on a large scale but not mild mannered. This beaver was as determined as any gold miner to hold a stake.

Emil growled his jaw to a square jut. Gossip said he had won Canyon City in a card game because he cheated. Others that the original city builder had lost the card game to be free of the beaver, selecting Emil for his successor because of a threat made to his wife.

No amount of nitro would dislodge the giant rodent's architecture; only a jar thrown down an open throat would have any effect. She hoped the beaver had a strong gag reflex and imagined Emil spiraling in the air with a pictured landing on a boggy shore. A smile curled one corner of her lip.

"Where did Merrell go?" Heston teetered as he stepped around a cluster of head-sized, pink-fleshed mushrooms that sprouted beneath a gold leaved birch to see more of the grounds and surrounding bluffs.

Emil snorted and lumbered away to storage shed. No doubt her pastor father would have something to say about her wish to see him blown skyward by nitro. Perhaps some wishes were too extreme to come true. Heston twitched a mosquito off his painted eyebrow.

"He's looking for a way through," she said. "Or around, or over," she finished with raised eyebrows.

"Is that Merrell?" Heston manually adjusted his binocular vision to the top of the opposite cliff.

"I hope he has no intention of flying," Gwendolyn murmured as her brother stood feet together, arms flapping. Arms that long might fly with a great coat spread, she thought.

"He's not going to jump, is he?" Heston swayed on the tips of his muddy boots.

"I doubt it. Merrell has proven to be quite attached to life," she answered.

"He, he..." Steam puffed out leaving a soot ring around Heston's nostrils. "He quite gets up to things, you know, his workshop, inventions, his travels." Heston looked away from Merrell to the shed Emil had gone into.

Gwendolyn followed his gaze and looked back at Merrell again. Perhaps he had crossed the river in their long boat or had dared to meet the giant beaver on its dam. Little more than a year ago he had stood still in a desert gloaming as a maned lion watched him with fire flicks in its eyes. These Yukon beavers were almost as big as hippos and just as volatile.

Merrell stopped flapping and stepped away from the edge. An eagle soared above him and turned into a mocking spiral. Able to match wit and cunning with anyone or animal, he had not yet attempted flight.

"Are we going to fly to the Klondike?" Heston scratched at a port behind his ear.

"We'll see what Merrell has in mind. The long boat won't make it past the beaver dams," Gwendolyn said as Emil came out of the shed at a heel to toe pace with a jar balanced in his uplifted palm.

"Well, everybody else has been getting past this," he sputtered and jerked. "Obstacle."

"Yes, on an expensive tram and switch to other transport on the other side. I'd have to leave all my sketch books and architectural drafts behind. Everybody but the goldminers are making money in this boom." She wondered if she and Merrell owned Canyon City by default if Emil blew himself up while they were here.

She looked at the leaning sod-roofed cabins, smoke threading up from a chimney like pus from a pore, limp brown grass limned with morning frost, the livestock shed with weepy longhorn cattle and one swaybacked horse too tired to swish flies away. Steel-wheeled tram carts rested empty on a rusted track, the next sternwheeler days away. An offal and manure stench hung in a miasma over the carbuncle in the gold birch and tamarack above the gully that Canyon City nestled in. As she watched, a pink mushroom wilted into a black lump.

A loud smack jolted she and Heston into an embrace. Emil wavered and bowed on the trunk wedged into the dam before he hurled the nitro into the pond and dove back to the muddy shore. A boom fountained water.

"Does a mud bath count?" Heston chirped. "That bet you had with Merrell?"

Emil stood up and wiped muck from his arms and torso, flinging it back to the ground. He was fortunate the beaver's tail hit the water and not him, Gwendolyn thought, and hoped that Merrell was on his way back. Face beet with rage, Emil was looking to vent on someone or something.

"Hey, there's Merrell. He got a ride, look at them go," Heston crowed, rubber finger pointing.

Paddles flashed a bow wake to froth. Merrell perched in mid-canoe, legs crossed and making notes with his pressure loaded pen in a leather-bound notebook. He paused, touched the skin hull, and wrote again as the canoe grounded on the pebble beach.

"Gwendolyn, Heston, this is Chuck and Lootz," Merrell gestured from stern to bow.

Lootz nodded, eyes black as the soot streaks drawn under his eyes rested for a half breath on her bosom before a long, smooth, brown leg stepped over the gunwale onto shore. He looked from Emil to Chuck, whose eyes were shaded by a conical woven hat set with copper discs.

Her fingers itching to sketch the hat and the boat, a warning bell chimed. She would ask Merrell if their wariness of Emil was based on their heritage or something else.

Graceful for all his height, Merrell stepped with care over a gut bundle, feet on ribs and keel to protect the skin hull. Behind him at Chuck's feet was a skin bundle.

"Is it possible to kill one of these beavers?" Merrell asked pen on his chin as he stepped around a damp spot.

"Skookum beaver," Chuck answered.

"Skookum is strong." Heston said.

Lootz peered into his glass eyes, followed a china cheek to Heston's collar and bowed over his rubber hands. He chatted in Athapascan with Chuck and they grinned at Merrell, admiration gleaming from every tooth.

"Plan is," Merrell glanced from Emil who scrabbled on his knees on the mud bank to his stoic sister and the two men. "Plan is to get the long boat adapted and travel on without delay." He tapped a diagram.

Gwendolyn folded her arms. "What are you not telling me?"

Eyes locked, Merrell twisted his neck and head. Gwendolyn refused to yield to his discomfort and stared in silence. Heston shuffled and blinked beside them. A raven gargled from a dead branch. Lootz slipped back into the skin boat and pushed them off to paddle upstream.

"Emil tried to keep a cousin of Lootz here." He closed his notebook and put it in a pocket. "She limped out, barely able to walk."

"I will protect Gwendolyn," Heston burbled through a steam cloud.

"As always my friend," Merrell clapped Heston's shoulder.

Surprised that Merrell had not included the ability to blush in Heston, rage burned on Gwendolyn's cheeks. "If he is so dangerous, why is he blowing the dam?"

"Does it make sense to blow the lowest dam when the long boat is above the highest dam? That beaver already has the hole half repaired and he'll have no nitro to do the top the way he's going." His smile was sad. "Like you, she was a beautiful young woman curious about other cultures."

Gwendolyn scrunched her nose. "Will you have time to build your escape invention?" No need to explore other cultures when each had the same percentage of groping males, she thought.

"Ah, I was designing a simple steam powered sluice. I've spent the last few day tanning skins and gut with Chuck and Lootz." He smiled, glad that she had been so absorbed with her sketches that she had not missed him. "We're almost ready to go. Heston, you took everyone's kit to the long boat?"

"Except the expendables." Heston's lips warped around the Xs.

So sweet the smile that quirked his lips, she wondered again why he had left his university to escort his young sister around the world. After Egypt, he had designed Heston as a perpetual watch dog. Gwendolyn squeezed her thumb in her fist, the brigand's knife flashing again. Gender had more bars than a gaol cell.

An odor of rotten eggs turned her head. Emil glowered at them, the worst of the black sludge wiped off.

"Thank you for all your efforts to undermine the beaver, quite a monster he is," Merrell said with a smile.

Gwendolyn stepped behind Merrell, pant skirt swirling with her disdain for groping eyes. "Let's go Heston, let the men talk." No doubt Merrell had a story concocted to soothe Emil's feelings long enough to get them free. Behind her Heston's boots beat a steady tromp on the shore path beside the tram's rails.

Beached to portage by the upper dam was the skin boat. Lootz and Chuck carried the skin bundle swung on a pole between them on the trail around the beaver's barrier. Gwendolyn picked up her pace to see Merrell's creation put together. Behind her, Heston puffed and trotted past a chickadee on a branch.

"Hello, you sing beautifully," he cheered as the bird flew away.

Gwendolyn remembered Merrell thanking a sparrow for its song when he was a ten-year-old boy. His psyche was stamped into Heston. What did that mean for the Creator of Man? Where did the Emils of the world fit in?

She stepped on chips as big as her hand hewn from cottonwood by the beaver scattered on the shore adjacent to the mud bank logs anchored in. No rippled V marred the calm of the pond.

"Did you know that dams and bridges have to be anchored at each end?" Heston prodded a vent to adjust the exhaust.

"Yes, there's a height and length ratio to anchor points as well. This dam also has a curve which slows the water, first near the shore which is slow moving shallow water, the drag slowing the fast-moving deep water in the middle," Gwendolyn pointed.

Chuck and Lootz paused in unrolling a skin to look at her. She folded her arms and smiled. White teeth, grey green eyes, auburn rolling hair, long legs, youth, it was still fun to stun men into gawping, groping being the problem.

"Brilliant and deadly," Merrell said as he strode up, not indicating if he referred to Gwendolyn or the beaver. "Let me give you a hand," he said to the Athapascans. He held the bow of the long boat to steady the bobs as Chuck and Lootz unrolled a double-layered skin under the hull.

"Why does it have holes in the bottom? Won't that let the water in?" Heston blinked feathered eyelashes against a swarm of flies.

"It's to let water and air out, Heston. Rather than venting all the hot air up, these tubes will pump hot air down which will provide more lift over shoals." Merrell unfolded a deerskin tube on a thwart.

Chuck and Lootz began to tie the skin to the long boat, knots used since youth in trap lines and travel. Gwendolyn looked at the scraped paint on the hull, knicks and scars acquired since Merrell and Heston had built it in the spring on the shore of Lake of the Howling Rock. Polished and oiled, the steam engine sat proud in the middle.

"Heston, could you grab the coal bags I sent you to stash this morning?" Merrell looked over his shoulder.

"This morning?" Gwendolyn choked her question out.

"You were still asleep, and Emil never follows Heston," Merrell replied as he hopped on board and tied tubes in place.

"Emil has followed me?" Gwendolyn stood arms akimbo.

"Yes, which is why we are leaving as quickly as we can. Can you help Heston with the coal please? It burns better than wood." With worry clenched jaw, Merrell double checked the strength of his knots and looked back towards Canyon City. "Yes, it has to be loose to allow the air to pump down but that stitching has to be as tight as possible, no leaks," Merrell confirmed to his Athapascan friends.

Another time, Gwendolyn thought, they would discuss this. She followed Heston into the gold leaved underbrush. Lips pressed together would keep her thoughts and feelings to herself. From under the branches of a windfall spruce, Heston pulled dusty bags of coal and handed two to her.

"There, Merrell wants us to hurry."

"He does."

Perhaps if he had shared his concerns, she could have helped with departure plans instead of sketching flowers and being leered at by a pervert. Heston almost stepping on her heels, they returned to the long boat.

"Excellent, almost ready." Merrell peeked through the jumble of logs on top of the dam. "No sign of Emil, one more trip for coal then."

"What about my clothes?" Gwendolyn looked at each man in turn.

"A few had to be left, Heston brought out most this morning," Merrell said as he threaded leather thongs around the smokestack.

All the men avoiding her gaze, Gwendolyn glowered at the thought of Emil's filthy hands on her silk hose and pant skirts. "Seems I do too much sleeping," she mumbled and followed Heston.

"The clothing left behind had been handled by Emil. I didn't think that you could wash it out," Merrell added.

She stopped and Heston looked back at her. Lashes blinked over his green sapphire eyes. It would be cruel to ask who had watched the desecration. Heston looked away, and head hanging down, traipsed down a moss and lichen covered trail.

A breeze soughed in the trees and brushed a tingle of fear from the nape of Gwendolyn's neck. Hands on the clothes she had hung to dry near the fire, fingers rimed with dirt poking at lace and silk. She grimaced.

"Here," Heston whispered. He looked around as if Emil were about to pop out of the cones of a pine.

He handed her two small bags and ignoring the soot, she clamped the bags under her arms. Returning, she followed the path they had taken and saw their footprints stamped in the moss. Heston was on a circuitous route back that went around trees but left less sign of their passage, a display of aspects to Merrell's character that she had never considered.

"Heston, where did you learn to do that?" She stepped off the path and made her own through trees and around rose hip laden patches.

"Do what?" Heston batted his eyelashes and meandered on.

Odd, she thought, that in trying to protect her she felt isolated, a rock protruding from a lake.

Worry about his smile, Merrell stepped out of the boat to meet them.

"This should get us close to Dawson City," Merrell said as he hefted the coal on board. "Let's get up some steam there, Heston." Long legs stretched, and he was back on board.

"Right away." Heston wobbled until Gwendolyn stepped out of his way.

"It's a pity we can't get the castor oil from that beaver," she said, watching as Heston handed coal bags up and stepped on a rock to climb on board.

Merrell grinned. "Think how long that would last."

Heston bustled at the mouth of the fire box, scooping shimmering chunks of coal in. Lootz had stopped tying on the leather shroud to watch him put gloves on. Chuck murmured a few words that produced a smile and Lootz went back to work.

"Would you like to fill the boiler?" Merrell was diffident.

Gwendolyn looked at her hands, clenched into her waist and took a deep breath. At least she was not exempted from sailing duties, she thought. One hand and foot on the gunwale, she swung on board and picked up a small pail. Lowered over the side, she tilted the mouth to catch the current and fill the pail. Drips ignored water rose in the fill window as she lugged pail after pail.

A flare sparkled in Heston's hands as he lit the fire box. He closed the door, orange flecks in his eyes, as the coals caught. Merrell went down each side to test knots that held the shroud with a tug.

"He comes," Lootz said with a nod to Chuck.

"Push us away please, Heston to the bellows. Thanks, many thanks to you both," Merrell said as he clasped their hands in turn. He sat and twirled an oar before dipping it into the water for a short back stroke to pull them away.

"They're very brave men, dealing with gold miners, Emils and giant beavers," Gwendolyn observed as Merrell rowed them away.

"He's running," Merrell said, long neck stretched.

"Sad day for him, first he has to take a bath and then he has to run," she quipped.

Merrell frowned. "We're not out of the pond yet. Heston, can you seal that leak?" Steam spilled out where a thong had worked loose in the damp. "Then back to the boiler."

Heston scurried to pull the leak closed and darted back to the firebox. No smile on his lips or Merrell's. Worry licked at Gwendolyn.

"Let's try the water lift." Hand off an oar, Merrell increased piston speed and opened a valve to force water into the skin sleeve beneath the hull. He dipped an oar in to turn the boat upriver as speed picked up. "Not sure how much distance we need, five furlongs was my guess with a full load."

Swans cackled, splashed, and fed near shore. She wished for their wings, shoulders aching from the strain of balancing to bring water into the boat and then standing to fill the boiler. A beaver nose, whiskers wriggling, stuck up over the dam. Serendipity, strain, and danger. She winced.

"This should be seven furlongs, Heston please raise the balloon," Merrell said, head tilted to confirm his shore mark.

Heston nodded and hurried to spread the sewn gut balloon across the bow. A gloved hand held the sides separate and twitched, his head turning between the boiler and the filling bag.

"Did you notice the beaver there?" Gwendolyn blinked splashed water from her eye.

"Can I get you to oil while the balloon fills?" There was a furrow between Merrell's eyes.

Gwendolyn looked from him past Heston to the beaver, grabbed the bulb and anointed every moving part before she jumped back to her pail.

"Let it go Heston, let it fly," Merrell called over the chugging pistons.

From tiptoes, Heston thumped down into a crouch. He wheezed himself upright and limped to the boiler. Shaped like a square sail, as large as the long boat, the balloon lifted above the bow. Lift from above and below had to be enough to get them over two dams.

"Water, water," Merrell yelled.

Gwendolyn glanced at the half-filled boiler window and hurled her pail into the white water that now frothed beside the hull. Speed and lift, she thought. Shoulders a dull ache she hauled and filled.

"Hang on," Merrell shouted as he turned a valve.

The long boat's bow dug and lifted. Balloon taut above, water spiraled out beneath the boat, breaking contact with the river. Gwendolyn looked down at churned froth, her white knuckles gripping the side.

"Just," Merrell said. Bark chewed off trees of the dam flashed beneath.

A paw with foot long claws flashed behind the stern and water sprayed over Gwendolyn. Merrell turned a valve back and the long boat skimmed down onto the beaver pond. She wondered if he had seen the swipe of the beaver's paw as they left the frying pan for the fire.

"Fill, fill, water and coal," Merrell hollered.

She and Heston scrambled to shovel coal and fill the boiler. From the corner of her eye, she saw Emil running along the shore waving at them. The beaver swimming behind the boat turned a gimlet eye from Chuck and Lootz paddling hard for the far shore to swim after the innkeeper.

"There's another beaver," Heston called, pointing at a head.

"There's likely a whole family of them, all angry right now. Boiler full?" Merrell grinned at her.

Guilt stabbed through her gut. "Yes," she yelped and dove for the bucket. Were it not for her, he would not be risking his neck in a pond of territorial beavers.

Heston squirted oil on connections as she pulled a bucket up and the boat lifted. Half the boiler steamed away as they soared over the second dam. She struggled to rise to fill the boiler as the boat settled on the rills of the shallows just beyond the dam and Canyon City.

"Do they eat people?" Heston asked as he shovelled a scoop of coal.

One beaver loped on shore while the other swam towards Emil.

"Looks like Emil's about to find out." Merrell smiled and patted the steam motor. "It worked, next port, Dawson City."

"Thank you both." Gwendolyn stretched her shoulders. "I hope that you don't ever have to save me again."

Author's Note: While Canyon City did exist in the Yukon Territory during the Gold Rush, giant beavers no longer made the territory their home. All characters are fictional.

NOT QUITE A DEER
BY
JONATHON MAST

Three nights without water. Silent lightning forked across the distant sky, so far away we couldn't hear the rumbling. The humid heat of the day refused to let up, even an hour after sunset. The herd was restless, refusing to bed down for the evening. The cattle lowed at the heavens, shifting on their hooves. Most of the boys were circling the herd, trying to keep them contained. It wouldn't take much for them to stampede.

Micah shoveled steaming beans into his trap. Ben had set up the campfire like normal, of course, and the boys were eating in shifts. It would probably be another sleepless night, but the *segundo* was sure they'd make Hope River tomorrow. Once the herd was watered, everything should be easier.

"They're real loud tonight," Micah said between bites.

Ben looked out toward the herd, sweat dripping down his face. "I haven't seen beefs this restless in a long time."

"Oh?" Micah kept shoveling. The faster he ate, the faster the next boy could eat. They tried to help each other out as much as they could, especially at times like this.

Ben shook his head. "Hope it doesn't come to that."

"The herd's stampeded before. We've always got them back under control in a few miles." Micah shrugged.

Ben sniffed. "Hope so, Micah. Hope so."

The herd screamed. Every single one called out to the sky, all at once. Micah leaped to his feet, plate in hand. He couldn't hear anything over the beefs.

Silence.

The fire crackled.

Micah couldn't move. He hadn't heard silence on the trail like this ever. It didn't happen. There was always some fool steer making a racket. There were all the bugs chattering in the weeds. Coyotes. Something.

No. Nothing.

Ben swore. "Micah, you stay here. You don't want to be riding out there."

"Like hell." He set down the plate and dashed for his night horse, still saddled from when he rode in fifteen minutes ago for his supper.

The steady chestnut shied from his hand.

"Come on, boy," he chided the horse.

It stepped back, its eyes white. It snorted.

Micah lunged to seize the reins in his calloused hand and swung himself into the saddle. "Come on!" And they were off into the night, toward the herd.

After just a minute, he met up with Freeman. "What's going on?" Micah asked.

Freeman shook his head. "No idea. They just up and stopped. Look at them! They're ready to run, all right."

Lightning lit the sky in a silent flash.

"I'll circle the other way. You keep them calm," Micah said.

Freeman spat. "Boy, I've been on more trails than you and your brothers combined! I know my business."

Micah rode away without another word. Sure, it was his first trail, but he was no fool. He knew how to calm a herd. He knew how to rein in a stampede, too, but he didn't want to have to. He should pass one of the other riders soon enough. There were fourteen of them, and they should all be circling the herd.

His horse's hooves thudded against dirt and grass. The beef, though. Not a single beef laid down. Not one. Even after three days without water, they should be tired enough that at least some would be tuckered out. They weren't moving, either. They weren't shifting from hoof to hoof. They weren't flicking their ears. They stood still.

Micah's breath came short and fast. Sure, it was his first trail, but his family always had a few head of cattle. He knew what was normal. He'd never experienced anything like it, and he'd never heard about anything like it in the yarns around the campfire. His heart thudded hard in his chest.

Movement.

There. On the hill, facing the herd. Silent lightning lit up the prairie. A shadow of movement before darkness returned.

Micah's hand shot to his pistol. Anything could make the herd run when it was this tense.

The back of his throat itched. They'd had to cut back on their water, too. His canteen had a few swallows of water in it yet.

What was out there? Hard to tell in the darkness from this distance. Probably not a rustler; didn't look human. Didn't look big enough to be a buffalo, either, thank God.

Another flash of light.

Just a deer.

Micah breathed a sigh. Some of the tension fled from his shoulders, but the itch in the back of his throat grew in intensity. His hand slipped away from his pistol. A deer. It would probably scamper off, silent and quick. Shouldn't bother the herd at all.

Shouldn't.

But something about the deer stuck in his head. The flash of light was so brief, outlining slender legs, body, antlerless head.

Another flash.

It had moved closer to the herd. The thing was fast. It stood still in the brief brightness, its head turned toward Micah.

Did it only have two legs?

No. Must have been a trick of the light.

Micah's hand wandered toward his pistol again. Tension returned to stretch across his shoulders.

His horse shied.

"No, we're circling the herd. Ain't no deer going to scare us," he said. He hoped he convinced the horse.

The chestnut hesitated, then obeyed.

Maybe one of the other boys would be coming his way soon. Should be, at least. If they were all moving, he should be meeting one of the others pretty quick, right?

Usually, they sang to the herd to keep the beef calm. No one was singing tonight, he realized.

Where were the bugs? Why weren't the cattle moving at all?

Another flash.

The deer stood not thirty feet away.

Just a deer.

No. It wasn't quite a deer. It had too many joints. No, not enough. Something about its legs. How many legs did it have?

It stared into Micah.

Darkness.

The beef stampeded.

The thunder of hooves swelled. The ground trembled. A bevy of pistol shots fired into the air—a signal from the other boys so everyone could tell what direction the herd was running.

The herd ran from the deer.

From the thing that was like a deer.

From the whatever-it-was that was staring straight at Micah. Even though the darkness had swallowed the thing up, Micah was sure it was still there.

His horse shook under him, and not from exhaustion. Or maybe that was just Micah shaking. Hard to tell.

The herd thundered away. The boys would be chasing them, trying to take the lead, to rope off the leaders and control the run.

Here was Micah, terrified of a deer. Just a deer. That's all it was. That's all it could be. He'd heard stories, of course. They all told their stories around the fire at night. It's what they did on the trail. He'd heard about the dead, the ghosts, the bloody tales. He'd heard about the not-quite-men who stole boys from the trail so their women mourned them. He knew about all that.

Ain't no one told him about a deer.

He should turn the horse. He should chase after the herd. Help keep it together. Get it back under control.

He should.

He couldn't move his arms. He couldn't kick his heels.

The humid air pressed in on him, squeezing his chest. His heart fought back. Breathing was getting hard. He coughed. Something scratched the back of his throat. Some of the beans must have lodged there.

Lightning lit the prairie with its cold and sudden light.

The deer.

The not-quite-a-deer.

It stood right in front of him.

His horse bucked. It kicked and screamed.

Micah fell out of his saddle. He snatched at the reins as he fell. They slipped from his fingers. His left foot tangled in a stirrup. Didn't matter. He was out of the saddle, and his horse ran.

He hung off the side of the horse, the ground pounding away out of control. The horse still screamed. Left foot in a stirrup, Micah clawed at his horse's flank.

The ground struck his head.

Breathe.

Breathe!

Micah inhaled sharp and fast. That's when the pain hit. He lay face-down on the ground. The dirt was cool against his face. Something rumbled—his horse. It was galloping away. Was he sleeping?

No. He had fallen. His thoughts came to him, gathered them up like a deck of cards that had fallen on the ground. His head hurt, and his left ankle burned. Something crunched inside his mouth. None of that was good. Hopefully, the boys would be able to find him after they regathered the herd. He could fire his pistol, of course, if he heard one of them close by. Should be fine.

Roll over. Staring at the dirt isn't going to help you, Micah.

He cried out as he flung himself over onto his back. He lay on a slight incline, his head toward the top of the rise. Above him stars shone bright until a border of darkness cut off their shine. The clouds. They were getting close. And the lightning was close enough now he heard its grumbling over the distant, distant herd.

Cold light flooded the grassland.

A dark shadow drank in the light about a hundred yards away.

The not-quite-a-deer trotted his direction.

He tried scrambling to his feet, but his head swam and his ankle gave out. He sprawled on the ground in the darkness. His pistol. He snatched at his belt. His pistol was there. He drew it. He tried drawing it. Something was wrong with his hand. With his arm. He was weak. Couldn't lift the weight of his pistol.

Another flash of light.

It stood in front of him.

It was no deer. Micah didn't know what it was. It was something else. Something older.

He tried to scream, but something in his mouth wouldn't let him.

***

When the boys found Micah's horse the next dawn, they knew something was wrong. Ben told them that Micah was gone, not worth searching for, but there was a loyalty among the boys. Most of them stayed with the herd and drove them toward Hope River, but a few turned back to find Micah.

They found him just an hour later. At least, they thought it was him. He looked like he'd been baked by the sun, untouched by predators for weeks. His clothes were tatters, his skin tight and brown against a withered frame. A small tree sprouted out from between his jaws.

On the ground nearby they found deer tracks, but nothing else.

CLAUDE
A TALE OF THE BAJAZID
BY
KENNETH BYKERK

Tak...tak...tak...

The pattern would not leave him. It had become an obsession.

Tak...tak...tak..., one...two...three..., tak...tak...tak...

The rhythm was simple, the meter consistent; three taps, a pause, and repeat eternal. This empty, unceasing repetition was spat out in a whispered, "Tak...tak...tak..." through yellowed teeth and a beard grown unkempt.

"Tak...tak...tak..., tak...tak...tak..."

Short, nearly imperceptible puffs of steam, breaths barely visible, pushed past his crusted and filthy whiskers, were torn and whisked away by the frigid blast that drove relentless up the canyon.

"Tak...tak...tak..., tak...tak...tak..."

His steps did not hold to the same pattern. They faltered and stumbled as he plod through icy snow knee-deep, a small, crude sled towed on a rope behind. He trudged on, slow and snow-blind, trusting to inevitability to achieve his goal. If he traveled west downstream, there was only one place he could end up, and he needed beans. He needed beans and candles, so downstream he went, stumbling and faltering and mumbling curses in between each insistent series of three.

The sun, newly risen over the crest of the mountain, was shining bright at his back, reflecting off the snow and turning the world before him a painful white. He had been walking for most of an hour. Most of that had been without aid of path through deep drifts and steep ground. Now that he was below where the Diski and the Idrar joined the Bajazid, he finally had the pretense of a path to follow, one carved wide enough and even enough for wagons to travel. There had been some steady work up the Idrar, and traffic necessitated at least such a road. The unbroken crust of snow before him spoke of how few had traveled it since the last storm. Behind, only his steps told of man or beast alive on the mountain, and that path terminated in a tomb.

He needed beans...
"Tak...tak...tak..."

***

It was near the Ides of December when the wind turned from bitter to brutal and snow began falling in earnest. By evening, the Kroeger brothers had wrapped up their daily endeavors and sat themselves before the small stove they had purchased and dragged up to their cabin. It was not much, neither the cabin nor the stove, but one kept the wind at bay and the other provided just enough heat to thwart the poor construction of its space. They did as they had done every night they had been on this mountain: Sift through their daily toil for easily culled grains and nuggets before placing the raw ore aside to be assayed. By the time they each crawled into their beds, low mangers stuffed with straw, the storm had turned into a tempest. Within the hour, the walls had begun to buckle in.

It was a hard-fought scramble when the walls came down and the storm chased them from their bunks. They grabbed what they could and fled in the fury for the safety of their mine. Once in, they struck the lantern kept inside and began to make themselves at home. They braced before the narrow adit poles and boards, scrap left over from the building of their doomed shack, to seal the entrance from the wind and drifting snow. Near the entrance, they built a small fire with the remaining scrap wood kept inside the narrow tunnel and after necessities were complete, they settled down to ride out the night as the howling of an angry wind stalked outside the safety of their cave.

The storm raged through the night as the brothers sheltered in restless sleep. When it was agreed the night should be past, when sleep was determined an enviable phantom elusive and cruel, they pushed through the barrier they had built to see what salvage could be made of their home. Snow covered the ground outside the adit, obscuring the world known the day before beneath a frozen blanket already two feet deep. Still the flurries fell, still the wind blew, but they braved the continuing assault to search for and salvage anything they could from their destroyed home. In that dull grey morning, with the sun obscured by low and heavy clouds, they rescued what they could and returned, poorer still, to the safety of their mine. Most of their small store of victuals survived the onslaught of the night, buried as they were beneath a sheltering wall fallen inward. The stove they salvaged and dragged with great effort into the mine followed by as much of their woodpile as they could before the storm increased beyond bearing. There they determined they would make their home, safe from the effects of the weather in their hole underground. Let the storm rage. Let it bury the mountain. They had shelter and they had their work to busy them through the storm. When the blizzard had passed, they could head to town and pick up what supplies they might need to rebuild, but until then, they were safe and dry.

***

He stepped with the slow certainty of the damned. This was a journey of necessity alone. Before the storm, before nature forced he and Claude to seek shelter below the earth, a trip to town was a welcome respite, one the brothers would plan for. On the edge of a wilderness where the effects of civilization are far and few between, the most provincial pleasures proved sufficient, and Baird's Holler held in its environs all a pair of lonely men might need. Now he walked alone, his path trailing behind him in a long line of broken snow. No expectations warmed his thoughts as he walked, no hopes of a warm bed shared for the night nor smoke-filled rooms hiding behind a hot hand and an open bottle. This was a trip of necessity. He needed beans.

"Tak...tak...tak..., tak...tak...tak..."

Provisions had run low. Beans were needed as were candles and kerosene. These things were needed. In days past, he and his brother would secure their belongings, lock up what they could and hide, buried beneath the boards of their shack, the treasure they had hoarded. Then they would travel with light step and expectations high. Now he traveled alone for Claude was gone. There would be no whores, no games, no drinking. No such desires remained. When Claude left, so did such hope. Now there was nothing left but the empty routine established of chipping away at buried rocks for treasures now bereft their promise. Now there was but nothing beyond the desperation of obsession in a lonely tomb and the ever-present need for beans, for beans and candles and kerosene and matches. Now there was nothing left but a broken, frozen trail in the snow and the soft "Tak...tak...tak..." of bitter repetition between curses for a brother absent.

***

The first days, if days could be counted in the hold of the earth, were replete with the activity of conspiratorial camaraderie. The two brothers laughed and joked about their situation and their forced seclusion. They pretended back to their youth the measures they would take to hide and to avoid the chores dealt out or the lessons the schoolmarm had assigned. A game was made of their predicament to pass the time, to provide amusements to assuage the empty hours. "Oh, the beating we will get when Papa finds us this time!" "Oh no, brother, Papa will never find this hidey-hole!" Thus, they kept their spirits best they could as they listened to the storm outside ebb and flow and flow again until they forgot at last to laugh.

He and Claude had been inseparable their whole life through. Born but a year apart, they were the last of a large family and overlooked in the disbursements of duties and boons. When one came of age and was called up, the other lied and together they soldiered a year in Grant's army. A decade more in uniform took them to places far and wide, ever west into lands untamed. When their service demanded their separation, they took theirs from the service instead at Fort Whipple in the Arizona Territory. Heirs to nothing but their names, they took up pick and shovel and followed the tales of gold in the Silver Mountains to their south. It was these tales that brought them to the Bajazid and to the town of Baird's Holler.

Now Claude was gone.

***

He did not feel anymore the ice caked within the insides of his boots. The frigid blast which stung his face he ignored. His thoughts were on one thing alone: Claude. Claude had left him. Claude had abandoned him and gone away, leaving him there in that hole alone to chip away at an empty fortune. Curses muttered, damnations directed to the one person in the world who had mattered, expressed his anger and disgust between clipped repetitions. The cold no longer mattered. Nothing mattered beyond beans and candles, kerosene and matches and yes, whiskey.

One foot in front of the other, the icy crust of the snow yielding to the advance of his knees, he walked. The sky was clear, cloudless, and cold. The sun, rising ever higher and brighter, remained devoid of heat in the face of the chill wind that swept the canyon. His eyes, accustomed so long to the depths of his hold, struggled against the reflected surface around. No signs of life, neither birds in the trees nor tracks of beasts large or small gave indication anything had survived in the world after the brothers had sealed themselves in. Even human habitation was absent at the only residence along the route. The house, belonging to a family with several children who would wave to the brothers whenever they passed, was abandoned. The broken structure sagged beneath layers of snow and ice, the windows empty and the door hanging on its frame. No thought of the occupants passed through his mind. No concerns for their absence bothered him. His thoughts remained fixed: bitter recriminations amid tedious repetitions selfishly focused. Claude was gone. Who mattered beyond? Who cared? Beans and candles and kerosene and matches and yes, whiskey. That was all that mattered, all that consumed him as he passed a silent sentinel, a frozen pillar piled high of snow that stood before the vacant door of that ruined house.

***

In the depths of a starless night, the music of the spheres remains unheard. Time passes in an eternal crawl, routine freezing in uncertain place the only markers of its passage. Their world was one glimpsed in faint illumination leaked from their stove and the candles placed down the length of their tunnel to aid their toils. Together they would crowd at the end of their main dig, chipping at the bedrock which had enticed their work. With but limited room to place tailings, they dumped them down a side drift they had abandoned early on, one which slanted downward near the entrance. A chimney pipe had been run out through the barrier, protecting them from the elements, and the melt ran down into this deeper tunnel. Here too they left their own waste, another indicator of time passed. Thus, they worked with small hammers, chipping in regular patterns at the veined stone that had arrested their advance, that became their obsessive hope.

Humor dies in darkness. Soon their conversations waned, and, in their stead, silence communicated the growing isolation they shared. Words were breaths wasted. Games they had played withered and soon silence reigned. Interest in the weather outside faded as the storms backed up one to the other until resignation of internment stayed their curiosity and hopes. Together they would crowd the tight end of their tunnel, each chipping tirelessly at the wall before them, the focused intent of their efforts leaving empty spaces where words had no place. Soon the only sounds were the shuffles of body function and movement and the soft tap of hammers chipping flakes of gold from a granite face.

***

As he approached the town of Baird's Holler, from the distance of a mile out, signs of life began to appear. The path began to be joined by others, footprints and hoofprints converging from disparate directions to merge and to press the snow down to hard, cold ice. Smoke blown from chimneys reached him on the rushing wind and soon sounds of frontier industry rose from the stillness about. The distant clang of the mill-stamp at the Mortenson Mine, the hammers of blacksmiths beating time over forges, and as he came over the last rise to leave the town spread before him, the complaints of life which fill the air of such frontier habitations.

The town was a scar amidst the world of white he had traveled through. The bucolic winter scene was betrayed by the ruin to which the town suffered. Swaths of the town had been razed, devastated in a fire the summer before and charred, skeletal remains of buildings burned poked up through the snow covering those abandoned places. The outlying neighborhoods where houses and hovels had survived were diminished by the ruination in their midst. Where once had been the impression of hurried growth, kinetic albeit haphazard and chaotic, now was revealed a poverty arrested and frozen, a promise stalled. Where the town still stood, the central hub of commerce and industry, few figures braved the frigid air and hied with intended step to limit their exposure to the wind and cold.

His goal, Devitt's General Store, lay at the far end of town, down near the bridge that crossed the creek and led to the mine which gave reason for the very existence of Baird's Holler. As he made his way through the frozen streets, mud arrested in carved ruts and broken by travel, none greeted him nor acknowledged his presence with more than a glance. He returned this refusal of recognition, his gaze locked into a stare far beyond his steps. None did he acknowledge, and none acknowledged him as he made his way past others singularly transfixed until he came at last to his goal.

**

Claude had shared everything with him and he with Claude. Theirs was a bond beyond the influences of greed or jealousy. Their silence was their last communion, their last shared connection. As they forgot about the world outside, they forgot the things that drew them together. Conversations stifled in confined closeness, the ever-present existence of another in increasingly isolated spaces drew forth slow but irrevocable resentments that had never existed before. It was this that led Claude to leave, to abandon this secluded cell. He recalled not specifically what it was that drew Claude away, nor did he notice at first Claude was even gone. In his solitary mania chipping away the stone before him, tak...tak...tak..., his notice left him until it came time to boil more beans and there were none to boil.

**

When the heat hit him, a thin green wave of nausea swept his body. He stood one step in the doorway, knob in his hand. Behind him, the cold sought entrance in forceful surges.

"Shut the damn door!" The cry was raised by more than one voice and each of those repeated their demands in earnest, increasingly unkind epithets thrown liberally in. He stepped forward and as he did, a boy slipped behind him and pushed the door shut to the cheers of the men in the room. There were half a dozen lounging on chairs and boxes beside a large iron stove. Another, apron-bound, stood behind a counter nearby. They all stared at him. He stared back. Their faces disturbed him, adding to the feverous sweat that sickened him.

"You need help, feller?" the man behind the counter asked.

He knew this man. He remembered him. He could not place the name. He knew the man and it was his store, Devitt's General Store, but he could not place the man's name. So, he just stood there and stared as the fraternal recriminations which had obsessed him gave way to an empty mind and a cold sweat. From beneath whiskers clotted with frozen mucus, that singular tattoo softly slipped, "Tak...tak...tak...".

"Feller, he asked you a question. You gonna answer it?"

None spoke, none he saw. The words were there, words he knew but didn't make sense. Soft, his mantra slipped his teeth. "Tak...tak...tak..., tak...tak...tak..."

"I think he might be dumb."

"I think you might be right."

Laughter rose from the vulgar things gathered. Words, more words than he could hear at once crowded each other out until one word singled itself: Claude. He turned his head ever so slightly in the direction his brother's name came.

"Hey, are you Claude or Hans? Which one is you? I say you is Claude."

"Tak...tak...tak..."

"That ain't Claude. Look at his nose."

"Why's he wearin' Claude's coat then, huh? Answer me that!"

"You're Hans, right?"

Hans made no movement, no nod or gesture of recognition. He simply stared while he absorbed that name he thought was his and repeated once again, barely audible, that which had consumed his thoughts. "Tak...tak...tak..., tak...tak...tak..."

"Ask him why he's wearin' his brother's coat."

"You ask him. He's right there, for chrissakes!"

"How do you know that's his brother's coat?"

"It is. I seen it 'afore, too. Recognize that coat anywhere."

It was recognizable and it was Claude's coat. It was a long coat, a light-gray canvas shell with a distinct tartan pattern in diverse symmetrical places throughout. The inside, padded thick, was of the same fabric, same pattern, as the bands decorating. It came with a great, padded hood, a luxury his own fur-lined leather jacket lacked. This he wore beneath Claude's overcoat.

"Maybe he ain't feelin' well."

"Nah, I wager he's dead."

"Why don't you ask?"

"Hey Hans? That's you, right? Where's you been? Where's Claude? We ain't seen or heard from you since the big one came through. What was that? Two months ago?"

"Tak...tak...tak..., tak...tak...tak..."

"You go simple up there? Where's Claude?"

"Tak...tak...tak..., tak...tak...tak..."

One of the men, dressed in clothes unfamiliar to labor, stood and walked toward Hans. Hans knew him, knew who he was but no name would associate. It was an empty face before him, a dead face, one waiting to rot and that face, haughty and severe, sought his eyes. Hans stared back with gaze wide, unfocused, seeing beyond the pale blue orbs that demanded his.

"You've been asked a question. Where've you been? How have you been holding up? Where's Claude?"

"Tak...tak...tak..., tak...tak...tak..."

"What type of answer is that? You feeling well? Where's Claude?"

This was something he understood. It was simple and clear, direct. "Claude's gone. Tak...tak...tak..." The words were flat, alien in his own mouth.

"Gone? Where? Where'd he...Holy God, man!" The man in fine clothes stepped back, his hand rising to cover his nose. "You stink of shit!"

The others passing their afternoon in gossip there recoiled together as the warming stench reached them. Exaggerated howls of disgust rose from those assembled. The reason was evident. Stained down the whole of his pants and trailing behind him was excrement, waste caked in his pants moistened by the long walk through the snow. The heat accumulated in that confined room was giving new life to old shit.

The imperious dandy began a wide, appraising circle to the rear of Hans. "Hans...I can call you Hans, yes? Do I need to remind you that one must lower one's drawers before defecating?"

Laughter and a torrent of increasingly crude assaults from lesser wits poured forth until at last the man behind the counter yelled, "Enough! I want that stench out of this store as fast as possible and you fellers aren't helping! My boy is right over there, and Margaret is in the next room with the girls! Have you no decency?"

"Y'all heard Mr. Devitt. Step it down, boys."

"Yes, Mr. Clayton," was the response of more than one, followed by the pleadings of pardon from Mr. Devitt.

"Thank you, Steve." Then turning his whole attention to Hans, Devitt asked, "What can I do you for today?"

Hans, who had stood golem-still during the deprecations of his character as if deaf, turned to Mr. Devitt behind the counter and said, "Beans. Tak...tak...tak..."

"You need beans? How much?"

"Beans, candles and beans. Tak...tak...tak..."

"All right, you got money? I don't just give things out here."

For response, Hans stepped forward and drew forth from his pocket a handful of gold nuggets, rolling them onto the counter. At this, those assembled braved the fecund air about the stranger and leaned forward for a better look.

"All right," the proprietor said without more than a glance at the gold himself, "What is it I can do you for? Beans, correct? Beans and candles? How much of each and what else?"

"You ain't really gonna..." one lurking ghoul began before Devitt hissed for silence. Undeterred, "I mean, he smells like shit."

"Tak...tak...tak..., candles and kerosene, tak...tak...tak..."

"Right now, he smells like a customer to me, Plinsky. If you find that offensive, you may wait outside." Devitt returned his attention to Hans, his eyes still avoiding directly the small pile of nuggets before him. "I'm sorry, Mr. Kroeger, is it? You said candles and kerosene?"

"Matches. Tak...tak...tak..., tak...tak...tak..."

"Beans, candles, kerosene, and matches. We'll get that for you right away, Kroeger. Do you mind perhaps stepping back some?" Devitt waited for an answer, staring into Hans' unresponsive face as Hans stared back in blank repugnance. After a stressed pause, realizing no true response was forthcoming, Devitt turned and raised his voice. "Timothy! Lionel!"

Two boys, both on the edge of the change that would carry them to manhood, came hurrying from the depths of the store. One, the boy who had shut the door, was a junior version of the proprietor down to the sandy blond hair. The other was as dark as the first was pale.

"Get Mr. Kroeger here a ten-pound, no, make that a thirty-pound sack of beans." Turning to Hans, "You got a way of carrying that much?" Then, after craning his neck toward the window and seeing the sled on the boardwalk, he turned back to the boys. "Lash it down tight to his sled. He's got a walk ahead of him and his money's good, got that?"

"Yessir!"

"Yes, Mr. Devitt, sir!"

Off the boys ran to get their intended burden and cord.

"Now, let's see about the rest of that list..."

"Whiskey, tak...tak...tak..."

"Whiskey, yes, we'll get you some of that, too."

Devitt busied himself, stepping quickly from the counter and the foul air gathered there. This left Hans standing alone with an audience of half a dozen bags of breathing flesh staring at him in stalled silence. Presently Clayton ventured to break the impasse. "So Hans, you ain't said where Claude went off to. He doing well? He get sick? Did he just up and go? I thought you boys were thick as flies on butter."

Hans just looked the man in the face and softly slipped the same three syllables in unconscious repetition.

"When you're being spoken to, answer. Where's your brother?"

"Claude's gone," came the reply followed by that ever-present tak...tak...tak.

"Maybe Claude's gone to the same place Hans' mind has?"

This comment from a short, bespectacled wit, brought forth a round of laughter from the loathsome assembly but elicited not a twitch from Hans. Magnanimously, Clayton acknowledged, to the delight of the nebbish ghoul, this coup in jest with a nod before turning his gaze hard on Hans.

"That ain't really an answer, Hans. Where'd your brother go? I mean, you're wearing his coat. Did he walk off into the snow without it or is there something you ain't tellin' us?"

"Claude's gone. Tak...tak...tak..., tak...tak...tak..."

Clayton spun around, hands wide, to those waiting in his shadow, "Can you believe this fellow? All he can say is 'Claude's gone,' and 'Beans and candles!'" This brought a fresh round of laughter, but the self-important intruder could not leave well enough alone. With serious mien, he looked hard at Hans. "Where's Claude, and if you just say he's gone again, we're gonna have words."

Hans' eyes focused, the distance in their gaze converging to arrest Clayton's own. The words that slid forth held a barely perceptible change, a directness of intent superseding the cold repetition involved. "Claude's gone. Tak...tak...tak..., tak...tak...TUK..." The last syllable was uttered with a definitive finality. Nothing further slipped from Hans' mouth for a full minute as he locked his gaze with Clayton's. It was only after Clayton, his expression slackening, shook his head and turned to his chair that the soft tak...tak...tak... resumed its whispered design.

The door opened and closed several times in the silence that followed as Devitt and his staff lashed a bundle of beans to Hans' sled. Added to that was a small gallon keg of kerosene, a jug of whiskey, and a tightly wrapped package containing candles and matches. The boys followed Devitt back into the store laughing, the adventure of running into the freezing wind for moments at a time appealing to their need for any break in monotonous routine. Devitt himself seemed cheered and brisked by the wind as he took off the coat he'd put on to step outside. He appeared pleased with himself, finally looking down to the gold on his counter.

"Well, Mr. Kroeger, we've got you set up quite nice. You shouldn't have any trouble with your sled on your way back. Is there anything else I can get you?"

Hans, who had been staring blankly into the store and over the heads of the six men now sitting somewhat subdued beneath his gaze, did not respond.

"Very well then, um, what you got here on the counter looks about right. Would you like a bill of receipt with this, Mr. Kroeger?"

Hans didn't answer. He had no need to. He was done. Without a word, he turned and walked from the counter without acknowledging the excess gold he had left. Behind him, whispered words reached his uncaring ears.

"You're robbing him blind, Devitt."

"He isn't complaining."

"Hell, Kevin, you know better than that. That must be a hundred times profit you're making there. Don't you feel no shame?"

"Fie on you, Caleb! Keep your numbers! You think he's coming back? You think we'll ever see Hans Kroeger again?"

And the door was pushed shut behind him by the young man who looked so very much like his father.

**

The path returned him slow and steady with the wind and now the sun at his back as he climbed higher and higher up the valley and up the mountain. Back through empty forest still undisturbed by life too timid to emerge. Up the Bajazid until the clang of the mill and the smoke from the smelter no longer disturbed his senses and intruded upon the blissful repetition that submerged his thoughts from the horrid present. Past the frozen house with its grim sentinel, past the separation of the Idrar and beyond to the confluence of the Diski.

In his thoughts, he dwelt bitterly still upon the disappearance of Claude. Together they had worked in silence for time uncounted, each tapping the rocks to patterns comfortable to themselves. Of the annoyances Hans suffered, the petty intrusions on personal space which served to sever their bonds, the one which mattered the most was found there. The repetition which had formed of habit with Hans, the tak...tak...tak... of his mallet was challenged in rhythm by the tak-tak...tak-tak... of his brother. There in the depths of that mine, deep against that granite focus, this incongruity of pattern slowly served to deteriorate this détente built between the two. For Hans, the tapping of his brother grew more and more unacceptable, more and more contemptuous. Tak...tak...tak... competed with tak-tak...tak-tak... in the still silence of that tomb. The rhythms struggled against one another; tak...tak-tak...tak...tak-tak...tak... in discordant competition, distracting Hans' focus slowly and surely, grating on his nerves as he became less and less aware of the source of his distraction.

Tak...tak-tak...tak...tak-tak...tak...

Tak...tak-tak...tak...tak-tak...tak...

Tak...tak-tak...tak...tak-tak...TUK...

Tak...tak...tak...

Tak...tak...tak...

Tak...tak...tak...

And then there was no further discord.

***

Hans Kroeger pulled his sled through the adit of his mine, squeezing it and dragging it rough over the piled garbage within the entrance. From the package, he pulled a forth the candles and matches and lit one, placing it on a rock which held the melted remains of its predecessors. He then replaced the boards which had provided shelter, tapping above them briefly to ensure a fall of gathered snow above would help seal the door. Ignoring the remaining supplies on the sled, he took another candle, lit it, and crawled back to the very end of the tunnel. There in that dim glow, he took up his small mallet and began tapping once again on that tombstone before him with a regular, comforting, and uninterrupted pattern.

He squatted thus at the termination of his tunnel, chipping away at an unyielding stone until the new candle beside him was half consumed. He tapped with focused clarity on the goal before him, the only truth that remained. He tapped and tapped until hunger reminded him. Taking the knife kept nearby, he pulled away the denim fabric that barred his progress and cut away at the cold thing beside him. He cut and tore at the meat until a piece pulled free. Then, with his jaws keeping time, oh, sweet, perfect time to his mallet, he resumed his slow assault on the stone.

Tak...tak...tak..., tak...tak...tak...

NIGHTSHADE LADIES
BY
MARILYN "MATTIE" BRAHEN

W ylie pulled a bite of his chewing tobacco off and set his jaw and teeth to it as he rode his horse down the trail. He glanced at Tom riding glumly and slumped on his brown and white mare to Wylie's right. He couldn't figure why a young man like Tom, barely past twenty-one, could be so sanctimonious over the death of a useless, ornery prospector in California.

Sometimes Tom acted like a dandy, always running his fingers through his curly blond hair to straighten it, brushing the dust from his clothes and spouting on like a preacher about right and wrong. Wylie wished he were as young and as lean, instead of pushing fifty years old with a weather-beaten face like old leather and a balding head more wisps than hair.

And griping, griping, griping about Wylie's killing that vagabond prospector when he tried to hide his saddlebag of gold nuggets from them, but Wylie had his gun out and shot the old man dead. The prospector hadn't laid claim to his find yet, and Wylie promised to put his own name on the stake and Tom's, too, if the kid shut up about murder.

Wylie had his story all laid out. He was the one prospecting, and the old man came at him with a gun to steal his claim. Tom would be his witness and they'd be on easy street once they put the claim on paper, legal-like. But Tom wasn't playing along, and it angered Wylie.

They rode along Sunset Trail hoping to reach Shasta, the nearest town to stake the claim, by the next afternoon, maybe bed down in this northern territory if they wanted a few hours' shut eye.

The night came on, that saddlebag full of the stolen loot against his horse's side making Wylie smile and not a bit sleepy yet. Sunset Trail had been sort of empty except for dried and cracked landscape with few landmarks along the way. No signs of the town anywhere until they rounded a bend, and what they saw was unexpected. A large, two-story log house loomed before them up ahead with a wooden-post fence around it and a small barn and corral with four black horses inside. As they neared the house, its door opened and a large-breasted woman wearing an alluring blouse and skirt, both bright scarlet, came out to greet them. She smiled up at them as they dismounted and tied the reins of their horses to the fence.

"Howdy, gents. Care for a little rest and relaxation. This here's Nightshade House, and I and my girls aim to please you weary travelers."

Wylie took in her coal-black hair, her voluptuous figure, her comely face and red painted lips. She wasn't all that young anymore, closer to his age. Tom was looking at her warily. Wylie almost laughed. Hadn't he ever seen a whore before? "Well, ma'am, we're clearly obliged to accept your invitation." He hefted the saddlebag over his shoulder. "And we can pay for our pleasures." He grinned.

The woman smiled back. "My name's Lucille and I'm in charge here."

"Well, I'm Wylie, Lucille, and this here is Tom, traveling with me."

She glanced approvingly at Tom. "Well, you and Tom come on in and meet my girls and have something good to eat. We've got beef stew, potatoes and biscuits all waiting for you." She laughed. "The girls are for dessert if you're still hungry."

They followed her into the parlor where four other younger girls in scanty clothes lounged on the sofa and chairs, giggling at him and Tom, who turned red as a beet when he saw them.

Wylie grinned broadly and sat down next to a busty brunette, flinging his arm around her shoulder. "I think I'm aiming to have my dessert first!" His free hand dived onto her ample breast and squeezed it, his mouth going for her cheek, then mouth. "What's your name, sweetheart?"

"It's Annabel, and ain't you the feisty one, darlin'?"

"I've got a rising feeling that just can't wait, Annabel, honey. Why don't we just go upstairs and have a little love nap before we eat?"

She giggled and pushed him away playfully. "Don't be so impatient, sugar. Your friend ain't hungry for dessert yet."

Wylie laughed. "I don't rightly think he knows what to do with ladies like you."

He felt a tug at his arm, just as his hand was attempting to slip under Annabel's skirt. He turned. Tom yanked his arm away more forcibly than he thought Tom could for such a skinny fellow. Wylie pulled his arm back from Tom's grip. "What are you doing, boy?"

"Trying to teach you some manners! Let's go in and eat, or the food won't be warm."

Lucille intervened. "Seems Tom is hungry, Wylie. You'll have lots of time afterwards for your just desserts." She smirked.

Disgruntled, Wylie shot a nasty look at Tom but rose from the sofa and nodded.

Lucille led them all into the dining room where a large table was set with bowls of food and pitchers of beer, plates and cups and cutlery set for eight. Lucille took her place at the table's head as Wylie and Tom sat beside each other in chairs on the left. The four pretty prostitutes sat across from them, amply filling their four chairs and leaning over the table invitingly as they watched the men fill their plates and cups, but took no food themselves.

Wylie glanced at the saddlebag on the floor at his feet. He'd make sure no one toyed with it as they ate, then had their fun and went on their way.

"What brings you fellows our way?" Lucille asked.

Wylie answered. "Came from Nevada to do some prospecting. We found gold and we're heading to Shasta to stake our claim. Right, Tom?"

Tom hesitated before saying, "I reckon that's our story."

One of the young whores, a blonde, reached across the table, nearly touching his hand, pointing at him. "You look unhappy, handsome. Gold makes you cry, huh?"

He shook his head, suddenly wanting to talk. "Had a hard life up till now. Never knew my pappy and my maw died about two years ago. Was working as a ranch hand when Wylie here, he was working the ranch, too, asked me if I wanted to travel with him to northern California."

Annabel, the brown-haired beauty, slid him a sly look. "And you and your buddy struck gold and you're rich now."

Wylie finished his meal and belched loudly. "As long as no rat tries to jump our claim and steal it from us. Well, I guess I'm about ready for dessert," he leered.

Lucille regarded him quizzically. "Well, we've got one other boarder who wants to fill himself up with that which satisfies the soul first."

Wylie glanced at her suspiciously, but he blanched with shock and terror as an old man came through a back door and stared at him.

Tom reacted swiftly, staring at the blood stains on the man's shirt where Wylie's bullets had ripped into his heart and chest. "God have mercy on our souls!"

"Yes," said Lucille, "I do believe you would want that right about now." Her girls giggled at them, but their eyes held a hard and vicious gleam.

Tom stood up abruptly, his chair falling back. "I didn't want no part of it, mister! Honest to God, I didn't. I didn't know Wylie would kill you for your gold!"

"Shut up, Tom!" Wylie snarled, his voice low.

The old prospector confronted Tom in a gravelly voice. "Yet you were going to back his story up, son."

Tom gulped and stole a look at Wylie, not moving from his seat, his hand inching to his gun in its holster. Tom wondered why Lucille hadn't asked for their weapons.

"I wouldn't do that if I were you." Lucille now trained her own gun on Wylie. Wylie lifted his hand, palm out to her.

Tom looked the dead prospector in the eye. "I told Wylie that to keep him from shooting me. He wouldn't have let me live if he thought I wasn't going to back his claim in Shasta."

The prospector laughed. "He would have killed you anyway. We're doing you a favor, killing the guilty first, here at Nightshade House. It sits here waiting for sinful men, liars, cheats, and murderers to come along and get judged. These ladies—" he waved his hand at the five women— "they serve both a higher and a lower power. They served their time on Earth, and now they take those guilty of sin down to Hell. You might say they're escorts to Hell. And I'm called to this court as the witness to your sins. And when I'm done this testimony, I get to claim my just reward, which is a bit higher than yours will be."

"Wait!" Tom shouted. "I didn't do anything. I didn't expect Wylie to kill you, and I sure as hell didn't approve of it. I was just trying to stay alive until I could get away from him."

Wylie recovered from his shock enough to shoot him another dirty look. "You yellow-livered milk sop."

The prospector coughed. "I ain't finished my testimony." He received their silence and continued. "I was minding my own business, checking my gold in my saddlebag before settling down for a good night's sleep before heading to Shasta myself to stake my honest claim, when this varmint—" he pointed to Wylie— "comes riding up. He don't even get off his horse but pulls out his gun, aims, and shoots me. And the last thing I see and hear before I pass out and die, is that young man shouting at him, 'Don't!' The young man was not expecting it; his face was damned terrified at this bastard's crime. Then everything went dark on me, like I was deep asleep until I woke up here and met you fine ladies to aid in your verdict. What's your name again, son?"

He answered in a breathy whisper. "Tom."

"Well, you ain't guilty, Tom. But he is, and his punishment may commence when you ladies is ready."

Wylie jumped up, knocking his chair over, and fled into the parlor, but no further. All doors into the Nightshade House were barred, the windows barricaded. Tom looked at him helplessly and horrified. Wylie grabbed his gun from its holster, grabbing Tom's arm and gripping him forcibly beside him with a strength borne of fear. He placed the muzzle of his gun against Tom's head. "I ain't going nowhere but away. You whores better open this door or I'll blow Tom's head off. That young blonde took a'hankering to him. You don't want her bawling her eyes out over him, huh?"

They were all in the parlor now. "Go ahead," the prospector laughed. "Blow his brains out!" They all watched him expectantly while Tom sucked in his breath and tried to pull away.

Wylie growled and pulled the trigger.

Nothing happened. Wylie pulled it again and again, furiously, only harmless clicks sounded. Tom slumped with exhausted relief.

Wylie cursed, stared at his gun and said, "What the hell—?"

Lucille opened her hand, revealing six bullets.

Wylie stared at them. "*How* the hell—?"

"Yes, exactly," said Lucille.

The sneers on Lucille's and her Nightshade ladies' faces turned demonic as they advanced on Wylie. He threw his gun at them, looking at the stairs going up to the bedrooms and bounded up. They followed him, not so much climbing the stairs as flying up them like birds of prey.

Tom, weak with shock, remained standing in the parlor with the prospector.

"You all right, son?" the dead man asked.

From the floor above, screams blasted the Nightshade House, along with Wylie's short-lived prayers, moans, and sobs. Then silence filled the house. The old prospector nodded. "Judgment's been carried out." He looked at Tom, still standing shakily. "The Nightshade ladies are all gone now. Why don't you bed down on that comfy sofa, boy, until morning. Then you can get on your way. Things will go better for you, son. I promise you."

Tom walked woodenly to the sofa and sat down.

The prospector went into the dining room and returned with his saddlebag of gold. He opened it and drew out two nuggets of gold and threw them into Tom's lap. Then he closed the saddlebag and hefted it onto his shoulder. "I'll be taking the rest of this with me to a new destination. God be with you, son." The prospector and his loot slowly faded before Tom's eyes.

Too weary to get up, despite his intense desire to flee the house, Tom fell onto his back on the sofa and passed out.

He awoke at dawn to the painful ache of sleeping on the hard-packed soil along Sunset Trail. The house was gone, as if it and its inhabitants never really existed. Wylie was gone, too, although if Tom had dreamt the whole thing, where was Wylie?

Both of their horses waited patiently nearby for their riders. The old prospector's bag of gold was missing from Wylie's.

Tom pulled some beef jerky from his saddle bag for breakfast and drank from his canteen. He waited an hour, calling for Wylie. Hoping he didn't answer.

Shaking his head at the mystery, he reached into his pocket to pull out his bandana to wipe the summer dust and sweat from his face. He also felt something hard inside the pocket.

He drew out two gold nuggets.

He saddled his mare and tied the reins of Wylie's horse to his saddle to follow behind. He mounted the mare, and holding the nuggets, bowed his head and said a prayer for the souls of the prospector and all the Nightshade ladies.

Then he headed for Shasta, hoping the beauties of the trail would refresh and heal his own soul. He knew where that gold had come from, but nothing in this world—or any other world—could make him go back for more of it.

AND HELL FOLLOWED WITH HIM
BY
JASON J. MCCUISTON

The black stallion pawed the sunbaked earth as Gideon Cain surveyed the desert valley below. He had finally come to Purgatory. The mining town was a small huddle of adobe and sun-bleached wooden buildings and was on its last leg. From his vantage, Cain could see the towering structures of the abandoned copper mine on the hill above.

The town seemed to cower from the ancient horror contained therein.

A gust of hot air sent a tumbleweed fleeing before a whirling dust devil, skidding through the sand and cacti. Somewhere in the brush a rattlesnake announced displeasure at the disturbance, causing the stallion to shy.

"I hate the desert." Cain spurred the horse down the hill and followed the buzzing telegraph lines and rusted train tracks into town. The heat didn't bother him, nor did the blinding sun, nor the choking thirst it inspired in a man. The desert reminded him of Palestine, where his nightmare had begun. But since the end of the War Between the States, Cain had found himself driven ever westward, spending over twenty years among the pueblos and peaks of the Mojave.

One of the last of his kind, Cain was hunted, and the noose drew ever tighter. His time was running out, but this town held the promise of escape and final release.

A pale wooden sign just below the local Boot Hill declared the town as PURGATORY, NV. POP: 42. The "42" was in relatively fresh black paint atop a patch of white. A pair of vultures perched on the cemetery's crooked gate gave him stink eye as he rode into town, sizing him up. The first person he saw on the town's only dusty street, the black-clad undertaker, gave him the same look.

Cain smiled, sending the man retreating back inside his bone-white parlor. Ordinarily, he would have said the mortician would be moldering in his grave long before Death ever came for Gideon Cain. But not today. Less than twenty-four precious hours were left to him if he didn't end the curse he'd borne for eight centuries.

That curse had brought Cain to the isolated town on this mid-September day in 1897.

Purgatory lived up to its name. With all the accoutrements of a thriving boomtown—a livery stable, a general store, a pair of saloons, a doctor's office/barbershop, and even a church/school building, surrounded by a scatter of adobe-and-timber houses—it gave the impression of prosperity. But closer inspection showed that most of the buildings had boarded-up windows and hadn't seen a coat of paint in years, or, like the falling-down hotel and the gutted train station, had been abandoned altogether. The town was trapped between life and death.

A condition to which Gideon Cain could well relate.

He tethered his stallion beside four horses outside the Number 6 Saloon, just across from the company store. He recognized the horses—a palomino, two roans, and a paint. He'd followed the men riding them from the rail station in Carson City, Pinkertons dispatched by the mining company to collect the "profits" from Purgatory's dwindling wealth.

Cain's spurs jingled as he stepped onto the wraparound porch and dusted the trail from his black slouch hat and long coat. He heard boisterous laughter from within the saloon, the jangle of an out-of-tune piano, and the crooning of an out-of-tune singer. He smelled tobacco, booze, and sweat clinging to every surface inside the building's front room. Unhooking the thongs from his guns' hammers, he stepped through the batwing doors.

The singing and the music ground to a clunky halt as every eye in the dim saloon turned on him. A thin man with a handlebar moustache stood behind the bar, beneath a gaudy odalisque. A trio of middle-aged locals, probably ex-miners, sat at a table trading coins and cards beside the front window to Cain's right. The four Pinkertons, bottles and glasses in hand, stood with a pair of scantily clad women beside the upright piano. This was nestled in the corner of the wraparound stair opposite the door. The heavyset pianist wore a careworn top hat cocked at an angle, a hand-rolled cigarette in his yellow teeth.

"Howdy, stranger." The barman smiled nervously. "What can I get you?"

Cain ignored him and took a step into the saloon, letting the doors flap behind him. He glared at the Pinkertons. "Let me guess. The till was short this month. Again. So the four of you have offered to cover the difference in exchange for 'favors.'"

The apparent leader dislodged himself from the more buxom of the two women and stepped into the center of the room, his brown bowler low over his pale blue eyes. He raised the bottle of rotgut like a weapon. "What's it to you? Who the hell are you, anyhow?"

"Me? I'm Gideon Cain."

Sobriety crept over every face in the room. Cain had earned a reputation for cruelty during the War, but the atrocities he'd committed in the decades since had put his wartime escapades to shame.

"You're... a wanted man," the Pinkerton in the bowler said. His comrades spread out behind him. The pianist and the soiled doves wisely cleared out. The old-timers moved as far away from Cain as they could without running.

"With a goodly-sized bounty on my head. Money like that could set a man up for a while. But, in all fairness, I should warn you: I won't be taken alive."

The Pinkerton in the bowler carefully placed the bottle of whiskey on the bar. No one moved.

A fly buzzed somewhere in the room.

The Pinkerton on the far left was the first to draw. Grabbing the Colt Thunderer in the cross-draw holster on his hip, he was dead before the short barrel cleared leather. His three companions followed in a matter of heartbeats as Gideon Cain filled the saloon with fire, thunder, and blood.

His Colt Walker Dragoons smoking as the four dead Pinkertons bled out on the floorboards. Cain had not moved, not even when a pair of bullets tore through his right shoulder and left hip. The pain was fleeting, the wounds sealing up before he felt the impact.

"Anyone else feel like getting rich?"

One of the girls spat on the dead Pinkertons before kneeling and fishing out a wallet. "Damn Pinks."

The barman set a dusty bottle of fine whiskey on the table with a clean glass. "Mr. Cain, I know you can't stay for long and they'll just send more in a couple days, but you just done us here in Purgatory a mighty fine service."

The old-timers eased to the doors at their back. Cain holstered his revolvers and let them go. He knew they were heading for the local lawman, but that was part of the plan. He needed a pure soul if he was to finally be free. Any man willing to dedicate his life to upholding the law in a godforsaken town like this might just have that kind of purity. Or, more likely, would be desperate and corrupt enough to gladly throw in with Cain, trading a local soul for Purgatory's freedom from the demon in the mine.

Cain accepted the whiskey as the undertaker rushed in to earn his keep, and his share of the dead Pinkertons' wallets.

Staring into the mirror behind the bar, Gideon Cain understood why neither of the sporting girls had come to congratulate him. Despite years of riding the high plains and desert valleys, his skin was still corpse pale and his eyes black as night. His short-cropped hair hadn't grown an inch in eight centuries. And though he couldn't smell it himself, an old Apache medicine man had once told him he carried the stench of the grave.

"Don't move, mister."

Cain had watched the lawman enter the saloon in the mirror. He finished his whiskey and put his hands in the air. "Looks like you got the drop on me, marshal."

Cain continued to watch the reflection as the dark-skinned man stepped forward. Revolver leveled at Cain's back, the marshal pulled the still-warm Dragoons from their holsters and slid them down the bar, well out of Cain's reach.

"All right. Let's go."

Cain kept his hands in the air and a smile on his face as they marched down the middle of the street. He noted a few curious faces at windows along the way. Cain touched the brim of his hat to each. "Not too many backwater towns like this would put a badge on a black man, much less a half-breed."

"About what I'd expect from someone who wore the Gray."

"I've worn just about every color of the rainbow in my day, marshal. And no offense meant, just an observation. White folks tend to get nervous around armed black men and Indians, in my experience."

They entered a solid adobe building with iron bars set in its small square windows. The word JAIL was painted in bold letters just above the words JIM BASS, TOWN MARSHAL beside a heavy timber door.

"Glad to make your acquaintance, Jim."

"Shut up and get in that cell."

Cain took off his hat and sat down on the cell's cot as Jim Bass locked him in. The jail was one small room with a smaller cage occupying one corner. The front wall housed the only door and two windows. The cell had one window overlooking the back. A hurricane lamp on the marshal's desk provided more light than any of these openings. By its glow, Cain saw a neat array of Wanted posters tacked to the adobe walls. Many of these had big red checkmarks across the hand-drawn portraits.

"Well, now I see where the lion's share of this town's prosperity comes from. Looks like you make quite the killing on bounties, Marshal Jim."

Bass smiled as he sat on the corner of his desk, his Remington still in hand. "And the reward for you might just bring in enough to hire us a preacher."

"An exorcist, you mean?"

The lawman's smile vanished.

Cain nodded at the unseen hilltop mine. "You figure you get rid of what's hiding in that hole up there, maybe Purgatory will come back to life?"

Bass nodded. "This town was founded by Forty-niners who stumbled on the copper deposits on their way to California. They decided to stake their claims here rather than go on and face all the competition at Sutter's Mill. In a handful of months, they were making more money catering to Gold Rushers than on the copper itself. That's how the town got its name. Somebody said it was like

Purgatory, somewhere between the Heaven of California and the Hell of Nevada."

"Then the mining company moved in and took over."

"Just made the place grow bigger and faster. At least until they discovered that... thing down in the mines in '65. But that was back before my time."

"Well, Marshal Jim, what would you say if I told you I could get rid of that demon in the mines for you? You let me out and take me up there, and I'll solve all your problems."

Bass frowned. "The mining company has sent in Pinkertons armed to the teeth, and the governor even called in the Army once. Bullets don't hurt the thing, and the mere sight of it kills grown men dead..."

Cain stood and got close to the bars. "You know what it is, don't you? I knew you had Indian blood in you."

Bass raised the revolver. "Sit down... My mother was Paiute."

"So you know that thing up in the mine is called Tse'nahaha, and that it's a giant demon that eats souls."

"How do *you* know that?"

"I know about lots of things like it." Cain smiled. "Let me tell you a story, Marshal Jim... You ever hear of the First Crusade? Well, I was on it."

Bass laughed, then his eyes widened when he realized Cain was serious.

"My brother Drogo and I were part of a conroi of knights who answered Pope Urban's call to drive the heathens from the Holy Land. After our victories at Dorylaeum and Iconium, we heard tale of a demon, what the locals called an Ifrit, living in a hole in the desert just outside of Antioch. Being young and stupid, nine of us went out there to kill it—ostensibly for the Glory of Christ, but in reality, to glorify ourselves.

"Which is probably why we failed. The demon didn't kill us, not outright. It mocked us and laughed as it cursed us to roam the earth for eight-hundred years, making war on the living, until Satan would drag us to Hell to be punished for our dozen lifetimes of sin.

"So, you see, Marshal Jim, I can't die." Cain did not tell him the whole truth as he pointed at the two fresh bullet holes in his clothing. Silver could end him just as quick as steel or lead could a normal man, as could some kinds of magic. And he feared the rites of the Church's holy exorcists, which would send him to Hell ahead of the appointed hour.

Bass narrowed his eyes. "That's why you're here, isn't it? You *want* to face that thing. But why?"

Cain told Bass most of the truth. "Because, while fighting for Hunyadi in Bulgaria, I met a Romani woman who told me that my curse could be lifted by... 'facing a demon in Purgatory.'" He did not mention the part about sacrificing a pure soul to it, however.

This time Bass did laugh. "Well, Mr. Cain, I will say that is one hell of a tale, and I thank you for it. But I believe I'll wire Carson City. Come this time tomorrow, you'll be somebody else's problem and we'll be placing an ad for a preacher in the big-city papers."

A knock at the door ended the discourse. A lovely dark-skinned woman and a boy of about five or six stepped inside. The smiling woman carried a covered basket against her flowing skirts while holding the boy's hand.

Bass turned at their arrival, smiling. "Annabelle."

"I heard about the shooting. I figured you might be spending the night here, so we brought you supper." The marshal's wife cast a nervous glance at Cain. When he smiled, she looked away.

The boy, however, stared at Cain with wonder and curiosity. Cain's smile widened as the marshal hurried his family out of the jail. "Now there is a pure soul if ever I saw one..."

***

The hardest part had been waiting, letting each precious minute fade away with the slow setting of the sun, knowing that tomorrow's dawn would open the gates of Hell for his soul. After eight centuries of what had passed for life, Cain now found himself without any patience.

He forced a smile while Jim Bass sat at his desk, eating fried chicken, cathead biscuits, pinto beans, and boiled potatoes. He feigned hunger and appreciation when the marshal put together a plate for him and filled a tin cup with fresh buttermilk before stepping to the cell door.

With the speed and grace honed from centuries of action, Gideon Cain came off the bunk. He blew a fine yellow powder off his palm and into Bass's surprised face. Cain had learned how to make the powder from a Caribbean woman in Baton Rouge years before. He always kept some hidden in his hatband for just such an occasion.

Jim Bass lay sound asleep in the spilled leftovers on the jailhouse floor. He did not see Gideon Cain don his hat before lifting the cell door off its hinges.

Cain knelt beside the unconscious lawman. He knew Jim Bass was a good man, but did he have a pure soul? Cain looked at the red marks on the Wanted posters. How many of those bounties had been collected on bodies shot in the back? What nefarious things might the marshal have done in order to keep the peace of his town? Had he justified them to himself, his family, and his community? There simply wasn't any way to be sure.

"And this late in the game, I've got to be sure." Bass's boy was the only sure thing Cain could think of at the moment.

The full moon crested the hills to the south. Purgatory appeared to be a ghost town when Cain stepped out of the jailhouse. He had bound and gagged the marshal. He could have killed Bass, but found himself reluctant to do so for some reason. He didn't waste time contemplating this as he strode down the street, headed to the Number 6 Saloon.

Through the saloon windows, Cain saw the bartender cleaning up by the light of a single lamp. It was a cool night, so the man had left the main doors open to air out the place. His tuneless whistling carried clear and shrill while he worked.

The whistling stopped at the sound of a spur jangling.

Cain stepped through the batwing doors and walked to the bar. As he'd expected, his Dragoons hung on a pair of nails just beneath the odalisque. A hand-written card pinned beneath identified his weapons with the date of "capture."

"Whiskey."

"B-but... I'm closed, Mr. uh, Mr. Cain, sir." The barman stepped cautiously toward him.

"And while you're at it, I'll be taking my shooting irons back as well."

"But—"

Cain lashed out. His hand closed around the barman's spindly throat. He lifted the man a foot off the floor before fixing him with his cold black eyes. "Forget the whiskey, then. But I'll have my guns, and the location of the marshal's house."

Tears bubbled out of the man's eyes, his face turning red.

"Look, barkeep, I ain't in no mood to waste time. If I ain't sacrificed a pure soul to that demon in the mine by sunup, then Satan himself is going to ride out of Hell to take me to eternal damnation." Cain pulled the terrified man close and breathed graveyard breath on his face. "I'm of two minds right now. On the one hand, I reckon I've killed enough in my time that I don't need to go adding to that tally with Eternity hanging in the balance. But on the other hand... What the hell, right?"

The bartender told him everything he wanted to know. Cain walked out of the saloon, his Dragoons in their holsters, the saloonkeeper weeping behind him.

When blades and bullets have lost their bite, one doesn't often find a need for stealth. Fortunately, in the long-ago days of his youth, Cain had known a girl in a village outside of Rouen. Her father had been one of the Duke's crossbowmen—and a light sleeper. Equally as lucky, the Bass residence was a single-story adobe with big open windows. Luckier still, the boy was sound asleep in the back room while Annabelle Bass read aloud to the family dog in the front. The dog had growled and whimpered, but Cain had made good his getaway before any alarm could be raised.

A small dose of sleeping powder applied to the boy's nostrils before taking him from his bed ensured his cooperation for the short, moonlit ride. Still, Cain had bound the child's wrists and ankles, as well as covered his head with a sack. No sense taking any risks, including allowing the boy to lay eyes on the demon before the deal was done.

The mine's structures jutted up against the starlit sky like the bones of a long-dead giant. Two riders on black horses stepped onto the trail just below the abandoned complex, barring Cain from his goal. The moon was already in decline.

Cain drew one of his revolvers while steadying the sleeping boy on the saddle behind him. He slowed his horse, but did not rein in. "You fellows have sure picked the wrong desperado to bushwhack, and damn sure the wrong night to do it."

He felt the fiery explosion of pain before he heard the shot. A flash of silver in the moonlight as the Colt Dragoon flew from his shattered right hand. The pain was so sudden and intense that he almost laughed, having long forgotten what real pain felt like. "Who the hell uses silver bullets?"

Realizing the shot had been fired from cover, Cain put spurs to horse and charged through the two riders. He swept the boy around to his front as he passed them. He couldn't afford a stray bullet robbing him of his prize. Another gunshot cracked behind him, the bullet zipping past his head. Cain hoped he could beat the riders to the mine's outbuildings, then take cover and pick them off as they rode into the clearing.

But the next shot struck his horse's head. The animal shuddered in mid-stride, its long legs losing strength and coordination. Beast and rider went down in a heap. Cain tucked the boy into his own body, shielding the child from the fall. This kept him from leaping clear and keeping his feet. He lay sprawled flat on his back when three black-clad riders surrounded him.

"Bonjour, little brother." The speaker had a Winchester propped on his hip. Moonlight glowed in his onyx-black eyes, on his face like polished marble. "Surprised to see me?"

"Drogo..." Cain pulled himself to his feet, broken bones resetting in loud pops and jerky motions. He made sure the sleeping boy was still alive and unharmed.

"So you haven't forgotten me." Drogo sheathed the rifle in his saddle and dismounted. "I thought maybe you had, since you didn't tell me about this place and what you came here to do."

"I told you about the prophecy three hundred years ago."

Drogo laughed. "When you didn't believe it, yourself. But you knew I was in Mexico and Ranulf and Rollo, here, were in Cuba. We could have joined you on this little quest. We are the last ones, after all."

"You mean you could have beaten me to the punch, freed the demon and yourselves while leaving me to be dragged to Hell."

"Isn't that what you're doing to us?" Drogo turned to fetch something from his saddlebags.

Cain flexed his shattered hand, almost relishing the exquisite pain pulsing up his arm. He chuckled, feeling a shred of humanity slip back into his soul. "I suppose it is. But, to be fair, I'm not the one who wanted to go find that Ifrit in the first place."

Drogo turned with a shrug. "Nobody forced you." With one quick motion, he looped a silver chain around Cain's neck and jerked him back to the ground. "Rollo, fetch the boy."

Cain gasped for air, his flesh sizzling at the touch of the silver noose. It felt like barbed wire digging into his throat. "What are you doing, Drogo? Silver bullets and now this?"

Drogo gave him a death's-head grin and held up gloved hands to show that he was protected. Climbing back on his horse, he looped the other end of the chain around the saddle horn. "No way out, little brother. We started this ride together; I reckon we'll finish it that way."

The three dark riders rode into the abandoned mine above Purgatory, half-dragging Cain behind them. They reached the entrance to the mineshaft, and the three riders dismounted. Rollo tossed the bound boy to the dirt like a sack of potatoes. The landing woke the child and his terrified wail rent the still desert night.

That scream stirred something in Cain. For the first time in centuries, he remembered fear. He recalled the night he had followed Drogo and the others into that dark canyon somewhere between Iconium and Antioch. He remembered how the Ifrit had billowed out of a tiny hole in the ground as purple smoke. It took the shape of a giant naked woman with eyes like stars, hair the color of midnight, and skin a glowing violet-indigo. Though beautiful in the most unholy of ways, her cruel laughter carried the cries of a thousand damned souls. Cain would have fled in terror had his pride not kept him rooted beside the others.

He imagined that same kind of soul-wrenching fear rampaging through the boy's mind, suddenly awakened, bound and blindfolded, torn from the safety of his home and family. Cain looked at the bullet hole in his right hand and felt a pang of regret for having brought the child into this nightmare.

Drogo shouted a challenge to the demon of the mine. "Tse'nahaha! We have come to parley! We bring you a soul in exchange for your help! The pure soul of a child to free you!"

Silence, save for the boy's muffled whimpers.

Cain took a deep breath, struggling against the pain in his throat. "Maybe this was a fool's errand after all, Drogo. I guess we should let the boy go and face our comeuppance like men."

Drogo tugged on the chain, dropping Cain to his knees in fresh agony. "This is your prophecy, little brother. Maybe you need to be the one to call up the demon."

Cain shook his head. "No. Let the boy go."

Rollo growled and drew his Peacemaker. "Hell with that. I'll kill the whelp before I give up on this last chance. Now do it or so help me—"

The ground shook and a deep rumble thundered from the mine. A howl like that of a gigantic coyote followed, twisting into the wail of a tormented soul at its ear-splitting crescendo.

And then the demon was before them.

Tse'nahaha crouched, gigantic and gaunt. The thing looked like an emaciated, leprous Indian with strands of greasy black hair dangling from its scabrous, balding skull. Huge, bloodshot eyes bulged from its skeletal face, its sagging skin glowing a sickly green. A black tongue slithered over yellowed fangs and blacker lips pulled tight in a rictus of demented glee.

It spoke in a voice of deafening thunder, but in a language Cain had never heard. The riders looked at one another. Drogo shouted again as he pointed to the child on the ground. "This is for you! Take him and free us from our curse!"

Tse'nahaha laughed. It was the same laugh of the Ifrit, and Cain was once again that terrified young mortal of eight hundred years before. He realized this was a terrible mistake. There was no bartering with demons, and this one was going to destroy them and take the boy as well.

Drogo and the others came to the same conclusion, drawing their revolvers and opening fire. The bullets had no effect. Tse'nahaha reached out a bony claw and snatched Ranulf from the ground before plucking his arms from his torso like a sick child torturing a fly.

The demon continued to laugh.

Drogo dropped the silver chain and ran for his horse. Instead of mounting, he pulled the Winchester from its scabbard, worked the lever, and fired. Tse'nahaha recoiled and howled as the silver bullet punched a clean, bloodless hole in its desiccated chest.

Cain struggled with the silver noose, scorching his hands in the process. Freeing himself, he looked at the bloody welts on his palms, then to the crying child curled into a ball at the monster's feet. Cain wrapped the chain around his right hand until it smoked, the pain almost blinding. Gnashing his teeth, he ran for the boy.

Rollo screamed as he was torn in two. The demon continued to laugh. Drogo continued to shoot. Cain grabbed the boy, tossed him over his shoulder. A giant bony hand descended on him.

Cain punched up with all his might. The improvised silver cestus drove a hole through the monster's palm in an explosion of glowing green goo. Tse'nahaha howled and recoiled. Cain pitched the boy behind a stack of old support timbers.

Cain turned to see Drogo reloading the Winchester as the demon swept him up in its uninjured hand. Drogo got off one shot, tearing a ragged hole in the monster's cheek just before Tse'nahaha bit his head off and spat it out.

Cain snarled in rage, remembering that he had once loved his brother. He remembered that he had once been a knight in service to God and His Holy Church. He gave the boy one last look to make sure he was safe, then turned back to the monster. Cain spun the length of silver chain as he charged Tse'nahaha.

The words that sprang from his throat surprised him: "*Deus vult!*"

***

Marshal Bass led a posse of six men up to the mine just before sunup. He was overjoyed to find his son safe and sound, if badly frightened, amidst the carnage. Bits and pieces of at least three men were scattered about the clearing while the broken body of Gideon Cain lay twisted beneath what appeared to be a giant human skull.

Bass held his exhausted son tight to his chest as the sun crested the eastern hills. A hot breeze stirred, then a gusting wind. Then a roaring dust storm kicked up from the valley floor. The men held their hats and hurried to find cover among the derelict buildings. Protecting his son and racing for a toolshed, Bass saw something he could not believe.

The whirlwind sweeping up the hillside was filled with flames and howling demonic horsemen. Terrified, Bass shut his eyes and closed himself and his boy inside the shed until the tempest was gone. When he and the other men emerged from hiding, the clearing outside the mine was empty save for one body.

Gideon Cain lay in peaceful repose on the ground, his hands folded upon his breast.

Bass didn't know what had happened at the mine that night, but he felt certain something profound had occurred. "Maybe we should change the town's name to Redemption."

THE RIDER OF THE DARK
BY
DARRELL SCHWEITZER

*"I see by your outfit,
"That you are a cowboy."
~ The Streets of Laredo*

I met him in a steakhouse in Denver in 1927 while waiting for a train, on my way home from college at Christmas break.

He slammed a silver dollar on the counter and said, "Give me a whiskey!"

As this was a steakhouse, and Prohibition was in effect, the man behind the counter could only gape and fumble with a towel and try to explain that they didn't serve alcohol on the premises.

"When I say I want a whiskey, I want a whiskey!"

I could see that this guy was what you'd call a "character." He was maybe seventy, a little hunched over, his face like old, gnarled tree bark, his beard a bristly white. His clothes were an unsavory mix of leather and denim, so worn they were shiny. Quite out of fashion.

As I drew closer, I noticed that he didn't smell too nice either.

"A whiskey!"

"Sir," said the cook behind the counter, "If you don't quiet down, I shall have to call—"

Nevertheless, my instincts were aroused. Here was source material, a *story*.

The old man looked at me, hard, then his look softened when I opened my jacket and showed him the silver flask in my inside pocket. Though a freshman, I had begun to move in sophisticated circles.

"It's all right," I said to the man behind the counter. "My grandfather is here to meet me. It's okay."

We sat down. I ordered steaks for both of us. The old man snatched the flask out of my hand before I could offer it to him.

"The name's Rufus T. Harris, and I ain't your grandpappy—"

"I know, but I had to tell him something. You were making a *scene*, Mr. Harris."

He took a long swig from my flask.

"Don't I have the right to? I can't find a decent saloon in this here town—"

"It's called the 18th Amendment to the Constitution, sir—"

"Well, *my* constitution needs a good snort now an' then." He drank some more. "Damn, boy, that's good hootch you got there! You shouldn't be drinkin' such stuff till you got whiskers on your chin, though surely this'll raise hair if anything will, uh—"

"Yes. Is there a problem?"

"You got a name, don't you, boy?"

"Oh," I stood up and extended my hand. "I'm so sorry. I have been impolite. My name's Blake, Robert Blake—"

He didn't take my hand, but finished my liquor and dropped the flask to the tabletop, then belched. I sat down again.

"I got you pegged, Bobby Blake. You're one of them writer fellows, ain't you, wantin' to meet a real older-timer who can tell you what it's like livin' life in the raw, back when the West was really wild? Ain't that so?"

"Kind of..." This was not the time to explain that I really wanted to be the successor to Poe and Baudelaire, rather than Jack London. "I *am* a journalism student," I hastily added.

"Well, ain't that grand? So, here's your story, Bobby Blake. No! Put that stupid notebook away! If it ain't worth rememberin', it ain't worth hearin'."

Just then our steaks arrived. As we chowed down, he began to tell me his story.

"It was a long time ago," he said, pointing at me with his fork. "I was about your age, which means I was so wet behind the ears I didn't know a longhair from a longhorn, but I was like you in a way, Bobby Blake. I wanted to experience the whole big, wide world. I wanted manly adventure, just like in the dime novels."

The first rule of journalism, even if you're not really intending to be a journalist, is knowing when to say nothing. Don't argue. Let him think what he wanted of me. Let him get on with his tale.

"So, I joined a cattle drive, back in the old days, when the railroads only came to Kansas City, and we had to drive the cattle north. My uncle Joshua convinced the trail boss, one Samuel Quintus Knight—now you remember that name, Bobby Blake, because Big Sam Q. Knight was the biggest, bravest, toughest cowboy there ever was. Why, the other cowboys told me he once shot the tip off the crescent moon with his six-shooter, and he split a man's skull at fifty paces by spittin' a chaw of tobacco."

He waited to see if I would react. I didn't. I just let him think I believed every word he said.

He went on with his story.

***

Yep [Harris said], I was just like you, Bobby, I was. I looked up to that man like he was God. I thought he could catch the lightnin' in his bare hands. He was everything I ever wanted to be. I was terrible, terrible grateful to Uncle Josh for getting me this job, and I stuck real close to Sam Knight, because I wanted to learn everything I could from him, and I wanted him to know I'd learned everything I could *from him*. So, I worked mighty hard. And, I tell you, it was the thrill of my life to be ridin' and ropin' beside him, and to sit near him around the campfire at night when he an' the boys would get out the harmonicas and guitars and make soft music to keep the cattle quiet.

I suppose that's how I come to notice the signs, then. I mean, there was something in the way Big Sam looked out into the darkness, how he watched a cloud pass over the moon and then turned his eyes away suddenly, how he made strange emblems like five-pointed stars in the sand around the edge of the camp each night, and muttered something I couldn't make out. And one night his voice faltered as he strummed a guitar and sang, "*Git along little shoggoth, it's your misfortune and none of my own.*"

Almost asleep, I rolled over in my sleeping bag and asked, "What's a shoggoth, Sam?"

He stopped playing. "You don't want to know, son," was all he said. "You just don't want to know."

And that morning two men were missing, the tall cowboy named Shorty and the right-handed one named Lefty. Their horses was still there, but no sign of them. There was nothing we could do.

I could tell Big Sam had somethin' on his mind. The way he looked up at them vultures circling. The time, in broad daylight, something *dark* and huge that the eye couldn't quite wrap itself around blotted out the sun for several minutes. There weren't no Injun smoke signals atop the mesas. Nothing like that. It was quiet, too quiet, all the way, and if I knew what more must Sam be knowing, that's what I wanted to know.

Bad signs. Of course, it was the place for it. We'd passed through the Superstition River Valley, near Hanged Man's Gulch, betwixt the Screamin' Skulls Mountains, just past Great Old Ones Canyon—and you don't have to know precisely where any of those places is. Let's say west of the Pecos and north of the Rio Grande.

That's enough. Bad place. Not where you want to be caught at nightfall with ten thousand head of cattle, but night falls when it does, and there we was.

I had a bad feeling about this.

But we made camp, there in the dark. There wasn't no moon that night, and not because Big Sam had shot it neither. Just no moon, and precious few stars, though it wasn't *cloudy* exactly. There was just somethin' funny about the air, like the air itself was thicker than usual and you couldn't see much farther than you could spit. Not countin' that Big Sam had once kilt a man with a chaw at fifty paces—no, I mean as far as any other ordinary feller could spit.

Nobody felt like singin' much that night, though the cattle was mighty restless.

So we was sittin' in the dark, just a-waitin' for somethin', for the sun to come up we hoped, but for somethin' real bad to happen, we was all afraid—then somethin' real bad happened.

There was a man a hollerin' out there in the dark somewhere. That's a real bad thing on a cattle drive, because the herd was already nervous, and anything that starts a stampede can get us all kilt real fast.

"Help me, fellas! Help me!"

We all got up. We reached for our guns. Somebody lit a lantern and shined it out into the darkness, where the cattle's eyes seemed to shine back at us like the eyes of wolves. It weren't natural. It was another sign. It was wrong.

Now, sudden-like, the herd was quiet, too quiet, and then there came staggering into the firelight none other than Tex Weinstein, the scruffiest, mangiest owlhoot in the outfit, with a beard like a tumbleweed and a little cloud of horseflies that seemed to follow him everywhere. But he'd always been good enough at cowboy work, even though he was just a bit of a moron, who would sometimes talk gibberish and just stare at you and say, "I don't know how," till you whapped him on the head with the handle of your six-shooter to snap him out of it... But that wasn't gonna do no good now because we couldn't help but notice as he come moseyin' into the firelight, his eyes was all rolled till only the whites showed, and the top of his head was chawed clean off.

He spoke in a weird, gurgly voice. "It's too late. You didn't help me."

Big Sam just drawed out his pearl-handled six-shooter and plugged Weinstein right through both of them blank eyes. *But he kept on comin'!* I tell you, it was the most god-awful thing I ever seen in my life. Sam shot him again and it took off most of his head, till there was just his jaws a' flappin' and slobberin.' *But he kept on comin'!*

So we all backed away as he came into the firelight, his hands out to grab us like they was claws, black ooze sputterin' from out of where his brain used to be.

Real quick, Sam drawed one of them five-pointed signs in the dust—*sigils* he called 'em—and when Tex Weinstein stepped in that he was caught somehow, and just blundered around, gropin' at the air, and Sam shot him one more time through the heart and he dropped down to the ground, stone dead.

Only it was obvious he'd been dead all along, living dead. I got out my own gun, just to be sure he was *dead* dead. But Sam pushed the barrel aside and said, "Don't waste your ammo, Rufus. You're gonna need it."

I looked down at the *dead* dead man who seemed content to stay that way.

"What happened to him, Sam?" was all I could say and what we all wanted to know.

"He be a *zombie*," said Louisiana Louie. "I seen things like that down in the swamps outside New Orleans. Them black folks can raise up a dead man like that with their African magic—"

"It wasn't African magic," said Big Sam, holsterin' his pistol. "It was a whole lot worse." And he told us then what nobody could believe if they hadn't seen it and what nobody could forget in all their born days if they had, how we just happened to be, at the worst time of the year in the worst place, because Great Old Ones Canyon wasn't called that fer nothin'. *Millions* and *millions* of years ago the Old Ones, monsters or devils or something, come down from the stars on a dark night like this, when there wasn't no moon and the darkness was... *thicker* somehow, like the air opened up and there was something even darker behind it. And these Old Ones was sleepin' in that canyon, waitin' for something like Judgment Day, when they could come up out of the ground and take over the whole world. But meantime, when the stars was *just right*, they could sometimes walk through the desert night in dreams—I didn't quite know what that meant, but that's what Big Sam said—and if you ran into a dream-ghost of a Great Old One, and you happened to be dead, that would turn you into a zombie, it stood to reason.

"But it *don't* stand to reason," I said, amazed and terrified that I would actually say something against the trail boss at a time like this, but it didn't, and I said so. "It *don't* stand to no reason because Tex *wasn't dead*. I mean, sometimes with him, when he gets funny, maybe you ain't so sure, but he ate his grub tonight, so I *don't think* he was dead—"

"The boy's right," said Coyote Jim the Halfbreed. "He wasn't dead, so he musta got turned into a zombie some other way."

"There is only one way," said Louisiana Louie. "For a living man to get turned into a zombie, he has to get bit by a zombie."

Some of the other cowboys joined in.

"That's why the top of his head was chawed off then?"

"Stands to reason."

It took them a while to work out the implications.

"That means there's *another zombie out there*!"

"Among the herd!"

"My God! We gotta protect the herd!"

Now what I wanted to know, and didn't have time to ask about, was why the whole top of Tex Weinstein's head was chawed off, because, well, a man's mouth ain't big enough to take a bite like that.

Just then a strange and eerie *mooing* came out of the darkness, like a long, lonesome wind, but with a voice, saying things you'd rather not hear.

I didn't have time to ask anything more because Big Sam shined the lantern out at the herd again, and we saw that every last one of them longhorn steers had its eyes rolled up all white, and them white eyes was *glowin'* like a million evil stars.

"It's too late to save the cattle," Big Sam said.

All of a sudden, Louisiana Louie let out a shriek, because a zombie-eyed steer had lunged out of the darkness and caught his head in its foaming mouth. He wriggled a bit, but it wasn't no use. The critter chawed off the top of his skull and sucked out his brain as we watched. Then he came at us, hands out like claws, all a' slobberin' and most of us together shot out his eyes—which distracted him long enough for big Sam to make another of them *sigils* in the sand. When Louie—or what used to be Louie—stepped into it, we plugged him in the heart and that was the end of him.

"How did you learn to do that?" I asked Sam, pointing at the *sigil*.

"When you're trail boss long enough, son," he said, "you learn all sorts of things that come in handy."

Again, my heart swelled up with sheer hero-worship. "Jeepers—"

But there was no time for that.

All of us high-tailed it right pronto. We couldn't even get to our horses, because we heard the horses screamin' and we knowed that the cattle got to them first. It ain't a smart idea to ride a zombie horse. So we ran on foot, the cattle closin' in, until we reached the base of a rocky hill.

There we made our stand, shootin' out the eyes of the zombie longhorns, which continued to distract them a mite, but didn't kill them.

And among the rocks, there was no place to draw a *sigil*.

And we was runnin' out of bullets.

Up we climbed, up, and up, the cattle comin' after us. Somehow a dead steer can climb a lot better'n a live one. Don't ask me why. Maybe it's just more determined to catch up with a living man and chaw out his brain.

Another scream, and one of 'em got Coyote Jim the Halfbreed.

Up. There wasn't much of any place to go. Fortunately we came to an open, sandy spot, where Big Sam could make another *sigil*, so we was able to plug what used to be the Halfbreed and a dozen of the cattle, but there was too many of 'em, and our ammo and our numbers was runnin' out, as the zombie cattle zombified one more cowboy after another.

At last, it was only me and Big Sam at the top of the hill, back to back. I can tell you I was scairt. Who wouldn't be? As far as we could see, in every direction, zombie longhorns with eyes like glowing coals was coming at us, up, up to chaw out our brains.

But that wasn't the worst of it. Maybe I was plumb crazy already, but I swear as I looked up into the sky, I seen *behind* what few stars there were, enormous shapes, faces, the dreaming ghosts of the Great Old Ones walking above Great Old One Canyon, and some of them had faces full of feelers like squids, and some had wings, and burning eyes, and none of them was like anything you ever seen on Earth; and I knew that they *hated* us more than words could express, and were just lookin' for the chance to wipe us all out like some goddamn vermin they think we are.

I had only one bullet left. I put the muzzle of my gun under my chin and said, "Well, Sam, I wanted to grow up to be just like you, 'cause you're my hero, but I guess I ain't gonna get the chance." I was sobbin' then, I am not ashamed to say.

But Sam he took the gun away from my chin and he said, gently, like a daddy would to his boy, "There is another way, Rufus. But only for one of us." He pressed what felt like a piece of smooth, cold stone into my hand. "This is something else I picked up 'cause it might come in handy someday. It's called a shining traphezohedron. Stare into it like you is looking far, far away. You'll see something movin' in there. Call it to you. Ask it for help. There will be a price you have to pay. But it is the only way. Do it. Now give me your gun, and I'll try to distract them a bit more so you have a chance."

He took my gun, and put his last six bullets into his own, yelled, "Yippie ki-yi-yo!" and charged down into the zombie herd, blastin' away. I don't think he got very far.

Then it was up to me. I held the shining traphezohedron in both of my hands and stared into it hard, and, yes, it was shining somehow, with light of its own, and then it seemed that a million stars flowed *out* of it like water out of a geyser, and I was *falling down* but into the sky at the same time, and the wind was howlin' all around me like the worst winter blizzard you ever heard with a hundred tornados joined in as chorus, and then I was lookin' out on *someplace else*, a different world, that was like a desert of blue ice, with three or four blue suns in the sky that didn't give off no heat at all.

And I saw, ridin' across that blue desert, a man all in black, but for his *silk mask*, which was yellow, and very strange because the bulges behind it didn't suggest a *human* face at all, not like he had a nose or a chin or anything... But Big Sam had told me what to do, and I done it. I called out to the rider of the dark, in something other than words, because when I opened my mouth there was only more howlin' of the wind, but somehow my *thought* was sent to him, and he heard me, and he turned in his course and came ridin' right at me, closer and closer, and I thought he was gonna ride me down, but at the last minute he grabbed me up like I was a little child and swung me up behind him in the saddle, and I clung to him as he rode down the rocky hillside. He didn't use his reins. His horse didn't need guiding. He had *black*, shiny six-guns in both hands, blazing away, and even after he'd shot a thousand times, he didn't run out of bullets, and somehow when he did it, as if *he himself was the sigil*, he kilt them zombies and zombie cattle, every last one of them. We rode on for hours, blastin' away, up and down the hill, all across the plain, into Great Old One Canyon and out again, shootin' and shootin' until there was nothin' left movin' anywheres, and then the sun come up, and the masked rider seemed to just fade away like mist, and I landed on the ground with a bump, and I didn't have no six-gun (because Sam had took mine), just the shining traphezohedron in my hand, and there was thousands of dead zombie cattle and dead zombie cowboys as far as the eye could see.

Then all I could do was walk, for days and nights without stoppin', without eatin' or drinkin', until I had become completely crazed, and it was all like a terrible dream that never, never ended. And I don't think it ever did end, even when I come to a farmhouse and fell down fainted on the floor. I remember thinkin', *Who was that masked man anyway?* and I remembered answerin' myself that he'd said his name was Nigel, Nigel R. Lathotep... Some kinda Irish name, I think. And I laughed and laughed at that like I didn't have no brain left at all, and the folks that took me in thought I was just delirious, but what did they know? They had not *seen* what I had *seen*, now, had they?

***

Old Rufus Harris was still laughing over the table in the steakhouse when he finished this. "Now what do ya think of my story, Bobby Blake?" he said. "What do ya think? Did I give you the *real stuff?*" And he went on cackling and wheezing and cackling some more, so much that I was acutely aware that people were beginning to stare.

"Please, sir," I said desperately.

He paused for just a moment to gaze longingly into my empty silver flask.

"I don't suppose you got any more of this fine concoction—?"

He started cackling again, louder and louder.

I had no choice. I got out the spare I carried in my boot. I had hoped to save that one for the holidays.

He snatched it from me and drained it.

"So, Bobby Blake, what'cha think?"

I measured my words carefully. I refrained from saying that, yes, he had given me the *real stuff*, because, having planned a career of writing about grotesquerie, horror, and the insane, it was helpful to make the acquaintance of a genuine, raving lunatic.

Instead, I merely asked him about the *price* Big Sam had mentioned.

"Oh, that," he said. He got out what looked like a shiny black stone, perhaps a piece of obsidian, cut strangely, with many angles, so the eye could not quite grasp its shape. It was, of course, the shining traphezohedron. He began to explain, in a voice that faded away as the wind roared louder and louder, how he had exchanged death for deathless bondage, how he was now an eternal servant of the Rider of the Dark, whose name was, more properly, *Nyarlathotep*, and it was his task to recruit more such slaves like himself, whether willing or unwilling, it did not matter. "Ain't no use fightin', boy," he said. "You can't get away nohow."

Then I heard nothing more, and, staring into the shining traphezohedron, I seemed to be falling *down* into the starry sky, and gazing, or floating, over the frigid blue desert beneath the cold blue suns, as the rider in the silken mask drew ever closer to me.

It was only with the greatest strength of will that I broke away. I pushed the black stone back at the old man, then ran screaming from the room, out into the street and across to the train station, where, I discovered, I had missed my train.

Then I fell down faint, into a delirium, and I heard a voice whispering in my mind, the voice which inspires all my nightmare visions, all the hideous and terrible and strangely beautiful writings for which I have since become famous.

We shall meet again, Robert Blake, it says. *Though you flee to the ends of the Earth, it is no distance. We shall meet again.*

BLIND FAITH
BY
ADRIAN LUDENS

The day Juleen Hardgrove's life changed, the midday sun cast its heat with palpable force. Juleen paused midway between the farmhouse and the well and let the empty water pail hang limp in her hand. She gazed at the Ridgeback Mountains jutting out of the earth on the far side of the valley. The scene never failed to inspire her. Someday, she'd cross those mountains. Someday, she'd build her own life.

The Hardgroves kept to themselves. Pa tended to the crops he coaxed from the fields. He worked dusk to dawn, as the unpredictable Montana weather allowed. Juleen didn't find that unusual. She had no knowledge of how farming was done elsewhere, and never questioned her father's nocturnal habits. He slept days. When his family had bathed and turned in, he rose and went out to work the fields.

Ma was a silent woman, taciturn, but loving toward her children. Juleen had never heard her mother speak. Each day she cooked, cleaned, tended the garden, and tackled a dozen other duties and chores. She and Juleen had worked out a series of hand gestures for when she wanted or needed help.

Elsabeth, Juleen's older sister, sat in her corner and sewed. The girl looked like a beautiful store-bought doll. Her sister had creamy, perfect skin, full lips the color of red ribbon, and bouncing sweet corn-yellow curls. Elsabeth sewed clothing for the entire family. She created fluffy quilts that staved off the bitter winter cold. She knitted with incredible speed and created breathtaking embroidered scenes. She did it all by touch. Elsabeth could not see. Juleen's sister wasn't just blind, Elsabeth lacked eyes. Sometimes Juleen cast surreptitious glances at her sister's face. The disconcerting pockets of darkness lurking behind her half-closed eyelids marred her otherwise remarkable beauty.

Juleen—boyish and stocky—often thought of herself as apart from the others. Every day and night, she struggled with a restless feeling. She wanted to travel the wagon-rutted trails that narrowed out of existence in the direction the sun rose, and in the direction the sun set. Juleen wanted to see more of the world.

Twice a year, on the vernal and autumnal equinoxes, Pa hitched their mule to the wagon and Ma made the journey to the nearest town. She'd leave at sunup and return at sundown. Pa never went, owing to his preference for the night, but he always labored over a handwritten list of supplies to be purchased. Juleen had a dozen questions. Did her mother speak in town? Did she simply show the shopkeepers the list? How did stores work? Did her family have money Juleen didn't know about? Did her mother trade for goods? The wagon always left empty and returned piled with supplies. Though Juleen begged each time to accompany her mother, her parents had never let her leave their homestead.

Juleen sighed, tore her longing gaze away from the sawtooth majesty of the Ridgebacks, and resumed her journey to the well.

Juleen turned the crank to lift the heavy wooden bucket from the aquifer deep in the ground. Motion on the horizon caught her attention. A colorful wagon came into view, an iridescent beetle trundling along the trail. Juleen kept her eyes on the slow-moving object as the bucket rose. She dumped the water from the well bucket into her own pail. Then she secured the rope and peered again at the approaching wagon. It rolled along, still miles away. Juleen carried the pail of water back to the farmhouse.

Excited to be the bearer of news, Juleen pushed open the door. "Ma, there's a—" she broke off when she saw her mother standing at the far window, watching the wagon's approach.

Juleen put the pail on the table and joined her mother. Ma put a finger to her lips and cast a meaningful glance at the room where her husband slept.

"Who is it?" Juleen whispered. "Can you tell?"

Ma's lips pressed into a thin line. She made a brisk motion with one hand. *Salesman.*

***

As the wagon neared, Ma and Juleen busied themselves preparing for a guest, or possibly, guests. In her corner, Elsabeth sewed in placid silence. Ma swept the floor while coffee brewed. Juleen couldn't stop herself from looking out the window to mark the wagon's progress.

At last, Ma signaled Juleen to go outside; it fell to her to greet their guests.

Shivering with anticipatory delight at the break in monotony, Juleen paced in the dooryard's dusty heat. She kept glancing at the wagon on the trail, the same way her tongue strayed to the empty socket whenever she lost a baby tooth.

As the wagon neared, she picked out more details. The wagon itself was black, but garish and colorful lettering decorated the side that she could see. Four horses—three black, one a dark brown—pulled the wagon. The man at the reins wore all black, with an old-fashioned stovepipe hat pulled down to his ears. The wagon slowed and the horses turned toward the farmhouse. The driver must have noticed Juleen standing in the dooryard watching, because he twitched the reins and the horses began to prance.

She studied the driver's face as he approached. He had smooth, sun-darkened skin. His dark eyes, shaded by his hat brim, conveyed both warmth and danger. His high-bridged nose sat atop a dark brown mustache that spread over soft lips like sleek bat wings.

Juleen's insides felt tingly. Her heart raced. The stranger pulled at the reins and the horses came to a standstill. The man doffed his hat and made a deep bow. He grinned.

"Hello, darlin'. Is your father here?"

"Pa's sleeping like always, but Ma has coffee ready for you." Juleen said. Caught up in the wonder of the moment, she added: "I'd like to see what you got inside your wagon!"

One side of the stranger's mouth lifted in a half-smile.

Juleen felt her face flush with embarrassment. "Beg your pardon. We don't get many guests." Not knowing what else to do, she kicked at some pebbles and waited for the visitor to speak.

"Well, now," the man atop the wagon said. "I'm always glad for such an enthusiastic greeting. Why don't you introduce me to your mother and we'll see about satisfying your curiosity later."

Juleen nodded. The man placed his stovepipe hat on the seat beside him and climbed down from the wagon. Juleen led the way into the house. Her mother rose from her seat at the kitchen table as they entered.

"Allow me to introduce myself. I am Doctor Alfred Moyle, madam." The stranger gave her a deep bow. "I am so pleased to make your acquaintance."

Ma acknowledged his bow and motioned for him to sit. Then she signaled to Juleen to speak on her behalf.

"Ma doesn't talk. She..." Juleen realized she couldn't explain something she didn't understand. "My mother's name is Judith Hardgrove."

Her mother smiled at their guest and poured him a mug of fresh-brewed coffee, which he accepted.

"Thank you, madam. And what is your name, young miss?" he asked.

"Juleen."

"And your father?"

"Sleeping, like I told you."

Moyle laughed. Juleen glanced at her mother, who gave her a reassuring smile.

"Yes, of course, but what is his name?" Moyle pressed.

Juleen's cheeks burned for the second time in as many minutes. "Pa's first name is Aleister."

Moyle sipped his coffee and then asked, "Is he ill? Perhaps I can be of service. I have with me a wide variety of miraculous cures gathered from the ends of the earth."

Juleen shook her head. "He isn't sick. He just sleeps during the day."

Moyle peered first at Juleen and then at her mother. "I see." He said at last, though Juleen realized Moyle found her father's habit unusual.

"Well, I don't," Elsabeth exclaimed, "because I can't!" She laughed at her own joke.

Moyle started in surprise. Juleen felt sure he'd have spilled his coffee if he hadn't set it aside. He stood up fast enough to send his chair skittering backward.

"I beg your pardon," he said, looking at Ma. "I didn't realize someone else was present." Moyle walked over to Elsabeth's corner.

"My! Aren't you the picture of beauty?" He bent and kissed her small white hand. "On my honor, you are as lovely as a porcelain doll." He took her other hand and kissed that as well. Elsabeth giggled and Juleen felt a prickle of envy.

"She's eleven," Juleen blurted. "And I'm nine." Moyle straightened. Ma sat rigid, watching Moyle. Juleen sensed something had gone wrong. Was it her fault? "My sister and I have the same birth month. Isn't that interesting, Mr. Moyle?" She knew she was babbling but didn't know how else to smooth things over; the mood of the room had changed.

Their guest strode back to the table and reclaimed his seat. "It's *Doctor* Moyle." He pinned her to her chair with a withering look. "I hope I won't have to remind you again."

"I'm sorry... Dr. Moyle." Juleen felt shocked and close to tears.

Ma made a pair of quick hand gestures and Juleen slid from her chair and left the table. A weight lifted from her spirit and buoyed her steps. Ma had told her to wake her father. Pa would set things right.

She tapped on his door. When he didn't respond, she knocked. "Come," he said, his voice groggy from sleep. Juleen entered her father's dark, windowless room. She closed the door behind her. *This is all Elsabeth ever sees,* Juleen thought. "Pa?"

"Yes, lamb?" her father still sounded drowsy.

"There's a man here," Juleen whispered. "He rode up in a funny looking wagon."

"I need my rest." She heard her pa yawn. "Are you sure you can't handle him yourself?"

"He's actin' fresh." Juleen danced from one foot to the other, anxious to have the stranger gone.

"With your ma?"

"With Elsabeth."

Her father made an inarticulate sound as he considered her words. She heard the whisper of his blanket and he drew it aside to climb out of the bed. "I'll get dressed."

Juleen left the blinding darkness of her father's room for the silent oppression of the kitchen. On her way, she passed her sister. Elsabeth stitched the hem of a gingham dress and kept silent.

Juleen gazed at her mother as she reseated herself at the table. She didn't look at Dr. Moyle. Awkward silence reigned.

At last, Juleen heard her father's approach. Moyle turned his head and broke into an impolite smirk he didn't try to disguise. "I see now who the living doll takes after!" he said, and followed his remark with a guffaw.

Unused to the light, Pa blinked like a mole as he surveyed the room. He reached Ma's chair and stood on tiptoe to kiss her cheek.

Then he made his way around the table with cordial solemnity and extended his hand to shake with Moyle. "I am Aleister Hardgrove. How do you do, sir?"

The doctor rose from his chair, towering over Juleen's father by more than two feet. Moyle went through his introductory speech again.

"Don't think we need any of what you have for sale, sir," Pa said, his tone mild but unapologetic. "We make do for ourselves. My wife, bless her heart, makes the most of the local herbs."

"Haven't met anyone yet who didn't end up buying *something* from my traveling medicine show." Moyle scowled down at Pa. The big man seemed to be taking mental inventory of his wares: "Pills, tonics, elixirs, remedies, cures, pamphlets, novelties, and entertainment."

Ma gestured and Pa spoke in reply. "That is a splendid idea, my dear." To Moyle he said, "Won't you stay for dinner?"

Moyle gave everyone in the room an oily smile. "Don't mind if I do. I take my steak rare, madam."

"There will be only stew, I'm afraid," Pa said. "But we'll have something made in no time, won't we?"

Ma nodded her assent, rose, and busied herself about the kitchen.

"Juleen, would you see to Dr. Moyle's horses?" her father said. "I'm sure they'd appreciate some fresh water."

Juleen rose and walked to the door. To her dismay, Moyle followed her.

"It's too late to move on tonight," he announced. "I'll just bed my horses down in your stable and be on my way in the morning."

Without waiting for a reply, the big man caught up with Juleen in three long strides. He grabbed her shoulder and spun her around to face him. Moyle bent and spoke into her ear. "Whatever you think about me, put it out of your head. I'll have what I want soon enough and then I'll be on my way."

***

"We're simple folks, Dr. Moyle," Aleister Hardgrove said. "Keep to ourselves most of the time, unless a neighbor needs help with a barn raising or Judith takes Elsabeth to a quilting bee."

Moyle studied Elsabeth for longer than Juleen thought gentlemanly. "That's why you know nothing about life," he said. "Out there is a world you cannot imagine." Moyle pointed expansively with his fork, a piece of potato still stuck in the tines. "I've been across this land and have learned a great deal." He shoved the bite of potato into his mouth and helped himself to the last of the stew. "Take those hills, for instance." Moyle indicated the general direction of the Ridgeback Mountains with his chin. "I bet you think they're something special. They're not." He slurped water and belched. "You ought to see the Rockies. Now those are *real* mountains."

Juleen noticed her pa hide a smile behind his hand and wondered what he found amusing.

"No one knows as much about medicine as me," Moyle announced. "Not bragging, just stating a fact. The list of folks whose lives I've saved with my expansive knowledge and expertise would fill your living room walls."

Juleen refused to swallow this obvious lie. "I don't believe you."

Moyle's face paled. Ma set down her coffee. Even Elsabeth recognized the insult and stopped eating, her head cocked.

"Now, Juleen," Pa said. "Don't disrespect our guest."

Moyle drew himself up in his chair and locked eyes with Juleen from across the table. "Explain your insolence," the doctor said coldly.

Juleen hadn't heard the word before but guessed its meaning.

"You talk real big, but I think you're a liar. If your medicine really worked, people would come to *you*. But you keep moving from place to place, and that proves you're nothing but a cheat."

The words Moyle said next dripped venom. "You are a loud-mouthed, rude, and stupid little girl, in need of a thrashing."

"She'll get one," Pa said. Juleen wilted. She could stand up to Moyle, but her father siding with the stranger stung.

Her mother tried to console her with covert hand signals but Juleen stared at her plate, her eyes swimming with tears. She refused to be consoled.

"An unfortunate way to end the evening," Moyle said. "But I suppose acknowledgement of one's betters is too much to ask of back-country yokels." He pushed back his chair and stood. "I'll be gone by morning's light."

As Moyle strode to the door, Pa spoke. "Juleen, help your mother wash the dishes. Then change clothes and meet me at the woodshed." His features looked solemn, even grim. "After twenty lashes from my belt, you'll be helping me in the fields tonight."

***

It took Juleen a moment to realize her father had trudged past the woodshed without stopping. Had he forgotten the whipping he'd promised?

The moon glowed overhead. The stars winked and sparkled in the heavens as father and daughter made their way through the wheat field. The crop's leaves brushed their legs, and the heads, heavy with kernels, bowed as if in deference as they passed.

Pa entered a small clearing and paused. Juleen reached his side and gasped.

An oblong stone of the darkest black lay at the center of the clearing. Juleen's immediate emotion was one of amazement. Then she realized this was where her father would beat her, and her muscles tensed.

Standing shoulder to shoulder, her father met her gaze. As if reading her mind, he said, "I have no intention of thrashing you, despite that traveling charlatan's outrage. In truth, I am glad you stood up to him. He's an empty-headed braggart."

Juleen felt weak with relief. "But why did you take his side at supper?"

"I needed an excuse to have you join me here—at the Sacred Shrine," her father said. "Time is short. We must offer a sacrifice tonight."

Juleen's fear returned—and multiplied.

"Steady, my daughter," her father said. "Surely you noticed your mother does not speak. She sacrificed her tongue. Last year, Elsabeth sacrificed her sight by giving up her eyes."

Aleister reached into his satchel and retrieved a jar containing an herbal mixture of his wife's creation. He removed the lid, dipped his fingers into the sticky paste, and smeared sigils onto the surface of the shrine.

"Our rites are based upon an ancient Eastern maxim about seeing, speaking, and hearing no evil. We sacrifice a sense in order to gain insight into—and power over—evil."

Juleen remained silent and wide-eyed. She'd never seen this side of her father. "Are we bad people, Pa?"

"Not at all, lamb!" he laughed. He finished his ministrations and closed the jar. "We are warriors, in opposition to evil. But I made a mistake; I delayed the completion of the rite, and now I fear we could pay a terrible price."

"Because of Moyle?"

"Yes, but if not him, there would have been another. It's my fault for letting you keep your hearing as long as I did. I will rectify that tonight. Once I have completed the rite, we will have one family member who is adept at each skill, and our power to stifle evil will triple."

Juleen opened her mouth to respond when an orange glow on the skyline over her father's shoulder arrested her attention.

Pa turned to look. Ma, her dressing gown billowing behind her in the night air, dashed toward them. She kept making a series of gestures with her hands.

"He's set the house ablaze," Pa translated. His lips pressed into a tight white line and his features darkened in anger. "And he's taken your sister—by force."

Juleen felt sick.

Ma arrived, gasping for breath, and fell to her knees, into Pa's arms. He held her until she broke their embrace.

"We cannot wait a moment longer," Pa said. He dug in his satchel again and withdrew a long-barreled revolver. Juleen felt her skin grow cold.

"Daughter," her father's words were gentle, "are you willing to make this sacrifice?"

***

Juleen stretched across the surface of the Sacred Shrine. The stone had soaked up the sunshine all day long and radiated heat beneath her, chasing away the chill she had felt.

What if Pa is crazy and all his talk is claptrap? Would Ma still allow him to do this? We need to save Elsabeth, not do this! And our home is burning to the ground!

Juleen gazed into the endless night sky and fought to silence her thoughts. The image of Elsabeth, held captive in Moyle's departing wagon, stuck in her mind like a cocklebur.

Ma spoke to her father through a series of gestures.

"No, she's *not* out of reach," Pa said. He peered into the darkness. "Moyle has his horses at a full gallop, but he's still well within striking distance."

Juleen had no cause to doubt her father; his night vision was much keener than theirs.

He dug once more in his satchel and withdrew something Juleen couldn't identify. He held his hand out to Ma. "Judith, take some beeswax to protect your ears during the ritual."

Juleen's eyes shifted between her parents as they pressed the beeswax into their ears. Her heart raced. *Please let the waiting be the worst part of this*, she prayed, although Juleen did not know who she expected to acknowledge her.

Ma took her hand. Juleen, despite her mounting trepidation, felt comforted.

Pa used his thumb to cock the hammer of the revolver. He placed the gun uncomfortably close to her ear and pointed the barrel away from her, into the wheat. He uttered a strange series of words Juleen couldn't understand.

He pulled the trigger while still speaking. Juleen's entire body jerked in shock. Her eyes watered—or perhaps she wept. Both seemed plausible. Her father had placed his free hand between the weapon and her face to protect her from the worst of the recoil. Juleen trembled. Her ears rang. *Just one*, Juleen realized. *The ear on Ma's side still works.*

The moment she realized this, her parents switched places. Ma took her hand again. Pa leaned down and spoke into her ringing ear. "Thank you for your noble sacrifice, my daughter. I love you."

He straightened, repeated the incantation, and pulled the trigger.

Utter silence fell.

No echo, no ringing, no humming. Juleen heard nothing to indicate even the absence of sound. She had entered the domain of ineffable silence.

Her parents helped her into a sitting position. Ma pulled a kerchief from the pocket of her dressing gown. She wiped away wetness from Juleen's ears and cheeks.

Juleen stole a glance at the kerchief and her stomach gave an unhappy lurch when she recognized her blood. She'd hurt herself before, was no stranger to blood, of course. This blood, however—trickling from deep inside her skull— seemed more intimate, more precious, somehow.

Pa knelt at the head of the altar. Ma took the space to his right. He motioned for Juleen to kneel at his left.

Take your father's hand and close your eyes, Ma signaled. When Juleen reached across for her mother's hand, Ma shook her head. She pressed her free hand against the black stone surface. Juleen did the same and closed her eyes.

Seconds later, she felt a dizzying sense of motion. She panicked and opened her eyes. Her father squeezed her hand in a gesture of reassurance. Both Ma and Pa kept their eyes closed. Their features seemed serene.

Juleen closed her eyes and the sickening motion returned. It lasted only a few moments before a shape swam into focus. *It's a glass jar,* Juleen realized. It held dried seedpods. The view changed, and Juleen was ready for the motion this time. It took getting used to, but she no longer felt quite as sick. More jars and bottles nestled against each other in carpetbags and crates. Juleen saw Elsabeth's delicate hands lashed together with strips of rawhide. Juleen leaned her forehead against the stone altar, stunned. She understood she was seeing what her sister would have seen—if she still had eyes.

That's part of the sacred magic, a woman's voice said. *Now that we are connected, we all see what she can't; we all hear what you can't; and I can speak here, but only because you are all with me.*

Though she had no memory of ever hearing it, Juleen knew this was her mother's voice. Girlish excitement intermingled with sorrow over their situation and threatened to overwhelm her. It was too much to take in; she couldn't—

"Juleen, look at all this neat stuff!" Elsabeth thought. "Thanks to you, I can see it!" She scanned the interior of the medicine show wagon, revealing animal pelts, antlers, exotic fruits and vegetables that neither of the girls recognized, and more. A pair of marionette puppets danced frenetic jigs as the wagon jounced over the trail. Juleen laughed, despite herself. In the semidarkness, they identified a deck of playing cards, a white banjo, a dark shotgun, and an assortment of other fascinating objects.

Then Ma's voice came again. *All right, girls. You've had a gander at Moyle's treasures. It's time we put an end to this.*

"Will you come rescue me, now?" Elsabeth asked.

We're sending help, Ma said. *Everyone be silent, but stay connected. Your father and I must converse with Awaxaawé and plead our case.*

***

Juleen never forgot what happened that night, nor did she ever fully understand it. Her perceptions of the events were like individual puzzle pieces but try as she might, she never assembled the puzzle into a coherent picture.

The name her mother had used was, "A-wa-ha-wa," but more nuanced and guttural in her pronunciation.

Juleen kept her eyes closed, kept holding her father's hand. She braced herself against the stone altar.

Pa seemed to be speaking to Ma in the real world, and Ma, in turn, communicated with their mysterious benefactor on the family's behalf. Awaxaawé's responses made Juleen feel as if an angry porcupine kept bristling inside her skull. She tried to understand its language but comprehended nothing.

Then, for a single prolonged moment, everything lapsed into darkness and silence.

The world beneath her quaked and shook without warning. The ground fell away, then rose and struck her. Juleen hurtled through the air, flailing her arms and kicking her legs. She tumbled and rolled through the wheat field like a dirt clod in a dust storm.

She lost sight of her parents and the black stone altar. Her skin stung from various scratches and scrapes. The nausea bothered her the most. Her mind's eye, like a looking glass, duplicated her physical state, and Juleen tumbled through endless inner space. Her instinct toward self-preservation forced her eyes open. If she could get her bearings, she reasoned, maybe the dizziness would subside.

The earth's violent tremors continued, as if following a pattern. The ground heaved like storm-tossed waters. She tried to tuck into a ball to protect her head and limbs each time she fell.

Then Juleen misjudged her position and hit the dirt hard enough to drive the air from her lungs. She lay on her back, fighting for breath. Juleen sought the moon for comfort—but could not find it. Even the twinkling stars had disappeared. Then the moon emerged from behind a towering cloudbank and glowed high in the sky. Some of stars reappeared as well, while others disappeared. The ground shook, and Juleen bounced and rolled. Now, however, she kept returning her gaze to the night sky. Something out there was moving; something colossal. *It blotted out the moon just now*, she realized.

A fresh shockwave sent Juleen airborne. When she landed, her head struck a solid, smooth surface. She fell unconscious before her brain realized she'd returned to the Sacred Shrine.

***

Juleen awoke to the touch of her mother's hand on her cheek. Her eyes fluttered open. Ma's face was smeared with dried blood and her hair was tousled and mottled with wheat kernels. Pa stood nearby, squinting at the sun's brilliance. He smiled at Juleen then turned his attention back toward the horizon.

Her mother stroked her face and helped her sit. Juleen saw Elsabeth riding toward them, astride the brown horse, and clutching its mane. The trio of black horses followed. Juleen remembered Moyle and chewed on her lip, contemplating his fate.

Elsabeth leaped from her perch and Pa hugged her tight.

The family faced each other. Pa said something and Elsabeth smiled. Ma gestured an approximation of his words for Juleen's benefit—something about riding the tail of a comet. To her right, a wispy column of smoke rose and smudged the sky. Their home, Juleen knew, lay in smoldering ruins.

The brown horse had wandered in close to the group and nuzzled Elsabeth.

Ma's hands flew, and Juleen tried her best to decipher her communication. *We'll ride the horses to the next homestead and seek help there. Moyle is dead. Elsabeth is safe. We, the Hardgroves, have won.*

Juleen didn't feel like they had won. She felt dazed, battered, and exhausted. She gazed across the valley at the Ridgeback Mountain range and frowned. Her perception of the world around her had altered, though she could not articulate how.

***

Fifteen year later, Juleen woke to the motion of her husband lunging from their bed. She sat up and watched Jeff pull on a pair of trousers. He grabbed his shotgun from above the door and hurried out into the night.

Juleen sat awake, waiting until he returned.

A fox outside the chicken coop, Jeff signed when he reentered the house. *I shot it.*

Juleen pondered the hens. Jeff had heard them, but she could not. Suppose they had not had the ability to communicate their terror in a way Jeff understood? How much damage could the fox have done, if left unimpeded?

Jeff returned to the bed they shared. He gave her a quick but loving kiss on the cheek and settled in beneath the blanket.

Juleen observed her husband as he curled back into the same position in which he'd lain before waking. Even though she had witnessed it, she perceived no discernable evidence that he'd roused, risen, dealt with the disruption, and returned to his slumber.

Suddenly, Juleen found it hard to breathe. Her pulse raced. In her mind, she returned to the night when the earth had rumbled and shook. She remembered the man who had destroyed their home and had tried to steal her sister. He had disappeared from the face of the earth. Juleen considered the moon and stars, blotted out for a moment, and then reappearing. She thought about the sawtooth peaks of the Ridgeback Mountains, mere miles from her childhood home. Nothing had looked, or felt, quite the same to her after the earth-shaking events of that night.

Sunrise found Juleen still awake, pondering the night she learned faith could move mountains.

BONNIE LEE AND THE BONEYARD BOYS
BY
MARTIN ZEIGLER

Open Arms, Wyoming, 1892

I must still have been asleep that morning when I opened my eyes to a skeleton standing at the foot of my bed and asked it straightaway, "Well, who in the wide world are you?"

Because, it seems to me, if I had been the slightest bit awake, and a skeleton was the first thing I laid my eyes on, I wouldn't have asked it a thing but instead taken a flying leap out my bedroom window and run the entire width of Lake Marvis without sinking once, all the while screaming to Saint Anyone for salvation.

And yet, if I had managed any sleep at all, it would've been a wonder. So much was weighing on me. The devastating fire, first of all, as vivid in my mind as when it happened two months before. Then all those sums and differences and other bookkeeping matters sprouting up from Father's old wooden desk like mile-a-minute weed. And a day didn't go by when one Cyrus Ackerny didn't ride out here to badger me into selling the land.

And here I was, barely eighteen years old, already knee-deep into adulthood, and without the slightest idea what to do.

In any case, sleep or no sleep, I was fully alert soon enough, and there most definitely was a skeleton in my bedroom, its white bones luminous in the early morning light. What's more, it was grinning a never-ending grin and drilling a look right into me.

The set of its jaw and the intensity of its cavernous eye sockets did send a chill through me, I confess, but the more I looked, the more I came to realize that, for a skeleton, the act of grinning and staring were about the most natural things in the world.

But when the skeleton let out a cough to clear its throat, as if it were about to make a pronouncement, why, that did not seem the least bit natural. It was one thing to ask a skeleton a question, as I had done; quite another to get a reply.

Nevertheless, I remained where I was and decided to hear it out.

"Why, Bo-Lee Marvis," it said. "Don't you recognize me?"

The manner of speaking was low and gruff, without an ounce of meanness to it, and only one man I knew had ever spoken like that. It was the same man, and only man, I ever let call me Bo-Lee instead of Bonnie Lee, my real name. And when I surmised how that hard working, stoop-shouldered man I once knew would fit perfectly over the skeleton's solid bones and curved spine, there was only one thing I could do: scream. Not in horror but in delight at both the impossibility and the truth of it.

"Uncle Cory? Dear Uncle Cory, is that you?"

The skeleton put its bony fingers to its ribs and took a bow. "At your service, m'lady. As are the rest of us."

"The rest of you?"

He turned to the open door and called out, "Come on in, fellas."

From where I lay I could barely see out into the hallway, and so I had no idea whom Cory was beckoning in. There was no one else living in the house, not any more. I then heard a hollow clattering on the hardwood floor, and the next thing I saw was two more skeletons marching into my bedroom, waving to me as they entered.

Uncle Cory moved over to give them space, and the three of them now lined up side by side at the foot of my bed as if presenting themselves for inspection. I sat up and looked them over, feeling every bit like a beginning medical student, until it hit me who they were.

"Manny! Cousin Parker!" I shouted, clapping with glee at how I was able to tell so quickly.

Uncle Cory looked equally surprised as his eye sockets grew wider. "Bo-Lee, you are a wonder."

But it only stood to reason when you thought about it. Manuel Barquero, the jack of all trades my father had hired on a whim, had been a heap of tight muscle squeezed into a short mass of a man, and only he could belong to that sturdy, compact set of bones in the middle.

Which could only mean skeleton number three had to be Cousin Parker. But I would have recognized him anyway. He had been a tall drink of water, a gangly bundle of nerves who, when he moved, strutted about with his arms dangling by his side, and when he stood still, which was seldom, did so in a knock-kneed kind of way as if embarrassed not to be moving. A fellow like Cousin Parker was made to order for that loose sack of bones on the right, in which each bone, it seemed, connected to the next by the merest thread.

"No, truly you three are the wonder," I said.

The sunrise through a far window drifted down the hallway and into my room, lighting my visitors from behind like a welcoming ghost.

Cousin Parker held one arm bone out to the light, then the other, turned this way, then that, as if showing off a brand new suit. "What-what do you think, Bonnie Lee?" he said in that nervous way of his. "T-took real elbow grease to scrub away all the-all the soot and carbon and whatnot."

Then Manny joined in, with one hand on his hip and the other in the air, which I gathered was his recollection of what a dance hall girl did. "You like?"

Sensing my puzzlement, Uncle Cory stepped in to clarify. "If you remember, Bo-Lee, last time you saw us, we were a mite spit-roasted."

I finally understood. And, no, I did not like. Not one bit. Especially now since the sunlight dancing on my bedroom wall was more and more beginning to resemble flames.

"Oh, you boys," I said, close to tears, "that isn't in the least way amusing. What happened that night had to be the most horrific thing I've ever witnessed in my life."

And in my mind, for the briefest of moments, I bore witness one more time.

***

I was out on the front porch, reading of romance and magic, when I finally set down my book in favor of the real things before me—the dusking sky, the calm of the lake, the ducks quietly painting ripples in the waning light.

A strange sense of peace overwhelmed me, and yet it wasn't the calm that instilled it. No, it was the voices echoing up from the boathouse down by the lake—Cousin Parker's incessant chatter, Manny's boisterous laughter, Uncle Cory's low-pitched and carefully considered words.

They could have been prattling on about anything—the weather, the weathered hulls of the older boats, whether Manny could beat Uncle Cory in a game of checkers. It didn't matter. There was an ache in a corner of my heart over the loss of my parents—my father to pneumonia, my mother a year later to cancer. It was an ache I knew would never go away, nor would I ever want it to, but simply listening to the rise and fall and quality of those voices on that clear night filled me with an assurance that the love and friendship of these three would accompany me for a long time to come.

But within a very short time I learned two lessons: That having hope doesn't guarantee it, and that tragedies don't always stop at one or two. Sometimes they can pile atop each other like cordwood in a shed.

For all at once, as if by a snapping finger, those comforting sounds of camaraderie turned into shouts of alarm. I smelled the smoke, then spotted the flame rising from behind the boathouse. Then, next to it, more flames appeared, poking above the rooftop, jabbing every which way like glowing demons.

Now the screams seemed to move from the rear of the boathouse to the front, the side I could see.

I shot up out of my chair, leapt off the porch, and ran in that direction.

The boys lived in a shotgun dwelling attached to the far side of the boathouse. My father had built it for them as a modest home until they decided to stake claims of their own. It was made up of three small bedrooms, one after the other, lined by a narrow hallway leading to a simple kitchen in back, where a door opened out onto a view of the lake. My father figured the sun rising over Lake Marvis would be a fine thing to see upon stepping outside each morning. The boys were much appreciative of the gesture, but I did recall them once confiding in me that a door at the front end would have been equally welcome.

The fire, I quickly suspected, had started in the kitchen, where the only door was, then spread rapidly to the bedrooms, where the only windows were, leaving the boys no choice but to head down the narrow hallway to the opposite wall.

From there they could proceed no further, for this was the wall where the desired door could have gone but never did.

And with the fire rushing toward them from behind, there was little the boys could do but scream for help and kick at the wall with all their might in the hope it would give way.

I was on the other side of the wall, a few feet from them, unable to see them, able only to hear them, and I whispered again and again to the wall to please give these boys a chance.

I thought of racing toward the tool shed, grabbing the axe, rushing back and valiantly swinging away at the siding, but in that instant of thinking, tongues of flame lashed out between the boards as if starving for the darkness.

Inside, the screams turned into shrieks, and the pounding grew more thunderous. Outside, the heat became unbearable, forcing me farther away. I couldn't have gotten closer again with an axe or the best intentions.

***

The skeletons had moved from the foot of the bed over to my side of it, where I was sitting up against the headboard. Uncle Cory laid the bones of his fingers gently atop the back of my hand. Cousin Parker, his jaw quavering, seemed to be searching for words. And Manny, bless him, found them.

"We should have not made a joke, Bonnie Lee," he said. "Please forgive."

I placed my free hand, in turn, atop Uncle Cory's, and looked at the others to show I had theirs, too. "Oh, applesauce," I said. "I should be the one begging forgiveness. I have no right to tell you boys how to recall your own horrors."

"Bo-Lee," Uncle Cory said, "you likely recall them better than us. We remember the flames from out of nowhere, then finding ourselves all burnt bone and no flesh, but what happened in between is empty as a desert."

"You remember nothing of the fire chasing you? Or you yelling for help? Or banging at the wall?"

All three shook their heads, as if ashamed. Uncle Cory said, "Seems like the ones in the midst of a calamity have the least to say about it."

"Maybe for the best," I acknowledged. "But do you recall anything about how you came to drop by here, in my room?"

Uncle Cory nodded. "I do believe we were of like mind that those pine boxes we found ourselves in were not yet meant for us. So we pushed up against the lids, then crawled our way through to the top of the top soil. If you were surprised seeing us, Bo-Lee, imagine how surprised we were seeing each other. Anyhow, we jawed a bit, tried in vain to catch up on what the hell had happened, and by and by came to a mutual understanding why we each had to dig our way out. And that's why we made our way from your family's gravesite to right here, where we're at right now."

"But why am I so important?"

"Because we-we wouldn't have gone-gone through all that work pushing outta the coffins if you-you wasn't important," Cousin Parker said.

A school teacher or two of mine might not have seen that as an answer, but it was answer enough for me. "Well, I have to say. You three are certainly a sight for sore eyes." And then I added, "I hope you can stay a while. I could sure use the company."

"How about the help?" Manny asked.

I hesitated. "Well, I don't know. I'm supposed to be an adult and all that."

"So what?" Uncle Cory said. "Being a kid means you always get the help. Being grown up means you know when to ask for it."

"In that case," I said, smiling, "I would very much appreciate any assistance you have to offer."

"Well, then," Uncle Cory said. "We'll step outside, while you get yourself dressed. We have work to do."

***

These boys could hardly be expected to saunter into Jake's Lumber Mill and purchase supplies on their own, the shape they were in. And so it was up to me. They told me what words to use and what numbers and sizes, and I took the horse-drawn wagon into town to use them.

By the time I returned, morning had inched up to half past noon and the boys had already torn down most of the damage, hauled it off to a far corner of the Marvis land to be buried during a lull. Gone was the burnt black beams and floorboards; the heaps of ash still smelling of smoke; the charred remnants of dressers, tables, and chairs; the picture frames and pictures gone to cinder; the reminders, for two months, of lives I thought I would never see again.

The part of the boathouse that truly housed the boats was blessedly spared the fire, thanks to most of it being above water. It was the shotgun attachment, where the boys had lived, that had suffered the brunt of it, to the point of being almost completely destroyed.

But now that I was back with all manner of hardware and lumber, we were ready to rebuild.

And, oh, did we have a ball as we went to work, as we unloaded the wagon, as we lifted things and carried them and handed them over and up, as we climbed and balanced and hammered, as we barked knuckles and swore and then laughed at our swearing, as we labored like the devil and kidded each other like angels.

We stopped for the occasional break, though the boys never needed one. They had no muscles to soothe, no brow to wipe the sweat from, no thirst to slake. The cool tartness of lemonade, which felt like a balm to my parched throat, would have only sidled down the front of their spines like rain along a spout. And yet they welcomed the respite anyway, for my sake.

In some matters the boys were the sole experts, and I deferred to them. I thought it best, for instance, that they put in that sought-after front door. In other matters, they left things up to me. Fetching supplies, as I mentioned, was one of them. Another was fending off, in a gracious way, the kindhearted.

Word had got out that restoration was underway at Lake Marvis. From far and wide, the good folk of Open Arms, Wyoming dropped by to offer an extra hand. Not a soul asked who the three men toiling away on the boathouse were, or why, in the midst of summer, every inch of them was covered in woolens, dusters, leather boots and gloves, wide sombreros, kerchiefs around the neck, and bandanas over the face. But I feared if I allowed these generous people to linger or draw nearer to the boathouse, they would soon discover the truth, and their panic would spread like a pestilence. It was not an event I wished to have happen. The boys had risen from the dead to be with me, not to scarify the daylights out of the fine citizens of Open Arms.

And for that reason, I expressed my gratitude but politely declined their offers. And, knowing how much I had endured regarding the fire, they took my response with good grace and went about their business.

Unfortunately, there soon came along that man on his high horse who was completely lacking in any form of grace.

***

First time I saw Cyrus Ackerny was a little under half a year ago. He was standing beside his horse, sporting a derby hat and a fancy suit, a shiny gold watch chain dangling from the vest pocket.

He knew my name and gave me his, then went on about how he had traveled here by train, having heard about the Marvis land being for sale. I told him he had heard wrong, and then apologized for his wasted trip.

"Well, it sure would fetch you a pretty penny, Miss Marvis," he said. "Plenty of grazing land, perfect for livestock. And you would be set for life."

"I appreciate the offer, but I inherited this land from my mother and father, and I'm living on it just fine."

"Offering rowboat rides is living fine? All due respect, but folks can row at other lakes for nothing."

"True, but they don't."

"Tell you what. You think about it. I'll be staying at the Wilford Hotel in town for a week or two. Ask for me at the desk, and I'll come right down. They serve a mighty fine meal there. We can discuss this like reasonable people."

I let him go, figuring he'd be gone soon enough. But he was here every day. And after two weeks, he still came around, constantly comparing my land to gold or silver or whatever mineral he could come up with.

And then came the fire, and after that, the funeral, when he stepped uninvited into my house and found me.

"Not today, Mr. Ackerny," I said. "Please, not today."

"Horrible, what happened," he said.

"Yes, it was horrible. Now kindly leave. I'm with friends."

"Aren't you and I friends by now? And please, call me Cyrus."

I was near to the point of tears, but I held them in. "Mr. Ackerny, I want you to leave."

"Heard what happened. Fire started in the back, where the kitchen was, worked its way to the front. Trapped your hired hands inside. Truly, truly horrible."

I looked straight at him, and not in a friendly way.

"I can see the pain in your eyes," he said. "The burdens thrust on you must be overwhelming."

"The only burden I feel right now is you."

"Good day, little lady," he said. "I'll be in touch."

Now, dismounting his horse and striding up to me in his same hat and suit, Ackerny seemed different in his demeanor. There was a swagger to his step, more of a shine to his pocket watch.

He said, "Work's started, I see."

"You're still in town, I see."

"What kind of greeting is that in a town called Open Arms?"

"Open Arms for most, not all."

His lips formed what some would call a smile. "Once my men start working this land and heading into town for relaxation, I reckon we'll see plenty of open arms."

"You're assuming something."

"I don't think so."

"And why is that?"

"That work crew of yours, Miss Marvis. Looks like they've mistaken August for January."

"How they're dressed is no concern of yours."

"Beg to differ. Three men held up a bank out in Dry Gulch, made a clean getaway. Maybe they figure the best thing is to hide in plain sight. Maybe you're the kind of gal who fancies the thieving type."

I said, "These men are not robbers. Let them be."

"Why don't I just mosey on down to that boathouse and have a little chat. What do you say?"

As he started down the slope, I yelled for him to stop. And when he turned to me and waited, I said, "They don't speak English."

"Well, then, I'll forgo the palaver and just have myself a look. See if there's any resemblance to what's posted up at the sheriff's office."

"Get off my property."

"Fine. I'll be back momentarily with that same sheriff."

"What do you want?"

He reached into the his suit and withdrew a single sheet of paper, followed by a thick roll of cash. "You know what I want," he said.

There was nothing else I could do.

"One more thing, little lady," he said, pocketing the signed paper. "Come morning, I want you and your three friends off my land."

***

"I had no choice," I told the boys. "If I hadn't done as Ackerny demanded, he would've exposed you, and all of Open Arms would've been in a fright. You would've been forced into hiding."

I sat back hopelessly in my armchair. The boys were standing about the living room, still in their work clothes, except with their sombreros at their backs and their bandanas down to their necks, so that I could look them in the face. Or, rather, in their skulls, which bore the creases of sadness and disappointment more than any human face could.

Finally, Uncle Cory said, "But Bo-Lee, listen. This was more than land, this was your family's land, land more important than the three of us."

I looked up at him, then the others. "Don't ever say that," I said. "You all mean more to me than acreage."

Cousin Parker slammed his forearm against the mantel. "What-what I'd like to do to that brute Ackerneck for black-blackmailing you like that."

"He's an awful man," I admitted. "I know something about him, and I should've used it, but I was in such a state. I feel terrible. How many more mistakes like this am I going to make in my life?"

Manny touched his hand to the back of the chair. "What do you know about him?" he said.

His question took me by surprise and made me hesitate. "Why—I think it best I keep it to myself."

The look passing between the boys told me they knew the answer. Uncle Cory spoke for them. "What we won't do to others, we can do to Ackerny. Just tell us what, Bo-Lee."

If I couldn't even handle my own land, how could I possibly know what to do about the man I sold it to? That man who had showed up from out of town one day and... and suddenly the answer came to me, a possible path to redemption.

"All I want is for you boys to welcome him with open arms."

***

Next morning, though I was supposed to be off the property, I was inside the house at a half-open window, hiding behind a curtain. By and by, Ackerny came marching up the stone path, swinging a set of keys, eager to revel in his new acquisition.

As he approached the porch, something drew his attention to his left. Perhaps he was curious why a mound of dirt was there, or perhaps not. Either way, three things poked up through the dirt like early spring blooms, and he froze.

I saw the things from the back, Cyrus did so from the front, and either way you looked at them, they appeared to be human skulls. Now dirt slid off the craniums as they rose up further, exposing shoulder blades and arm bones, ribs and backbones, and finally pelvises and leg bones. To me, they looked remarkably like Uncle Cory, Manny, and Cousin Parker. To Ackerny they likely looked like something that should be dead and unmoving rather than striding toward him with arms stretched wide in a gesture of welcome.

The shaking joints and bones of the tallest skeleton looked as if they caused a particular degree of agitation in Cyrus, because that's when he cried out, "Back away!" as if to an unleashed dog.

But the skeletons, tall or short, did not back away. However, Cyrus did.

And now the trio began to chant, in unison and in as natural an intonation as you're likely to hear, "Friend, pleased to have you join us."

That is when a dark circle appeared in front of Cyrus's trousers like spring water bubbling up from the earth.

Within seconds, he swung around, made like a bandit toward and onto his horse, and, with a slap of his derby against the animal's flank, vanished in a cloud of dust.

Not much later, thanks to a messenger from the Wilford hotel, the deed was back in my hands, and Cyrus Ackerny's dirty money was back in his.

***

Following a hunch and feeling a tremendous urge to put icing on the cake, I rode downtown to meet the one o'clock train. Blessed be to hunches, for there was Ackerny at the station, pacing back and forth alongside an empty track.

I hitched my horse and walked on over. Ackerny turned to me and said, "Not enough you got your rowboats back?"

"Just wanted to make sure you get aboard safely."

"Oh, I will. I intend on steering clear of your haunted land for good."

"Wise choice, considering the only ones the ghosts don't abide are cold-blooded killers."

"What's that supposed to mean?"

"It means, you once made mention of the fire starting in the kitchen and making its way to the front. Only way you'd know that is if you were there."

He opened his pocket watch for the time, though he likely already knew it.

"Way I figure it," I said, "you took a skiff across the lake and landed behind the boathouse, then set fire to one room after the other. Clearly to throw me into such a fit of despair, I'd come begging you to buy my land."

"You got no proof," he said.

"First thing out of an innocent man's mouth is, 'I'm innocent.' First thing out of a guilty man's is, 'You got no proof.'"

"You still got no proof."

"I do or I don't. Either way, I won't pursue it. I've seen enough of you on my land. You think I want to see more of you in a court of law?"

He stared at me for the longest time. I stared right back until, without a word, he picked up his carpetbag and made his way to the train that was slowing to a stop.

***

Outside the station, someone was shouting my name, and shouting it to the point of exhaustion.

It was Billy Meadows, a young sprite whose family lived three miles down from me, which made them my next door neighbors.

"Miss Marvis! Guess what I saw!"

"My goodness, Billy. You ran all the way down here?"

He stopped and pressed his hands to his knees to catch his breath, barely able to get out a, "Yes, ma'am."

"Take your time, Billy."

"I saw three skeletons in front of your house. They sprung up from a patch of dirt. Scared the stuffing out of guy in a suit."

This did not bode well. "Oh, Billy, what a lively mind you have."

"No, ma'am," he said. "'Cause later I saw them putting on clothes and going to work on your boatshed. You got skeletons working for you. Did you know that?"

Fearing the answer, I asked the question anyway. "You haven't told anyone, have you?"

"No, ma'am. Only Tommy, my brother. I ran back home and told him."

"Is that all?"

"My ma and pa were there when I told Tommy. And then there was Stevey and the Cameron twins and Mrs. Carter, my teacher. And Joe, Suzy, and Ralph. And Fred, my best friend, who lives five miles from us, and Mr. and Mrs. Vale who own the dairy, and old Charlie Jeffers, who's good friends with the sheriff, and..."

He went on and on, reciting a list that would have stretched from one end of Main Street to the other.

***

On the way home, I became certain beyond a doubt that the thing I feared most—about the boys being discovered as skeletons and all of Open Arms getting in a lather—was about to come true. And not because of a murderous, unprincipled land grabber but because of a rambunctious, innocent boy.

Then, as I rounded the bend and pulled onto the Marvis land, I came upon a scene that dropped my jawbone and pretty near widened my eye sockets.

There they were—Uncle Cory, Manny, Cousin Parker—alongside each other, not in woolens, hats, and scarves, but just as they had appeared to me at the foot of my bed—as full-fledged skeletons.

And gathered around them was every person Billy had told, as well as everyone he had not told, not a single one of them cowering in terror, but instead clapping the boys' scapulas, shaking their phalanges, hugging their ribs—all of them, to the man and woman, to the boy and girl, laughing and carrying on as if the boys had just returned from a long journey and there was a heap of catching up to do.

All around my cherished land, with the boathouse a finishing touch from completion and Lake Marvis a stride away, everyone was treating each other as if there wasn't a lick of difference between them, as if one man having a schoolbook anatomy and the next man having just bones was no different than one man having blue eyes and the other brown.

It was a town fair, a centennial, a gathering of open arms.

DEADFALL
BY
GREGORY L. NORRIS

Turley stared at the sprawling ruins. The rubble was scattered across the majority of a slope covered in brittle stalks of dead sagebrush, which added to the element of wrongness emanating from the vast circle of stones.

"Medicine wheel," Ghent said.

The voice of the other man, riding beside him at the reins of the prairie schooner, shattered the spell of silence. No birds sang or circled overhead. Even the horses had stopped their snorts and chewing the bits. Turley swore he could feel the earth's tenseness vibrating through the wood and metal spokes of the wagon wheels as they traveled past the ominous landmark.

The four bodies baking in the covered section along with all they owned in the world grew restless.

"Griffin, what is it?" Iselin Turley asked.

The damp lace of his wife's sunbonnet brushed the side of Turley's face, unleashing a phantom tickle that was terrible on the skin, like the unwanted caress of a spider or some bloodsucking insect.

"Mister Ghent believes we have come upon a medicine wheel," Turley said, his voice not much louder than a whisper. "Only..."

What he didn't add in the unfinished sentence was the size or the age of the curiosity, which looked to be as old as ruins in Rome and Greece. How many sweltering summers had cooked the stone circle here at the end of the world? Hundreds by his estimate. Thousands. And why was it here, on a hillside far from Arapaho, Sioux, or Cheyenne settlements?

It's a warning, thought Turley. The day's heat, already miserable, seemed to double in intensity. Fresh sweat poured down the nape of his neck. His flesh itched.

"We need to go," Ghent said, giving form to the panic building in Turley's gut and pulsing through his blood.

Nodding, he clucked to the horses. They jolted out of their sluggishness and trotted forward at a faster clip.

They were lost, had been since Independence Rock. Lost in territory best vacated in haste and never seen again.

Turley listened to the groan of the fine furniture standing upright in the wagon, the occasional clank of cooking pots and pans, and a sob from Ghent's daughter, Madeline, all of it sounding louder in the tenebrous calm. His heart galloped in response. The sensation that they were being watched returned, unleashing a shiver down his spine. That, too, was unpleasant, warm instead of icy, which made its slither along his backbone worse.

***

Lost.

Reaching Oregon and the new life waiting for the Turley and Ghent families was no longer their mission.

"I'd settle for California to be free of the Wyoming Territories," Albert Ghent said what felt like long hours later—long enough for the sun to have crossed a merciless sky devoid of clouds.

Not one single cloud, but by dusk, a dark gray mist drifted down from the surrounding buttes, noxious to breathe in and reeking of brimstone. The foul shroud made the way ahead impossible to navigate. Turley stilled the horses and gagged on the clotted air.

"Daddy, I'm scared," Madeline mewled.

Ghent patted the girl's hair, damp and clinging to her father's neck. "Be brave, Maddie," he said around a deep cough.

For years, tall tales had circulated among settlers headed west about smoking holes in the angry earth in a part of the territory brooded over by canyons and peaks of yellow stone, the rumors originating with the expedition of Lewis and Clark. But the proof of those mad hallucinations now surrounded them in jagged, smoldering gouges in the hardscrabble and the ever present gurgle of bubbling mud.

A full moon lurked behind the mist in the sky, sallow-tinged, an enormous Cyclops eye that tracked their slow progress. For days, Turley had suffered the phantom chill of eyes upon them, though it could have been weeks in the confused lapse of time since they passed Independence Rock, the way station now far behind them and last sure landmark telling them they were on course before falling under the shadow of Big Horn Mountain. The feeling was back. Turley tipped a look up at the moon, the connection brief. Any longer, and the voice in his head warned him that the Cyclops eye would blink and, long last, he'd snap, driven insane in this charred landscape straight out of Hell.

Ghent's wife, Thea, spoke his name, the tremor in her tone clear. Turley imagined her and Iselin exchanging worried glances. Maynard, of course, would stay silent, though his son's eyes, Turley guessed, spoke volumes in the covered wagon's dark shelter.

"We can't," he started, choking on the words, the sour air painting a foul taste on his tongue. "Can't keep going. The horses could step into those cauldrons and then—"

"Agreed," said Ghent.

"But Griffin," Iselin persisted. "We can't stay here. By all the Saints..."

They couldn't go forward. There was only the smoking earth, the noxious air, and the unblinking eye of the moon staring down at them through the mist.

Turley barked at his wife to be quiet and instantly regretted the harshness. Guilt followed regret, because it was the loudness in his voice in the night rather than whom it had been directed to behind the original emotion. What was out there, gazing down and listening from the mist-cloaked slopes? His imagination wandered from wolves and mountain lions to horrors standing upright on two legs. Things with fangs and claws. Worse.

"We don't have a choice," he said in a voice less gruff and far quieter. "We'll get far from this place in the morning, at first light, I promise."

He reached a hand behind his flank. Iselin took it, her slender fingers in their satin glove clammy against his bare flesh.

***

They ate rations of cured meat that hit Turley's stomach hard. Sipping a ladle of warm and grainy water from the jug worsened the effect. His gorge threatened to rise. Turley willed his guts to unknot and settle. Somehow, the unpleasant meal stayed down.

The boy sat beside Madeline at the back of the wagon, his feet dangling over empty space, fear showing clearly in his eyes.

"Think of the stories we'll tell in Oregon," Turley said. Then the irony struck him. Maynard hadn't spoken a single word in his nine years.

He ran the fingers of his right hand through the boy's hair, a bit of play between father and son that should have reassured them both but didn't. The silent boy's hair was brittle, his scalp oily to the touch.

"Just like Misters Lewis and Clark, no one'll believe us!"

The wind rose, its disembodied howl stirring the mist. The moon solidified overhead, more face now than eye.

Turley doubted he'd sleep but was wrong.

***

In the dream, he heard their screams; saw the terror in their unblinking eyes—buffalo and wolf, coyote and bear. Eyes wide, like his son's, by the thousands they fixed him with pleading, insane looks as the animals sank into the ground. Though he couldn't see how far the bubbling mud holding onto legs and hooves measured, somehow he knew they were deep down there, the mud dragging centuries of prey to their deaths.

The screams intensified. Now, the doomed were human—Arapaho, Cheyenne. Those that followed were a kind of man, not quite modern... dwellers from the distant past. Then giant cats with saber teeth and things that resembled elephants from the African continent only with enormous, twisted tusks and bodies coated in fur. Giant lizards like the dragons in Chinese mythology. Things with scales and armored plates and mouths filled with sharp teeth, all shrieking in alien voices, devoured by whatever was down there lurking in the mud and brimstone.

Turley bolted upright. He trapped his own scream behind his teeth before it could emerge and wake Ghent sleeping beside him on a blanket beneath the wagon. The sensation of being watched crawled worse over his skin. Turley pinched his eyes. Thick tears spilled between his fingers. Invisible ice formed over his flesh, turning his sweat frigid. He expelled the breath bottled and boiling inside his chest.

He willed his crippled muscles to move and craned his neck toward the edge of the wagon. The mist had thinned, diffused by the wind. The world glowed silver beneath the full moon's light. A ridge of time-eroded buttes rose directly ahead of them, ghostly gray stone fingers clutching at the sky beyond the filter of fog.

A hand. A giant stone hand, Turley thought.

The arrival of dawn did little to change his view that something monstrous blocked their path. Something buried deep in the earth but clawing its way up from the depths.

***

"Is that Bridger Pass?" asked Thea Ghent.

Turley wanted to believe that it was. "I'm not sure."

The truth was, he didn't know. Turley was having a difficult time focusing and thinking rationally. Giant stone hands? Nausea gripped his stomach. He felt dirty and in need of absolution. Thoughts of plunging beneath the surface of some cool, clear pond seduced his imagination.

"Griffin?" Ghent asked.

The vision shattered. "What?"

"I think we should take the chance. That looks like a clear shot out of this valley." Ghent aimed a dirty pointer at the gap between stone forefinger and thumb. "Anything to be free from this place!"

Turley nodded. "Let's go."

He remembered the dream and began to tremble despite the morning's heat. The sun rose over the mountains, a fiery red orb whose light promised little comfort. They approached the line of buttes.

The horses complained. Turley forced them onward with a reminder from the whip. Iselin's breath rained across his neck, too warm, too close. Turley shifted, making his temper known. They trudged closer. The nearest of the buttes towered over them, the different strata of rocks reminding him of the knuckles in a finger. The giant's thumb boasted six instead of two.

The prairie schooner passed between thumb and forefinger. A haze of mist drifted over the space directly beyond, at first making it impossible to identify the lay of the land. But the sun soon burned off the fog, revealing the last thing they expected to see.

A town—a bona fide *town*—spread out across the center between buttes. A town where none should be! An elegant wooden sign on the trail leading through stretches of lush green prairie grass and bright yellow flowers declared the little oasis was Deadfall.

"It's beautiful," said Thea. "Don't you agree, Maddie?"

"Oh, yes, Mother," Madeline said.

For a second, Turley gave in to the sense of relief that engulfed their small expedition. According to all that greenery, there would be fresh water. The wooden structures, some three stories tall, offered shelter. They'd find food in Deadfall, delicious but more importantly agreeable on the stomach.

As though timed precisely to that moment, the buttery smell of fresh bread teased Turley's nose. His gut burbled, unleashing a sound similar to that made by the bubbling earth at their backs, the music of hunger at its worst.

"Do you smell that?" Ghent asked, a wide smile breaking on his mouth to show yellowed teeth and several gaps.

"Yeah," Turley said, the lone word juicy on his tongue. He realized that he was salivating.

"They're *barbecuing*."

Turley narrowed his gaze on the other man. "What?"

"I bet there's a whole steer down there roasting on a fire as big as this prison." Ghent smacked the hard wooden side of his seat, indicating the wagon.

Turley didn't smell meat on the breeze or see any smoke. Only after they started their decent down the winding trail toward the town did one other disturbing fact register.

They didn't see any people either.

***

"Hello!" Turley called. Ghent followed suit with a similar beckon and received the same lack of a response.

"Is anyone there?" Iselin's voice, dulcet on the echo, carried in the hot air with a haunting note like a question posed underwater but made in the throb of hazy ripples rising from the sun-blanched earth.

On the outside, the town maintained its shiny façade. There were storefronts and a saloon, a boarding house according to one painted sign, and troughs for horses, though they were empty.

"It's like everyone just up and left," said Ghent.

"And left all of their belongings behind," Iselin added.

Turley and his wife's glances met, and the next part of their conversation passed in looks without the need for words. They hadn't seen such largesse since Fort Laramie, a million miles behind them in who-knew-what direction. Any life waiting ahead in Oregon would be gritty and primitive by modern standards, likely disappointing in expectations. Here, there were shops filled with ladies' dresses and bolts of fabric, a saloon whose shelves sat laden with bottles, beds— real beds in the rooms of the boarding house, and shelter. And by all outward signs, the gift was theirs and theirs alone.

Turley glanced up. The buttes beyond the town, those fingers of yellow and gray rock, rippled in the waves of heat and, for a terrible instant, appeared to flex, as though closing in around them.

***

Turley hunched down, aware of the ache in his knees and the popping of tired joints. Pain had seeped past his bones and into his marrow. The position put him almost level with Maynard. The boy's face reminded him of a scared animal's.

"I want you to protect your mother while Mister Ghent and me explore the town."

The scared animal eyes opened even wider as his father handed him the pistol, holding it by the barrel, the grip offered. Maynard shook his head.

"Son," Turley said.

Reluctantly, the boy accepted the ominous gift. A sense of lightness came over his expression. The wildness left his eyes. Only after he and Ghent set out, each man armed with a rifle, did Turley realize that it wasn't bravado or even acceptance in his mute son's eyes but surrender.

***

The arid wind slithered around posts and eaves, its whine irritating on the ear like a mosquito's. They moved cautiously onto the saloon's wooden veranda, the scuffle of their steps heavy in the heat. The saloon's door groaned in protest when opened, the sound of hinges that hadn't been tested in some while.

The inside was a humorless expanse of empty tables sitting gray in the poor light offered by a pair of windows. Dust lay thick on surfaces. Turley discovered that the rows of bottles on shelves were as empty as the horse troughs and tables.

He pitched one of the empty bottles at the floor. The thunder Turley expected never erupted. The noise registered as dead—a gasp from the bottom of a well a thousand feet deep.

"What is this?" Ghent asked.

The other man reached for the nearest table and toppled it with a hard shove. The table splintered upon contact with the floor, the pieces kicking up dust.

The pieces shattering *into* dust.

The clothes on the dress forms in the ladies' shop dissolved beneath Turley's touch like burial rags exhumed from an ancient sepulcher.

Up close, the town bore none of the illusion of newness or welcome that it had projected from a distance.

"We're leaving," Turley said.

Ghent swore before voicing his agreement.

The two men turned toward the location of the prairie schooner. And then someone screamed. A single gunshot followed, both noises robbed of their sharpness.

Turley tore across the street. A wall of hot air attempted to slow his progress, but he put on a burst of speed, aware of the agony infecting his marrow, and cut past the saloon and those dust-filled water troughs in time to see all their horses evaporate.

Like Ghent earlier, Turley cursed as his heels skidded to a stop on the desiccated ground.

There one instant and gone the next, the four horses renounced a dimension from three to two, taking on the appearance of a yellowing photograph in an old piece of newsprint. An empty moan reached his ears, a scream missing its peal. A stagnant afterimage painted on the insides of Turley's eyes, only there now between blinks: the horses bucking in agony right before they vanished from sight.

Ghent invoked God's name. From the corner of his eye, Turley realized the same weathered patina from the town stained their covered wagon, leeching the sturdiness out of the wood, rusting the iron, and corroding the canvas cover. A smell of swamps and upturned graves hung over the place. In the surge of panic that followed, Turley tried to not think about the fetor's origins.

Iselin, Maynard...

That lone gunshot. He called his son's name, the futility not lost on him. His son would never answer in Deadfall any more than other towns.

"Thea!" Ghent shouted. "Maddie!"

The oppressive heat threw the man's voice back at them, as though the air was clotting and the sky no longer there.

"Where are they?" Ghent asked, his words rising to a howl. "Where is my family?"

Gone, thought Turley, unable to fathom that so, too, was his. The ache in his bones had jumped onto his skin and rang in his ears. It painted itself thickly on his tongue. And then it shook him almost off his feet.

Whatever malevolent abomination existed here was feeding upon him, as it had the horses—as it had his wife and son!

"Run," he shouted at Ghent, wondering if the order reached the other man through the haze of his grief and the thickening air.

Without waiting, Turley ran.

And ran.

* * *

The town proper waned, replaced by the green at the limits, a belt far lusher than anything they had seen since Nebraska. Unnaturally so. *A trap*, Turley thought.

Thick sweat broke at Turley's hairline and poured into his eyes. He reached his free hand up to wipe it away and his wrist came away red. It wasn't sweat but blood.

The thing was eating him.

Turley dropped the rifle and swiped at the air in an attempt to drive off whatever sipped and slurped upon him the way the horror in his dreams had feasted upon predators as far back as the great lizards. Whimpers and broken words flew from his lips as the dusty trail passed underfoot. His mind raced, accessing flashes of memory that weren't solely his.

"*Croatoan*," Turley said, the word tasting foul and of fresh blood on his tongue.

The path beneath his old boots vanished, replaced by gray and yellow rock. Turley skidded to a stop. He forced his eyes up. The buttes had closed ranks. The stone fingers of the giant's hand were clenched into a fist, sealing off the valley, making escape impossible.

Turley whirled. The town was gone.

He had seen the giant's fingers, its lungs, and its stomach. Now, he saw its mouth and the sharpness of its many teeth.

ABOUT THE AUTHORS

Jason J. McCuiston has been a semi-finalist in the Writers of the Future contest and has studied under the tutelage of best-selling author Philip Athans. His stories of fantasy, horror, science-fiction, and crime have appeared in numerous anthologies, periodicals, websites, and podcasts. His debut novel, *Project Notebook*, is now available from Amazon. Connect with him on the internet at www.facebook.com/ShadowCrusade. You can find most of his publications on his Amazon page at www.amazon.com/-/e/B07RN8HT98.

Bradley H. Sinor has been published in anthologies by BAEN, DAW, Warner, Dark Owl Publishing, and others, including The Grantville Gazette and several Ring of Fire books. He also has a 1632 novel, written with his wife, Susan Sinor, published by BAEN. His solo novel was published by Airship 27, and he has a forthcoming novel to be published by Ring of Fire Press.

Gustavo Bondoni is a novelist and short story writer with over three hundred stories published in fifteen countries, in seven languages. His latest novel is *Test Site Horror* (2020). He has also published two other monster books: *Ice Station: Death* (2019) and *Jungle Lab Terror* (2020), three science fiction novels: *Incursion* (2017), *Outside* (2017) and *Siege* (2016), and an ebook novella entitled *Branch*. His short fiction is collected in *Pale Reflection* (2020), *Off the Beaten Path* (2019), *Tenth Orbit and Other Faraway Places* (2010), and *Virtuoso and Other Stories* (2011). In 2019, Gustavo was awarded second place in the Jim Baen Memorial Contest, and in 2018 he received a Judges Commendation (and second place) in The James White Award. He was also a 2019 finalist in the Writers of the Future Contest. His website is at www.gustavobondoni.com.

Kevin M. Folliard is a Chicagoland writer whose fiction has been collected by The Horror Tree, Flame Tree Publishing, The Dread Machine, and more. His recent publications include his 2020 horror anthology *The Misery King's Closet*; his novella *Tower of Raven* from Demain Publishing; "Bumper-to-Bumper," published in the Jolly Horror Press anthology *Coffin Blossoms*; "Home by Dark," collected in Transmundane Press's *On Time* anthology; "Headless Viper," in *A Celebration of Storytelling* by Dark Owl Publishing; and "Satyr," featured at The Dread Machine. Kevin currently resides in La Grange, Illinois, where he enjoys his day job as an academic writing advisor and active membership in the La Grange and Brookfield Writers Groups. When not writing or working, he's usually reading Stephen King, playing Super Mario Maker, or traveling the U.S.A. You can learn more about his writing at www.KevinFolliard.com.

John B. Rosenman was an English professor at Norfolk State University where he designed and taught a course in how to write science fiction and fantasy. He is a former Chairman of the Board of the Horror Writers Association and has published 250 stories in places such as *Weird Tales, Whitley Strieber's Aliens, Fangoria, Galaxy, Endless Apocalypse, The Age of Wonders*, and the *Hot Blood* erotic horror series. John has published two dozen books, including SF action-adventure novels such as *Beyond Those Distant Stars, Speaker of the Shakk, A Senseless Act of Beauty, Alien Dreams*, and the Inspector of the Cross series (Crossroad Press). He has also published a four-book box set, *The Amazing Worlds of John B. Rosenman* (MuseItUp Publishing). In addition, he has published two mainstream novels, *The Best Laugh Last* (McPherson & Company) and the young adult book *The Merry-Go-Round Man* (Crossroad Press). Recently, he published a three-book box set, *Starfighter Chronicles and Crash*, both of which are part of his Inspector of the Cross series. He also completed a science-fiction novel, *Dreamfarer*, that is the first in a new series and soon to be published by Crossroad Press. Two of John's major themes are the endless, mind-stretching wonders of the universe and the limitless possibilities of transformation—sexual, cosmic, and otherwise. John B. Rosenman is on Facebook, Pinterest, Goodreads, and LinkedIn, and has Amazon Author Page. You can find him on Instagram as @jrosenman and on Twitter as @Writerman1.

Stuart Croskell lives in the UK. He teaches Drama to kids with special needs and plays bass guitar in a band called The Siddhartha James. You can find more short stories by him on his Amazon author link: www.amazon.co.uk/J-Stuart-Croskell.

Matias Travieso-Diaz is a Cuban-American engineer and attorney, retired after half a century of professional practice in Washington, D.C. Following retirement, he has taken up creative writing and authored many short stories of various lengths and genres. His stories have appeared or are scheduled to appear in about forty short story anthologies, magazines, audio books and podcasts in the United States, the U.K., Canada, Australia, and New Zealand. You can look up his works at www.amazon.com/-/e/B08L8QMT27 and visit him at https://mtravies.wixsite.com/mysite.

Charles Wilkinson's publications include *The Pain Tree and Other Stories* (London Magazine Editions, 2000). His stories have appeared in *Best Short Stories 1990* (Heinemann), *Best English Short Stories 2* (W.W. Norton, USA), *Best British Short Stories 2015* (Salt), *Confingo, London Magazine* and in genre magazines/anthologies such as Black Static, *The Dark Lane Anthology, Supernatural Tales, Theaker's Quarterly Fiction, Phantom Drift* (USA), *Bourbon Penn* (USA), *Shadows & Tall Trees* (Canada), *Nightscript* (USA) and *Best Weird Fiction 2015* (Undertow Books, Canada). His anthologies of strange tales and weird fiction, *A Twist in the Eye* (2016) and *Splendid in Ash* (2018) appeared from Egaeus Press. A full-length collection of his poetry came out from Eyewear in 2019, and Eibonvale Press will publish his chapbook of weird stories, *The January Estate*, in 2021. He lives in Wales. More information can be found at his website, www.charleswilkinsonauthor.com.

Jonathon Mast lives in Kentucky with his wife and an insanity of children. (A group of children is an insanity. Trust me.) His first novel, *The Keeper of Tales*, is published here with Dark Owl Publishing. You can find him at www.jonathonmastauthor.com.

Alistair Rey began his career in Romania writing political propaganda for post-authoritarian governments. He has since advertised himself as an author of "fiction and parafiction," an archivist, a political satirist, and a dealer in rare books and manuscripts. His work has appeared in the *Berkeley Fiction Review, Juked* magazine and *WeirdBook*, among other publications. A complete list of works and stories is available at the Parenthetical Review website (www.parentheticalreview.com).

Gregg Chamberlain has enjoyed reading tall tales for longer than he cares to mention. His weird western story is a fantasy revision of an American Midwest folk tale about a way station along one of the early American stagecoach runs that was known for its shady operations. Gregg lives in rural Ontario, Canada, with his missus, Anne, and their cats, who let their humans think they are in charge. He writes speculation fiction for fun and has several dozen published examples of the fun he has available at *Daily Science Fiction*, in magazines like *Ares, Mythic, Polar Borealis*, and *Weirdbook*, and in various anthologies.

Dwain Campbell is originally from Sussex, New Brunswick. After his university years in Nova Scotia, he journeyed farther east to begin a teaching career in Newfoundland. Thirty-six years later, he is semi-retired in St. John's and studies folklore in his spare time. Contemporary fantasy is his genre of choice, and Atlantic Canada is a rich source of inspiration. He is author of *Tales from the Frozen Ocean*, and has contributed stories to *Canadian Tales of the Fantastic*, *Tesseracts 17*, and *Fall into Fantasy 2018*. Neil Gaiman is his hero of the moment, though he will reluctantly admit to a lifelong fascination with Stephen King.

Vonnie Winslow Crist, SFWA, HWA, is author of *The Enchanted Dagger*, *Beneath Raven's Wing*, *Owl Light*, *The Greener Forest*, and other books. Her stories appear in *Chilling Ghost Short Stories*, *Amazing Stories*, *Cirsova Magazine*, *Killing It Softly II*, *Creep*, *Unreal*, *Villains*, *Curse of the Gods*, *Black Infinity Magazine*, *SLAY: Stories of the Vampire Noire*, and elsewhere. Believing the world is still filled with mystery, miracles, and magic, Vonnie strives to celebrate the power of myth in her writing. For more information: www.vonniewinslowcrist.com.

Steve Gladwin has hit sixty and isn't happy, so he gets over it by writing stories. He is also a storyteller, teacher, and workshop leader, who last year, with his partner Rose, set up a website to help people deal with change and loss. Then COVID hit, so he is now relatively happy reading, writing, blogging, and interviewing fellow writers, artists, musicians, and storytellers for a proposed book. In 2014, his first published YA novel, *The Seven*, was short-listed for the Welsh Books Prize, and he has also collaborated on *Fragon* and *The Raven's Call*. He is also working on a collection called *Gods and Sods*, pitching a new fantasy TV pilot, and writing an opera blog/book from having watched far too much of it over the last year.

John A. Frochio lives in Western Pennsylvania and has retired from developing and supporting computer automation systems for steel mills. He's had stories published in *Interstellar Fiction*, *Beyond Science Fiction*, *Twilight Times*, *Aurora Wolf*, *Liquid Imagination*, *Mythaxis*, *Kraxon*, *SciFan Magazine*, *Helios Quarterly* and anthologies *Triangulation 2003*, *Triangulation: Parch* (2014), *Time Travel Tales* (2016), *Visions VII: Universe* (2017), *2047: Short Stories from Our Common Future* (2017), *The Chronos Chronicles* (2018), *Third Flatiron's Hidden Histories* (2019), *Breathe: An Anthology of Science Fiction* (2020), and *A Celebration of Storytelling* (2020), as well as his general fiction novel *Roots of a Priest* (with Ken Bowers, 2007) and a short story collection *Large and Small Wonders* (2012). His wife Connie, a retired nurse, and his daughter Toni, a flight attendant, have bravely put up with his strange ways for many years. His author's webpage is https://johnafrochio.wordpress.com/.

Lawrence Dagstine is a native New Yorker, video game enthusiast, toy collector, and speculative fiction writer of 20-plus years. He has placed more than 450 stories in online and print periodicals during that two-decade span, especially the small presses. He has been published by publishing outfits such as Damnation Books, Steampunk Tales, and Left-Hand Publishers. He is also author to numerous novellas and three short story collections, including *Death of the Common Writer*, *Fresh Blood*, and *From The Depths* (TBA, w. Illustrator Bob Veon). His work is available on Amazon and B&N.com. Visit his official website at www.lawrencedagstine.com. Or visit his Amazon author page at www.amazon.com/Lawrence-Dagstine/e/B001K8UG5K.

Q Parker is a novelist and screenwriter from coastal NJ. They're the author behind *Nova EXE* and *These Walls Don't Talk, They Scream*, among many other works written under many names. When not writing, they're probably working out or hanging around with their pet chickens.

Peter Prellwitz was bitten by the writing bug at an early age and has never been cured. Starting with an awful (but produced!) Thanksgiving play in fourth grade, Pete's writing skills fortunately have improved over time. With ten novels, a dozen short stories in multiple anthologies, and multiple awards, Peter also writes as H.K. Devonshire, Mars' most popular Martian author, whose first Terran editions of *Company A* (2019) and *The Bombala Mines Fast Draw* (2020) are now available. Two more Martian westerns arrive from Mars in 2021. Pete and his wife Bethlynne live in Jeffersonville, Pennsylvania with two dachshunds. Learn more about his work at http://ShardsUniverse.net.

J.B. Dane is a pseudonym of a multi-published, multi-genre novelist who goes by many names. Not because she is in Witness Protection. Really not in Witness Protection. Really. She may start hiding from citizens of Detroit since her Raven Tales urban fantasy comedic mysteries have populated their fair city with neighbors who might be supernatural, paranormal, or legendary beasts... or not so beasts... but probably *are* beasts. They could be hungry, too. She tampers regularly with the lore of the Claus family, you know, the one at the North Pole, and hopes this does not land her on the Naughty List, even if Nick Claus and his great-great-grandfather Frank have both landed on it frequently themselves. Dane might be found at www.4TaleTellers.com, but leave a message to be picked up by a disguised courier and delivered to a secret location. Ditto via www.facebook.com/JBDaneWriter or @JBDaneWriter on Twitter.

Stefan Markos lives in Tulsa, Oklahoma with his wife and two cats. He has resumed writing science fiction after a hiatus of some years, and is a member of Oklahoma Science Fiction Writers. In addition to writing, he also enjoys camping, hiking, fishing, bicycling, and participating in historical presentations and performances.

L.L. Hill. Resident in northern Canada, Laura plants wildflowers and takes photos in her spare time. She also hopes for a COVID-free near future.

Kenneth Bykerk lives in the ghost town of Howells in the mountains of central Arizona. Living on the land his great-grandfather mined a century ago, Kenneth claims his rare moments free as a single father to an autistic child to tell the stories of those ruins which haunted his own childhood play. The Tales of the Bajazid take place in one of the many ghost towns of central Arizona. These tales are connected through geography and time, each standing alone yet together helping to restore the history of this forgotten place. Two more of these tales are also in *A Celebration of Storytelling* from Dark Owl Publishing.

Marilyn "Mattie" Brahen has published fiction in thirteen magazines and anthologies in the U.S. and U.K. to date. Her 2003 first fantasy novel, *Claiming Her*, and its 2009 sequel, *Reforming Hell*, received good reviews. A third novel, *Baby Boy Blue*, a police procedural mystery set in Philadelphia, was published in 2011 and resold to Linford Mystery Library (large print edition) in Great Britain in 2014. Her short story collection, *Seastruck and Other Fantasies*, was also published in Autumn 2019. She is currently working on a sequel to *Baby Boy Blue* and other creative projects. Mattie is also a singer/songwriter/guitarist and artist and lives with her husband, author/editor Darrell Schweitzer, and their cat Lillyput in Northeast Philadelphia.

Darrell Schweitzer is the author of about 350 published stories and four novels: *The White Isle, The Shattered Goddess, The Mask of the Sorcerer*, and *The Dragon House*. His short fiction has appearance in many magazines and anthologies, including *Twilight Zone, Amazing Stories, Fantastic, Interzone, Postscripts, Cemetery Dance*, and the *Black Wings* series. His story collections include most recently *Awaiting Strange Gods* from Fedogan & Bremer and a two volume, forty-year retrospective from PS Publishing, *The Mysteries of the Faceless King* and *The Last Heretic*. His fiction has been nominated for the World Fantasy Award and the Shirley Jackson Award. He won the World Fantasy Award (shared with George Scithers) as editor of *Weird Tales*, a position he held for nineteen years. He has also edited many anthologies, including *The Secret*

History of Vampires, Cthulhu's Reign, That is Not Dead, Tales from the Miskatonic University Library (with John Ashmead), and *The Mountains of Madness Revealed*, these last three from PS Publishing. He is also a poet, essayist, and interviewer. He has published books about H.P. Lovecraft and Lord Dunsany.

Adrian Ludens is a rock radio afternoon host and hockey public address announcer. He lives in the Black Hills of South Dakota with his family. His interests include reading and writing dark fiction, listening to all types of music, and exploring abandoned buildings. Adrian's fiction has been published in *Alfred Hitchcock Mystery Magazine, Dark Moon Digest*, and several dozen anthologies, the newest of which is *Violent Vixens* (Dark Peninsula Press). You can follow him on Facebook via @AdrianLudensAuthor or on Twitter via @AdrianLudens.

Martin Zeigler writes short fiction, primarily mystery, science fiction, and horror. His stories have been published in a number of anthologies and journals, both in print and online. Every so often (okay, twice), he has gathered these stories into a self-published collection. In 2015 he released *A Functional Man And Other Stories*. More recently, in 2020, a year we will all remember with fondness, he released *Hypochondria And Other Stories*. Besides writing, Marty enjoys the things most people do. And besides *those*, he likes reading, taking long walks, and dabbling on the piano. Marty makes his home in the Pacific Northwest.

Gregory L. Norris. Raised on a healthy diet of creature double features and classic SF TV, Gregory L. Norris writes regularly for national magazines, fiction anthologies, novels, and the occasional script for TV and Film. Norris once worked as a screenwriter on two episodes of Paramount's *Star Trek: Voyager* series and has had two feature films optioned. He, his gigantic rescue cat, and emerald-eyed muse live at Xanadu, a grand century-old house located in the outer limits of New Hampshire's North Country.

THE DARK

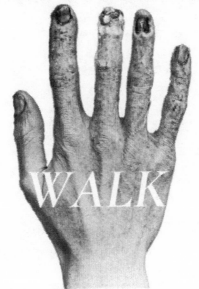

WALK

FORWARD

A HARROWING COLLECTION BY
JOHN S. MCFARLAND

Available in paperback and on Kindle from
DARK OWL PUBLISHING, LLC
www.darkowlpublishing.com

The Anthological Festival of Tales

58 stories by 39 authors designed to honor the art of writing
by including a fair, festival, or celebration in each telling.
From fantasy to sci-fi, from thrillers to mysteries,
we know readers will truly enjoy this feast of fables.

Now Available from   Dark Owl Publishing, LLC

www.darkowlpublishing.com

THE LAST STAR WARDEN

"A rare and refreshing level of pure pulpy fun."
~ Gregory L. Norris.
Author of the Gerry Anderson's Into Infinity novels

Written and Illustrated by
JASON J. MCCUISTON
Author of Project Notebook

VOLUME 1 NOW AVAILABLE!

VOLUME II COMING NOVEMBER 1, 2021

www.darkowlpublishing.com

Made in the USA
Columbia, SC
21 March 2022

57952644R00183